# strictly business

# strictly *business*

*a novel*

## JENSEN PARKER

Made for More Publishing, LLC

"An addictive enemies to lovers that hits the spot."

- Holly Whitworth, author of *Over the Fence*

"Still swooning over Finn and Michaela in *Strictly Business.* I wasn't sure how Parker could top *Until Now,* but she rose to the occasion and packed in even more heat! Run, don't walk to devour the *Strangers* series!"

- Claire Isenthal, author of Amazon Bestseller, *The Rising Order*

# Playlist

**Easy** - Alexandra Kay
**that way** - Tate McRae
**Unmiss You** - Clara Mae
**Young & Free** - Dermot Kennedy
**champagne problems** - Taylor Swift
**Over You** - Daughtry
**Painted Him Perfect** - Alexandra Kay
**Break Her Heart** - ZZ Ward
**Talk is Cheap** - Miley Cyrus
**greedy** - Tate McRae
**Something to Someone** - Dermot Kennedy
**Healing** - Riley Clemmons
**Nervous** - Maren Morris
**Get'cha Head in the Game** - Troy
**What Do I Mean** - Jonas Brothers
**Everleave** - Alexandra Kay
**you broke me first** - Tate McRae
**things i wish you said** - Sabrina Carpenter
**Sad Beautiful Tragic (Taylor's Version)** - Taylor Swift
**Tailspin** - For You
**Happy Once** - Alexandra Kay
**Once** - David J
**Jaded** - Miley Cyrus
**Treacherous (Taylor's Version)** - Taylor Swift
**I Don't Wanna Love You Anymore** - LANY
**messier** - Tate McRae
**Sympathy** - The Goo Goo Dolls
**You Were Mine** - Forest Blakk
**chaotic** - Tate McRae
**hate myself for loving you** - Mackenzie Arromba
**Forget About Us** - Perrie
**I Can Do Anything** - Alexandra Kay
**bad ones** - Tate McRae
**Call Me Maybe** - Carly Rae Jepsen
**All I've Ever Known** - Alexandra Kay
**underwater** - Mackenzie Arromba
**Go Get Her** - Restless Road
**I'm in Love With You** - The 1975
**Don't Throw it Away** - Jonas Brothers
**California King Bed** - Rhianna
**Wide Awake** - Katy Perry
**Change** - Djo
**Levels** - Nick Jonas
**Lose My Mind** - Dean Lewis

*Apple Music*

*Spotify*

*For those of us who don't have it all
figured out... You still have time.*

# Part One

*"I could easily forgive his pride,
if he had no mortified mine."*

*- Jane Austen, "Pride and Prejudice"*

*one*

*Michaela*

**WHAT SHE DOESN'T KNOW** won't hurt her…or me. Caitlin hasn't sent me a warning text yet. I must be safe, I hope so, because I am *so* late. Shocker, I know. Me, late? Never.

I zigzag through the crowd on Columbus Circle, regretting my choice in heels this morning — these things are *not* made for running through the streets of Manhattan. Crossing over Eighth, I throw a stern glance at the tourist who bumps into me, almost spilling my coffee. I do not have time to deal with a coffee stain on my white shirt. Again, probably not my best fashion choice for mid-July weather. I can feel sweat already wetting certain parts of my shirt as I walk into our office building.

Each time the elevator dings, I feel the anxiety rising in my chest because I'm not sure what awaits me when I get there. *Twentieth Floor,* the robotic voice announces. The doors part to reveal DV Designs in big, bold letters. Caitlin leans over the front desk, reaching for something, and Bella rolls her eyes before handing her the office phone. Bella's eyes glance to the elevator when she hears the door open and motions for

Caitlin to turn around. Meeting my stare, Caitlin breathes a sigh of relief, "You're here! Finally. Bethany called, she said—"

"Cait, stop. Is she here?"

A grimace, "In your office."

"Shit," I sigh. "Of course, *she's* running early when—"

"You're late," a familiar voice says from behind her.

Caitlin offers a sympathetic smile before I take a deep breath, put a smile on my face, and look over her shoulder to see my boss and best friend, Nina Villa. Owner of DV Designs and co-owner of Villa Inc., with her older brother Kai. We've been friends since my freshman year at Rosecliffe University. She stands with a smirk by the reception desk, a little girl clinging to her black blazer.

The girl's face lights up when she recognizes me. "Aunt Michaela!"

"Hi, Leia," I bend down to hug her.

"Caitlin, can you take Ophelia? Michaela and I have some things to discuss," Nina instructs.

Dead. I'm so dead.

"C'mon Leia, I'm pretty sure I saw some popsicles in the freezer yesterday. Then we can go bother Jaime."

"Who's Jaime?" Ophelia asks taking Caitlin's hand and following her down the hallway.

Without a word, Nina turns on her heel and expects me to follow. The one time (okay, maybe not the one time, but still, the one time) I'm late, Nina decides to show up on time. Not just on time, *early*. It's very Nina...

Her corner office overlooks the expansive cityscape, but more importantly, it overlooks Central Park — her favorite place in all of Manhattan. Not surprising, say I blame her, considering it's where she and her husband finally stopped trying to act like they weren't made for each other. It only took a little push from yours truly. A glass-top desk with marbled legs faces the door. Bookshelves line the wall to the right full of books and knicknacks she has picked up throughout the years. A conference table sits in front of the shelves, offering a private meeting space away from the prying eyes that lurk outside the usual conference rooms — she typically reserves it for more private clients. In the far-left corner, a white sofa with an extra-long chaise. Blue-gray pillows are set to appear as if they happened to land that way. A blue oriental rug rests beneath a marble coffee table. She designed her space, but let me handle the rest of the office. Her office is much grander than mine, but I suppose that's to be expected since you're the big boss.

I close the door but don't turn to face her yet, I can't.

Trust me, I deserve what's coming. Nina has given me a lot of "second" chances, and I keep messing them up. I'll be lucky if she doesn't fire me, but I think my luck is about to run out.

I twist the locket around my neck between my fingers and finally turn to face her. She sits on the edge of the desk, arms crossed, with an expectant look on her face. "Let me just start by saying I'm sorry, I know—"

"How many times this month?" she asks.

"This is only the fourth time!"

Nina scoffs, "Fourth time… Questa settimana. The fourth time this week, Michaela." She runs a hand through her hair, frustrated. Rightfully so. I didn't think she knew how often I've been late lately, but things have been… Look, I have a good excuse, I can't tell her. I *should* tell her, she is my best friend, and she'd understand, it might even save me the lecture, but I'm not ready to share it with anyone. "Do you know what day it is?" A rhetorical question. "It's *Thursday*, the fourth day of the week. I didn't promote you so you could come and go as you please. I need someone who's going to be here. Someone I can trust. What kind of an example is it for everyone else if you're showing up late every day?"

Excuses start swimming through my mind, and I'm

grasping for anything that will keep me off the ledge for a bit longer. "I have meetings, I have—"

"That's not what I'm talking about." Nina sighs, "Yes, you have duties and responsibilities that require you to be out of the office, but the days you don't, you're supposed to be here. *On time.* You're supposed to be available because I can't be. I can't be everywhere at once."

"I'm sorry, Nin. I don't want to disappoint you. I don't — I just have a lot going on right now."

Her eyes soften a little, and her shoulders fall with a sigh. "And that's fine, Michaela. You've had a lot going on, at least that's what you say, but I need to know you can handle this despite everything else. If not, I'll find someone who can."

"I can, I promise. It won't happen again. Not even one minute."

"You have one month, Michaela."

Fuck, she said it.

"Two."

"One."

"One and a half?" I try one last negotiation, but Nina doesn't budge, her arms crossed tightly over her chest. I can't blame her; she's given me more chances than anyone else would. To ask more of her wouldn't be fair.

"What's going on with you?"

"Nothing," I groan, and it feels like a child on the receiving end of a lecture from their parents. "Everything is fine, Nin."

Nina's brow quirks in response. She knows I'm not telling her the truth, but will she ask? Nope. She'll let it go…for now. She has too much other shit going on to worry about whatever mess I've created. But, I have to be careful because her trust and patience with me are starting to wear thin.

"Is David home?" she asks changing the subject. "You're welcome to bring him over for dinner later. Haven't seen him in a while, Kai will be there. He's picking up Ophelia."

"No, he's in D.C. I don't think I'll make it tonight, Nin; I have some stuff to do around the house."

"Do it tomorrow." She bats her bright green eyes at me. Normally, that might work, but I'm not in the mood to spend the night with the Villa siblings. "You can't skip out on dinner; Ophelia would be heartbroken." Nina sits behind her desk and the wall between boss and best friend comes down. "You do look kinda tired, Mic. Why don't you go home after you meet with Angela? Get some rest, and come back refreshed tomorrow. I can take care of whatever they need around here."

"When's the last time you ran an office?" I meant it more as a joke, but I can tell by the tightening of her jaw she doesn't find the humor in it. "I just mean, you're not running them — the offices. Not really. You have other people do the dirty work for you. There's a difference."

Nina laces her fingers together and leans forward on the glass top. "I have ten offices across this country, and I know what's happening in each one, but please, if you have something to say, ti suggerisco di sputarlo."

I stay quiet — it seems like the safer option right now.

The Italian flows quickly, and without pause, I have a hard time keeping up with no idea what she just said, but I know it's nothing good. I swallow the lump in my throat. Honestly, I'm not sure what possesses me to do it, but the filter between my brain and the mouth falters when the next thought enters my mind. "Just because you're upset you haven't fucked your husband in over a month doesn't mean you can take it out on the rest of us."

"Fuck you, Michaela." The calmness when she speaks doesn't match the look in her eye, and it sets my nerves on edge.

Okay, so maybe what I said was a little uncalled for (a lot uncalled for) and highly unprofessional, but she should know I didn't mean it that way. "Nina—"

"Un mese, Michaela," she says through gritted teeth. "Un mese. Se non riesci a mettere insieme la tua merda—" A knock interrupts her before Bella steps into the office.

"Hey, Nina… Oh! Sorry, I didn't —"

"It's fine, Bella. Michaela was leaving." Nina glares at me, "Go home and get some sleep. Be ready for our meeting with the Adler twins tomorrow morning."

She doesn't need to add the "or else." It's pretty obvious.

Nina raises her hand when I try to apologize, and I take the hint. Bella pats my arm in what is meant to be comforting as I pass through the door, but it only makes a new wave of nausea roll over me.

"Bella," I hear Nina say. "Tell Angela she'll be meeting with me today. You can send her to my office when she arrives."

*two*

*Michaela*

**"HONEY, I'M HOME,"** I say, not expecting an answer when I open the door to my condo. It's nothing fancy, but it's home. 201 East End Ave, Apartment 13E checked all my boxes when I moved to NYC two years ago: Upper East Side, low fees, over 400 square feet, at least one bedroom, and parking. Settled on the thirteenth floor, it has incredible views of a park and the river from the living room and a private balcony. I was ready to sign the papers when I stepped inside.

The condo is *cozy*; that's how Mom describes it anyway. It isn't Nina's four-thousand-square-foot penthouse at the Plaza. Yes, you heard me. *The Plaza.* New York City landmark hotel where "nothing unimportant ever happens." That Plaza. Not long after signing the paperwork on the New York office. The whole thing seemed fitting, really (very Nina), Nick wasn't kidding when he nicknamed her Princess.

When she decided to purchase a house in New York, Nick had initially been against it. "We don't need this, Nina," he said.

"You're right, but I want it, so I'm gonna get it," Nina

argued. I was sure Elizabeth and I were about to witness their first argument as a married couple. "Besides, you're gonna say no to that view?" The view was pretty spectacular, the 18th-floor condo had fourteen windows with unobstructed views of Central Park.

"Nina…"

"You get to live in The Plaza, Nick. It's like being the real-life Eloise!"

Nick shared a look with me, pleading for my help, but I shrugged. What did he want me to do? The girl had already made up her mind.

"Don't look at me; I'm team Nina," Elizabeth said when he turned to her.

"Our kids are not growing up in New York, Davina," Nick finally conceded.

"Don't be such a downer." Nina rolled her eyes, but Nick was unamused. "Besides, what if you get the job at that firm in Chelsea?"

Unsurprisingly, Nick *had* gotten the job in Chelsea, but what was surprising, he turned it down. He didn't want to move to New York, not really. He was happy accepting the job in Charlotte, where he wasn't far from his new wife and their home. Nina wasn't happy about it, she felt like he was missing out on a great opportunity, but Nick still refused. It didn't matter though, a year ago he took over the Architecture and Development department at Villa Inc.

So no, my condo isn't The Plaza, but it's more than some of the two-hundred and some square feet ones I had seen. Besides, it has doubled in value in the last two years — I could easily afford to upgrade, and David wanted to, but I've grown attached to the little shoebox overlooking the East River I call home. The kitchen is stuck in the 1970s, but I recently bought new stainless-steel appliances, and I plan on repainting the cabinets and replacing the hardware to make it look more up-to-date. What sold me was the walk-in California closet and large bedroom. I can deal with an outdated kitchen as long as I have some breathing room. I don't see the point in selling, David spent the majority of the last year in Washington D.C. since he got the job with Barnes and we—

Wait, did I leave the bedroom light on?

I don't think so.

No, I'm ninety-seven percent sure I did not.

What is this suitcase doing here?

And, this box filled with…

That. *Fucker.*

"You're kidding me." Pushing the bedroom door open, "You can't come in here when you feel like it. You don't *live* here anymore." Standing like a thief caught in the act…David. "What are you doing here?"

"It's my condo too, Mic," he says, tossing a box of hair trimmers into the moving box. He's never used them. They've sat in the box since I bought them months ago. "I'm allowed to stop by and check on the place." He rummages through the nightstand drawer. "Look, I'm not trying to fight, I just came to get the rest of my stuff."

"The rest of what stuff? This is *my* condo and *my* shit. You haven't lived here for three months."

"So, these are yours?" He holds up the trimmers.

"If you want to be technical, yeah. I bought it."

"Oh, come on, Mic. Don't be childish."

"I'm gonna ask you once, nicely, get the fuck out of my house."

How did we get to this point? Fighting over pointless shit like hair trimmers. Things had been okay. We were happy, at least that's what I thought… There had been some rough patches, but we were making it work. We even got married last August.

"Michaela, I'm sorry," David says, his face pulled into a

frown as if it hurts him to see me. I flinch when his thumb grazes my cheek. "I never meant to hurt you."

I try to fight the longing when he cradles my cheek, involuntarily leaning into his touch. A smirk on his lips fades into a small smile. I know better than to trust the doe-eyed man in front of me. I know the game he's playing, but it has been *so* long, and I'm feeling exceptionally lonely today. Without warning, he crashes his lips to mine, a moan mingles between us.

I should've gone to Nina's.

David squeezes my ass before pushing me on the unmade bed. I whimper as his lips leave a blazing trail along my neck. A warm hand finds my breasts under my shirt, no bra to protect the sensitive skin of my nipple from the assault. His teeth graze the skin of my neck. He better not leave a mark. The last thing I want to do is explain to Nina why I have—

"Attention right here," David tsks, and his fingers fist in my hair bringing me back to our current position.

"Fuck you, David."

"You already are, sweetheart," he whispers in my ear, the words spreading goosebumps across my body.

This is a terrible idea and only going to cause more problems. It definitely won't help fix things and it won't make me feel better. But, his mouth is moving in the right direction and... "Stop."

David freezes. "What do you mean *stop?*"

"We're not doing this." I shove him to the other side of the bed. "Get out." I fold my arms over my chest refusing to look at him. I should've stopped him when he kissed me. But, I...I miss him. No matter what happened, I ~~love~~ loved him and it has been hard to let go. For the past two months, I've been telling myself I don't love him, I *can't* love him because he isn't mine anymore. Looking back, I'm not sure he has been for a while. Even if I thought there had been a chance of saving this, coming home from Italy to divorce papers made it clear there wasn't. It only reaffirmed he had gone to Italy intending to tell me it was over and there was nothing I could've done to stop it. We spent almost two weeks together on a romantic getaway only for him to end our marriage on the last night there. Tonight is a reminder I have to let go.

David scoffs and readjusts himself before pulling the hair trimmers from the box he'd been packing. He tosses them on the dresser — the clatter sending a shock wave through my system — and stops in the doorway. "I'm done playing these petty games of yours, MJ. Sell the condo and hand over the ring." My thumb absentmindedly traces over my left ring finger — the indentation still there. "You're making this harder than it has to be. Do us both a favor and stop being so difficult for once in your life. I'm ready for this to be done and over with."

The way he talks about us breaks my heart all over again. *I'm ready for this to be done and over with* as if we meant nothing to him. As if our relationship (our marriage) — and ending it — was another task on his to-do list he's been putting off.

I cringe when the front door slams and make a mental note to call a locksmith.

Bright red numbers glare in my face — *7:47 AM* — I have exactly thirteen minutes to get ready and leave for the office. The room begins to spin, a blur of orange and cream and green, and a wave of nausea floods my senses when I sit up. I want nothing more than to call Caitlin and tell her I won't be in today, that I must've picked up a stomach bug. But, if I do that, Nina won't have to wait a month for me to get my act together, she'll fire me on the spot. So, I better show up bright-eyed and bushy-tailed *on time* today.

"Fuck," I groan. We have a big meeting this morning and I have no idea how I'm going to get through it. After David left, I spent the night hugging a bottle of white wine on an (almost) empty stomach. When I finally dragged myself to bed, I had three hours until my alarm was set to go off. Admittedly, probably not my best idea.

Coffee.

I need coffee.

And ibuprofen.

Maybe some Gatorade.

Definitely some food. Something greasy to soak up the remnants of last night.

The sun casts a bright light through the condo — not good for a walking hangover — which means today is a glasses, no contacts, kind of day. The empty wine bottle sits on the white coffee table next to a vase of dehydrated daisies, mocking me. The TV still binges "The Office" and my black knitted blanket is strewn on the floor. The comfy scene calls to me, it sounds so much better than a boring meeting with... Who are we meeting today? I don't even remember. Nina was the one who set it up last week.

"Be on your best behavior," she had warned me when she called about it. How happy is she gonna be when I walk in today?

I push forward. There is no way I can miss this.

Hot water dribbles into the coffee pot, and I breathe in the aroma of freshly brewed coffee, trying to suppress the nausea still crawling at the back of my throat. A glance at the clock tells me I have six minutes before I need to leave. God help me, today is going to be a long day.

The shades of Nina's office are drawn per usual making it impossible to determine if she's gone or ignoring the knocking on her door. Bella had pulled me from my meeting with Nina to handle a vendor issue and it took longer than expected, which meant Nina had to end the meeting with the Adlers. I have no idea what happened. I knock one final time before opening the door to an empty office. Well, at least I know she's not ignoring me.

Closing the door, all eyes quickly avert their gaze. I subtly check myself — everything is in place. The hushed conversations make it seem like everyone is trying to be respectful of their colleagues, but it's pretty obvious the chatter is not about work. What in the hell is everyone talking about? If one more person looks at me like that, I'm going to…

"If you all have something to say, go ahead and say it," I snap when I catch the eye of an intern before she quickly looks away. "If not, I suggest you get back to work. And, if you don't have something to do, let me know — we have plenty of work that needs to be done."

The silence is deafening.

"Okay, everyone." Cait steps out of her office. "Enough. Let's get back to work." For a brief moment, they stare at her before returning to work. She gives me a smile and motions me toward my office.

"What is their problem?" I hiss.

"You really want to know?" Caitlin asks closing the door, and I wait expectantly. "Bella told a few of them about the little disagreement she walked in on yesterday, between you and Nina."

Shit.

"I guess everyone thinks you're on shaky ground. I mean, can you blame them? If it were one of them, they would've been fired a long time ago." She's not wrong. Nina has given me a few too many chances, and it's finally catching up with me. "You're a good boss, Mic. You need a little more structure."

"I'm working on it, Cait. A lot is going on right now, but I'm trying."

"I know you are."

"Who's that for?" I motion toward the stack of samples in her hands.

"Grace. I want to get ahead on some of these projects, so everything is a little less hectic while you're gone."

While I'm gone? Am I going somewhere?

Caitlin opens the door where Bella stands, her hand raised to knock. "Oh! Hello, Bella."

"I tried to phone you, but you didn't answer," Bella says past Caitlin. "Your mom called. She wanted to remind you about the party for your dad and Uncle next weekend."

"Fuck, I forgot," I sigh.

"She said you would, that's why she called."

"Did I book that flight?"

"A while ago."

"I need to buy them something, I don't even know what to get. What do fifty-something men want?"

"To see their daughter and niece," Caitlin answers. "You haven't been home in almost a year, so I think seeing you would be a gift enough."

I haven't seen much of my family since the wedding last year. Normally, we'd split the holidays between our families, Thanksgiving with one, and Christmas with the other, but last year we were in Richmond for both.

"I'll just ask Elizabeth, she'll know what they want."

Caitlin rolls her eyes. "I'll see you ladies later, Grace will have my head on a platter if I even think about being late."

I don't bother with a response as she closes the door behind her and Bella. When I open my phone, I find unread texts from Alex, Nick, and... David.

David? What in the hell does he want now?

**David Reed**

**Are you ready to talk like adults?**

Sorry, no hablo fuckboy.

**Very mature.**

Have your lawyer call mine, honey :)

*three*

## Michaela

**MOST TIMES, I HATE** this place, but I still miss it. I miss home. The warm feeling it brings when you drive down familiar streets and know what lies around every corner. You can turn the GPS off and coast because you know exactly where you're going — you've done it over ten thousand times. The way of a stranger as you pass each other on the street, never thinking twice about it. Everything stays the same as it always has been.

I had always dreamed of leaving Bridgeport, I thought moving to would solve my problems. Things were starting to look up: David and I had been going steady for a while, I had just gotten a promotion (with a corner office), and I was finally moving to my dream city, New York! What could go wrong? Everything. Okay, maybe that's a little dramatic, but one by one, it felt like everything started to crash and burn. And now, I'm left wondering who the hell is Michaela Jane Davis?

I follow the winding road toward the back of my parents' subdivision. Each home sits back from the road a few hundred feet on a wooded lot with at least three-quarters of an acre. Pulling into the driveway of my childhood home, I feel some of the tension melt away. The split-level home is a combination of white siding and gray bricks with a door as dark as midnight that Josh and I helped paint years ago. We may or may not have gotten into a small paint war and ended up with black smudges on us for days. Mom's rose bushes that line the front of the house are in full bloom, and it makes me smile; she loves her rose bushes. Tending to them was one of her favorite pastimes, something neither Josh nor I picked up on. Maybe this will be good. Maybe getting away from the city will help me wade through the swamp of thoughts that have settled in my mind. Until tomorrow, when I'll be staring one of them in the face.

*Nope.*

Nope, not gonna think about it right now.

I'm going to focus on how it feels good to be home. I haven't spent much time in Bridgeport since I moved two years ago. I was never a fan of the small-town living. I suppose it's because we didn't get many opportunities to travel while growing up. Sure, Mom and Dad tried to treat us to different trips occasionally, but we never got to spend holidays away. Spring breaks were spent traveling to Hilton Head or Wilmington — in eighth grade, they splurged and took us to Disney World. Summers were for sports and work. Winters were for work and family.

I spent most of my childhood dreaming of living in the big city, and I don't mean Charlotte. That was our "treat" growing up. New York City has always been the goal. Nina and I bonded over it, so when she offered me the opportunity to take over the office, it felt unreal that I'd get to live my dream.

And, it was a dream…for a while.

I don't attribute my lackluster experience to David; I won't give him that much credit, but a small part of me knows he has something to do with it. New York was supposed to be our fresh start. The place where we could build their lives together.

But, as time went on, I found myself wishing for some of the charm of my hometown. I'd never tell anyone that. Especially not my parents. They were too excited about me moving, and then David popped the question only a month after we moved. It was everything I ever wanted... I can't stand the thought of their disappointment when they learn the truth.

My mother swings the door open before I reach the bottom step, and I'm swept into a tight embrace. "Finally!"

"Hi, Mom."

"You're skin and bones, MJ. Have you been eating?"

"I'm fine."

"Patrick, look at her. She's smaller than the last time we saw her." I roll my eyes. She always says the same thing. "Don't roll your eyes at me, missy. It's my job as your mother to worry about you."

"Leave the girl alone, Jen," Dad steps down into the foyer pulling me into a hug. "C'mon, your brother and Elizabeth will be here soon. Dinner is 'bout done. Let's get you settled before they get here." He picks up my bags and carries them downstairs to my bedroom.

"Honey, where's David? I thought he was coming with you," my mother asks, following us inside.

"Oh... He had to work." The lie comes out easier than it should, but lately, I've had to come up with more and more excuses as to why no one has seen my husband in the last two months. "Barnes needed him last minute for some meeting."

"Don't act so surprised, Jen," Dad says returning from downstairs. "He barely got away for their honeymoon." He sounds more annoyed than usual. Dad has always found David's lack of boundaries when it comes to work annoying, but he doesn't usually express his displeasure so outwardly.

"I'm just sayin', it would be nice to see our son-in-law from time to time."

"I'm going to go change before dinner," I excuse myself

before they ask me anything more about their soon-to-be ex-son-in-law.

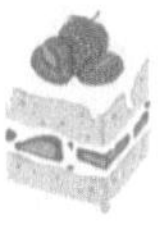

My parents told me they had asked Nina for some pointers on redecorating the house, including my old room, but I didn't think it would be like this. There isn't an ounce of me left. Long gone are the lime green walls, pink comforter, and widespread photo collage that took up half a wall. They'd even taken down my *Empire Strikes Back* movie poster. It had all been replaced by white walls, grey sheets, and a photograph of Mount Kirkjufell, which I recognized as one Elizabeth had taken on our family trip to Iceland a few years ago after Dad retired. I wonder if they finally did the same to Josh's old room… It had remained the same after he moved out, ready and waiting for him anytime he returned. I guess I won't be afforded the same luxury.

"Knock, knock," the gentle voice of my sister-in-law cuts through my thoughts. She leans against the door frame with a small smile. Her blonde hair has been lopped off, now resting on her shoulders. It's very different compared to what I'm used to. I almost don't recognize her. "Can I come in?"

"Of course."

Elizabeth pulls her legs underneath her when she sits on the bed. When my brother started dating Elizabeth, she always ensured I felt included — unlike most of his other girlfriends. I think it comes from her traumatic past, but whatever it is, I'm thankful for the friendship their relationship has brought me. Sometimes, I forget how much I loved being able to have a sister's night whenever we wanted. Living in New York, I can't call her up and invite her over on a random Tuesday night; I only get to see her whenever one of us is in town. "So, wanna talk about it?"

"I guess it depends on what 'it' is."

"I may have heard things didn't end so well when Nin was in town."

I laugh, "Of course she told you."

"Technically, she didn't tell me. She told Nick, who told Josh, who told me, and then I may have asked her about it."

"What did she have to say?"

"What do you think she said?"

"I'm on my last leg, one wrong move, and I'm out."

"Something like that," she says. "What's going on, Mic?" Elizabeth reaches across the bed and takes my hand in hers. "This isn't like you. I mean, yeah, you've always run on 'MJ Time,'" we both laugh because it's true, "but this is different. It's not five or ten minutes here and there; you're constantly late or missing things. It seems like ever since we got back from Italy something has changed... You've barely talked to anyone; you bite our heads off when you do."

"Everything is fine."

"Look, you don't have to tell me if you don't want to, but I'm here if you need to talk."

"There's nothing to worry about. Everything is perfect." I can tell she wants to fight me on this, but squeeze her hand reassuringly. "If something was wrong, I'd tell you. I promise." I hate the way the lies flow so easily. Kind of feels like the truth and I aren't related right now.

"There you are," Mom calls from the doorway. "Elizabeth, Josh was looking for you."

Wait a second, did Elizabeth just roll her eyes? That's odd...

"I should probably go," Elizabeth sighs, "he has an early morning tomorrow." She squeezes my hand and gives me a brief smile. "I'll see you on Saturday?"

I nod before she gives Mom a brief hug goodbye. When

she's gone, Mom slowly makes her way into my room — cautious. "Dad'll bring up your stuff soon," she still stands a few feet from me. "I figured you'd want to go through it on your own time. Decide what to keep and what to get rid of."

"Didn't waste any time getting rid of me, did you, Mom?"

"Don't be so dramatic, MJ."

"Drama is my middle name."

Mom rolls her eyes and pulls me up from my bed by the shoulders. She leads me in comfortable silence to the kitchen, where two red mugs sit on the counter.

"I'm surprised Nin let you repaint the cabinets black." Nina loves a clean look, rarely does she use dark colors on top cabinets.

"She liked 'em, especially with the new countertops," Mom says and stirs the contents of the mugs. The fairy-white quartz countertops and white farmhouse sink do brighten up the space, despite the black. I wouldn't have picked it, but whatever makes them happy. "You're not upset we asked her, are you?"

"She's here, it made sense."

She isn't really, but I couldn't tell Mom that. Nina had been spending a lot of time in Los Angeles and West Palm Beach handling the new offices, but she didn't want my parents to know. She made the time to run home and handle everything with their project herself. She asked me if I wanted to take over, but I assured her I did *not* want the task of helping my parents remodel my childhood home.

Per usual, Dad went to bed not too long after dinner, he has an early morning on the golf course — retirement looks good on him. So, it's me and Mom for the rest of the night. Mom pulls the chair out next to me and pushes a warm cup of hot cocoa towards me. My mom's homemade hot cocoa is one of the things I miss most about not living at home anymore. I've tried many times to recreate it, but can never seem to get it right — there is something special about the recipes only your mom can make for you.

"You wanna talk about it?"

Why does everyone keep asking me that? Am I that obvious?

"Oh c'mon, MJ. I know something is bothering you. It's written all over your face, not to mention I could tell the last few times we've talked."

"Everything is fine, Ma."

"I believe that like I believe your father eats the lunches I pack for him every morning." Daddy has never been known to eat his lunch. He usually passes it off to one of the guys opting to go out to lunch with a few friends. "Is it David — are you guys having trouble?"

"No, we're fine."

Lie.

"Are you sure? I mean, every time you talk about him, it seems—"

"I said, *we're fine.*"

"You know you can talk to me."

"Everything is fine, there's just a lot going on for both of us. Barnes keeps him extremely busy."

My mother's smile doesn't quite reach her eyes over her mug, "There always is."

*four*

## Michaela

**"WHEN ARE YOU GOING** to do it?" I stab a piece of chicken and lettuce before meeting Alex's wide eyes. Alexander Davis — cousin and (hopefully) soon-to-be partner at Abbott/Lowell Law Firm. Somehow, he managed to get the afternoon off, which meant I'd have something to get me out of the house and away from more of my mother's prying. Besides, it's been at least six months since I've seen him. When Alex told me he was moving to Charlotte not long after graduation from law school, I was shocked. He had two job offers at amazing firms in Boston, but he chose to move back home (almost) and take a job at Abbott/Lowell, instead. He said the opportunity was better, but I think he wanted to be closer to Uncle Jimmy, not to mention he'd get to stay close to his brother. He and Nick have always been close, and the time they had spent together in Boston was good for both of them.

"I don't know what you mean."

"Alex, it's been what, four years? You worship the ground she walks on."

He sighs and reaches into his jacket pocket to pull out his

35

phone. A quick search pulls up what he's looking for before he hands it to me. On the screen, an image of a beautiful ring — a simple silver band with small diamonds and a large princess cut in the center. "I'm gonna ask her on our trip to France next month."

"This is beautiful! Did you pick this out yourself?"

"Nick helped, I pick it up from the jeweler next week."

"He was home long enough?"

Alex laughs. "He's been home a little more recently and trying to travel with Nin; I think he's worried about her. You know how she gets — works too much, doesn't give herself a break. Gets a little…testy." The way he says it, I know what he's implying. "I hear you guys had a little run-in while she was in New York."

"Your brother has a big mouth."

"That's the pot calling the kettle black." Alex chuckles and I stick my tongue out at him. "I was hanging out with Nick when she got home and told him about it."

"It wasn't *that* bad."

"No? I didn't know telling your boss she can't run an office was the best way to work towards a good Christmas bonus."

I roll my eyes. "You don't expect me to let her walk all over me, do you?"

"Michaela, you cannot be serious. You expect me to believe that Nina Villa is being the unreasonable one?"

"She can be."

"She *can* be, but not about this. You told me not long ago you've been getting in late and struggling with adjusting to some of the changes since moving. She's given you a lot of slack, but it's been two years; it's time to grow up. Take responsibility for your mistakes."

Grow up? I've done more growing up in the past two months than he knows.

"It's not *that* bad. I'm just stressed and it doesn't help when she comes in and she's so on edge. I guess I can't blame her for having so many doctor appointments and being away from Nick so much."

"Back up — doctor appointments?"

*Shit.*

How did I let that slip? The look on Alex's face tells me there is no going back, I have to tell him the truth. Because if I don't, he won't stop until he gets it, even if that means going directly to Nina.

"What do you mean?" He pushes.

"Okay, what I'm about to tell you... You cannot tell Nick."

"Is something wrong?" The fear swims behind his eyes and I realize he's worried this will be another Aunt Evie situation.

"Alex. Swear you won't tell him. Relatively speaking, no. She's healthy as a horse, but she's gonna kill me if he finds out. I'm not even supposed to know!"

"If something is wrong, he deserves to know. That's his wife and if she's dealing with something, she needs to—"

I roll my eyes, "She's not dying."

"Then, what's wrong?"

"Promise you won't tell Nick."

"I can't do that, Michaela."

"Then, I can't tell you."

After a moment, he sighs, "Fine, I won't tell, Nick."

"Alex..."

"I promise!"

A deep sigh before I lean in a little closer. "Nina can't get pregnant. She's been going to specialists. She tried one in Charlotte, one out in Boston... Now, New York."

"That's why she's been there so much — not the office?"

"The office, too. I'm kind of under the microscope, remember?"

"Maybe you shouldn't be late all the time." He laughs when I throw a balled-up straw wrapper at him. "When is she going to tell him?"

"I don't know, she's supposed to go back soon, but it's not looking good. As long as I've known Nina, she's always wanted kids, I can't imagine—"

"This is gonna crush him, but it's not like he's gonna leave her."

I push scraps of lettuce around my plate. "Nina knows how much he wants a family, and she may not be able to give that to him. Whether we want to believe it or not, this could change things for them."

"Michaela, you can't be serious."

"I'm just saying. This is a big deal, it changes things."

"I don't think you're giving my brother enough credit. Sure, he's going to be pissed she didn't tell him, but not because she can't get pregnant, because he wasn't there for her."

I've tried to reason with Nina, telling her the same thing, but she's made up her mind.

"Look, I'll talk to her," Alex says.

"No! She'll know I told you. Alex, you can't say anything. Listen, I'm already on thin ice with her. If she knows I told you, that's it. I'm done."

"She isn't going to fire you because you told me."

"Have you met Nina?"

"Yes, and I know she can separate when it comes to business. If she *is* going to fire you it's for not doing your job."

"Shut the fuck up, Alex."

"Am I wrong?" He ducks when I throw one of the croutons at him. "That's not a no."

*five*

*Michaela*

**"I COME BEARING GIFTS,"** I say walking into the kitchen with the cake for today's party. Elizabeth clears a space on the counter and sets up the multi-colored polka dot cake stand. I open the lid when she finally turns to me, and the smell is heavenly — fresh vanilla and strawberry waft through the air. "Freshly baked this morning by the famous Ellen."

"It smells so good." She's practically drooling as she removes it from the box. The layered strawberry shortcake from Ellen's Bake Shop is always a must at Davis family functions, now that Aunt Evie isn't around to make her famous red velvet. Mom and Elizabeth have tried to recreate it, but unfortunately, no one makes it quite like her. The top is covered in a layer of cream frosting and fresh strawberries, each layer of cake separated by more frosting and berries, and fresh strawberry sauce drizzled on top. You must add Cool Whip, per Ellen, before serving, but not before. The whole thing looks magnificent sitting on its pedestal.

"I think we should skip lunch and go straight to dessert," Kai says joining us with Ophelia on his hip. "What do you think, Leia?"

"Yes!" Ophelia rubs her hands together and licks her lips.

"You don't want to spoil your appetite, do you?" Elizabeth boops her on the nose. "I made your favorite — dino nuggets!"

"Absolutely," Kai laughs, but Ophelia struggles, her eyes trained on the cake. She loves dino nuggets but loves cake more, ultimately agreeing with her dad.

"We at least need to wait for your Uncle Nick, don't we?"

Oh wow, Elizabeth is playing the Nick card. That's dirty. She knows Ophelia wouldn't dare leave her favorite Uncle out.

"Daddy, we have to wait," Ophelia says crossing her arms with a pout.

"This is blasphemy," Kai laughs, "you're supposed to be on my side, kid." He turns to Elizabeth," I can't believe you used Nick against me." Elizabeth shrugs, a large smirk on her lips as she rearranges more food. Ophelia squirms out of her father's arms and runs out of the kitchen towards the living room. When he is sure she's gone, he asks the question we're all wondering, "You sure he's even coming?"

"Said he'd be here," she says and leans back against the counter taking a sip of lemonade. "He was supposed to have landed last night, but Nin said he got held up at a dinner. His new flight should have landed about twenty minutes ago."

"Anyone heard from him to confirm that's real?" I ask.

"His flight got delayed," Nina says walking into the kitchen wearing high-waisted navy blue dress pants, a cream satin camisole, with a tan blazer and leopard print heels.

"You look like you just came from a board meeting," Kai taunts her — at least I'm not the only one who thinks so. I feel undressed in my jean shorts and a dark green button-down.

"Nick isn't going to make it," she ignores her brother's comment and doesn't acknowledge me.

"How long until the others get here?" Elizabeth takes another sip of her lemonade.

"Alex said they were leaving as I pulled up," I add swiping one of the carrot sticks from the veggie platter. "And, Mom and Dad should be here any minute."

"Where's Josh?" Kai pulls a beer from the fridge. "I haven't seen him yet. I thought he was on burger duty."

Elizabeth doesn't answer, her attention turns back to the food spread. It's quiet for a moment while we wait for her answer, but she never does. I look between the siblings who share a knowing glance, a private conversation I'm not privy to, before Nina motions toward me.

"Okay, well, I'm gonna go see if Mom and Dad are here yet," I say, but no one acknowledges me. Only after I step outside do I feel like I can breathe again. The vibe quickly shifted to something much heavier when Kai brought up Josh. Now that I think about it, that's the first time Nina hinted at knowing I was in the room — her eyes quickly shifting toward me before glaring back at her brother. I was missing a piece of the puzzle, something between the three Villa siblings that the rest of us weren't aware of. I don't know what that could have to do with my brother.

I take a quick step back when a black Escalade pulls into the circle parking in front of the steps. Tinted windows hide the driver from view. Who the hell is this?

Seconds later, a white Mercedes zips down the driveway pulling into the garage — found Josh.

"I didn't know they were offering valet service."

That voice. There's no fucking way. They wouldn't invite him. He's not even family. Shouldn't he be in Prague or Amsterdam or whatever the latest party city is in Europe right now.

"Why the long face, Shortcake? Not happy to see me?"

Finnley Sheffield.

God, I wish I could smack that smug look off his face.

"I thought that was you!" My brother clamps down on

Finn's shoulder disrupting our stare-off. "Glad you could make it."

"You know I wouldn't miss a chance to hang with the fam."

"What is he doing here?" I hiss at Josh.

"Oh, c'mon, Shortcake, don't be like that. I know you missed me." Finn outstretches his hand toward me like he's going to ruffle my hair, but I swat him away.

"Don't call me that." I despise the nickname. *Shortcake.* He has always called me that and I cringe every time. Where did it come from? I have no idea, probably because I've always been the shortest person around. I can't help it if I was the only one in the family not to inherit the Davis height genes. I turn back to my brother, "What is he doing here?"

"We ran into each other in town yesterday, so I invited him over," Josh shrugs like it's no big deal. "Mom and Dad will want to see him before he jets off again."

"I'm going to be sticking around for a while," Finn says. He opens the back of his Cadillac and pulls out a decent-sized box covered in wrapping paper with the poop emoji on it. So glad to know we've all grown up.

"What did Mommy and Daddy cut off your allowance?" I roll my eyes when Josh shoots me a glare.

"From those split ends and your outfit, I'd say Nina did too."

"Alright, you two, enough," Josh laughs. "Can't we agree to get along for one day?"

"Easier said than done, Joshy-boy," Finn says walking past me up the steps.

Josh rolls his eyes but turns to me with a pleading look. "For Dad and Uncle Jim, can you please *not* start any shit today?"

"I'm not the one who started it!"

"Just behave for one day; that's all I ask."

Is Josh telling me to behave? He invited the devil himself

to our family party. You can't invite Jabba the Hut to the party and expect me to be okay with it.

Behind us, I hear two cars pull up; they park behind Finn's Cadillac in the circle. Josh wastes no time turning away from our conversation to greet them.

"The party has arrived!" Dad says before rushing to the passenger side to help Mom out of the car. One of the small things he's always done for her — opening the door whenever she's getting in or out of the car, absolutely refusing to let her do it herself, even if it means getting soaking wet in the rain or sweating his ass off a few second longer in the summer heat.

"We were starting to think you got lost," Josh jokes, hugging our parents and then Uncle Jim.

"Your father decided this morning was a good time to trim the trees around the house," Mom remarks shooting him a glare.

Dad shrugs, "Needed to be done."

"Well, c'mon. Everyone else is here and food should be about done. I just have to throw the burgers on the grill." Josh ushers them up the steps and into the house, shooting me another warning glare on his way.

So much for today being relaxing.

"Is it just me, or does everyone seem a little on edge?" Alex asks, plopping down on the couch next to me.

"Definitely not just you." I follow Finn's movements as he plays some imaginary game with Ophelia in the corner. She screams with delight as he swoops her off her feet, spinning in a circle, and crashing into the large pillow fort she had built with Dad earlier. Ophelia lands on top of him when they fall, and she uses her body to cover his chest, giggling the whole time. Uncle Jimmy appears from the kitchen and counts to three declaring Ophelia the winner.

"I beat you, Uncle Finn!"

Since when is he Uncle Finn?

Alex pokes me in the arm pulling my attention away from the duo. "Hello, earth to Michaela."

"Huh? Sorry, what'd you say?"

"I asked if David was in D.C. this weekend?"

"Probably."

"Probably? You mean, you don't know?"

"I think he said they were traveling this weekend. He doesn't tell me everything, you know. He was home for a day last week, that's the most I've seen of him."

Good Michaela, really good, keep digging the hole deeper.

"That's why you're so on edge — haven't gotten any action lately?"

I roll my eyes. "For your information, the only thing bothering me right now is the fact my brother invited that asshole to the party."

"Who, Finn? Oh, you've got to be kidding, Mic. Are you still hating on him? It's been like ten years."

"Your point?"

"Grow up," he laughs.

"You should stop staring, might give someone the wrong idea," Finn interrupts before I have a chance to tell Alex to fuck off. Looking around, the room had cleared out leaving only the three of us.

"I was making sure you weren't being inappropriate with my niece."

"Michaela," Alex hisses.

Finn looks unimpressed with my comeback, and honestly, so am I. It was lame, but what else am I supposed to say? I *was* staring.

"Finn, she didn't mean that."

"I know she didn't." The smirk that spreads across his lips infuriates me. "She can't admit to staring at me, now can she? Like I said, might give someone the wrong idea."

"In your dreams, Sheffield," I scoff.

"You have no idea, Shortcake." Finn's voice drops lower than I've ever heard before, and it sends a shock straight to my core. He winks and holds my gaze for a second too long before turning back to Alex. "Josh still in the kitchen?"

"He and Dad went to his office before I came in here," Alex says skeptically. When Finn is out of earshot Alex turns to me with a wide look. "Did really he just say that?"

"Don't take it to heart. He's always saying shit to get under my skin."

"But he—"

"Wouldn't be the first time, probably won't be the last." I finish the rest of my sangria before leaving him to get a refill.

"Oh good," Elizabeth says when I walk into the kitchen. "Can you grab Nina?" She swipes crumbs from the counter into the palm of her hand before washing it down with a sanitary wipe. "She was on the phone out front, we're about to do cake."

"You got it, boss." I offer her a small salute before heading towards the front door.

At first, I don't see her, but after a second, I hear her boots pacing the asphalt up and down the circle. She doesn't say much to whoever is on the phone, but from the look on her face, the conversation is not going well. She pauses at the far end of the circle and ends the call, but she doesn't turn to come back inside. She lets her shoulders fall and releases the breath she has been holding. I'm torn between interrupting her and leaving her alone. She needs a moment to decompress, but with how things have been going today... I don't know if I want to come back empty-handed.

Nina straightens herself and prepares to walk back inside, to put up the mask once again, but freezes. Something catches her eye from the driveway I can't see. And the first real smile I've seen all day tugs on her lips before a dark-haired blur rushes towards her — Nick. He lifts her off her feet and kisses her. I don't know how they do it. Spend so much time apart. It used to kill me being away from David for a week, I can't imagine going two, three, or more at a time.

"Uncle Nick! Uncle Nick!" Ophelia? When did she get here? She barges out the door towards them tackling Nick's legs.

He laughs and kneels to her level, "Oh my goodness, is that Ophelia Jade? I swear you've gotten ten inches taller since I saw you."

"Nu-uh!"

"You sure? You're almost as tall as me." Nick moves his hand from the top of his to hers.

"Because you're on the ground," Ophelia giggles.

"Sorry, she slipped past me," I say joining them.

"I'm always happy to see my OJ," Nick says. He ruffles Ophelia's hair much to her dismay. "C'mon, let's go see everyone."

Ophelia jumps at the opportunity, taking his hand and babbling the whole way leaving me and Nina alone. I think about saying something to her, apologizing for the last time we saw each other now that we're not around everyone else, but Ophelia's words stop me, "Uncle Nick, is Aunt Nina okay?"

Oh no.

The world stops. I told Nina that kid was listening that day in the park. There's a questioning look on Nick's face as he glances down at her and back at his wife. He bends down to her level again. "Of course she is, Leia. Why would you ask that?"

Ophelia looks at Nina before beckoning him closer.

Using her hand, she cups her mouth to his ear and whispers something. His gaze narrows on Nina, but she doesn't react. Damn, I wish I had as good a poker face as her. Then, his gaze meets mine, and I know we're screwed.

"You're too smart for your own good." Nick kisses Ophelia's forehead. "Go inside, Leia. I'm right behind you. Tell Grandpa Jim it's time for cake, okay?"

"And then I can help with presents?"

"And then you can help with presents."

Ophelia wastes no time running back inside. Before the door even closes, Nick turns to face both of us.

"Nick—"

"We'll talk later, Michaela," he stops me. "Go inside."

I share a look with Nina, who nods, but I don't want to leave her. "Michaela, go," she insists. After a moment, I finally give in. "Nick, let me—"

"Doctor, Nina?" His voice a low hiss. "What in the hell is going on?"

"I'm okay," she says as I reach the door. "I will explain everything at home, I promise. Can we please go enjoy the party? For your dad and Patrick, Nick… Please."

Alex stands in the doorway. "Everything good?"

"Nick knows."

## six

## *Michaela*

**NICK MOVED INTO NINA'S** house on the outskirts of Winchester not long after their elopement, and from what I could tell, it had been an easy transition. He didn't have much, but it didn't matter because Nina already had everything. Much to my surprise she cleared out some of her closet for his clothes and gave him free rein to make changes in the house. "It's his home, too," Nina said with a small shrug. He didn't change much, instead, he opted to take over one of the spare rooms on the lower level turning it into his office and man cave.

I've always loved Nina's house, it's warm and welcoming, but as I approach the entrance to the Villa-Davis home today, I feel anything but welcome. Through the paneled windows on either side of the door, the house is dark. Nick stands in the open door, arms crossed tightly over his chest. His jacket from earlier gone, sleeves rolled up to reveal a new tattoo on his forearm. It looks familiar — a mountain range. Haven. It's the mountains surrounding their home in Haven. "Hey, Michaela." His greeting is simple and nice enough, but his tone betrays him.

"Nin home?"

"Yep."

"Am I interrupting something?"

"You could say that."

I sigh, "Nick, don't be too mad at her. She just... She didn't want to worry you."

"My wife forgets she's my wife sometimes. Forget there's another person involved — it's not just her anymore."

"She was trying to protect you."

"And, who's protecting her?"

"What do you want, Michaela?" Nina's voice resonates from further inside the house. Nick sighs and finally steps to the side allowing me to enter.

The house is dark sans the light flooding the living area from the kitchen. Nina stands on the other side of the Calcutta marble island, still dressed in her party attire, but her makeup looks worn. She's been crying. I picked the wrong time to visit, but I leave in the morning and need to make things right with her. I'm starting to think a phone call would've been better.

"Before you say anything, I have something to say to *both* of you," Nick says before I can start.

"Nick," Nina pleads, she sounds tired.

"No, Davina." Oh shit, not the full name. He really is mad. "I'm going to say what I have to say, and you're both going to listen. How could you keep this from me? Am I not the other half of this relationship? We are a team, Dee. You and me. You're not alone anymore. And you," Nick looks at me, "I would've thought you'd tell me."

"I wanted to, but—"

"No buts, Mic. The second you knew, you should've said something. Did you at least go to the appointments with her after you found out?"

She wouldn't let me. I only found out the time before this

last trip, I—

"No?" He turns to Nina, "So, you did this alone?"

"We didn't want to worry you," I plead.

"What did you think was gonna happen when I found out? You knew I'd find out eventually."

"I was hoping it wouldn't come to that," Nina's voice is firmer.

"You weren't gonna tell me?"

She doesn't respond and that tells him everything he needs to know.

"Nina," I sigh. Of course, she wasn't going to tell him, not if the tests came back with positive results. She was hoping for the best, hoping for some kind of miracle so it wouldn't have to come to this. To avoid this exact moment. By the look on Nick's face, I know this conversation is far from over — Nina's admission hurt him far more than he will ever care to admit. I really should leave. "Look, you guys need some time. I can just call you tomorrow, Nin."

"No, it's fine." Nick's eyes never leave his wife. "I'm gonna go for a drive." The door slams behind him, echoing around us, but Nina doesn't flinch.

She takes a breath and closes her eyes. "Michaela, I am not in the mood. Whatever you have to say—"

"I'm sorry, Nina," I say it anyway because I need to.

Nina sighs, "I need a drink." She disappears into the pantry returning with a bottle of whiskey. "Wine isn't going to cut it."

"No, it's not," I laugh as she pours two glasses. "Look, Nin... For years, we have been able to draw a line between business and our friendship; I'm sorry that I crossed it." I try to finish reciting the speech I practiced my entire drive over, but she stops me.

"Michaela, I know. Okay? I know you're sorry, and you came to apologize, but I don't want to hear it." I swallow the lump in my throat. "What I want... I want you to get your shit together. You are so much better than this. So, if you want to apologize, just get it together because I don't wanna fire you. But, I will fire you if I have to. This is not personal, it's business."

"I know."

Nina lets her shoulders fall with a deep exhale and downs her whiskey in one gulp.

"It's gonna be okay, Nin. He'll get over it."

"Maybe tomorrow, but not tonight."

"So, you really weren't gonna tell him?"

Nina smiles and pours another glass. "If everything came back fine, why worry him?"

"But, they said—"

"Wishful thinking, I guess."

Without a second thought, I hug the woman in front of me. She takes a shaky breath, but when we part there is no sign of the brokenness moments earlier. Taking a step back, she pours another glass and downs it without so much as a wince and asks, "So, are *you* ready to talk?"

"I'm not sure what you mean." I step into the living room a few paces behind her, falling into the large sofa. The coffee table is littered with wedding debris — menu cards, a seating chart, floral arrangement examples, and color samples. How does she ever get any sleep when she has constant reminders of things that need to be done lying around?

"Oh, come on, Mic. Something is going on," Nina scoffs, rolling her eyes and taking a rather large sip of wine. "You've been acting weird for *months.* You're falling behind at work, you're always late, you were rude to Romy in Italy, you're avoiding your parents, and—"

"Everything is fine. I promise."

"Is it David?"

"Why does everyone keep asking me that?"

I avoid her gaze, but she leans down into my line of vision

and says, "Maybe because he hasn't been around lately."

"David hasn't been around since we moved to New York."

"This is more than normal," she argues. "Sure, Barnes keeps him busy, but I haven't seen him once in the past few months. Are you guys having problems?"

"We're fine." The statement comes out harsher than I mean for it to, and she puts her hands up in defense. I repeat myself, softer this time, tracing the rim of my glass.

She stares at me for a moment then shakes her head and goes to the kitchen to make another drink. Just like Elizabeth, she doesn't believe me, but she's not going to push it. Pouring more whiskey into the glass, "Oh, I forgot to tell you. I need you to help me with something in the coming weeks." The smirk tugging on her lips when she finally meets my stare tells me I'm not going to like what she has in store. "I have a project at corporate that I need covered, and I think you're just the person for it."

"Corporate? Nina, what are you—"

"You wanted a change, right? I'm giving it to you."

"Wait, does this mean you *are* firing me?"

"No," she laughs. "I'm trying something out *and* giving you a little extension on your timeline."

"Who's going to run the office?"

"You have some time to figure that out, you'll be at the office Monday and Tuesday. Take that time to get everything prepared. I need you at corporate starting Wednesday."

## Michaela

**CHAMPAGNE STONE BUILT THE** walls of the estate home Nina rented for our time in the Estranei countryside. She had chosen it because it reminded her of her home in Haven — a secluded, private estate with stunning views. Complete by an expansive garden and a pool overlooking the lush Italian countryside with five buildings on the grounds: the main house, an annex, a pool house, a barn, and servants' quarters. A courtyard separates the annex from the main house — Nina and Elizabeth share the main house, while I will be in the annex with Nina's long-lost cousin who has yet to arrive. At the top of the courtyard, a dining terrace off the kitchen features a wood-fired pizza oven and an extra-long farmhouse table. Two more terraces hold a smaller dining table perfect for morning breakfast and an outdoor fire pit with seating.

Being here feels like living in a fairytale — one I'm not sure I want to leave. And for the last day and a half, Elizabeth and I have been taking the opportunity to enjoy some peace and quiet before what is sure to be a long two weeks.

"She's here!" I hear Nina call from the main house.

*She* being Romy Beaumont, the daughter of Audrey Beaumont and granddaughter of Caterina Villa, sister of Lorenzo Villa. Lorenzo was Nina's grandfather who moved to the United States following the death of his parents. Caterina left Italy two years before their death when she turned eighteen to pursue a career in fashion, much to her parents' dismay. After leaving Estranei, she lost contact with her family until her daughter, Audrey, got in contact with Nina's dad before his sudden death. Unbeknownst to his family, until Audrey reached out to Nina almost a year later. When Audrey introduced Nina and Romy, there was an instant connection, like long-lost sisters.

Romy and Nina have spent the past year pouring over the work their parents had done, delving further into the history of the Villa family and its roots. They knew Alessio, their great-grandfather, worked in a vineyard in the Province of Ancona and notes from Audrey pointed to the name Vitali. There are two vineyards in the province that trace back to the name Vitali, and only one with a potential connection to the Villas. Bacami Vineyard in Estranei — the owners Camilla and Enzo Vitali, siblings.

The discovery of Bacami Vineyard was three months ago. Since then, Nina and Romy have been planning this trip to learn more about their family. Unfortunately, Audrey isn't healthy enough to join them.

I'm not sure what I was expecting when the long-lost Villa cousin stepped out of the black SUV, but it was not a paler version of Nina. Same height and hair color. It was like someone hit copy and paste with a -3 on skin pigmentation. Romy speaks excitedly into her phone in a language I don't recognize. French, maybe? Her eyes practically roll out of her skull before she bites back at the person on the other end. She says something into the phone before ending the call abruptly and turning to us. "Davina!"

"Romy!" Nina embraces her cousin. "Com'è stato il viaggio?"

"Perfetto," is the only word I understand as Romy begins to say something in what I think is Italian. Nina nods, and they giggle. "Oh mio... Sono Elizabeth e Michaela?" Nina confirms. "No Italiano?"

"Minimo."

Romy shares a tight smile before she turns to me and Elizabeth. When she removes the large shades from her face, I notice she has the same green eyes as Nina, but they are much bigger, rounder — like ovals. Her dark brown hair is pulled into a tight, slicked-back ponytail on top of her head. The poet-sleeved sheer white shirt over a tank top shows off her exceptionally slim hourglass figure. As she approaches, I notice she, unlike Nina, has a full face of makeup — foundation, contour, blush, shadow, lashes, lipstick...

"It's so nice to meet you!" Her English is perfect with the slightest French accent. "Davina has told me so much about you both." First, she hugs Elizabeth, who welcomes her with open arms, but when she turns to me, I only offer her a tight-lipped smile. She pulls me into a hug anyway. There is something I don't like about Romy, but I can't quite place my finger on it, or maybe I'm being too quick to judge.

"You'll have to forgive us, as long as we've known Nina, we still haven't quite picked up much Italian," Elizabeth says.

"Nonsense. I need to practice my English, anyway."

"Come inside, Elizabeth just made brunch. We have plenty," Nina ushers Romy towards the house.

"E colazione liquida?"

"Plenty of it."

I smile stepping into the warm morning sun with a fresh cup of coffee. I'm almost convinced we're living in the wrong country because I could get used to this. I retreat from the dining terrace down to the lower level terrace — planters filled with different flowers surround a wicker patio set. Each terrace has a little garden with a few samplings of the expansive greenery surrounding our vacation home. Despite the conversation outside my window last night, dinner was completely normal. I overheard Nina and Romy talking about my less-than-welcoming remarks to Romy at the pool earlier in the day. A conversation I wasn't supposed to hear, but it flowed through my open window. "Mi dispiace per quello che ha detto Michaela," Nina said and I'd heard that sentence more than once in the years. She was apologizing for what I said.

Romy started to reply in Italian, but said, "I think she's worried."

"What is there to be worried about?"

"Davina, how would you feel if some person showed up in Michaela's life, supposedly her long-lost family member and she flew across the globe to meet them." Nina didn't respond. "Esattamente." Nina returned to Italian. That time, I wasn't sure what she said. I didn't have to wait long because Romy asked, "Strange how?"

"We can't talk here," Nina said before a long pause. "La finestra." *The window.*

I had expected some kind of confrontation at dinner, but it never came. Then again, I knew Nina would wait until the right moment to strike.

I settle on the couch, taking a large sip of coffee, and my mind immediately wanders back to my phone call with David the day before leaving home.

"What do you mean you can't come?" I hissed. I had called to confirm what time I should pick him up from the airport, but instead, he informed me he wouldn't be coming home.

"We leave tomorrow, David."

"I can't get away right now, Mic. There's too much to do."

"You're telling me Jonah can't handle things for a few days?"

"A few days? Michaela, it's *two* weeks! That's a long time. I can't just—"

"Yeah, you're right, your work is important, and Barnes needs you there."

"Don't do that," he sighed. "Don't be a brat." After a moment of silence, his voice was softer when he spoke again. "Look, I'm sorry that I can't up and leave like Nina and the rest of 'em. This isn't a job where I can decide not to go to work today because I don't feel like it. I'm sorry I can't be there to see you off, but I'm needed here in D.C. Maybe when you're back, you can finally come down here for a change." That's always the solution. I have to come to D.C., I have to be the one to come to him, or I won't see him at all. "I think you'd like it here."

"I think you like it there. I'm not having this conversation right now, David."

"You never do," he sighed. "Look, I gotta go. We have a dinner tonight and—"

"Sure, yeah, go ahead. I'll talk to you later." I hung up without saying goodbye. That's how it's been — constantly bickering, going back and forth, taking little jabs at one another — truthfully, it got worse after we got married last August. Saying "I do" that day in the little chapel, I never imagined our life would end up like this. Sure, he's always been a little rough around the edges, but that's what I liked most. I thought we'd get to live happily ever after like we had always talked about, but it seems the only happily ever after on the agenda is his. It wasn't until he started playing pretend with the big wigs in Washington that I noticed he wasn't who I thought he was.

I take a deep breath of fresh country air, soaking in the warmth of the Italian sun. Long blonde strands blow in the breeze before I tie them up into a haphazard bun. Sipping my coffee, I think back to when we first met almost four years ago…

I sprinted through the doors of Charlotte Douglas International Airport with exactly ten minutes to get through security and to my gate before they closed the boarding door. There was no way I was going to make it. Reaching the ticket counter, I resigned myself to the fact I was going to miss the flight and the friendly smile of the counter associate didn't do anything to help my anxiety. "She's going to murder me," I muttered to myself pulling out my passport.

"I'm sure she'll understand, dear."

"I appreciate the vote of confidence, but you don't know Nina." Digging through my purse for my phone, I dreaded the phone call I was about to make. "When is the next one I can get on?"

"Well," the older woman typed on the computer. "Looks like we have some room for you on the noon flight."

"Okay, that's not bad. I can be there pretty early still."

"That'll get you there about 7:00 PM."

"7:00 PM? That's too late! Don't you have any—"

"Sorry, sweetie. All my nonstops are booked. You gotta take a layover in Salt Lake before you land in San Diego."

"Fine," I cursed. "Okay, whatever gets me there. Now she's *really* gonna kill me." The older woman — Doris, her name tag read — gave me a sympathetic smile over the computer. After a few moments, Doris handed back my passport and a fresh set of tickets.

"Good luck with everything, sweetie. Hope your friend doesn't get too mad."

"She's probably expecting it, let's be honest." I sighed and pulled up the familiar contact. I needed to get my shit together if I wanted her to even consider me for a bigger position in the company — aka the New York office, she had plans for in a few years.

I stuffed my sweater into my purse before shoving it through the X-ray machine. My carry-on behind it. The line for bodies was held up by a group of young twenty-somethings who were flirting with the two TSA agents on the other side. Wasn't that the opposite of what was supposed to be going on? Where were the grumpy TSA agents who kept the line moving? I could see the bags piling up on the other side of both X-ray machines.

"Oops! Sorry. I moved again," I heard one of the twenty-somethings giggle. Finally, a female TSA agent stepped in relieving the flirtatious ones. She motioned for the young women to proceed to an older agent who was waiting to search her on the side.

"Thank God," I heard the man in front of me huff, and I couldn't help but express my own relief.

He was a tall glass of water. His hair was black and styled to perfection. His back muscles strained against his sky-blue dress shirt. Not to mention the way his gray pants put his ass on display. If he was this handsome from the back, I could only imagine what he looked like from the front.

"Ma'am, please step forward," a different TSA agent beckoned me forward to a secondary scanner. I cursed him for missing the chance to see what my mystery man looked like.

With no sign of him when I made it to the other side, I slung my purse over my shoulder and reached for the handle of my leather duffel bag. I was mentally preparing myself to wait another four hours before my new flight would start boarding. At least, the gate was nearby one of my favorite bars — I could get a drink before this long ass trip.

"Excuse me," a deep voice called behind me. I heard them, but I didn't stop. Surely, they weren't talking to me. "Excuse me," it called again, closer. A sudden jerk on the bag in my hands stopped me.

"Hey! What the hell?"

"Would you stop?"

My suspicions were correct. Tall. Dark. And, *extremely* handsome. Stormy grey eyes glowered down at me. A full beard matched the color of his hair, but it didn't hide the sharp jawline beneath.

"Are you going to just stare at me or are you going to give me my bag?"

Wait, did he say *his* bag? I looked down at the bag in my hands and the one in his own. They looked similar, but not quite the same. Mine was a shade lighter and had a front pocket, but the one in my hands did not.

"You speak English, no?"

"Um, yes. Sorry. I didn't—"

"Are you going to hand it over or... Y'know, some of us have places to be." I quickly handed over the bag and caught mine before it landed on the ground. He continued to mutter to himself as he walked away.

Later in the day, I stifled a yawn following the other passengers on board my connecting flight in Salt Lake. I stuffed my carry-on into the overhead bin before falling into the seat that would be my bed for the next two hours. Just as I started to let myself slip into a state of unconsciousness, I felt something fall halfway into my lap — a suit jacket. The owner grumbled to themselves stuffing their belongings into the overhead bin. Opening my eyes, I came face-to-face with the same stormy eyes from early that morning.

"Try not to steal my bag when we leave this time," he says, but this time it's less assholey. The smile that tugged on his lips told me he was, in fact, making a joke as he fell into the seat next to me.

"Sorry about that," I said handing back his coat.

"It happens. I'm sorry I was such a grump this morning, it has not been my day."

"You can say that again." The seventy-eight text messages on my phone told me exactly how things in San Diego were going. Nina had been laying into people left and right and after the first ten messages, I decided it was best to ignore it until I got there.

"Vacation?"

"No, work."

"Hitman?" The laugh busted out of me at his outrageous assumption. "I mean, what else would bring you all the way across the country?"

"Anything else," I chuckled. "Literally anything."

"I'm David," he stuck his hand towards me. When I returned the gesture, his hand swallowed mine whole.

The crunch of gravel from the black Mercedes Benz making its way up the driveway interrupts my thoughts. Weird, we aren't supposed to leave for the vineyard for another hour and a half. Maybe Angelo is dropping off more groceries. "Hey, Angelo!" I stand to meet him but freeze when another man steps out of the passenger seat. "Nick?"

"Hey, Mic!" Nick, dressed in black khakis and a black polo, retrieves his bag from Angelo before handing him a few bills even after Angelo refuses.

"What are you doing here?"

"Didn't feel right not being here, ya know?"

I smile, "She's gonna be happy to see you."

"Well, I'd hope so," he laughs. "Besides, someone else wanted to join the fun." As he says it, the man I'd been thinking about moments ago steps around the other side of the SUV.

"David? What are you doing here?"

"Boss told me I needed a few days off," David's response light as he drapes his arm across my shoulders. We follow Nick up the steps. "Heard I was supposed to be in Italy for a family reunion and kicked me out."

"I told him I was heading out last night, so he decided to

join," Nick calls over his shoulder as we reach the kitchen door.

Dark wood-beamed ceilings, contrasting the sand-colored walls, are featured throughout the entire villa. The country-style kitchen features black-stained cabinets and black marble counters, modern appliances, and marble floors. Open shelves float above the sink, and more shelving is tucked into a small alcove to the right of the stove. Elizabeth washes pans from breakfast. "Mic, that you? Can you grab Romy so we can eat? Nin should be back any second from her run."

"You make enough for six?"

Elizabeth drops the pan in her hands at the sound of Nick's voice. Her jaw drops when she turns around. "What are you doing here?" She engulfs him in a large hug. "I thought you had work."

"I did, but this is why I have people who work for me. They can handle it while I take care of important things like this."

"Oh! David, you too?" Elizabeth seems more shocked than me to see him. It's a known fact that my husband rarely gets time away from his job with Senator Barnes.

"Senator kicked me out," he squeezes my side gently before offering Elizabeth a brief smile.

"Did I miss something?" Romy stands in the doorway dressed in high-waisted jean shorts and a tucked white button-down, much more relaxed than yesterday. "Oh," her words are lost when she finally sees the faces of the newcomers, specifically my cousin. "Hello, handsome." She flits towards him, her long fingers tracing the opening of his polo, nails lightly dragging across the skin.

"Sto interrompendo qualcosa?" Nick doesn't hide his smirk at the sound of *her* voice, and all eyes turn towards the door except his. I'm sure he can already see the look on her face. Her skin flush from the run she's come back from, chest rising and falling with each breath as she wipes at the sweat on her face.

"Davina! This lovely gentleman—"

"Is Nick," she interrupts her cousin and Romy looks between them before quickly taking two large steps back.

"I didn't know. Oh, mon Dieu. I am so sorry."

Nina doesn't hide her smirk, finally meeting her husband's gaze. His lips fall into a soft smile, and she returns it. "C'mon, I'll show you the room," she extends her left hand towards him, the ring on her finger sparkles in the sunlight from the window. Did she know they were coming? She doesn't seem that surprised to see him.

"It's nice to finally meet you, Romy," Nick says before following Nina up the stairs.

"Oh my gosh," Elizabeth giggles when they are gone.

Romy's face turns a deep crimson. "I can't believe I just did that."

"C'mon, I'll show you our room," I whisper to David, leaving behind a mortified Romy and an amused Elizabeth.

The rolling hills of Estranei surrounding the Bacami Vineyard and Estate look more like a painting than a real-life landscape. The estate began operating in 1891 and would release its first wine two years later. It sits on two hundred and thirty-five hectares of land — close to five hundred and eighty acres — most of which are dedicated to the vineyards, divided based on which side of the estate they sit. Red grapes were planted closer to the coast, while white grapes were planted on the inland, mountainous side of the estate. One of their main goals is to preserve the originality of each wine — each stage of production is done on the estate.

Lorenzo Villa, Nina's grandfather, grew up here. His father

worked as an estate groundskeeper. After the tragic death of his parents, Alessio and Gaia Villa, Lorenzo sold everything the family owned and moved to the United States. He would never return to Italy, much to the disappointment of Tommaso Vitali, his childhood best friend and son of the estate owners.

"Our grandfathers were the best of friends," Camilla Vitali, one of the current co-owners, tells us as we enter the tasting room inside a large barn. "We still have some photos of them up over here." She leads Nina and Romy around the corner toward the back of the tasting room.

"You wanna get out of here?" A deep whisper tickles my ear and a hand tugs on mine, pulling me a few steps behind the rest of the group. "Not like anyone would notice."

"I think they'd notice. C'mon, this is important to Nina, which means it should be important to us."

"It's not our family," David huffs.

"But Nick is mine, and Nina is his, which makes her family mine."

"Whatever, Mic. You just want to be around that Enzo guy." David drops my hand and takes two steps away from me.

"You cannot be serious." Today has been going a little too well, and I've been waiting for the moment things implode. Houston, we have arrived. "David, are you starting this right now?"

"I'm not the one who started it."

"For the love of God." I roll my eyes and leave him to rejoin the others. As I turn the corner the group disappeared around moments ago, I meet the curious eyes of Enzo Vitali — brother of Camilla and the co-owner of the Estate.

"Oh, hello Michaela," Enzo says. His accent makes me melt. There is nothing better than a man with an accent. He whispers something inside the office before closing the door, turning to me with a small smirk. "Did you get lost from the group?"

"Something like that."

"No worries, I'll help you find them." I hesitate briefly but take his arm when he offers.

David immediately apologized when we returned from the vineyard that night. And as much as I wanted to stay mad, I couldn't. We don't get much time together and I wanted to enjoy vacation, not spend the rest of it arguing.

On the last two days of our trip, David and I decided to stay in Rome while the others traveled to Lake Como; though I am a little sad I won't see where Anakin and Padme got married. Minus the fight at the vineyard, this trip has been exactly what David and I needed to reignite the spark we seem to have lost a few months ago. However, I am a little worried about what happens when we go home.

Will we go back to the way it's been? I don't think I can bear it. Being so far from him for such long periods isn't working… for either of us. In the beginning, we thought he would at least get to come home once a week, but that rarely happens. He wants me to move to D.C., but I can't — I don't belong there, I belong in New York. My entire life is there.

"What are you thinking about?" David asks as we walk side-by-side through the ancient streets after a romantic dinner at Aroma, a restaurant with amazing views of the Colosseum It's our final night in what might be the most magical place on Earth.

"Just how nice this has been," I sigh and loop my arm through his, but he feels limp in my grasp. He only nods. Come to think of it, he's been extra quiet today. "I don't want to go back home, back to reality."

A soft chuckle.

"When do you go back to work?"

"I'm flying straight to D.C."

"You can't even come home for—"

"Michaela, I've been gone long enough, I have to get back to work." He stops abruptly, "Look, Mic," he stops abruptly. He pinches the bridge of his nose and takes a long, deep breath. "We need to talk."

My stomach sinks at his words, but I try to laugh it off. "Isn't that what we've been doing?"

"You know what I mean."

## *eight*

### Michaela

**"I'M SORRY, MICHAELA, BUT** he's not budging," Elias says from across his oversized mahogany desk. The man across from me isn't who I imagined when I found his law firm online. I pictured an older man — slicked back gray hair, glasses, maybe a bit of a gut — but that is not who I found when I walked into his office almost three months ago. Elias Donovan reminds me of Rufus Humphrey — if you know, you know. He removes his glasses from the edge of his nose and looks up from the papers in his hands. "He wants it back, in its entirety."

"What is he going to do with it — propose to his next wife? That's a little tacky, even for him."

Elias tries to hide the smile in the corner of his mouth. "The center stone is very important to the family and—"

"I said he can have that one back."

"And the condo? He wants to sell it, split the proceeds."

"It's *my* condo, he's barely—"

"You're both on the deed, Michaela. He has just as much right to want to sell as you do to want to keep it."

I roll my eyes, I knew putting him on the deed was a

mistake. "I bought that condo, Elias. He didn't put a penny down on it, I just—"

"Doesn't matter, he's on the deed." Elias offers a sympathetic smile. "Look, we can work on it, but we still have the ring to worry about. If you don't want to give the whole thing back what are *you* going to do with it?"

"Throw it in the Hudson, probably."

He can't hold back his laughter. "Well, please refrain from doing so before the divorce is finalized."

"No promises, Elias."

Elias sighs and pulls a cloth from the desk drawer to wipe invisible dust off his glasses. "Michaela, you realize this could have been finalized if you weren't holding onto the ring. I'm almost positive we could get him to budge on the condo if you'd give the ring back." Setting his glasses back on his nose, he folds his hands in front of him. "What good is it to drag out the process for something you're not going to keep anyway?"

He's right, but that's not the point. It's the point that my husband blindsided me with a divorce without any room for discussion or the possibility of fixing it. "I'll think about it."

"So, what exactly are we doing here?" Caitlin follows me through the revolving door of the Woolworth Building — home of Villa Inc., NYC — the next morning.

I wave at the security guard sitting at the front desk, and she waves us through. "I wish I could tell you, Cait," I press the call button for the elevator. "I know as much as you. All she'd tell me is there's something she needs help with at corporate. It's pushed back my probationary period, so I guess I shouldn't complain."

"At least we're not late."

"Sure about that?"

She checks her watch with a groan. "You're a terrible influence."

We aren't late, yet, but we will be by the time we get upstairs.

The ride to the twenty-eighth floor takes less than a minute, but it's the longest minute of my life. When the elevator doors open, big, bold letters greet us — *VILLA, INC.* Underneath them a young redhead with bright red lips talks into the phone, and she holds her finger up to us when we approach the desk. The person on the other end drones on about something she doesn't care about based on the look on her face, but the smile never falls from her lips. "Okay, well, unfortunately, I can't give you that information. You will have to wait for a response from Mr. Fields... No, it doesn't matter who— Well, I'm sorry, but that's protocol. You can take it up with him when he gets back with you. Have a great day!" I wait for the smile to falter, but it never does as her attention turns to us. "Morning ladies, they should be in conference room two waiting for you."

*They?* Who the hell is they — I thought I was meeting Nina.

"How is she this morning, Liv?" Caitlin asks.

"Seemed to be in a good mood when I got here, she'd already been here by the time I got in, but that was a while ago, so who knows what someone around here could've done by now."

"You're not inspiring any confidence."

"I wouldn't worry about Mrs. VD as much as her counterpart." Before I can push for more details, the phone rings and she instantly picks it up.

"Sounds like we're in for the time of our lives," Caitlin says, looping her arm through mine. She begins to tell me more about the guy she has been seeing for two months as we walk through the halls. Apparently, he's too good to be true, and in my experience, that means he is, but, I don't want to burst her bubble. Besides, it worked out for Nick and Nina, right? That should give everyone a little hope.

The environment of Villa Inc. is drastically different from DV Designs. It's nowhere near as warm and inviting, more executive. Offices are closed off, and the ones with windows have the blinds drawn for extra privacy. DV offices tend to be open and airy, with glass walls and splashes of color throughout the decor. Nina never wants it to feel like a typical office setting, she wants it to inspire creativity and make people feel comfortable. Unlike the feeling I'm getting right now.

"You've got to be kidding me." The words tumble out before I can stop them walking into the conference room. At the far end of the table sits my worst nightmare — one of them, anyway. "What are *you* doing here?"

This has got to be some kind of joke, Nina cannot seriously be putting me on a project with *Finnley Sheffield.* I step outside and double-check the number on the outside of the door — Conference Room 2.

Fuck.

"You here to take my coffee order or something? I'll take an Americano—"

"We are not your errand girls," I cut him off.

"Then, you must be in the wrong place because I have a meeting with—"

"Michaela!" Nina hustles through the door with Eddie, her assistant, hot on her heels. "Oh Caitlin, I didn't know you were coming."

"Michaela asked if I'd accompany her, in case an extra pair of hands were needed," Caitlin smiles briefly.

"So, who's running the office?" Nina's question is directed at me.

"Jamie and Erin are working—"

"Caitlin," Nina interrupts, "head back over. I want to be

sure the place doesn't burn down and I can't trust Jamie won't start a fire. Michaela will be perfectly fine, they'll have all the help they need right here."

Caitlin offers me a sympathetic smile and mouths, 'Good luck,' before Nina closes the door behind her.

"Sheff, how was the flight?" Nina asks, settling into one of the seats across from him. Eddie falls into a chair next to her, typing away on his phone. I've been there, helping Nina take care of things on the back end, but that was when we were still a smaller firm... I can't imagine what it must be like now.

"Davina, can I talk to you? Privately." Finn glares at me from the corner of his eye.

"Finn, we need to— Okay, okay. Fine. Michaela, give us a moment, would you?"

She cannot be serious.

"Michaela, please."

With a sigh, I push out of my chair and step out into the hallway leaving the door partially open so I can still hear their conversation.



"You cannot be serious," Finn hisses. "You want to put *her* on this project? Nina, she doesn't have any kind of experience with this type of thing."

"She's one of my best assets, Finn. She's a hard worker and very detailed, you need someone like her if you're going to make this work."

"Josh said you were about to fire her last week."

Nina sighs. "Michaela is one of my best employees—"

"You mean friends."

"Employee, she always has been. I truly think she's the best person to fill in while I'm gone."

**Cait**

**He seems like a real joy.**

Oh yeah, a true ray of sunshine.

"You came to me, remember? You asked for *my* advice. My help, I–"

"Exactly, *your* help! Not some random person from your office. If I wanted someone with no experience, I would've picked someone off the street. Instead, I came to you—"

"I have been more than fair to you with my time and resources, Finnley Sheffield." The bite in her tone leaves a silence in the air. "While running not one, but two companies, I have helped you beyond what I should have without hesitation. I—"

"We're both benefitting from this, Davina."

"You want to continue to receive my help? This is me offering that to you and more… Take it or leave it."

"I can't believe this." Second later, the door swings open to reveal an extra pissed-off Finn. He doesn't seem at all shocked to see me standing in the doorway listening to what was meant to be a "private" conversation. His eyes narrow. "Don't fuck this up," he grumbles and pushes past me.

Nina continues to glare after Finn even though he has turned the corner out of sight. I swallow the lump in my throat when cold green eyes meet mine.

"Well, he's a real treat," Eddie whispers without looking up from his phone.

That's one way to put it.

"Can we discuss what happened earlier?" I ask stuffing a piece of a California roll in my mouth. Nina offered me dinner at her place before she leaves to meet Nick somewhere out West in the morning, and I couldn't refuse.

"What is there to discuss?" She refills her glass with Chardonnay.

"The fact that you want me to work with the most impossible man on the planet."

Nina chuckles behind her wine glass. "You wanted a change, right?"

"Anything would be better than working with him. *Anything.*"

"You're being a little dramatic, don't you think?"

"I hated him growing up." I make sure to emphasize the hated. "He has always been an asshole, I don't know how Josh and Nick have stayed friends with him this long."

"You didn't seem to mind him at Josh's wedding."

"There were hundreds of other people there to keep him preoccupied, and I did everything I could to stay away from him."

Not that it worked, we still managed to run into each other.

"Look," Nina sighs, "he's a little rough around the edges, but Finn is not that bad. I've been helping him, but I don't have the time to keep focusing on it. Besides, I think this is exactly the thing you need."

"How is this the thing I need?" I stuff another piece of sushi in my mouth.

"It'll help get you out of whatever rut you're in. It's only two weeks, that's about all the time left before it goes to the board, anyway; but, in two weeks, if you're still adamant about it, I'll pull you off the project."

Two weeks, huh? I can do that. I'll make it work. After two weeks, I'll ask her to take me off. Except two weeks will be the end of the probationary period she put me on. If I ask to be taken off... I bite my bottom lip, unsure if I want to ask this next question. "What happened to my month's probation?"

"We'll see how things play out."

Her smile doesn't quite reach her eyes, and for the first time, I see how tired she looks with dark circles under her eyes showing through her makeup. If she's been working on the new DV offices *and* helping out with corporate *and* helping Finn with this project... I can't imagine. Nina has always been there for me and helped me, continued to put up with me when I messed up, the least I can do is suck it up for two weeks.

"Fine," I sigh. "I'll help him. I won't like it, but I'll do it."

"You can always call me."

"And bother you when you finally have a chance to get away from the devil himself? I don't think so."

Nina rolls her eyes and finally asks what she's been wanting to know since she invited me for dinner earlier. "Where's David, by the way? I was hoping he'd be in town,"

No, she wasn't, she's just nosey.

"D.C.," I lie avoiding her gaze. It's not a total lie, I assume he is in Washington with Barnes, but I don't know for sure.

"Everything still okay with you two?"

"Yeah, we're fine. Busy, you know how it is." Without having to tell her, Nina knows something is going on, but she'll wait for me to come to her. I should tell her. She won't judge, but if I tell someone, that makes it *real.* And I don't think I'm ready to admit this is happening to anyone but Elias.

"Listen, you don't have to tell me, but I'm here when you want to talk."

"He's been traveling more than normal with Barnes," I shrug and pick at the remaining pieces of sushi.

"Aren't they usually on recess right now?"

"Not yet, still another week or two." At least, that's what I remember looking at the calendar last November. "The work never truly stops, does it?"

A soft sigh in return, "No, it doesn't."

*nine*

*Michaela*

**SIFTING THROUGH BOXES OF** old shit is not how I wanted to spend my weekend, but it was better than waiting around for Monday morning to show up. My dad arrived in the city Thursday morning with a truckload of boxes labeled *Michaela's Room.* It was crazy to see my entire life packed into a few boxes, but I can't deny it was a nice trip down memory lane. We spent Thursday together before he flew home that night.

I was hoping I would wake up this morning and last week would be a bad dream, but I guess I'm not that lucky. "Two weeks," I whisper in the final seconds to myself before the elevator doors open.

Liv waves briefly from behind the desk talking to someone on the phone. She's my favorite part of working at corporate. I got to know her better at the end of last week while setting up the temporary office space Nina offered to Finn and me. The space overlooks a small green space between our building and the Four Seasons Hotel. It's not the nicest view, but I shouldn't complain. At least we will have somewhere to work without interruption.

Reaching the door to the office, I take a moment to brace myself for what's on the other side. I remind myself this is what I need to do to prove to Nina I'm capable of continuing to work for her. With a deep breath, I push the door open... to an empty office.

Thank God, I get a few minutes to breathe before Finn gets here. I claim my spot at the conference table in the middle of the room. Last Friday, I brought in some office supplies, an espresso machine, a mini fridge filled with snacks and almond milk, and a blanket because my favorite way to work is snuggled under a warm blanket with a latte. I'm going to be stuck here, I might as well make it as comfortable as possible, and surprisingly enough, the corporate people don't have an espresso machine.

I go through my emails, scanning over a few between Caitlin and Jamie about a current project in Brooklyn before a new email pops up in the corner.

*Try not to have too much fun. - N*

Thanks Nin.

The time next to the notification catches my eye. *10:16 A.M.* Did we not agree on ten?

Great, the bullshit is already starting...

"Mr. Sheffield has already arrived, he's in your office," Liv says when I step off the elevator the next morning.

"You mean he decided to show up to work today? Goody," I huff earning a small laugh from her.

Needless to say, I gave him two hours yesterday before I called Nina. Did she answer? No. Did I text her ranting about him? Yes.

**Nin**

Handle it, Mic.

How was I supposed to handle it? It's not like I'm his boss. Technically, she is... Isn't she? I mean, it's her company. Or is it Kai's? Both? It doesn't matter. What does matter is I have no idea how she wants me to *handle* it.

"If I hear screaming, no, I didn't," Liv calls over her shoulder as I walk down the hallway towards the office.

Through the open door, Finn sits with his ankles crossed on top of the oak conference table, a steaming cup of coffee in one hand and the *New York Times* in the other. His navy blue jacket hangs on the back of the chair, and his sleeves are rolled up to his elbows, showcasing strong arms struggling against the taunt white fabric.

"Can you not act like a caveman for two seconds?" I push his feet from the table.

"You first," he says from behind his coffee mug.

Another deep breath. "Look, we just need to get survive the next two weeks and then we never have to speak again."

"I'd rather we not speak now."

"Ditto."

"Do you even know the first thing about running a business?" Finn finally looks up from the newspaper to glare at me.

"Do you?" I snap back.

"From what I hear, you're not the best at it. Seems you are on thin ice."

I scoff, "You don't know what you're talking about."

"So, Nina didn't give you one month's notice to get your shit straight or get out?"

"You know what..."

His smirk never falters as he waits for me to finish my statement. I'd like nothing more than to reach across the table and slap the shit out of him, but if I have to keep my cool. I cannot let him get the best of me. "I'm waiting," his smirk grows wider.

Don't do it, Michaela. Don't fall for it. He wants you to say something snarky, so he has a reason to be even more of a dick.

"Nevermind," I say between clenched teeth.

"Good, let's keep it that way, huh?" Finn folds the newspaper and tucks it under his arm standing from the table. "I have some errands to run. You can handle this, right?"

"You're leaving?"

"Got shit to do, Shortcake. I expect..."

"Don't call me that."

"...a full report of what you did in the morning." He tosses his jacket over his arm and slings his bag over his shoulder.

"You weren't even here yesterday! How are we going to get this done if you keep not showing up?"

"According to Nina, you're the expert. You figure it out."

"You're insufferable."

"At least that's something we can agree on." He smiles and finishes his coffee. "See you in the morning, Shortcake."

I snarl at the nickname, and it makes him smile before he leaves. He has got to stop calling me that. I let out a frustrated groan when he's gone. I don't know which is worse, Sheffield, the arrogant teenager, or Finnley Sheffield, the trust fund baby pretending to be a businessman.

This whole thing has to be a joke. Some kind of test. Nina cannot seriously think I can finish this project when the person in charge doesn't even show up to get anything done.

What infuriates me even more is the fact that if Nina were here this wouldn't be happening. He'd be here every morning, ready and willing to do whatever it took. What irritates me more is the fact she won't help me get him under control.

I might as well start packing up my office on Columbus Circle because at this rate I can kiss my real job goodbye. It's like she's trying to find a way to fire me. Is this her way of having an easy way out? No, no she wouldn't do that. If she wanted to do it, she would just do it... Right?

"It seems like you guys are getting off on the right foot," Liv says, leaning against the door frame. Her red lips are pulled into a smirk, and small copper ringlets escape from the bun on top of her head.

"I can't do this, Liv."

"Sure you can!" She encourages me through a smile, placating me.

"No, really, I can't do this. I can't work with him."

"Funny, he said the same thing about you." She giggles falling into one of the chairs next to me. "Can't you guys put your differences aside long enough to get through this? And then you never have to see each other again."

Ever the optimist. I won't get away from him that easily, he's still one of my brother's best friends.

"Kind of hard when he doesn't show up for his own business."

"What are you working on anyway? I've been super curious since Nina started meeting with him last month."

I pull up yesterday's PowerPoint and turn the computer toward Liv; there's a curious shift in her expression. "Foster kids?" I nod. "Interesting, so this is like a nonprofit?"

"Guess so. It's a company that helps kids find homes or reunite them with their families. Also, they want to take over one of the old buildings in Brooklyn and turn it into a type of housing and learning center. He's calling it Sheffield House."

"And this was Finn's idea?"

I shrug, turning the computer back to me. "Wanna trade jobs?"

"As fun as *that* sounds... No."

"What does he need to do this for, anyway? It's not like he needs the money. He has plenty of it in his trust fund. And foster kids — what does he know about helping foster kids?"

"Maybe he wants to prove he can do something on his own. Something good."

I scoff.

"I'm just saying," she lifts her hands, "we all have our reasons for doing things. Maybe you should try to figure out his. It might make this a hell of a lot easier."

*ten*

## Michaela

**I SHOULD'VE KEPT MY** big mouth shut. Can we go back to when he *wasn't* here? Turns out him being here is ten times worse than having to figure it out on my own. Everything I've said today has fallen on deaf ears with no sign of it getting better anytime soon. He sits at the other end of the table with his computer open and if it weren't for the small *FS* icon at the top of the document I'm editing I'd think it was all for show.

"Nice of you to show up this morning," I smirked when he walked through the door earlier. "Albeit ten minutes late, but at least you showed."

"How could I not when someone decided to run and tattle to Mommy?"

Shit.

"I didn't tattle! I just—"

"No? Then why did I get a call from Davina at eleven o'clock last night?"

Okay, so *maybe* I finally got ahold of Nina and *maybe* I told her what he's been doing the past two days. That still doesn't make me a tattletale. I only want him to do his part for his company. Is that too much to ask? I still don't understand his choice of clientele; it's very un-Sheffield, but at least he's finally doing some good in the world.

"Because you're a tattletale," he answered himself and fell into the chair at the furthest end of the table.

"You can't get mad at me. This is your project, Finn! You should be here working on it." My words go ignored because he had already shoved his AirPods into his ears, effectively tuning me out. "Asshole."

And that's how we've spent our day. Me, working through marketing, and him sulking on the other end of the room.

His phone vibrates on the table and he quickly answers quietly, "Yeah?" He leans back in his chair, stretching long limbs that have been set in stone for hours now. "Tell him not to worry about it." Finn rubs his temple and takes a deep breath. Seems the person is more annoying than being stuck in the same room with me for the moment. "The twenty-third — No! No, you don't need to come here for— Because it's not necessary." He scrubs a hand down his face before his gaze catches mine. I quickly avert my stare not wanting to give him any reason to start an argument. "Look, Mom, I can't talk about this right now." After another minute of listening to his mother on the other end, Finn hangs up and drops his phone on the table.

"That's cute, Mommy calling to see if you need her help with your special project?" Good job, Michaela. Way to avoid an argument.

"Fuck off, Michaela," he sighs.

Normally, I'd twist the knife a little bit more, but something tells me his mother already did that. Am I supposed to ask if he's okay? I mean, it's Finn. We don't do stuff like that. That would be weird...

"You... okay?"

"Fine." His eyes bore into his computer screen and he

reaches for the coffee mug next to him, but it's empty. That's the third time he's done that since he finished it an hour ago.

"You've been out for a while; I can go get some if you want."

"I can get my own damn coffee." Finn slams the laptop screen and pushes back with a little too much aggression shaking the table and spilling the remainder of my cup all over the stack of papers next to me. "Dammit, Michaela! That's the numbers for—"

"You're the one who shoved the table." I try to shake some of the coffee from the documents. Besides the paper being a little brown and some ink bleed, they'll survive. Might be a little hard to read some of the numbers, but it should be easy enough to guess… I think.

"Why do you have to ruin everything? It's like you were put on this Earth solely to make a mess of things." Finn snatches them from my hands. "This is why I didn't want you to work on this project. You're going to make a mess of things. You always do."

Finn's words take me back to that night, walking the streets of Rome when David told me the divorce was my fault because I couldn't follow the plan. "What plan, David?" I asked. "The plan was to move to New York, get married, maybe have a kid or two… Barnes, D.C., living separate lives, that was *never* the plan!"

"We were supposed to be in this together, Michaela," David said simply. "Washington was always the plan. You knew that, even when New York came up. I was always going to end up in D.C., and you stayed with me anyway."

Tears burned my eyes while standing in front of our hotel. I couldn't believe this was happening. I couldn't believe he had flown to Italy *just* to end our trip by asking for a divorce.

"And now, you've ruined everything. You always do."

The office door slams, and I realize I'm alone, again.

"God, he is such an ass! It wasn't even my fault the coffee spilled, he was the one who knocked my mug over trying to get up. How is that on me?" I take a rather large gulp, wincing as the now room-temperature beer hits my tastebuds. "Why did Nin agree to help him? And why did she choose me to take over when she couldn't be here? And, I mean, *why* do I have to do his job for him? It's such bullshit, he's an adult, why can't he—"

"Mic, breathe," Alex chuckles on the other end of the line. "If this is only day three, I'm scared to see you at the end of two weeks."

I roll my eyes and stab through my fried rice. "This isn't funny, Alex."

"I'm not laughing," he says, not even trying to hide the fact that he is indeed laughing. I'm so glad he finds my frustration amusing. "Look, you're not supposed to be working for him, but *with* him."

I scoff, "Hard to work with someone when they won't even show up. How will he run a successful business if he isn't there?"

"Pot, meet kettle."

"Just shut up and agree with me, would you? I didn't call you for you to be the voice of reason. If I wanted that I would have called Josh or Nina. You know who I should've called? Nick. He would agree with me."

"I'm stating facts here. You're being childish, Mic. Can't you suck it up and get along with him long enough to help Nina out?"

"That's what I've been doing."

He hums in a way that says, *Yeah, mhmm, sure.*

"Well, if we're stating facts. How about you start by sharing the facts of your trip to France?" The other end goes silent. "Hello?"

A soft sigh.

Oh no, that can't be good.

"She said no."

"What do you mean, she said *no*?" It comes out a lot louder than I meant for it to. How could Anna possibly say no? They live together! They go on vacations together, they have a dog… They're basically already married.

"She isn't ready, doesn't know if she ever will be."

Ouch.

"I want to be married, Mic," he sighs. "I want the house, the dog, the car full of kids… But, I want it with her."

"It's only a piece of paper, Alex."

"Says the girl who has dreamed about being married since she was like five." Yeah, look how that turned out. "It sucks, but I'd rather know now than in five years."

"You gonna be okay?"

"Eventually, but right now, I'm just taking everything day by day. She moved out on Sunday. It doesn't feel right being here without her."

"I'm so sorry, Alex."

He changes the subject to me. "Have you and David decided what you're going to do? I mean, you can't keep living in two different cities!"

"Sure, we can."

"Not happily. I'm surprised you haven't divorced his ass by now, honestly. This is like the opposite of what you wanted."

I almost tell him. Almost let it all tumble out, but the words get caught in my throat. I can't do it. Saying it makes it real and I'm not ready for that yet.

"Maybe this is a sign you're not meant to be in New York."

Maybe.

*eleven*

*Michaela*

**I HATE THAT DAVID** and I have reached the point of having to communicate through lawyers. I mean, we were together for almost four years, shouldn't we be able to handle something as simple as a divorce? I mean, we're splitting amicably, for the most part. There's just the matter of the ring...and the condo... "Where's your ring?" Mom asked when I was home. She continued to glance down at my left hand where the ring finger lay bare.

"Oh, it's at the jeweler." The lie came out way too fast. I hated that I had to lie to her, but I couldn't admit my marriage of less than a year had failed. She and Dad had been married for over forty years! She would never understand. Not to mention, there was still a small amount of hope we could fix things.

"It been there a while, huh? You didn't have it on last time we FaceTimed, either."

"There was an issue with one of the diamonds after I got it cleaned last time," I shrugged. I don't think she believed me and I'm surprised she didn't push harder. Jennifer Davis is anything but subtle, she will not hesitate to ask a million questions until she's satisfied she has gotten the whole story. So, why was she holding back? Unfortunately (or probably fortunately), Dad interrupted our conversation, requesting my presence in the garage. He wanted to show me the new lawn mower he'd rebuilt.

"He still wants you to sell the condo and split the profit," Elias says from across the table. We agreed to meet at the coffee shop down the street from his office trying to make a sad situation a little less…sad. Did it work? Not really, but I'm not one to say no to free coffee and pastries.

"That's bullshit!" I lean forward in the plastic chair. "I bought that condo on my own. Just because his name is on the deed doesn't mean he has a right to—"

"Legally, it kind of does. According to him, you were having talks about selling anyway."

"Elias, that was before he decided to move to Washington permanently. We talked about selling or renting it out and buying a bigger place *together*."

Elias shrugs, "Don't shoot the messenger. David seems to think he has a claim to whatever profits you'll make on selling and wants it sold."

"All of this over a stupid ring? He's going to come after everything I own until I give it back."

"I told you this might get ugly," he says simply, taking a sip of coffee. "You've insisted on holding onto that ring."

"Isn't there anything you can do? I mean, can't you talk to his lawyer, get them to understand—"

"I've already tried that, Michaela. The only way to make this go away is to hand over that ring in its entirety *and* sell the condo."

"You see that email from Nina?" Finn asks walking back into the office with two coffees from Five & Dime downstairs. Damn, two coffees this late in the day? Seems a little excessive, but okay. I watch suspiciously as he walks towards me, setting the extra one in front of me, and goes to sit down like he didn't just set a ticking time bomb in front of me.

"What is this?"

He takes a sip and raises it towards me, "It's this thing called a coffee. Typically thought of as a morning beverage, but can also be enjoyed throughout the day."

"I know that, you smartass. I meant, why did you put one in front of me?"

"Figured you needed one, you looked like you were about to fall asleep."

My eyes narrow. "Did you poison it?"

"Now, there's an idea I hadn't thought of."

"Asshole," I mumble, finally taking possession of the warm beverage.

"Did you see the email?"

"There's no email."

"This is why I got the coffee." He quirks an eyebrow as he sits back in his chair and points towards my computer, "3:26, check your email."

I roll my eyes finally taking a sip — latte, vanilla latte. Basic, safe, but one of my favorites. Toggling towards my email, I see that he's right, there is an email from twenty minutes ago. Subject: *Monday.*

Shit.

# twelve

## Michaela

**I SHOULDN'T BE THIS** nervous, but the butterflies in my stomach don't seem to understand that. They've been fluttering since I got the email on Friday...

*Kai and I will be in town on the 12th, we'll want to see how things are going. Be ready first thing. - N*

It's not like this is the first time I've had to present my work to Nina, but something about it feels different. Not to mention, it's only been a week since I took over. Even less since Finn started cooperating if you can call it that. Why couldn't he be so cooperative from the start? Don't get me wrong, Finn Sheffield is still as rotten as ever. Our time together hasn't exactly been pleasant, but it hasn't been as bad as I anticipated either, and he's been putting in the effort, now.

"Huh, I was sure I'd beat you this morning," the smooth voice wraps around me, and goosebumps rise across my bare arms. Looking up from my screen, the wings in my stomach flutter even faster, but for an entirely different reason. The blue and white striped dress shirt exposes the strength in his arms normally hidden beneath a jacket. Pale yellow suspenders bare down on his broad shoulders, desperately clinging to the waist of his gray slacks. My fingers involuntarily curl around nothing as the dark blue paisley tie begs to be ripped from his neck. "You okay, Shortcake?"

How many times do I have to tell him *not* to call me that?

"You look a little flush."

"No, no... I'm good. Great! Just you know..."

"Stressed?" The smirk on his face infuriates me as he drops a paper bag on the conference table, a drink carrier with two steaming coffees in his other hand. I wouldn't be stressed if he'd done his part sooner.

"No. Why would I be stressed?"

"Because *both* of your bosses are stopping by today and not because they miss your gorgeous face."

I narrow my eyes at him. What's with him this morning? He seems to be in an extremely pleasant mood. Should I be worried?

I roll my eyes turning back to the business financial statement projections for the next three years. I need to finalize it before Kai and Nina arrive. Getting their input will be vital to determine if things are heading in the right direction. But, I can't stop thinking about the man on the other side of the table.

Has he always been that fit?

How have I never noticed how hot he is?

"Probably because you were too busy chasing after douchebags."

"What are you yammering on about?"

"You asked why you haven't noticed how hot I am before, and I said–"

"No, I didn't."

Shit. Oh my God, did I say that out loud?

"Hate to break it to you, Shortcake, but you did." Finn begins to empty the contents of the paper bag: two black to-go containers. "Don't worry, I won't tell if you won't." He winks handing me a container as I do my best to hide the burning in my cheeks.

Throwing open the lid, my senses are blinded by the delicious smell of fresh bread. Not any bread... A rainbow bagel. And not any rainbow bagel... An egg, ham, and cheese rainbow bagel sandwich with a scoop of jalapeno cheddar spread on the side...from Bagel World. "What is this?"

"Most people call it a sandwich."

"Yeah, all the way from Brooklyn."

It's his turn to avoid my gaze digging into his breakfast.

"Not that I don't appreciate getting breakfast from my favorite bagel shop, but why did you go all the way to *Brooklyn* to get breakfast? You could get a rainbow bagel sandwich from literally anywhere in the city!"

Finn shrugs taking a bite of his sandwich.

"I don't understand, you–"

"Michaela, just shut up and eat the damn sandwich."

"How did you come up with this idea for Sheffield House?" Kai questions fingering through the packet I put together.

"Helping these kids means a lot to me," Finn answers. His hands wring together under the table. Wait, is he nervous? This might be the first time I've ever seen him nervous. Not even during the big rival football games at Bridgeport did he ever show any kind of nerves. He's always been calm, cool, collected...and I've always hated it. "A lot of them don't get the same opportunities I do, so if I can give them a fraction of–"

"I think it's great," Nina says, returning from the hallway. "Not to mention, I think going the nonprofit route is a wonderful idea. We've been talking how the company needs to do more charity work, Kai."

A simple hum in response, and Nina rolls her eyes. Kai was supposed to take over the company when Ric died four and a half years ago. Then Eileen got pregnant, and Nina decided to take on a bigger role at corporate than she had anticipated. She wanted her brother to have time to adjust to his growing family and it wasn't until recently that he started showing up more. I think it annoys Nina; she's been running both DV Designs and Villa Incorporated for almost four years — not that the board knows because Kai always showed up for the important stuff. "We have to look like a team," Nina always said when I asked her about it.

"So, these events... You have some time before the big presentation." Kai still hasn't looked up from the papers, but I can practically see the gears turning in his mind.

"Are you suggesting we do one of them?" I ask.

"Why not?" Kai finally looks up.

"Well, for starters, we don't have the time or monetary resources right now."

"Says who?" Nina asks.

"Says the pending approval from the board. This hasn't even been launched, and we don't even know if—"

"I think we can pull some strings," Finn interrupts me.

"I think having some kind of physical evidence on top of the figures is a great way to prove to the board what you're doing here," Nina shuffles the papers before filing them in her bag.

"Great, then it's settled." Kai stands from the table and reaches his hand out towards Finn. "Make sure you let us know when you selected a date, we'd like to join."

"Of course," Finn says and grips Kai's hand. "I'd be happy to have you guys there."

"Up for a drink?" And just like that, the switch has flipped from business to personal. It's honestly kind of shocking how quickly it happens.

"Kai Villa, you know the way to a man's heart."

"Don't tell my wife."

They share a chuckle before Finn turns to me. "Same time tomorrow?"

"I'll bring the bagels." I smile and Finn returns it grabbing his bag; he presses a chaste kiss to Nina's cheek and follows Kai out of the office. Turning away from the door, I'm met with the smirkiest smirk I've ever seen on Nina's face. "Don't start," I warn.

*"I'll bring the bagels?"* She mocks me. "I'm sorry, but what happened to not being able to work with someone as arrogant and self-absorbed as Finnley Sheffield? What was it you called him... Oh, right, the Devil himself."

"He's not that bad," I grumble.

"I'm sorry, what? I couldn't hear you."

"I said, he's not that bad."

Nina giggles as she picks up her purse. "Nick should be landing in a few. You should come over for dinner."

"I don't want to impose–"

A tight smile on her lips, "I said, you're coming."

"He brought you breakfast?" Nina practically screams. I shush her not wanting Nick to hear in the kitchen. "Don't shush me!"

"It doesn't mean anything! He was having a momentary lapse in judgment."

"Bagels from Brooklyn is not a momentary lapse in judgment, Michaela."

"Finn brought you bagels from Brooklyn?" Nick appears from the kitchen with a fresh glass of wine handing it to his wife before kissing the crown on her head.

"It doesn't mean what you think it means," I say.

"And what do we think it means?"

"You think Finn bringing me breakfast all the way from Brooklyn has some significant meaning, when it's probably because he was over there looking at the space he wants to purchase. It doesn't *mean* anything. Nothing. The bagels were *just* bagels, nothing more."

"Who are you trying to convince?" Nick asks. "You don't have to convince us, but it sounds like you're trying to convince yourself."

Nina smirks behind a sip of red wine. God, they're obnoxious. Not everyone is secretly in love like them. Not that it was much of a secret, they were too damn stubborn to apologize and move on. "I'm just glad you guys are getting along, even if it's only for the next week. I still don't understand why you didn't get along anyway."

"Because he's an asshole," I say simply.

"If you think he's bad, meet Oliver."

Oliver Sheffield — Finn's father — his very wealthy, very obnoxious father. I've only had the displeasure of meeting him a handful of times, but I've heard plenty of stories. Every one proves the apple doesn't fall far from the tree, but I'd still take Finn over his dad any day.

"The only person I know who didn't hate him was Daddy," Nina says. "Even Brina hated him, that should tell you something."

"That's because he was afraid of your dad." I roll my eyes. "Your dad was what Mr. Sheffield wants to be and more, so of course, he's gonna be nice to him. Even if he talks shit later."

Nina shrugs, "Daddy always called him an ass, but said he wasn't as bad as everyone said. Then again, when you're married to Brina Villa, everyone probably seems like a saint."

"Dee," Nick sighs.

"Well, am I wrong?"

No, she's not. Her mother is even more of an acquired taste than Finn. Not only was she cheating on Ric with Nina's ex-boyfriend (yeah, you heard me), but she was just an overall bad person. Brina would have been happy if they had stopped having kids after Kai and made sure Nina knew it. Don't even get me started on how she treated people who worked for the family… But, now she lives a modest life somewhere in SoHo. She got knocked down a few pegs when Ric left her nothing in his will, not to mention he was about to divorce her before his accident…

"Look, Mic, all I'm saying is Finn isn't that bad," Nick says, trying to steer the conversation away from Brina. "He's rough around the edges, and a little bit of a prick, but overall he's a good guy. You guys have had this feud since we were all kids, don't you think it's time to put it aside and grow up?"

"I already told Nina I'd put my differences aside for two weeks to help her with this project, but I refuse to promise anything more."

"I don't think *you* have to do anything," Nina snickers.

"Seems like he's making the effort for you," Nick adds. "If David doesn't start coming home, he might have some competition."

"For the love of God, it was just breakfast!" I huff and fall back onto the couch.

"From Brooklyn."

*thirteen*

## Michaela

**"THIS IS ALL YOUR** fault, you know." I walk through the door Finn holds open to Birch Coffee. This morning has been anything but normal since the moment I woke up. The first thing I thought of was whether or not I should return the favor and bring breakfast for the two of us. After mulling it over as I got ready for work, I decided yesterday was a one-off and not to expect anything to come of it. I'd probably walk into the office to find your typical grumpy, uptight Sheffield waiting for me. The second I walked in, he was surprisingly pleasant. He suggested we head out of the office to work, and get some fresh air and coffee to get the creative juices flowing. All I could think was that Hell had frozen over or the world was ending or both.

"And, how is that?" Finn laughs. I feel the warmth of his hand on the small of my back guiding me towards the small line at the register.

"You're the one who said we could pull money together for something on such short notice!"

"Well, we can."

"That doesn't mean we *should*. The company isn't even up and running yet."

"And I think Kai is right. Something like this will show investors why it's important." He smiles at the barista stepping up to the counter and when I try to hang back to wait and order, he demands I let him pay for me. Either he thinks I'm poor, or he's being extremely nice, and it's starting to worry me. Maybe he's dying. Is he dying? He doesn't look like he's dying. He still looks normal…

"Stop staring at me like that," he hands over my latte.

"I'm not staring."

"Yes, you were. Now stop it."

"Finn, I have to say this. You're going to take it the wrong way, but I have to say it."

His brow quirks as he holds open the door again, letting me walk out first. Has he always been such a gentleman? "I don't like the sound of that."

"What in the hell is wrong with you the last two days?"

"What do you mean?" He sips the black coffee with cream, no sugar…*just* coffee. That's disgusting.

"You brought me breakfast yesterday and today—"

"I can't be nice?"

"No! You're never nice, not to me. And vice versa. We don't do breakfast. We don't do whatever *this* is."

"It was just a sandwich, Shortcake."

"From Brooklyn."

"Where I happened to be before I came into the office." That's exactly what I told Nick and Nina last night, so why do I feel disappointed when he says it? I knew he wouldn't go all the way to Brooklyn to bring me coffee and a bagel. "And as for today, we have a lot of work to do. I figured treating you to some nice coffee, and not that shit you've been making in the office, was the least I could do. Today is going to be hell."

"Oh."

"Don't worry, your secret is safe with me."

"What secret?" I whip my head to look up at him.

"Well, obviously, you think there's some reason for it other than what it is."

"I do not!"

"Whatever you say, Shortcake," Finn smirks behind his cup.

I knew the days of us getting along weren't meant to last. We spent the rest of the morning walking through the streets of Tribeca, going through the list of possible event ideas. I thought he should keep it simple, do a small cookout-type thing at one of the waterfront parks, but Finn had other ideas. He wanted to go big or go home. He wanted to buy out Luna Park for a day. Do you know how much that would cost? Neither do I, but I can imagine it's not chump change. You can't just rent out Coney Island! He didn't care. He wanted to do and that's how it was going be.

That's where our days of amicability ended.

"Sasha can meet us on Thursday," I say walking back into the office with containers of food Caitlin dropped off on her way home. I told her we could order delivery, but she insisted. I think she wanted to see how things were going after I spent over an hour venting earlier. Sure, I had already given in to him, but I had to finish getting it out.

**Cait**

it's not your problem. if he wants to spend all his money on renting out an amusement park, let him.

Cait was right, it's not my problem. I only have three more days to deal with this, and then I'm free. I won't have to worry about any of this ever again. So, why should I care how he wants to spend his money? He's doing what I wanted him to do in the first place — run his own business.

"Did you hear me?"

Silence.

"Helloooooo, Earth to Finn."

Nothing.

"Fine," I toss the container in front of him. "You want to act like a child, be my guest."

Finn laughs, "I learned from the best."

"Oh fuck off, Finn."

"Young ladies shouldn't use such language, Michaela Jane."

"Good thing I'm not one."

He gasps, "Something you wanna share with the class?"

"I'll show you mine if you show me yours."

With a soft chuckle, he leans back in his chair. "You couldn't handle it, Shortcake." A warmth spreads across my skin from the heat of his stare. He licks his lips, and it sends a shiver down my spine. When I meet his gaze again, there's a twinkle in his eye that I've never seen before. Is he challenging me?

"Fuck you, Sheffield."

Finn rises from the chair and my body vibrates with anticipation. He gently pushes the hair from my shoulder, leaning in close, his breath ghosting across my skin before he whispers, "Only in your dreams, Shortcake."

# *fourteen*

## Michaela

## Ten Years Ago

**TONIGHT IS THE NIGHT** I have been waiting for! I apply a layer of my favorite lipstick, "Tell Me More" from AK Cosmetics. The muted mauve purple goes with anything, and it's perfect for the outfit I've picked out for tonight. Heath Samson finally asked me a date — I've only been waiting for the past two years. It's been a back-and-forth game since we met at one of his infamous parties when his parents were out of town.

As excited as I am, I'm keeping it a secret...from Josh. I always tell him about these things, he wants to know who he needs to beat up if something goes wrong but this isn't his business. I don't have to tell him every time I have a date, besides he's going to flip out. He and Heath got into some big argument when Josh was home for Christmas break last year, Nick had to step in and break it up before Josh did something stupid. Naturally, when I asked what happened, my brother said, "Just stay away from him, Michaela, he's an asshole."

What was that supposed to mean? He's never been an asshole to me. Well, except that one time when... No, never mind. He's better now.

I tuck my black turtleneck into my high-waisted white mini skirt and straighten out the nude stockings, at least they'll fight off the cold weather that has stuck around longer than normal.

"Where are you going dressed like that?" In the mirror, I meet the stare of none other than Finnley Sheffield. He leans against the doorframe, arms crossed tightly over his chest. I roll my eyes ignoring his question. What the hell is he doing here? Josh isn't even home yet.

*Shit,* I freeze, is Josh home? A glance at the clock tells me he shouldn't be home for another hour. I planned everything perfectly so he would arrive home *after* Heath picked me up. But if he's home now... No, he's not home. He would've come upstairs by now. I would've heard him downstairs, at the very least.

"Go away, Finn," I say picking up the locket Mom and Dad got for my eighteen birthday last month. The silver chain holds a heart-shaped locket with a floral imprint on the front cover. I try to secure it around my neck, but the clasp refuses to cooperate under the burning stare of the man standing at my door. Why is he still here? Doesn't he have someone else to annoy? I steal a glance at him in the mirror and instantly regret it. Fuck, he looks good. Really good.

Wait, what?

No, Finnley Sheffield does not look *good.*

But, damn, can he wear the fuck out of that cable-knit sweater. The cream color looks delicious against his warm, tanned skin. Dark denim hugs his legs, but I'm pleased to know he doesn't wear skinny jeans. His hair is longer than the last time I saw him. I can only imagine how soft it is.

Pull yourself together, MJ. This is Finn. Sworn enemy.

Asshole. You cannot imagine how soft his hair is...

"Let me help," he says gently standing behind me. Shit, I hope he didn't notice me jump. When did he get so close? I swallow the lump in my throat as he takes the chain, his fingers brushing against mine. His skin is as warm as I imagined. He makes quick work on the clasp before resting the chain gently around my neck, but he doesn't move away — not like he should. His eyes meet mine in the reflection, and there's something there I can't quite place. Something new. Softer. Gentler. Heat rises under his stare, and I hope he doesn't notice the blush on my cheeks because they are burning hot right now.

"A date," I say, answering his question from earlier, watching the way his jaw ticks in response. "With Heath."

Chocolate eyes narrow, the warmth gone. "You're fucking joking."

"Why do you care?"

"Oh please, don't be stupid, Shortcake." That fucking nickname. "Samson? After what he said about you, I can't believe—"

"What are you talking about?" I turn to face him. "What did he say about me?"

"You know what, never mind." Finn backs away, hands raised in defeat. "Enjoy your evening with *Prince Charming*."

Is he serious?

"What the fuck, Finn? You don't get to do that! You don't get to come in here judging my outfit, judging my makeup and hair, and then talk shit about my—"

"God, you're so delusional," Finn scoffs. "Do you think he just decided he likes you out of the blue? You've been chasing after him like a lost puppy for years. Last I heard, he was fucking Miranda Caldwell, Hannah Norris, *and* Isla Hurley at the same time. You're still in high school for god sake. You're not special, Shortcake."

The tears prick the corners of my eyes, but I try to fight them off. "Fuck you, Finn."

"And for the record, you look like a hooker, all that's missing are the boots." I try to ignore the pair of black boots sitting outside my closet, but my eyes betray me. His eyes follow mine, and a smirk tugs on his lips. "Guess you have everything to fit the part, huh?"

When he's gone, I take a deep breath and swallow back the tears threatening to spill over. I will not cry over Finn Sheffield. Tonight is supposed to be my night, and I refuse to let him ruin it.

# *fifteen*

## *Michaela*

**HIS TOUCH IS LIKE** fire against my skin, rough and warm, as his lips devour mine. A soft whine escapes me when we part, and I open my eyes to meet warm chocolate orbs staring down at me. Our chests heave trying to catch our breath.

Holy shit.

Did we just… I take two large steps back. "What was that?" But from the look on his face, he seems just as shocked. "Finn…"

"Michaela, I advise you give me a minute."

"Why? Oh!" I smirk seeing the tightening of his dress pants. Even through his pants, I can tell he's big. I thought he might be, but damn— I mean, no, I never thought about it. He's my brother's best friend. I have never thought about him like that. "You get that hard from a little kiss? Damn Sheffield, how long's it been?"

"Truthfully, a while."

"So, you decided to kiss me?"

"Me kiss you?" He scoffs. "You're sadly mistaken, Shortcake. You're the one who kissed me."

"Oh, don't flatter yourself."

"You did, you kissed me." Finn steps closer, "And you liked it… I heard your little whimper when I pulled away."

I can't lie. It was a good kiss.

No. No, it was not a good kiss. I don't think about him like that. I can't think about him like that. This is Finn. *Finnley Sheffield.* I don't find him attractive… Damn, he does look good right now. No, stop it Michaela. But, with the top buttons of his dress shirt undone, sleeves rolled up, and his hair slightly tousled from running his hands through it in frustration he looks really good. Okay, so maybe the idea of him fucking me on the table isn't so bad, but it's *only* because I've been a little extra lonely since David left. Something about that kiss felt… right. That's crazy, though. It doesn't make sense.

"Admit it, Shortcake. You liked it." I jump slightly when his fingers graze the skin of my shoulder, pushing my hair back. His eyes bore into mine before he bends down pressing a kiss to my collarbone. I gasp as his tongue trails up my neck to my ear, he whispers, "Say it."

"No," I whimper.

He scoops me off my feet, and I desperately clutch to him in surprise. My dress slides to the top of my thighs when he sets me on the table. His eyes glance down at the newly exposed skin, and he lets out a harsh breath.

"Such a cliché."

"You've wanted it since the day I walked in."

"You wish," it's breathless, but it makes him smile.

His tongue pokes out to wet his lips, and he glances down at mine. He grunts when I press myself against him a little further, his fingers digging into the skin of my thigh just below my Pisces constellation tattoo. We've never been this close before. There's an electric current flowing through my veins, it radiates from every place he touches my skin. Meeting his stare, it's the first time I notice his brown eyes are ringed with the prettiest gold. He presses his mouth against mine and his teeth catch my bottom lip in a soft bite. A shiver runs down my spine. When he begins to move his mouth against mine, plying it open, I lose all thought. His tongue dances against mine – stroking in a desperate embrace.

Holy. Fuck.

This is happening — I'm kissing Finn Sheffield. This cannot be a good idea. I should stop this. He's Josh's best friend, for fucksake; I am *not* supposed to be doing this. But, when Finn starts to pull back, I pull his mouth back to mine.

God, I am so screwed.

Finn pushes the burgundy dress further up my legs before his fingers brush lightly over the damp fabric of my panties. He twists his hand in my hair and tugs. He chuckles when the same whine from earlier sounds at the separation. "You're a needy little thing, aren't you?"

"Fuck off."

"Patience, Shortcake." Finn presses a chaste kiss to my lips before pulling me to the edge of the table. He doesn't break our stare when he hooks a finger and tugs the only thing barring him wholly from me. Sliding it off my legs, he stuffs my thong in the back pocket of his dress pants, I guess we're keeping souvenirs. What's mine? His fingers trail my legs, and my breath catches when his left hand pauses at my center. I'm too focused on his fingers taunting me, the anticipation it brings… His right hand gingerly pushes hair behind my ear and tilts my chin to meet his stare. There's a warmth in it that was missing moments ago. It reminds me of that night years ago when he found me getting ready for a date with Heath Sampson. There was something in his eyes that made me feel…whole. He grips my chin and pulls my mouth to his.

Finn's tenderness surprises me. The kiss is slow and languid — he plies my mouth open, and I tangle my fingers into his hair to pull him even closer. This kiss is different and it makes me wonder why I never tried this before. His lips leave a burning trail down my neck to my chest.

"Shit," I gasp when his thumb brushes over my center, a small taste of what's to come.

He smirks against the skin between my breasts, nipping at the soft skin before lowering himself to the ground and lifting my legs over his shoulders. He drags me even closer to the edge of the table. I feel like I might fall, but his grip is deadly. "Be a good girl, and don't move." His eyes bore into mine. "Can you do that?" My reply gets caught in my throat. "Answer me, Michaela."

I nod.

"Use your words."

"Y-yes."

I gasp when his tongue swipes up my center. My body involuntarily moves to fall back onto the table, but he has other plans.

"Eyes on me, Shortcake."

Another swipe of his tongue before he pushes one finger inside me, then another. I want to grind against him, to help create more friction that my body so desperately craves, but I know I shouldn't. I have a feeling if I disobey him, I'll be on my own tonight. And fuck, this feels way too good to let it end. His lips find my clit, and he grips my thighs. He refuses to let me pull away from him continuing his assault. A moan falls from my lips and it makes him smile. His name falls from my lips at the mounting pressure building through me and my legs tremble against his hold. His tongue replaces his fingers, and it takes every ounce of willpower not to let my hips buck off the table. Warmth spreads through my belly. I prepare to dive headfirst off the cliff he's brought me to, but he pulls away milliseconds before I can jump.

"You get to come when I say," he responds to my whine at the loss of contact, "and it won't be on my fingers."

Fuck, this man is going to be the death of me.

His pants and underwear fall to the floor in a heaping pile, and I grip the front of his shirt pulling him back to me. My fingers fumble with the buttons to free him of the restricting garment, but he stops me. He gently pushes me back until I'm laid out before him like a Christmas feast.

"Fuck Michaela," Finn groans. "Seeing you laid out like this..." He shoves my dress up a little more and kisses my abdomen. "...all for me." My mouth falls open when he rubs his crown against me. He slowly guides his dick inside me. "Fucking hell," he moans when he sits fully inside me, and he waits a moment allowing me to adjust before he begins to move.

His name is like a prayer as he thrusts in and out of me. I reach the edge of the cliff in no time. His pace is brutal, each pump bringing me closer and closer. One hand reaches up and grasps my breast through my dress.

"Finn," I gasp.

"You want to come, Shortcake?"

I lift my head to meet his gaze and it sends a wave of heat crashing through me. He fucks into me from the edge of the table and it's the hottest thing I've ever seen.

"Go ahead, baby," he whispers and his command makes my orgasm roll through me. His hold tightens on my hips as I come holding me in place so he can continue to fuck me through it.

I whimper when he pulls all the way out, but he rolls me to my stomach and pushes into me again. The stretch even more delicious than before, and it pulls a moan from deep in my chest. He grips my waist fucking me over the edge of the table and I grasp for something, anything, but my hands find no purchase — nails scrape against the sealed wood. One of his hands reaches around, rubbing my clit, and I feel it, that burning fire deep in my belly. It's stronger than before and like nothing I've experienced before.

"Wait for me, Michaela," he demands, but I'm not sure I can. "You *will* wait for me." His movements slow, and he pulls all the way out before slamming back in. "Fuck, you take me so good." All the way in. All the way out. "I wish you could see yourself, how sexy you look." In. Out. "This what you've been wanting, Shortcake?" In. Out. He lifts my hips slightly, and I feel him at a new, deeper angle. "There it is," he gasps. He reaches around again to my clit, this time the assault much faster. The coil tightens even further, and I know I'm not going to last. "Come," he demands, and I do. He tangles his hand into my hair and thrusts two more times before his movements stall as he comes.

The aftermath of having sex with someone for the first time is always the same… Awkward. Quiet. Weird. You redress yourself running through the events of what just happened and asking yourself how in the hell you let it happen. At least, that's what I'm doing right now.

I run a hand through my hair, pulling it into a high ponytail, trying to hide the fresh sex style it now dones. Finn adjusts himself before tucking in his shirt, then buttoning and zipping his pants.

The silence is maddening. I can't take it anymore. "What was that?"

Nothing. Not a fucking peep.

"Look, it's probably best if we…forget this happened. I mean, it's not like we're going to—"

"Nothing happened."

"You call that nothing?"

"I call that a normal day at the office." The words make my stomach sink. Is he fucking serious? *A normal day at the office.* What office does he work at? "Don't worry about it, Shortcake. It won't happen again."

"Good... We agree to never speak of it then." I am not one of his playthings he can call up when he needs a release.

"Already forgotten." Finn packs up his stuff and I find myself unable to look away. Knowing that mere moments ago, he was fucking me into this same table, and now we're fighting about what it meant.

"So, we'll just go back to the way things were before."

He slings his bag over his shoulder, "They never left."

# sixteen

## Michaela

**I STAND ACROSS BROADWAY** debating whether or not to go back inside after last night. I mean, what was that? It feels like a fever dream. The feeling of his touch on my skin is the only thing I've been able to think about since I left this very same building not even twelve hours ago. Fuck, I'm so screwed. Am I supposed to act like last night didn't happen? I can do that...

No, I can't.

I'm already late. I could say I'm sick, not coming in. But that would look even worse, wouldn't it? Avoiding him will only make it more awkward than if we face the situation head-on.

At least I know that he won't tell Josh. I'm safe from my brother's wrath and from having to explain sleeping with someone who isn't my husband. How do I find myself in these situations? Taking a deep breath, I straighten my shoulders and walk toward the front door. It's only two more days, I can do this...

"He's not here," Liv says when I step off the elevator. "And you're late."

"What do you mean he's not here?"

"Sent a memo that he'd be working from home today." A smirk tugs in the corner of her lips. "Said you had a long night getting things prepped for meeting Sasha tomorrow."

That's one way to put it.

"I'm surprised you're here this early if that's the case."

"I considered working from home but there's a lot that needs to be done. And if he's going to play hooky, someone needs to be responsible."

"Well, if you changed your mind, I wouldn't blame you."

Part of me thinks it's a better idea not to go back into that office because all I can think about is his head between my legs. God, just the thought sends a shock straight to my core.

Opening the door, nothing looks out of place. There's no evidence of our heated work session. But that doesn't stop the aching between my legs that reminds me it did, in fact, happen... Honestly, it's a good thing he isn't here because something tells me we wouldn't be getting any of the right kind of work done.

Fuck, I'm in so much trouble.

"You wanna grab dinner?" I glance up from my computer. Liv stands in the doorway, ready to leave for the day, Caitlin at her side.

"Cait, what are you doing here?"

"I told her you'd been holed away for hours without food or water."

Cait starts to pick up my purse, "C'mon, we can go get some bánh mì and get some—"

"I don't want to go out. I have a lot to do before I meet Sasha tomorrow. Have you ever tried to plan a fundraising event in less than a week? It's not as easy as it sounds!"

"Get up, we're going to get food and take it back to your place so you can spill your guts," Cait demands.

"Spill my guts about what?"

"What's going on between you and Finn."

Five minutes of arguing and a little over an hour later, we're walking into my apartment with a bag full of fresh bánh mì and fries from McDonald's that Liv couldn't live without. I haven't let anyone come over since David left, and I'm praying to God this doesn't bite me in the ass. "David not home?" Cait asks kicking her heels off by the front door. Liv follows suit before plopping onto the couch with her fries.

"Nope."

"When's the last time he *was* home?"

"Um, it's been a little bit." Not a total lie.

I pull a bottle of Sauvignon Blanc from the fridge and grab three plates from the cabinet. As I reach for the bag of food, I see my phone light up with a text from 'Jabba.' I'm right back where I started... Thinking of Finn Sheffield and the way his mouth felt against my skin, the fire of his touch, the way he made me feel beautiful and sexy and—

"Who's David?" Liv asks.

"Michaela's husband, I'd think he was made up if I hadn't been at the wedding," Cait snickers.

Shit, I almost forgot they were here. Note to self: ignore the text, and do *not* think about Finn or last night while the girls are here.

"I didn't know you were married!" Liv's mouth hangs open as I walk out of the kitchen with dinner and wine. "You don't even wear a wedding ring. Wait I thought—"

"David isn't home much, he works a lot," I shrug. "I don't always wear it, with it being a family heirloom and all."

Sure, let's go with that.

"What's he do?"

"Works for a Senator. It's decent work, but—"

"He wants her to move to D.C.," Cait rolls her eyes and pops the bottle of wine.

"You don't want to?" Liv asks.

"Not really, New York has always been my dream."

"What would you even do out there? It's not like we have an office," Cait says like she doesn't know the answer.

"He makes enough money. I could stay home, play housewife, just like his mother," I say.

"So, you live apart instead." It's not a question, and I wonder if Cait knows more than she lets on. Cait finally looks up from filling our glasses to meet my gaze and I'm too tongue-tied to answer. She hands me a glass of wine continuing, "I'm not judging. It's strange, but you gotta do what works for you. Every marraige is different."

"I'm going to be completely honest, I thought you and Finn had a thing going on," Liv says. "The way you guys go back and forth all the time." She blows out a breath as if she were hot, then quirks an eyebrow and pops another fry into her mouth. I practically choke on my wine.

"If I didn't know any better, I'd say the same. You could cut the sexual tension with a knife," Cait agrees.

"Oh my God, shut up," I beg taking a large gulp of wine. This cannot be happening right now.

"You can't say you've never thought about it!"

"Seriously! I mean, have you seen him?" Liv giggles.

I chew on my bottom lip just thinking about his body.

Because yes, I *have* seen him.

"OMG, you're blushing!"

"Can we please talk about something else?" I plead and pull the sandwiches from the bag, separating them on the plates. "Seriously, anything else."

There's hesitation in Cait's voice before she and Liv share a glance. Liv nods before Cait says, "Mic, you know we love you, right?"

"I'm starting to question it a little."

"We're worried about you. You've always been all over the place, but it's been worse than normal."

"What is this some kind of intervention?" They share the same look from moments ago, they don't believe me. Hell, I don't believe me. "You guys, I'm fine. I promise, I just—"

I should tell them. It's not like I'll be able to keep the charade up much longer. Once the divorce is final, it's going to be hard to maintain the illusion. And what happens when David moves on and gets married again? It'll be the big spectacle his mother always wanted and I didn't allow.

"We're not here to judge," Liv squeezes my hand gently. "We want to make sure you're okay."

I can do this. I can tell them. It'll be good practice for when I tell my family. I just have to do it… Like ripping off a band-aid. I down the rest of my glass hoping to find confidence at the bottom, but all I'm left with is more nerves. "David and I are getting a divorce."

They don't say anything, and I wonder if they heard me because I barely heard it myself. As much as it hurts to say it aloud, to admit my marriage failed, there's a weight lifted off my shoulders. It feels good to know I don't have to pretend anymore. At least, not with them.

"Shit," Cait sighs. "Mic, when did this—"

"Italy."

"That was three months ago!"

Liv downs her wine, the shock written all over her face. Can't say I blame her. Not only did she learn I'm married, but I'm getting divorced too, all in a matter of ten minutes.

"Why didn't you tell me?" Cait murmurs.

I shrug. "No one else knows."

"You haven't even told your parents? Michaela!"

"I know! Okay? I know," I sigh. "I don't need the lecture, Cait. It's been hard enough. I'm aware it's messed up, but I just... The thought of disappointing them, I can't bear it. They've been married for over forty years; they don't believe in divorce. They'd never understand."

"I'm sure they'd understand if you explain it to them."

Maybe.

Maybe not.

I think that's the real reason I've avoided telling my family. What happens if they don't understand?

"Does Nina know?" Liv asks and I shake my head. "Michaela!"

"I know, she's going to kill me for not telling her," I cover my face with my hands.

"This explains a lot, honestly," Caitlin sips her wine and steals a fry from Liv. "You've always been a little spacey, but it's been worse lately."

"Just promise you won't say anything to anyone." I look up at both of them. They wear identical sympathetic looks — eyes full of pity hidden behind small smiles. "I'm going to tell everyone, I just... I need to figure out how to do it."

"That's not our place," Cait shares a nod with Liv. "You need to tell them."

"I will," I nod and repeat the words, more for myself than them. My stomach rumbles as I begin digging into one of my sandwiches, I didn't realize how hungry I was until I smelled the delicious scents of Vietnamese food walking into the restaurant. Probably shouldn't go so long without eating next time.

"Oh, and I slept with Finn."

We spent the rest night giggling like a bunch of school girls, watching shitty rom-coms, and drinking wine... It was exactly what I needed. Being able to talk freely was refreshing. It was nice not having to worry I might say the wrong thing. There is absolutely nothing that can bring me down from the high I'm on. Except the face staring back at me when I open the office door.

Shit, he already looks annoyed, and it's not even 9:00 A.M.

"No breakfast today?" I joke but it only earns an eye roll.

Brown eyes avert to the screen in front of them. God help me. This is going to be so awkward, I'll take fighting and bickering for three hundred, Alex.

"You like him," Cait said last night when Liv went to the restroom. I tried to deny it, but she wouldn't let me. "It's okay, you're allowed to find happiness after David."

"It's not exactly *after* David, is it? We're not even officially divorced yet."

"You've been separated for three months. Fighting over a ring is a pretty lame reason to hold up the process, but hey, what do I know?" She shrugged and slipped into her heels when Liv rejoined us. I hugged them goodbye and spent the rest of the night thinking about everything we talked about and facing Finn in the morning.

"We have to meet Sasha at twelve outside the park. At that time of day, we need to leave by eleven—"

"Great. Since you've got this handled, I'm going to head out." Finn slams the laptop closed and stuffs it into his bag.

Without another word, he stands from his seat and begins to pack his bag.

Liv opens the door. "The board is requesting—"

"Whatever it is, Michaela can handle it. I have a flight to catch."

"A flight?" I stand from my chair. "Finn, we have an event to plan!"

"You have an event to plan. You're still on this project for two more days. That was the deal, right? I have somewhere to be."

I lean across the table taking hold of his phone before he can grab it and run. "This is your event. Your business. You can keep running off—"

"Just because we fucked Shortcake, doesn't mean you can tell me what to do." The glare he shoots at me sends a chill down my spine. He grips the phone and tugs it ever so slightly. "Now, hand over the phone. I have a flight to catch."

# Part Two


*"Don't let people tell you who you are.
You tell them."*


*- Serena van der Woodsen,
"Gossip Girl"*

# seventeen

## *Finn*

**PLEASE TELL ME WHY** I agreed to this. Spending time with my family is not the highlight of my life, and I woke up angry this morning with the knowledge that I was about to spend the entire weekend with Oliver and Hayley Sheffield. I feel bad taking it out on Michaela but seeing her was also a reminder of what happened between us, and I *cannot* think about that. She is Josh's little sister and he'd kill me if he knew what happened. But fuck, I'd be lying if I said I haven't been able to get her out of my mind since. I thought I had myself under control after taking Wednesday off but seeing her walk in this morning in that outfit… Tight jeans. A white satin camisole. Tan blazer. *Fuck.* I was ready to bend her over that conference table and—

"Finn, it's good to see you!" Uncle Jack knocks on the car window interrupting my thoughts. Thank God. I can't be late to this party because of a hard-on thinking about Michaela.

Uncle Jack has always been the fun one between him and my dad. Looking for a good time? Call Uncle Jack. Looking to score some goods? Uncle Jack is your man. Need to get away? Uncle Jack can help you do that, no questions asked. He's the only one who knows how bad it has gotten between me and Dad in the past. We always tried to keep it hidden behind the red door of the Bridgeport mansion, but some things were just too dark to hide.

"You didn't need help getting settled?" He asks when I step out of the car.

"Not this time." I shake his hand before he pulls me into a tight embrace with a quick pat on the back. "Nina's been helping me out."

"Villa?"

"Villa-Davis," I corrected.

"Ah, yes. The one Davis boy scored big."

"I don't think he sees it that way. If anything, he keeps her in line."

"Good, she needs it." We laugh before he drapes an arm around my shoulders pulling me towards the house. "So, what's got you hanging out in the city with Davina for this long?"

"Working on something. I'm thinking about moving permanently, kinda like it more than I thought."

"You mean you like that it keeps you away from Oliver."

"Something like that."

"Kind of ironic since this weekend is all about him."

I couldn't agree more. This weekend is supposed to be all about Dad as he celebrates the big 6-0. If it had been up to me, I would've skipped the festivities and stayed in New York to finish planning the event happening on Sunday. But, I knew if I didn't show my face for at least some of the weekend, I'd be in deep shit. Besides, Michaela would be better suited for the party planning anyway…

"How are things going?" Mom asked last week — the simple question was the real reason for her phone call. She had spent the ten minutes prior pretending to care about what I had to say, and she'd grown tired of the niceties. She wanted to know what was going on in New York and when I was coming home. The answer to that last part... I'm not. She didn't have to know that, not yet. Bridgeport isn't home to me, and I'd be happy to never go back again.

"Things are fine." Except for the fact that I'm putting together a nonprofit. I don't think that's what my father had in mind for my life.

"Will you be ready for the board?"

"If Michaela gets her shit together, yes."

"Michaela Davis? Josh's little sister? I thought Davina was helping you."

"She put Michaela on the project."

"She pushed you off on some assistant? How could she do that? You should be her main–"

"Nina has a lot going on, and Michaela isn't an assistant, anymore. She's been running the New York office."

"You just said–"

"She's fine," the statement came out a little harsher than I meant it to. "She and I have different work methods, but we're...figuring it out. That's all I meant."

"As long as she knows what's at risk."

"That's none of her concern."

"Finn, please tell me you understand what's at stake here. I don't want this to be another one of your failed attempts to prove something."

"I have to go, Mom," I huffed opening the heavy metal door to the gymnasium — the screeching sounds on the court echoing inside. "I'm meeting Colin."

"Colin MacFarlane? That boy from–"

"Yes, he's in New York." Colin waved from the other side of the gym, a basketball under his arm. "Look, I have to go."

"Sure, honey. I'll see you next week for your father's birthday?"

I hung up without accepting the invitation as I reached

Colin.

"Sheff, finally! Thought you were gonna bail." It still surprises me every time I see him how much he's grown up from when we met fourteen years ago — I had just turned eighteen, and Colin was eleven. Colin's mom had enrolled him into the Big Brother, Big Sister program after his dad passed. She hoped it would bring him out of his shell. At first, he didn't seem interested. He would come to the meet-ups, and we'd chat a little, but it wasn't until he noticed my Iron Man key chain that he finally started to open up. Comic books were something his dad loved and they had bonded over them. Once I knew that, it was easy to get him to open up and we instantly clicked. But long gone was that little kid, only to be replaced by a six-foot-two Marine.

"I'm not even late," I chuckled tossing my gym bag on the bleachers.

"Well, after the beating you took last time–"

"You wish, Mac." From the corner of my eye, I saw him plant his feet. He thought I wasn't paying attention, too preoccupied mentally preparing for our game, but his smirk fell from his lips when I caught the ball without blinking.

"You never let me have any fun," he chuckled.

"I guess it just comes naturally." I tossed the ball back to him and pulled my hoodie over my head so we could get started.

My phone buzzes once, twice, three times in my pocket. Then again. There are only two people who text like that. I have a feeling I know who this is. Pulling it out of my pocket, my suspicions are confirmed. "Will you excuse me for a second? I need to take this," I say to Uncle Jack.

"Best I can do is five minutes," Uncle Jack chuckles opening the front door.

"I'll take what I can get."

The group text between myself, Nina, and Michaela

continues to buzz with each message Michaela sends. This could have been an email, but apparently, she thought sending photos and instructions from Sasha was urgent enough to be a continuous text chain. Another one comes through detailing how the kids are supposed to check in on Sunday, where they should go and who to speak with, what the different color wrist bands mean, and...

"For the love of God, Michaela, stop texting!" I look up to see Nick helping Nina out of the passenger seat, her phone pressed to her ear. She tells Michaela to put everything in a single email and send it over when she and Sasha are finished walking through the details. When she hangs up, she mumbles something in Italian, only for Nick to hear.

"That's your friend," Nick snickers.

"That's your cousin."

"She's got you there, Davis," I say as they reach the front steps. We shake hands before I pull Nina into a quick hug. "I'm so glad you guys are here."

"I'm not," Nick says. "I voted to skip out, but someone said we had to be social."

"I did too, but Mom vetoed me."

"She wouldn't let you skip to finish the getting ready for Sunday?"

"She's letting me leave Saturday night, so I can be back in time for Sunday."

"So, Michaela..."

"Will be fine," I interrupt him. "Sasha can handle anything that may need attention with the event, I already spoke with her."

"Sorry to interrupt," Uncle Jack opens the front door, "but, you guys are the last to arrive and your father is wondering where *you* are."

"And, so it begins," I murmur earning a pitiful smile from everyone.

# eighteen

### Finn

**"SO, HOW WAS MY** sister?" My stomach drops at the question, and I look up expecting to see Josh locked and loaded, but he casually leans back in his chair. His face is neutral, unreadable... Shit, does he know? There's no way he knows. Michaela wouldn't tell him, but she might tell Elizabeth. I'm so screwed. Guess I found the reason he wanted me to come over.

"W-what do you mean?"

"On Sheffield House," he chuckles. "You were practically ready to throw in the towel when Nina told you Mic was taking over."

"Oh," a breath of relief. "Yeah, she was fine, I guess. Annoying as ever, but I didn't expect any less. She did have the idea for Coney Island, so I guess, something good did come out of it."

"Careful, someone might think you're starting to like her or something."

Suddenly it feels a little warmer in here. I wipe my palms on the thighs of my jeans and adjust in my seat. "She was helpful. What else do you want me to say?"

"Relax, man, I'm just making sure she didn't screw around."

Is he fucking with me?

"I know how important this is for you."

"Did you only invite me over to interrogate me about your little sister?"

"Hey, I have the inside scoop at my disposal, why not take advantage of it?" Josh smirks. He has always been an informed big brother. Always kept an eye on his kid sister. Always let her hang around even if the rest of us didn't want her there. In some ways, I understood, it was better than her getting involved in the wrong crowd, but hell, if it wasn't a downer when we had this little kid getting in the way of our teenage fun. If Michaela was around, we had to be on our best behavior, or at least pretend to be — there are plenty of times we did things when Josh looked the other way. Eventually, we all got used to her being there. The others saw her as one of our own, adopting her as their little sister, but not me. She and I were always at odds with one another, constantly bickering, picking fights, and talking shit to each other. I know it got on everyone's nerves, but we couldn't help ourselves. It kept us entertained.

"You have an inside scoop with Nina, too."

"Are you kidding? Nina doesn't tell me shit. Girl code and all that."

"She's ratted Michaela out a time or two."

"Sure, but only when it's really bad. Besides, Mic usually tells on herself anyway. You know she can't keep a secret."

"No shit." I roll my eyes. If anyone knows that I do — Michaela is why I spent my Junior year of high school at a boarding school in Tennessee. Not that it did any good; if anything, it did the opposite of what my parents hoped. What do you expect when you let teenagers live with very little adult supervision? "That little shit has never been able to keep her mouth shut."

In more ways than one. The sounds of her moans echo in my mind and my pants feel a little tighter. Shit, not now, Sheffield. Do not think about fucking your best friend's little sister with him right in front of you.

"The way you guys hate still each other blows my mind," Josh laughs. "You'd think you were the brother instead of me."

"Dude, don't say that."

"I'm serious!"

God, Josh. Just stop talking.

"Where's Ellie?" I ask attempting to change the subject. I've been here most of the morning and have yet to see Elizabeth once. Normally, she would have been here to greet me with a hot breakfast and coffee. Even if she had a shoot, she'd always stick around to greet you before leaving.

"Oh, I think she had a meeting down in Charleston."

"What does that mean — you think?"

Josh shrugs but doesn't meet my curious stare, finding his phone much more interesting. "She's been down there a lot recently — lots of shoots for some family or something. She should be home any time now."

"Josh, why in the hell is our— Oh, Finn!" Elizabeth walks into the kitchen from the mudroom looking like a kid caught sneaking in past curfew. "Sorry Josh, I didn't know you had company. Finn, what are you doing here?"

"It's Oliver's birthday," Josh says flatly. Normally, he would cross the kitchen to scoop his wife in his arms and plant a fat kiss on her lips, but he stays on the other side of the kitchen island. Elizabeth looks around before setting her purse in the empty place next to me, but she doesn't completely let go. She seems stiff and uncomfortable, a stranger in her own home. "I told you he was coming over this weekend," Josh says fiddling with the cap of his water bottle.

Elizabeth turns to me, "That's right, I'm so sorry. My weeks are starting to blur together more than I realized. How is Oliver?"

"Oh, you know... Oliver," I say.

She huffs a small laugh, but her smile doesn't quite reach her eyes.

"Will you make it on Sunday?"

"Sunday?" She seems genuinely confused.

"The Coney Island event for the thing he's been working on," Josh says with a little more annoyance than necessary.

"Shit," Elizabeth sighs, her shoulders falling. "Finn, I'm sorry. I don't think I'll make it. I have to be in Asheville for a shoot tomorrow and then Charleston on Monday for—"

"Don't forget our appointment on Monday."

Elizabeth finally meets his stare. A silent conversation before Elizabeth sighs and turns back to me. "I'm sorry, Finn. Things are just extra crazy right now."

"No sweat, Ellie." I wrap my arm around her shoulders and give them a gentle squeeze. "As long as you make it to the big party next month. You gotta take a break and celebrate occasionally."

Another sad smile. "I promise."

"Don't hold your breath," I swear I hear Josh mumble.

"Well, I have to go pick up the dry cleaning, I need one of the shirts for tomorrow." Elizabeth squeezes my arm gently before grabbing her purse. She leaves without another word and doesn't even kiss Josh. And it leaves me feeling... lost. What in the hell did I just witness?

"Dude, what was that?"

"What?" He turns from the fridge with two beers.

"*That.* What in the hell was that? She didn't even tell you goodbye. Elizabeth never leaves without telling someone goodbye, let alone her own husband. She didn't even kiss you!"

Josh shrugs, "Sure, she did."

"Josh—"

"Finn, just drop it. Okay?" The glare he shoots me is enough for me to end the conversation, for now.

I'm happy to accept the glass of whiskey Uncle Jack hands over after my day with Josh. Honestly, I was relieved to get back to pretending to be a happy family. That's something I never thought I'd say. Usually, I'm chomping at the bit to get away from my parents, but today I was glad to get back to some sense of normalcy. Tonight was the big birthday bash for all of Dad's closest friends, if you can call them that. The backyard had been transformed into a 1920s speakeasy including a makeshift entryway that required a code word to enter. I had to hand it to my mom, she and the party planner outdid themselves.

Dad takes his glass plopping into one of the brown leather chairs of the men's club across from me. His smile tells me I'm not going to like where this is going. When I was younger, I used to dream of what it would be like to join my father and Uncle Jack in the club. I wanted to be part of the secrets behind that giant mahogany door that concealed this room from the rest of the world. I was never allowed inside and that made it feel sacred...special. Until I found myself on the other side of the door on my sixteenth birthday. I learned this was nothing more than an over-glorified cigar and whiskey room where Dad would bring his friends to discuss business and talk shit. I wish I could tell my younger self not to romanticize it so much. Maybe I could have saved myself some of the disappointment that came with being accepted into the "club."

"So, Finn, how's your little project going?" Dad taunts.

I share an annoyed glance with Uncle Jack. Of course, Dad would bring this up now in front of the others. We're joined by three of his business associates — Jake Carpenter, finance guru; Alex Black, vice president of the local bank chain; and Cooper Lewis, owner of a sports team (baseball, I think) and my father's former business partner. All successful businessmen who know me as nothing more than Oliver Sheffield's failure of a son. Every venture I've ever attempted has failed, and I'm sure they all expect this one to be no different. That's why I went to the best of the best for help on this one...

"It's fine."

"Not as easy as it looks, hmm? Your mother says Davina isn't even the one helping you, some assistant is."

"Nina has been a little busy. She is—"

"You mean, she knows it's not worth her time." He smirks lighting a cigar. "You could always wave the white flag. No one would judge, we all understand how hard it can be." He and his friends share a laugh, but Uncle Jack just rolls his eyes.

"Isn't that enough business talk, fellas?" Uncle Jack interrupts before I can say something I might regret. Fighting with Dad isn't going to do me any good, it's only going to make things worse. And I can't afford to make things worse.

"Relax, Finnley," Dad takes a long drag of his cigar. "I'm just interested in what you're doing, that's all."

"That'd be a first," I mumble and down the amber liquid in my glass.

"So go ahead, give us your best sales pitch."

*nineteen*

*Michaela*

**"HONESTLY, SCREW YOU GUYS,"** I hiss, following Cait out of the cab. "I shouldn't even be here right now."

"Of course you should!" Cait loops her arm through mine, and Liv does the same on the other side as they lead me toward the entrance to Luna Park, where the check-in table has been set up.

Sasha's smile widens, and she waves excitedly when she sees us. "Michaela! I thought you weren't coming."

"I wasn't, but these two kidnapped me."

There I was, minding my own business when a knock at the door turned into a full-on kidnapping. Cait and Liv stood on the other side of the door ready to gag and bind me if I refused to come with them. I woke up this morning with a new lease on life. Thank God I get to go back to my office tomorrow. It felt so good to leave corporate on Friday knowing I didn't have to come back Monday morning. When Nina called Friday night asking if I wanted to spend another week helping Finn, I turned her down. "Best I can do is Sunday," I said. It wasn't fair of me to turn her down, and I knew I should help her, but I couldn't spend another week working with him. Scratch that, I couldn't spend another week doing all the work for him. I was finally free and did not plan on going backward. I'd be happy if I never saw him again — but, I'd never be that lucky. Not when Josh is my brother.

When I woke up this morning, I decided I wasn't going to torture myself today by attending the fundraiser. Not even my brother could convince me...

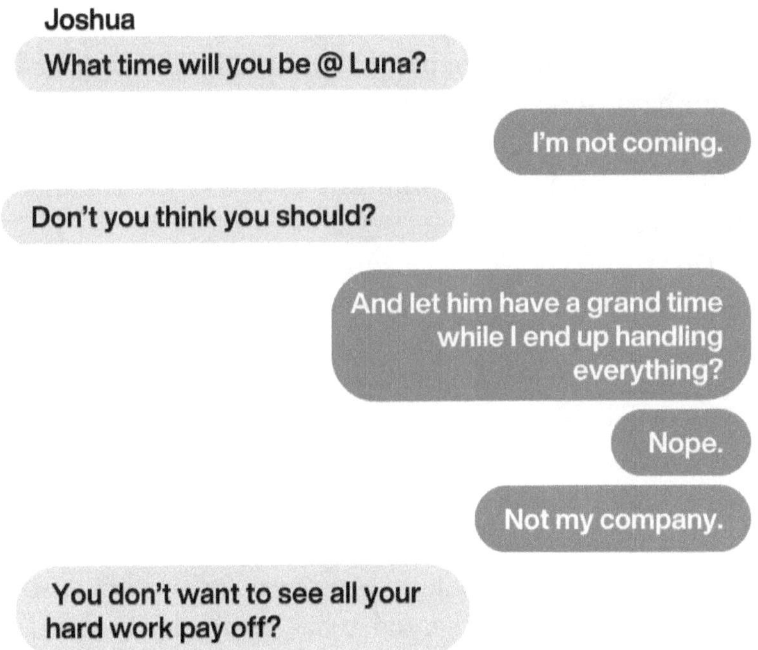


I rolled my eyes. I wouldn't have had to work so hard if *someone* had been doing their part. Instead, he was too busy having a good ole time — typical Finn, always looking for the next party. And, I would much rather spend my day at home catching up on the new season of *The Boys*. I mean, who wouldn't want to stare at Karl Urban for a few hours?

However, that plan was ruined when the two women dragging me toward the park entrance showed up. At least they brought donuts.

"Well, I'm glad you're here. You should reap the benefits of your hard work!" Sasha wraps one of the bright pink bands around my wrist with a wink.

"That's what I said," Caitlin says as one of the volunteers applies her band.

"Don't worry, we'll make sure to turn that frown upside down!" Liv says, lifting the corners of my mouth and shoving me inside the blue gates.

So far, so good... We have been here for two hours with no sign of Finn. I can't lie, today has been a lot of fun. I've never been to an amusement park when you're the only ones there but it's pretty great. No lines. No rude customers. The workers even seem relaxed and happy to be here. I don't think I'll ever be able to go back to normal amusement park living after this. I wonder if I can convince Nina to do this every time we want to go somewhere... Just imagine having somewhere like Disney World all to yourself.

"Well, look who decided to show after all." Nina stands with a smirk on her lips as she lifts her sunglasses. "I thought you told Josh you weren't coming today?"

"We couldn't let her bail," Liv says.

"Well, I'm glad you didn't. This has been a great event, Mic. You outdid yourself." Nina smiles and I feel a weight lift off my shoulders. I know I'm not totally off the hook yet, but it feels like she has some restored faith in me. "We still have some things to discuss, but... You did a wonderful job."

"Thanks, Nin."

"There she is!" Nick pops out of the crowd carrying Ophelia who clutches a lollipop bigger than her head.

Behind him, Josh, Kai, and Elieen break through the crowd. Eileen carries a teddy bear, surely a prize won for Ophelia from one of the carnival games. The crowd parts for one final member of the group, and I fully expect to see Elizabeth, but instead, Finn steps through. He's walking shoulder to shoulder with a younger boy, no more than fourteen or fifteen, who looks like he just graduated from boot camp. He's clearly one of the kids part of the event, but they look way too comfortable to have just met. Seems weird that Finn would know one of the participants from today. Why would he? The whole idea of him being invested in helping foster kids is still weird to me, it's such an odd charitable need to pick.

Finn stands out among the crowd dressed in black slacks and a blue button-up, the top buttons left undone, and the sleeves rolled up. The rest of the group is dressed down a bit — while maintaining a certain level of professionalism required by our positions.

"Aunt Michaela!" Ophelia squeals and Finn's attention is pulled from his conversation. His eyes are hidden behind a pair of black Ray-Bans, but I can feel his stare burning into me. Ophelia squirms from Nick's arms and crashes into my legs.

"Hey, Leia." I bend down to her level trying to ignore the two newcomers. "I haven't seen you in so long, how are you, sweet girl?"

"Uncle Nick won me a teddy bear!"

"He did? That was nice of him."

"Yeah, Daddy tried, but he wasn't very good at shooting the ball."

Kai rolls his eyes, "Thanks, Leia."

"Don't worry, man. We all know sports are your strong suit," Nick laughs gripping Kai's shoulder.

"C'mon Leia, let's go ride the Rainbowheel before we head home. It's almost nap time." Kai extends his hand towards her, and she looks up at him with the biggest puppy dog eyes I've ever seen. "Don't look at me like that. You know I can't resist those eyes."

Ophelia pouts a little more but finally gives in when Eileen gives her the mom look. She sighs and hugs me goodbye before taking her father's hand and disappearing into the crowd.

"We're actually about to head out too," Nina says leaning into Nick's embrace. She turns to Finn, "Don't stay out too late, Sheffield. We have a long week ahead of us."

"I promise to keep him on his best behavior," the boy says.

"I'm holding you to that, Knox."

Knox salutes her, and I can't help but smile. He seems like a sweet kid. Wonder what he is doing with Finn?

"I'll email you with some times that we can meet this week," Nina says to me.

"Damn, I thought I was off the hook," I laugh.

"Not quite. Between the two of you, I have my work cut out for me."

"Just remember, we love you, Nin," Finn says before he is pulled to the side by an older woman. I recognize her as one of the volunteers and social workers that Sasha introduced to me on Thursday. She wraps Finn in a tight embrace, and her gratitude is palpable as she holds his face between her hands when they part. The woman beckons a young boy closer from a few feet away.

"Put your eyes back in your head," my brother snickers ripping my attention from the scene. I realize we're the only ones left standing here — Nick and Nina have left, and Caitlin and Liv have gone to get a funnel cake from the stand a little ways down.

"What are you yammering about?"

"If you don't stop staring at him like that, someone might think you like him or something."

"Oh god," I choke on imaginary vomit. "I think I just threw up a little… Josh, that's disgusting." He doesn't seem convinced. "You think I like Finn?"

"I didn't say that."

"You implied it."

Josh shrugs. "Do you?"

"What?" I practically shriek catching the attention of the group a few feet away. I can see the glare Finn shoots me through his sunglasses before he turns back to the woman with an apology. "Josh, how could you even ask me something like that?"

"It's just a question, Mic. Maybe that's why you guys have always hated each other… It's secretly your love for one another."

I think I might throw up. "Josh, stop talking."

"You didn't deny it."

"We do *not* like each other, not like that… I can promise you that."

"Good thing considering you're married. Or are you? I haven't seen him or your ring in a while. Come to think of it, I haven't heard you mention said husband in a while."

Okay, yep, going to vomit. Where is the trash can? Scanning the area for the nearest one, I meet concerned brown eyes under raised sunglasses. He continues the conversation in front of him, but his focus has shifted to me. Knox notices and takes control of the conversation allowing Finn to step away. "You okay, Shortcake?" The concern in his voice catches me off guard. "You look a little pale."

"She's good, man. Just being a little dramatic."

"Michaela," it's forceful, yet soft. He touches my arm, fingers wrapping around my wrist when I jump slightly. "Are you okay?"

"Dude, she's fine," Josh reassures him, but Finn doesn't budge. "Finn."

"Yeah," I breathe out, but I know that I'm going to have to put on a show for my brother. Especially after what Finn just did. I rip my arm from his grasp. "I'm fine, Sheffield. What's your deal?"

Finn's features straighten and his eyes narrow as he towers over me. "Good, then stop causing a scene. Today isn't about *you.*"

I swallow any hope of a comeback.

"Alright, you two, break it up," Josh rolls his eyes. "Now isn't the time."

"Everything okay?" Cait asks when she and Liv return with funnel cakes.

"Take her home," Finn instructs them taking a step back finally. "She's had enough fun for the day."

"You don't get to decide when I leave." I try to follow him, but Josh holds me back reminding me we have an audience.

"Be a good girl and go home, Shortcake."

*Be a good girl.*

The words stir the fire in my core and from the smirk on his lips, that's exactly what he meant to do. That fucker.

"Josh, thanks for coming, man." He shakes my brother's hand before returning to Knox, who has since started showing the little boy how to play one of the carnival games involving a water gun.

"Asshole," I whisper. "How can someone so obnoxious and

rude think they can run a nonprofit to help foster kids? He doesn't even know the first thing about them!"

"I think he knows more than you," Josh scoffs. "He was one."

*twenty*

*Finn*

**"SO, HAVE THEY GOT** you hooked up with a little brother yet?" Colin asks, securing the strap of his bag over his shoulder.

"About four weeks ago. Cool kid. A little quiet but he just needs help coming out of his shell. Reminds me of you. I took him to the Coney Island buyout you bailed on two weeks ago."

"Hang out with you or go visit Saylor." He uses his hands to weigh out the options, and clearly, the Saylor option wins.

"Yeah, yeah, I know. I'm not as pretty as she is." I flip imaginary long hair from my shoulder as we step out of the gym onto the streets of SoHo. "How's Mama June doing, by the way? Anniversary's coming up."

Colin shrugs. "I mean, she's happy. Tom has been really good for her, but it's always hard around this time of year."

"How are you holding up? This year is what, fifteen years?"

"I'm trying to focus on the positives. That's what Dad would want. Oh, before I forget, Shey told me to ask if you wanted to come over for dinner when she gets back next week."

"Just tell me when and I'm there."

"You are being ridiculous!" A deep voice catches our

attention. Across the street, a man towers over another person as he berates them. This isn't the typical place for this kind of scene, so it draws attention. Passersby try to act like they're bothered, but they just want to know what's going on.

"Probably an assistant who got the wrong coffee," Colin snickers.

"Why can't you act like an adult for once in your life — is it really so hard for you?" The man shouts again.

"Or not."

The other person finally seems to break free of whatever hold the man has on them stepping into view and I feel like I've been punched in the stomach. You've got to be kidding. Is that... "Michaela?" I shout without thinking, catching everyone's attention.

"You know her?" Colin follows me across the street.

"Mic, hey! That is you."

"Who the hell is this guy?" Asshole glares down at her.

Who the hell is he?

"Finn, what are you doing?" Michaela ignores him. Dark circles I've never noticed hang under her eyes. She's dressed in bike shorts and a hoodie, her honey-blonde hair pulled into the messiest bun I've ever seen underneath a baseball cap – drastically different from her normal attire.

"I was over at the gym and–"

"Who's this — your newest fuck?" Asshole interrupts me.

"Hey, watch your mouth," Colin straightens to his full height — at least two inches taller than me at five-eleven, and I stand at least two inches taller than Asshole. I watch Asshole's eyes widen slightly. "There's no need to talk to a lady like that."

Colin, ever the gentleman.

"You okay?" I touch her hand trying to ignore the stare burning into the side of my head.

"Fine," she hisses and tries to rip her hand from mine, but I don't let go.

"Yeah, she's fine," Asshole tries to step between us, but I don't budge. "You can go now. We have a conversation to finish."

"Actually, your conversation is finished." I rest my hand on her back pulling her further into me despite the tension. It slowly dissipates as my thumb grazes the skin of her neck, a warmth blooming under my touch. "C'mon," I glance down at her, "let's go home."

"So, you are fucking him!" Asshole scoffs.

"What's it to you?"

"I'm her husband."

*Husband.*

Wait… She's married? I knew Josh had said she was seeing someone a few years ago, but nothing ever seemed to come out of it. Where's he been the last month? Obviously, not interested in his wife's whereabouts. He hasn't shown his face one time. I don't remember even hearing her mention him. Not once. That means she was married when we fucked in the office… Great, this is just great.

"And, considering she refuses to sign the divorce papers, I think I'm entitled to know who my wife is whoring around with."

I stick my other hand out to restrain Colin when he takes a step forward keeping him from doing something he'll regret. "No, I don't think you do and I don't appreciate you talking about my girlfriend that way. If you ever speak to her like that again, Colin over there will be the least of your problems. If you'll excuse us, we have somewhere to be." Like Michaela giving me an explanation as to what in the hell is going on. Uncertainty swims in the ocean eyes under her baseball cap, but I squeeze her shoulder gently. "Isn't that right, *Shortcake?*"

"Y-yeah. Yeah, we have, um, plans. Bye, David."

"Hand it over, Michaela," David hisses.

"You know, I don't think I will." A tight smile tugs on her

lips and she leans further into my side. Her voice becomes more confident with each word, "Especially if you're going to continue to come at me in such a threatening manner."

"Unbelievable. You'll be hearing from my lawyer, again."

"She knows where to find me."

This is going to continue until one of them walks away, and no one wants to be the first one to blink. So I do it for them, guiding her down the street. Colin hesitates briefly, he's still considering turning around and beating David's ass. He cannot stand a man disrespecting a woman, but especially not their own wife. David calling her a whore was the final nail in his coffin, whether Colin knows her or not. And right now, he thinks she is my girlfriend. So, David has not only disrespected Michaela, but me.

We turn onto Sixth Street from Grand, and Michaela tries to pull away, but I keep my hold on her. I know better than to stop this soon in case David follows. I guide her across Sixth to Broome and finally release her. "What in the hell was that, Michaela?"

"Fuck off, Finn. It's not your business."

"I find you in a screaming match with your *husband* in the middle of SoHo, and you tell me it's not my business?"

"It's not your business!"

"Michaela—"

"Okay, what is going on here?" Colin interrupts. "You failed to mention you were dating someone, Sheff. Let alone someone who is married."

"Soon to be divorced," Michaela corrects.

"We are not dating," I correct him. "Colin, this is Michaela, the one who was helping me with the House. Josh's little sister."

"Davis? Oh, shit. You're dating his little sister? He's gonna kill you, dude."

"We're not dating!" Michaela and I say at the same time.

"Like that would happen," Michaela mumbles.

"What's that supposed to mean?" I hiss. She'd be lucky to date someone like me, especially after what I just witnessed.

"I'd sooner go back to my ex-husband."

Ouch.

"From the sound of it, he's not your ex yet."

"You know what, I don't have time for your shit today." Michaela looks towards Colin, "It was nice to meet you, whoever you are. Finn's friend who knows my brother. I didn't catch your name, but I have to go. And Finn," she returns to me, her nostrils flare slightly and her blue eyes narrow, "stay out of my life."

"Strictly business here, Shortcake."

Michaela rolls her eyes before she huffs off down Sixth — she weaves through the small crowd like a fish swimming against the current.

"Dude," Colin says, catching my attention. "What the fuck are you doing?"

# twenty-one

## *Michaela*

**OKAY, SO FINN KNOWS** about the divorce. This is fine. Everything is fine... Right? I mean, I've successfully avoided telling anyone close to my family for the past three months, and I was hoping to keep it that way until things were settled. Or fixed. Deep inside, I guess I hoped David would change his mind. He'd show up on my doorstep saying he messed up and didn't want a divorce. As you can tell, that hasn't happened yet. The longer this drags on, the more I have accepted that it's over. As if coming home to an empty house every night isn't enough of an indication. Maybe that's why I've held out on the ring for so long. Thinking he'd come back...

And, then there's Finn.

The way he stepped in to stop David from causing even more of a scene, pretending to be my boyfriend without a second thought. The way he was so protective, the warmth from his touch... I've been searching for something similar since that night in the office, but nothing has even come close.

"Good morning!" Bella waves from her desk when I step off the elevator at DV Designs. "You're here early."

"Had a few things to catch up on since I had to leave early yesterday. Any messages I need to know about?"

"Nope, but I should probably warn you, there's someone here to see you."

"Bella, it's," I check my watch, "seven-thirty in the morning. Who the hell is here this early?"

"Morning, Shortcake." Every inch of my body tenses at the sound of his voice. Shit, I should've seen this coming.

"Surprise!" Bella whispers and holds up an iced coffee. "He even brought me a coffee."

I thought I had more time to prepare for this conversation. Scratch that, I thought I could avoid it all together since I don't have to be around him anymore, but I knew better. He's going to have a lot of questions – rightfully so. Not that I really have any answers. While I've spent the part of my night thinking how good his touch felt, how safe I felt by his side; I've spent the other half waiting for a phone call from my brother. I was sure Finn couldn't wait to tell Josh what he witnessed.

"You're looking a little pale."

"I'm fine." I try to avoid eye contact, pushing past him to head for my office. Despite my quick pace, I know he's right behind me. One of his strides is equal to two of mine. I could close the door in his face, but he'd come in anyway.

"You hungry?" He asks closing the door behind him. "I brought some danishes from the bakery down the street."

"Nope," it's quick and concise. It should send the message that I am not in the mood to talk. Sitting at my desk, I turn my focus to my computer logging into my email — the first thing in my inbox is an email from Kai. That's weird, Kai never emails me.

*You did good, Michaela. Board was impressed with everything and they're going to invest in the company. Nina and I have been talking, we think you'd be good at corporate...*

*If you're interested. Let me know. - Kai*

Corporate?

They want me to move to corporate?

What would I even do there? It's not like I'm "Villa Inc." material. Everyone who works there is so… uptight. So well… corporate. The opposite of my entire life. Except for Liv, but she's the front desk girl. She doesn't have to fit in with the rest of them.

"Are you going to—"

"No. I don't want a fucking danish. I don't want coffee. I don't want anything from you. Can you just *stop?*"

His brow quirks and he leans back in the chair in front of my desk. A small smirk tugs on the corner of his mouth before he laughs.

"What is so fucking funny?" I rub my temples. This can't get any worse, right? "Can you please leave? I cannot deal with your shit today."

Finn's arms cross over his chest, straining against the sleeves of his navy blue jacket, and he settles further into the chair. Guess he isn't going anywhere. "Fine, I'll go."

"Sit down, Shortcake." It's not a suggestion. He hasn't moved an inch he doesn't look at all bothered by my outburst. He motions to my chair. "Sit." Whether I want to or not, my body follows his command. "Now, you're going to tell me what is going on."

"I don't—

"Don't lie to me, Michaela Jane." Did he just use my full name? That was kind of sexy… Wait, no. No, it wasn't. Finn leans forward, forearms resting on my desk, hands folded perfectly in front of him. "What in the hell was that yesterday?"

Do I tell him? It's going to be kind of hard to lie my way out of this one. And if he hasn't told Josh yet, he definitely will if I don't start talking soon.

"Did you tell Josh?" I ask.

"Not yet."

"Not yet?"

"Well, it's not my place, is it? Besides, I don't know what's going on. So, I figured I should get the whole story before I rat you out." His attempt at humor does nothing but irritate me. "I'm kidding, Michaela. I've been worried about you since you left."

"You're worried about me?" I laugh, "You couldn't care less."

"That's not true."

"You've never cared, Finn! I was always just some dumb kid in the way. So, please spare me your pity now."

"Shortcake–"

"And stop calling me that, for the love of God."

He chuckles and leans back in his chair, "Okay, *Shortcake*."

"Dammit, Sheffield! I mean it."

"Alright, alright." He lifts his hands in surrender, a small smile on his lips. "Look, you don't have to tell me, but you should tell your family. I mean, does Nina even know?"

"It never came up," I shrug.

He shakes his head and reaches across the desk — I'm suddenly aware of how big his hands are when his right hand engulfs mine. The skin of his fingers is rough, it was the strangest sensation the first time I felt it — I would assume he had perfectly soft, manicured hands. But, his touch is soft and warms my skin. "Tell them, Michaela. I know they'd want to be there for you during this."

*twenty-two*

## *Michaela*

**MY PHONE DINGS FROM** the top shelf where I've kept it since my little conversation with Finn on Friday. I'm surprised it's still alive and breathing, but I guess that happens when you don't use it for two whole days. So, to answer your question, no, I haven't told my family about David yet. Instead, I spent the weekend holed up in my office working on project after project to keep myself preoccupied. It's been great workwise. Though, I think I should probably go home and take a shower...

Rising to my tip-toes, I stretch my fingers to grasp my phone from its position at the furthest point of the shelf that I could reach.

**Cait**

> I know you're alive because I've seen your emails, but where in the hell are you? Text me. Call me. Something.

I sigh scrolling through her other one million messages

before looking at the other unopened messages waiting for me. Liv. Josh. Nina. Alex. Mom. Elizabeth. Finn... Finn? Opening his messages, I'm surprised to see a total of five messages since Friday. The first one was about two hours after he left my office.

**Jabba**

> You need to tell them, Michaela. They'd want to be there for you.

> I'm assuming it's still a secret since I haven't heard from Josh.

> I know you're mad, but you could at least tell me to fuck off or something.

> You haven't opened a single one of these.
>
> Are you alive?

> I'm sorry if I was harsh the other day. I was just a little surprised to learn you were married after we...
> You know.

Suddenly, the three little dots bounce up and down as he types another message. They disappear but quickly return a few seconds later, a cycle until finally nothing comes through. Maybe he will leave me alone now that he knows I'm alive and have opened his messages... Thank you read receipts.

But, it's so strange. Why is he so concerned? This is not the same Finnley Sheffield I've always known. This is some alternate universe version... The one I've always kind of wished he would be.

I don't respond packing my stuff to head home. I need to take a shower, eat something, and sleep for the next twenty-four hours.

A knock on the door pulls my attention from my rewatch of *The Mandalorian.* Who in the world? I finally got back to everyone — minus one — about an hour ago and let them know I was alive and well, just consumed by work all weekend. I told Cait that I'd be taking tomorrow to stay at home and catch up on sleep since we don't have anything that requires me to be in the office.

If I pretend to be asleep, maybe whoever it is will go away.

Another knock before a muffled voice comes through the door. "C'mon, Shortcake, I know you're in there. I can hear the TV."

You cannot be serious. What does *he* want?

I grumble the whole way to the door, but I have to answer it because he isn't going anywhere unless I do. "What do you want, Finn?"

"I brought soup." Finn proudly holds up a plastic tub of chicken noodle soup. He's dressed in jeans, a black T-shirt, and a black jean jacket. Damn, he looks good. *So good.* Besides his gym clothes from last Thursday, I haven't seen him in anything other than a suit since he graduated high school. He needs to dress more like this. It's so casual, but damn...I like it. It's sexy.

No, Michaela, he does not look sexy.

Yes. He does.

"Thank you," he chuckles. His smirk tells me I just said that out loud. Shit. "I brought soup because I thought it might help make you feel better."

"What are you talking about? I feel fine."

"Well, I figured you must be dead or sick since you didn't answer my texts."

"I don't have to answer you anymore — that ended the day I was freed from you."

I reach for the container, but he holds it away from me. "Can I come in?"

"Hard pass."

"Oh, c'mon, Shortcake, just a quick in and out, I promise."

Trust me, there is nothing short or quick about him, I promise you that.

A smirk lights up his face as Finn finally steps past me to come inside. "Nice place you got here," he says. I snatch the soup from him and take it to the kitchen. I catch a whiff, and it smells heavenly. Yeah, I'll be eating that for a midnight snack later... Okay, time to get him out of here. Stepping out of the kitchen, I watch his eyes roam over the decor, stopping on the original trilogy posters that hang above the couch, before glancing down at my "Tell that to Kanjiclub" shirt. "Still a *Star Wars* fan, I see."

"Yeah, so."

"No need to get defensive, it's cute. You always were obsessed with it."

Okay, I've had enough of nice-guy Finn. He's never been this person, why is he suddenly trying to be nice to me?

"What do you want, Finn?" I huff.

"I can't come to check on a friend?"

"We're not friends."

"Sure we are, Shortcake." Finn winks, and I feel something deep inside that I haven't felt since that night in the office. I'm not supposed to think about that. It meant nothing, absolutely nothing. I haven't thought about it one time since that night...

With two steps, he's right in front of me, and the smell of his cologne fills my senses — rich, warm scents of blue cypress and vetiver — it's intoxicating. Slowly, he pushes a strand of hair from my face before his fingers trail down my jawline, and his thumb rubs along my bottom lip. Warm brown eyes meet mine before they flicker down to my lips.

Wait... Is he... No, he can't be.

"Finn," my breath catches as he slowly leans in, his lips ghosting over mine, but not quite making contact. I should stop this. End it before it even starts. There's still time to turn back, but I don't want to. Instead, I run headfirst into what can only be a disaster, and close the space between us.

*twenty-three*

*Michaela*

**"SHIT," FINN PULLS AWAY** and takes two large steps back. "Shit, I'm sorry." He tugs at the ends of his hair before straightening out his shirt.

"Finn—"

"I don't know what came over me, I—I shouldn't have done that. You're... You're still married and—"

"Finn." Finally, he meets my stare, fingers clench at his sides before his gaze falls to my lips, and he moistens his own. I can't remember the last time someone made every nerve feel like it was on fire, definitely not David. My heart beats rapidly at the anticipation. "Shut up."

That's all it takes for him to close the gap again. His kiss is rough, contrary to the one we shared moments ago. Fingers thread through my hair giving a soft tug before he nips my lower lip. His mouth is hard and demanding, and his tongue probes deeply taking what he wants. "Strawberry," he murmurs against me. His lips leave a burning trail from my jaw to my ear, "I always knew there was a reason I called you Shortcake."

My fingers clench the fabric of his t-shirt when he takes

my mouth again, a moan echoing between us. He pushes me against the wall of the hallway, chest flush against mine — he devours me. The way he dominates every part of me is delicious.

His teeth graze my neck before sinking into the skin earning a small gasp that seems to please him. He hums against the skin. A combination of nibbling and sucking is sure to leave a mark, but his tongue follows to soothe the pain.

Finn cups my ass and squeezes lifting me off my feet. I wrap my legs around his torso, where I can feel his erection stiff against me. The aching between my legs intensifies thinking about it. Remembering how he felt when we—

"We can stop," he whispers, nipping at my ear. I take a shaky breath when his almost black eyes pierce mine, filled with nothing but desire. "Forget this happened. Forget it's happened before. Go back to the way things have always been." He flexes his hips, and I bite back a moan at the feeling. "You want that, Shortcake?"

"No," it's breathless. No, I most certainly do not want that. The only thing I want is him on top of me. I can feel his pulse beating rapidly under my touch when I bring his lips back to mine. "I need you, Finn."

That's all the validation he needs to keep going.

His hands tighten their hold and carry me to my bedroom. I swear my heart is going to beat out of my chest. My mind races in a million different directions now — What happens in the morning? Are we going to regret this? Are we supposed to go back to the way things were? *They never left,* is what he said last time. What about this time?

Finn drops me on the edge of the burnt orange duvet and shrugs his jacket off before pulling his t-shirt over his head in one swift motion. My eyes must have grown ten times their size by the way he laughs. "Damn." I tentatively reach out toward him, allowing my fingers to dust over his tanned skin, and his body trembles slightly under my touch. "You've been hiding this the whole time?"

"You've been looking?"

A blush creeps into my cheeks. What am I supposed to say? I can't admit to checking him out. I mean, no, I have not been checking him out. Definitely not.

He kisses me gently, "Don't worry, baby, me too."

Fuck me.

"Don't worry, I plan to," he chuckles.

Did I say that out loud? Shit, I've *got* to stop doing that.

Finn slowly drags my oversized T-shirt up my torso, his fingers leaving a burning trail in their wake. They graze the sides of my bare breasts, and his eyes brighten, realizing I'm not wearing a bra. I chew on the corner of my mouth. He lets my shirt fall to the floor and his eyes freely roam every inch of my skin. Without hesitation he bends to capture my lips in another kiss, this one softer than the others. His tongue massages mine in slow, languid movements. It's the most sensual thing I've ever experienced. David was not a sweet lover, he was a hit-it-and-quit-it kind of lover. Finn takes his time — exploring, tasting, and enjoying himself.

His warm hand reaches to cup my breast, and his fingers knead the doughy flesh before he pinches my nipple. My core throbs in need. I tug for the waistband of his jeans, fingers fumbling with his belt. Why is this thing so difficult to undo? He chuckles under his breath and he gently removes my hands. He undoes the belt himself. My cheeks burn waiting for some smartass remark, but it never comes. Instead, he lifts my chin to meet his gaze and the only thing in his eyes is want and need.

"Aren't you going to finish what you started?" The words send a shiver down my spine and my fingers make quick work of the rest of his jeans.

A soft intake of breath falls from his lips when I softly cup him over his briefs watching as his eyes darken. Fuck, he's hard. So hard. I can feel his pulse under my touch. It sends a jolt of electricity straight to my core. My mouth ghosts over his matching the light graze of my fingers across the fabric covering his cock.

"Stop teasing," Finn warns.

"Who's teasing?" I smirk, unsure where the sudden confidence comes from as I push my sweats down my legs, stepping out of the heap on the floor. There's no going back as I stand completely bare to him.

"Fuck, Michaela." His eyes practically roll in the back of his head before they drink in every inch of me. "Look at you," he murmurs, and I've never felt like this before. Under his ravenous stare, I feel pretty and powerful. He reaches out to trace my curves, "God, you're beautiful." Finn pushes me back and I reach for him as he climbs on the bed. He cups my entrance, his fingers gently teasing me. His lips ghost across my jaw to my ear, a soft purr in his tone, "You're already so wet for me, Shortcake."

He slides one finger inside me, and his lips capture mine. His tongue flicks against mine – claiming, stroking in a desperate embrace. I gasp when he pushes another finger inside me. My back arches from the bed when his thumb finds my swollen clit beginning a relentless assault. I begin to grind against his fingers in time with his movements. "I need you," I whimper.

"Not yet," he mumbles. "I want to taste you when you come. I didn't have the pleasure last time." His words raise goosebumps across my skin. One more kiss, hard and deep, before he stares deep into my eyes. And in this moment, I don't need anything else but him – for tonight, this man is mine. "Would you like that, Shortcake?"

"Yes," I gasp when his fingers curl inside me. "Fuck yes."

Soft nips down my neck and collarbone send a shudder

down my spine before capturing my left nipple in his mouth. His tongue moves in time with his thumb against my clit, sucking and nibbling on my hardened bud. I can feel the fire building deep inside my belly as he moves to my right breast, doing the same.

"Finn." His name is barely above a whisper as my fingers tug his hair.

"Not yet, Michaela." His tone is unmistakably dominant pulling his fingers from me. I gasp at the sudden loss. Fuck, I was right there. I squeeze my thighs together, trying to find some kind of relief, but it's not enough. His lips ghost over my left thigh, his tongue traces the outline of my tattoo on my left thigh. "I knew I saw a tattoo last time," his voice is cocky, and I swear I can hear the smirk in his words. Like he's been thinking about the last time we were intimate. A soft whine resounds in my throat needing more of him. "Trust me, baby," Finn spreads my legs, "you'll like this much better."

I cry out when he puts his face between my legs, his tongue licking a long stripe up my entrance to my clit. A guttural groan sounds deep in his throat when he delves deeper into me. "You taste delicious," he mumbles against my core slipping a finger inside me. The tiny bundle of nerves between my legs throbs under his assault and I'm losing myself in him. Willing to give myself over to him without a promise of tomorrow because all that matters is right now.

"Oh my God," I gasp when he reaches up with his right hand to pinch my nipple. He smiles, slipping another finger inside me. I can feel that coil deep in my belly begging for release. I lift my right leg over his shoulder, desperate for more friction, and I find myself bucking against his tongue. Long, lazy licks turn to quick, teasing ones, and back; he knows exactly what he's doing. "Don't stop," it's a low whimper, but I know he hears me when his lips capture my clit. He suckles on the small bud, and that familiar fire ignites.

Finn moans and tightens his grip on my legs pulling me further into him. "Go ahead, baby. You don't have to wait. You don't have to wait, okay, Shortcake?" He's not going to torture me with waiting, not this time. When his lips find my clit again, a wave of pleasure crashes through me again and again.

When I come down from my high, Finn stares at me with the sweetest smile that sends a different wave of emotion through me. I do my best to suppress it because there's a big chance this is a one-and-done thing. I mean, there's no way we're going to do this again... Right? He pushes a strand of hair behind my ear. "You look so sexy when you come, y'know that?" He kisses me. It's soft and sweet and I taste myself on him when he deepens it.

I slip my thumb into the waistband of his boxers, but he stops me. "One sec," he kisses me and steps off the bed. Reaching for his slacks, he pulls his wallet from the front pocket retrieving a condom.

"You want one of those *now?*" I laugh.

"Don't you?" He asks with a raised brow.

"Didn't seem to bother you last time."

Finn chuckles but rips the foil with his teeth anyway and shoves his underwear down his legs. I know I've seen him before, but I can't help but stare. "Shortcake," his voice brings my gaze back to his face. I rise to my knees and meet him at the edge of the bed. I thread my fingers in his sandy-brown hair pulling his lips to mine, but he pulls away. "Are you sure, Michaela?"

A little late for that, I think.

I nod, my words soft. "I want you."

"Good, because I need you." Finn lays me back against the bed and pushes inside me. "Fuck," Finn hisses pressing his forehead against mine. I don't respond as I adjust to the sweet stretch of him, my nails digging into his shoulders. This feels so much better than last time. "You okay?" I finally open my eyes to meet his sweet brown orbs and melt at the concern in them.

"I'm great." The final word drags out as he thrusts into me. *So great.* Subtle pulses before he pulls out and slams back in again. He finds a rhythm that sends me spiraling. I thank God we're alone because I can't contain the sounds I make.

He smothers my moans with a deep kiss and wraps my right leg around his waist lifting my hips slightly to dive deeper. This new angle sends currents of electricity to my aching core, and I writhe beneath him. "You take me so good, baby girl."

My skin feels like it's on fire. And it's almost like he knows it as his thrusts become agonizingly slower than before. Like he's savoring each one. I rock my hips against his trying to find that release, but he refuses to give it to me.

"Please," I beg.

"You want to come?"

"Please, Finn, yes. Please, let me come."

Stubble scrapes across my skin as he hums against my neck before he bottoms out inside me. He doesn't give me time to adjust before pulling out and slamming in again. He does it repeatedly; each time, it's quicker than before, his movements wild and unruly. And it's there, that coil begging for release tightening more and more. His thrusts grow more staggered before he finds his release. He captures my lips in a brutal kiss, his fingers reach between us to capture my sensitive bundle of nerves. "Let go, baby girl," he demands, and I do. That blinding white heat rips through me, and he holds me as the final waves of release subside.

Sunshine filters through cream curtains casting a warm

glow on my face, but I won't let the sun win. My alarm hasn't gone off which means it's not time to get up, but I know it's morning from the birds chirping outside my window. My head rests on something much softer than how I remember Finn's chest feels. Lazily, I reach across the bed searching for him, but my hand meets cold sheets instead of a warm body. Okay, so Finn isn't a morning cuddler because I'm clutching a pillow instead of him. I peel open my eyes to look around the room, but any sign of him is gone. His clothes have been picked up from the floor and my pajamas have been folded neatly on the dresser. The only real evidence I have of the night before is the ache between my thighs.

You've got to be kidding me.

Of course, he would be gone before I woke up. Why would I expect anything else?

Pulling a Rosecliffe sweater over my head, I trudge to the kitchen to start a pot of coffee. Maybe it's good I'm up this early. I was going to stay home. Try and sleep, but maybe I'll go into the office anyway. I don't think I want to be home right now, I might go insane.

## twenty-four

*Finn*

**I CURSE UNDER MY** breath checking my watch. It's been over forty minutes since I left, she is probably up by now. Which means she probably thinks I left like some douchebag. Hopefully, today is one of those days when she plans on being late to the office. Otherwise, I won't make it back before she leaves.

My God, why is this elevator moving so slowly?

As the doors open to the thirteenth floor, I'm immediately greeted by a resident who feels the same way about the elevator. He doesn't even bother to look up from his phone or mumble an apology for practically running me over.

"Hold the elevator!" A woman shouts from down the hall, and just to piss off the other guy, I do. I can hear her quicken the pace before she rounds the corner and I'm face-to-face with Michaela.

"Going somewhere?"

"Finn? What are you doing here? I thought–"

"I went to get breakfast," I say. I lift the tray of coffee and breakfast sandwiches. Stepping out of the elevator, I finally let the door close.

"Breakfast?"

I kiss the crown of her head, "Mornin', Shortcake."

Michaela stands in shock for another moment even after I begin the walk back to her condo. She digs through her purse mumbling to herself as she walks, but I dangle the spare I found on the key ring in the kitchen. "Would this help?"

Her eyes roll before snatching it from my hands and unlocking the door. "You were gone when I woke up, so I figured—"

"Thought you'd be hungry. I was hoping to be back before you woke up, I'm sorry I wasn't. The line was longer than anticipated."

"So, you didn't leave and come back pretending to have been gone to get coffee?"

I laugh, "If I had planned on leaving for good, why would I take your spare key?"

"So, you could sneak in and murder me later."

"You have the wildest imagination, you know that?" I hand over a sausage, egg, and cheese English muffin. "It's not Bagel World, sorry." Michaela stares at it like it might bite her before meeting my gaze. "It's just a sandwich, Michaela." Finally, she snatches it from my hands and falls back onto the couch. I set the coffee and give her knee a gentle squeeze. "Hey, I'm supposed to get dinner with Colin and his girlfriend tonight, but they had to cancel. Would you like to join me instead?"

Michaela's brows raise. "You want to get dinner?"

"Of course."

Her mouth opens and closes as she fiddles with the lid of the coffee cup. "Finn, I— We don't *do* dinner. We don't— That's not— What is this?"

"What do you mean?"

"Not even five weeks ago you couldn't stand me. And now... You're asking me to dinner. We just slept together, for the second time!"

"Who said I didn't like you?"

"You!"

"Me?"

"Every time I'm around you." She lifts her hands in exasperation. "You're an asshole, what am I supposed to think?"

I can't help but laugh. "I mean, you can be a little annoying, but—"

"This isn't funny, Finn!" She begins to pace. "Is this some way to mess with me or—"

"No," I stop her pacing. "No, it's not like that." I don't know what *this* is. Sure, she has always gotten on my nerves. She's my best friend's little sister — the annoying little kid who never wanted to leave us alone, but it wasn't that I didn't like her. She was just...Michaela, but now...

"What is this?" she practically begs.

I don't have an answer for her because I don't know.

"If this is some way for you to get under my brother's skin—"

"No! No, that's not it."

"Maybe it's best if we just forget it ever happened. I mean, it was fun, but... I'm already dealing with one asshole, I don't need another screwing up my life more than David already has."

Fuck, she's right. I mean, she's not even divorced yet. When I came to check on her last night, it was not my intention to end up in bed together. One thing led to another, and I prayed to God she would stop me, but she didn't and I couldn't stop myself.

"I think it's best if we chalk this up to a two-night thing we never speak of again." Her sigh throws salt in the wound, and I want to tell her she's wrong. I don't want it to be a 'two-night' thing, but I can't say that if she doesn't feel the same way.

"I think we should go," she picks up her bag from the small white circular dining table and waits for me to follow — I guess the conversation is finished.

The elevator ride is awkward, to say the least. I don't think I've ever heard her this quiet. It's a little unnerving and I feel bad. How could I put her in this position? I've just made everything ten times worse.

When we get to the street, she hails a passing cab and I step in front of her to open the door. "Well, I guess, I won't be seeing you around," I say with a smirk as she slides into the backseat. Our faces mere inches apart when I lean down into the cab. "It was good while it lasted, Shortcake. Be a good girl, okay?" She bites down on the corner of her mouth and readjusts her position but refuses to look at me. "Columbus Circle," I tell the cabbie before handing him a fifty.

## Finn

"WHAT'S YOUR PROBLEM?" KNOX has never been one to beat around the bush. "It's pretty obvious something's on your mind."

"Nope, all good here."

He studies me for a moment before turning back to the gelato cup in his hands. For someone who told me they hated gelato not that long ago, he sure eats the hell out of some peanut butter gelato nowadays. Gelato in the park has become our Monday afternoon tradition, but once winter comes, we're going to need to find a new one.

"How'd your English test go today?" From the shoving of another bite in his mouth, I assume not so well. "Wanna talk about it?"

"Nope, all good here."

I roll my eyes, ever the smartass. "I thought you said you understood it."

"Yeah, I mean, I did, but then she was asking about what we thought the author was trying to say and relate it to real-world problems."

"Fitzgerald was trying to expose the illusion of the American dream and the dangers of holding onto the past."

"Well, how in the hell am I supposed to know that?"

"Just eat your gelato."

Coming to the fork just through Greywacke Arch, we walk the rest of the way in a comfortable silence, only to be broken as we step onto Fifth Avenue. "You ready to talk about it yet?" Knox asks tossing the empty cup into the trash can.

"Whatever problems I have going on in my life shouldn't be pushed onto you."

"But, I'm supposed to be your little brother, right? Brothers tell each other what's bothering them."

Dammit. Got me there.

"I promise, it's boring."

"Can't be too boring if it's got you this deep." Knox shrugs off his school jacket now that we've left the cover of the trees. "Is it a girl?"

"Want a hot dog?" I ask approaching the steps of the Met, where a line of street vendors wait to feed hungry tourists who are taking in the sights.

"It is a girl!" Ignoring him, I roll my eyes and motion the vendor to give us two hot dogs. "I never thought I'd see the day Finn Sheffield has girl trouble."

"Shut up, Knox," I mumble handing over a twenty. "Keep the change," I say, taking my hot dog and continuing down Fifth Ave. We should turn down 86th Street to get to the train, but I get the distinct feeling he isn't ready to part ways yet.

"I thought you didn't do relationships."

"I *do* relationships, I just haven't been in one in a while… The last one was a real doozy." And part of the reason I had to ask Nina for help in the first place.

"So, what happened — this girl shoot you down or something?"

"Or something. Look, I really shouldn't be talking to you

about this."

"I don't see the problem," Knox shrugs. "You're teaching me valuable life lessons to help me in the future when I have my own girl problems."

"Can't have girl problems if you don't put yourself out there, Knoxy-boy."

"Shut up, Finnely. We're not talking about me; we're talking about you."

Expletives roll off my tongue when a guy rams into me from the other side of the sidewalk spreading the hot dog across my shirt — red, yellow, and green stain the crisp white linen. Are you fucking kidding me? That is going to be impossible to get out, and I just bought this fucking shirt. The smirk in his voice makes my blood boil, "You should watch where you're going next time." Oh, you've got to be kidding me. Looking up from my shirt, I find it harder to contain my newfound anger.

"Dude, what the fuck?" Knox looks between us. "You ran into him!"

"Knox," I stop him. "It's all good."

"Yeah," the asshole taunts. "It's all good."

"What? Finn, he just—"

"I said, it's fine," I say through gritted teeth.

A satisfied smirk crosses the other man's lips, "Oh, and tell my *wife* I said hello."

"What happened to you?" Colin tries to cover his laugh when I move so he and Saylor can come inside my apartment.

"An asshole."

"Do I even want to know?" This time he doesn't even try to conceal his laughter when I glare at him. "Relax, man, I'm messing with you."

"Leave him alone, Colin. He's having a bad day," Saylor says and offers me a smile. "I know an old trick my grandma taught me that might help get some of it out."

"That's okay, don't worry about it, Shey," I assure her, but she won't hear it. It won't do me any good to go back and forth, so I unbutton the shirt and hand it over. She scurries over to the kitchen sink to work whatever magic she has up her sleeve.

"I thought you guys couldn't make it tonight," I ask Colin when I return from my bedroom in a fresh shirt.

"Shey wanted to stop and say hi. She leaves town day after tomorrow, so she wanted to make sure she got to see you." Colin and Shey started dating in high school, she stuck by him through the military, and now vice versa while she works as a traveling nurse. She's been working out of Colorado for the past six months, and it's the furthest they've ever been from each other. I don't think Colin will be sticking around New York much longer if they don't move her closer anytime soon. "So, who's the asshole?"

Grabbing a water bottle from the fridge, I explain how Knox and I were ambushed on Fifth Avenue by none other than David.

"You sure it was on purpose?"

"I'm fairly certain when a guy says, 'Tell my wife I said hello,' he meant to do it."

"Please tell me you're not sleeping with a married woman," Saylor looks up from the sink.

"Technically, she's in the middle of a divorce," Colin defends.

"Oh Finn," she sighs. I hate the pit of my stomach when she says it like that. *Oh, Finn.* It reminds me of my mom when I've had to tell her I've screwed up...again.

"Finn isn't with her, but her husband thinks they are."

"So you're not sleeping with her?" Saylor asks me.

"No, they—"

"Well," I grimace interrupting Colin. Guess it's time to let the cat out of the bag.

"You didn't," Colin sighs dropping his head in his hands.

"I didn't mean to. We were working on that project, and it just kind of happened."

"Jesus, Finn." Colin shakes his head.

"And then, last night I went to—"

"Last night? Finn, that's not once, that's two times! I thought you said you didn't like her. When I asked you about her last week, you said—"

"I know what I said, Colin."

"Does Josh know?" My lack of response is enough. "Oh shit, you are a dead man."

"We're adults, Colin. We can sleep with whomever we want." I try to ignore the nagging feeling that won't settle inside me. "Not that it matters, she wants to forget anything ever happened. It was a two-time thing. She's coming out of a marriage, now isn't the time."

"You *like* her," Saylor says with a small smile, and that simple statement hits me like a ton of bricks.

"No, I don't, Shey."

"Oh yes, you do. It's written all over your face!" Saylor smirks. "Wow, I haven't seen you this smitten in a while."

"I don't like her! At least, not like that." They don't believe me. Hell, I don't believe me. "She's Josh's little sister." I can hear the defeat in my voice, "I can't like her."

But, that hasn't stopped me yet.

*twenty-six*

*Michaela*

"ANY PROGRESS?" CAIT ASKS twisting a fork into her linguine. I spent the majority of the week avoiding anything and everyone. Cait had enough of my reclusive activities by Friday because she stormed into my office a little before four-thirty demanding I come to dinner. That's how I found myself sitting across the table at Finestra stuffing our faces with carbs.

"On what?"

"Let's start with David, seems like an easier topic to discuss."

I chuckle before taking a bite of risotto. "Is it?"

"We could start with Finn and how he went from asshole to best sex of your life back to asshole again."

"I never say that."

"You didn't have to," she winks.

I blush and roll my eyes — we are not discussing my sex life. "David still wants the ring, wants me to sell the condo, *and* now he wants an annulment, not just a divorce."

"On what grounds? They don't just hand out annulments for no reason."

173

"I coerced him into getting married to get access to his money."

"But you make—"

"I'm aware, but he comes from money… His family is well known and they're coming from the angle that I was in it for the perks, not him. They're saying, I lied about who I was and my intentions."

"Oh, Michaela," the sympathy behind her eyes makes me sick to my stomach. "I'm so sorry, you don't deserve this."

I shrug, "I guess it's better to find out who he is now than after twenty years of marriage."

"You're sure it's him? I mean, I know he was always kind of a dick, but I wouldn't think he'd do something like this."

"I'm sure his mom has something to do with it, she's always hated me. Especially after she didn't get to plan the extravagant wedding she always dreamed of." I finish the rest of the wine in my glass and pour another. "Just kind of sucks, y'know? It hurts to think he'd want to pretend like we never happened. Because that's what it is… Pretending like we never got married, like we never mattered."

"You'll be better off without him."

Tears burn behind my eyes, but I don't want to waste any more on him, I've already given him too many the past two days. It is strange to think I'll be better off without the person I thought I would spend the rest of my life with. How is that possible? When I said, "I do," I meant it, but I guess that's not how our story was meant to end..

"And Finn," I sigh. "Cait, I—I don't know what is going on."

"What do you mean?"

"We slept together again."

She drops her fork, and a few eyes look our way at the sudden commotion. "You what! But you haven't even seen him; you're not working with him anymore. When did this happen?"

"Sunday... He came over because I had been ignoring him all weekend."

"Why were you ignoring him?" She asks picking up her fork.

"Cait, he knows."

"Knows what?"

"Last Friday, David cornered me in SoHo and Finn ran into us on the street. He knows."

"Holy shit."

The pit in my stomach continues to grow bigger and bigger.

"Wait, did he tell Josh?"

"No, not yet anyway," I sigh. "He came over to check on me, one thing led to another and... I doesn't matter. I told him we need to forget whatever that was."

"You *like* him!"

"No."

"Yes, you do. Oh my God, you like Finn." Caitlin's smile grows with each word.

"No, I don't. He's a grade-A asshole." I take a drink of wine.

Caitlin sighs, "Well, *you* told him to forget it — not the other way around."

"I didn't tell him to go back to his old ways."

"I guess he took it literally."

"I didn't mean it *literally*." I thought it was best if we pretended like nothing happened, even if those nights we spent together are something I'll never forget.

"I'm just saying, he's a man, they're not mind readers even if we want them to be."

"If he was a mind reader, he'd know I didn't mean it." My eyes widen at the admission. Shit, I didn't mean to say that. God, I have to stop doing that. "Shut up, Cait," I say when she smirks.

"I didn't say a thing."

Cait turns when I walk out of the restaurant, she tries to hide her smirk. I swear, she's had one on her face from the moment I told her about Finn round two. "You missed a call."

"Whoever it is, I'll call them back tomorrow." I pull my jacket over my shoulders before taking my purse from her. I'm trying to maintain the good mood spending time with my best friend has put me in. Whatever disaster needs fixing can be handled in the morning.

"Sure about that?"

"Yes." I eye her suspiciously. "Why?" She hands over my phone, her smirk now on full display. When I click on my home screen, my eyes widen at the top notification: *1 Missed Call: Finn.* (Yes, I changed his name from Jabba to Finn. I thought it was time, right?) Why is he calling me?

"I think you should call him back."

"I don't think that's a good idea. He most likely wants to bitch at me about not telling my parents about the divorce yet."

"Michaela. Call him."

Before I can second guess it, I click his name, and it rings… and rings…and rings. It's not that important if he can't even answer when I—

"Where are you?" His gruff voice sounds over the speaker.

"Hello to you too?" I scoff.

"Are you home?"

"No, I'm out to dinner with Caitlin. I won't be home for a while." I shrug in response to her suspicious look. "Look, if you're calling to yell at me because I haven't told my brother, it can wait until—"

"Never mind, just forget it." Finn hangs up leaving me even

more puzzled than before. I stare at my phone, at the blank screen, as if it's going to give me some answer to what in the hell that was about.

"What did he want?" Cait asks.

"He didn't say."

"Well, he said something!'

"He asked if I was home. Why would he want to know if I'm home?" I look between the phone and her.

"You cannot be that dense." Cait grips my shoulders. "He is making the first move."

"What are you talking about? There's no move to make."

"Michaela. He's making the first *move*. This is it, the grand gesture!"

"Where's the boombox outside my window, then?"

Caitlin smirks, "Waiting for you at home."

I roll my eyes and hail the cab across the street. This is not a conversation I want to have. "Call me when you get home," I yell towards her opening my cab door.

"I think you're going to be a little busy," Caitlin sing-songs. "Call me tomorrow, give me all the juicy details. Better yet, maybe I'll just happen to be in the area tomorrow and stop by with coffee."

"Goodbye, Caitlin." I close the door and give the cabbie my address.

Pulling up to my apartment exactly eight minutes later, I can't help but laugh when there's no sign of Finn — or a boombox — outside. Of course, there's not. So why do I feel disappointed? I knew he wouldn't be here. It's not like I actually thought he'd be here waiting for me to pull up. Pfft, no way. I know better than that because Finnley Sheffield is not that kind of man.

# *twenty-seven*

## *Finn*

**THE HOUSE PHONE INTERRUPTS** my current rewatch of *The Boys*. Damn, talk about quick delivery time. I only ordered my food twenty minutes ago. "Paul, food already here?"

"Um, no sir. You have a visitor." A visitor? I check the clock on the wall, a little after 9:00 P.M. Who the hell is here after nine on a Sunday? "A pretty one," he adds in a hushed tone as if he's trying to avoid the person overhearing. "But, she doesn't seem too...happy."

"A pretty one, huh?" There's no way she showed up here. She doesn't even know where I'm staying. "I'll be down in a few. Keep an eye out for Mr. Joseph, will ya?"

Hanging up the phone, I slide my feet into a pair of slippers by the door. If she is here, what is she doing, and how did she figure out my address? Probably the same way I figured out hers — Liv. She can't possibly know I showed up at her place earlier... Can she? I didn't mention it, I only asked if she was there. That doesn't mean I was standing outside her building hoping to ring the buzzer and tell her even if we're going to put what happened behind us, that doesn't mean we have to go back to the way things were before. That I don't want things to go back to how they've been.

Stepping off the elevator, I'm greeted by the bright smile of Mr. Joseph, the delivery man and owner of the Thai restaurant. "Mr. Finn! Your food."

"Oh, Mr. Joseph, hey. Can you give me one—"

He lifts the bag towards me when I try to step past. "Don't worry 'bout it; it's on the house this time."

"What? No! That's not necessary. Here," I pull my wallet out of my sweats pocket, but he shoos my hand away.

"On the house. You overpay every time." He finally shoves the bag into my hands and waves goodbye over his shoulder as he turns the corner to the main lobby. "I'll see you end of the week."

God, this food smells amazing. I hope she doesn't put up too much of a fight because I'm starving. Maybe I can convince her to come upstairs, we can fight while I eat. Shit, I'll even give her some if that means getting to go back upstairs sooner. Compromise, right?

Rounding the corner, I'm greeted first by Paul's tight smile and then the most annoyed look I've ever seen on Michaela's face. She sits on one of the benches along the window, her arms crossed tightly over her chest as she waits. "She says she knows you," Paul motions towards her.

"Looks familiar, but the girl I know doesn't pout so much."

"I'm not pouting, you ass. Tell him to let me upstairs," Michaela glares at me.

"How'd you get my address?"

"How'd you get mine?"

"Touché," I chuckle and give Paul the okay. "I'll take it from here. Thanks, Paul."

He offers a small salute before heading to the door to open it for Mrs. Daniels.

Turning to go back upstairs, Michaela doesn't follow,

sitting in the same position. "You coming, or are we going to do this down here in front of everyone?"

Michaela's eyes inspect every inch of the condo when she walks inside. I wouldn't expect any less from someone who has spent their career working under one of the best designers in the business. But I can't take credit for anything done here; I'm only renting the place. Whoever did decorate it, had decent taste, but they still wouldn't be my choice of designer. Michaela moves to the middle of the living room, her arms still crossed, her lips pulled into a straight line, and her brow creased in thought. Her eyes stayed glued to the view from floor-to-ceiling windows — overlooking Tribeca with an unobstructed display of One World Trade. Even underneath the brown checkered overcoat, I can see the way her blue jeans hug her curves and it draws my attention straight to her ass. Stop it, Finn. Pull yourself together. This is not why she's here. "Pretty cool, huh?" I ask from the kitchen ripping open the bag of food.

"What do you want, Sheffield?" Her words are so blunt, I have to do a double-take. Michaela finally turns from the window. She steps up to the other side of the island, her arms still crossed looking more irritated with every passing moment.

"I should be asking you that question, you're the one who showed up at my place, remember?"

"We haven't spoken since Monday when you put me in the cab and told me to be a 'good girl.' Seemed final to me, but now you call asking where I am, asking if I'm home, like some stalker." Her blue eyes soften when they meet mine again. Her voice is softer when she speaks again, "I've had enough of the game, Finn. What do you want?"

"It's not a game, Shortcake." I step around the island, but she takes a step back.

"Not a game?" She scoffs. "You sleep with me one minute, and the next, you treat me like I don't even matter. Quite sure that's the definition of a game."

"You don't get to put this all on me, Michaela. You're the one that said—"

"God, this was a mistake."

"No." I grab her arm when she tries to walk away, and her eyes flare, hot as a blue flame. "You don't get to walk away because you don't want to hear what I have to say. You started this. You showed up here, so now you're going to listen." I point at the couch, "Sit."

"I'm not a child, Finn."

"Then stop acting like it."

She considers fighting back but huffs and sits on the white cushion without another word. Her legs cross and she places folded hands on top of her knees. I sit on the chaise leaving a space between us.

"You wanted this, Michaela, remember? You wanted to go back to the way things have always been. Pretend like what happened didn't happen."

"You didn't exactly fight me on it."

"I won't pressure you into something you don't want. You want to forget it ever happened? Fine. That's what we'll do. I won't—"

"But, I don't want to go back to hating each other."

"I don't hate you, Michaela."

"Sure," she scoffs.

"Trust me when I tell you that hate is the furthest thing I feel for you." That's the God's honest truth. I could never hate her. "Are you annoying as hell? Yes. Do you get under my skin?

Every damn day that I'm around you. But, I don't hate you."

"Oh no," she laughs, "are you about to tell me that you've secretly loved me all these years?"

"You wish, Shortcake." I pat her knee and squeeze gently. "Lord knows, I couldn't stand you when you were younger. You were annoying as hell and..."

"Hey!"

"...never got the hint to leave us alone."

"You weren't exactly the life of the party."

"I know plenty of people who would say otherwise, including your brother."

Her mood instantly falls, "Josh will murder me if he ever finds out about this. And you...there would be no evidence. You'd be gone without a trace. He can never know."

"So, what exactly are you suggesting because you're giving mixed signals."

"We—We can't... We can't do this." She pushes up from the couch, her hand slipping through my fingers when I reach for her. "This was a terrible idea. I don't know why I thought—"

Michaela reaches the door, but I place my hands on it so she can't leave. Not until we have this conversation, even if it means putting this behind us for good.

"Finn," my name a sigh on her lips, and it sends a jolt straight to my dick. I can't help but think about her under me, my name the only thing on her mind as I fuck her nice and slow. Reminding her exactly who she belongs to.

Shit.

I am so screwed.

"Michaela..."

"I shouldn't have come here. I'm sorry."

"Shortcake." The name stops her. Big blue eyes look up to meet mine, and I'm a fucking goner.

# *twenty-eight*

## *Finn*

**I WRAP ONE HAND** around her waist and cup the back of her neck, pulling her to me, my lips covering hers. She *has* to tell me to stop, I need her to. Tell me she doesn't want this. I'll end it here and now...even if it's the hardest thing I'll ever have to do, because I want her. There is nothing I want more than to push her up against this wall and fuck her senseless. I want to feel her body tremble underneath me as I worship her over and over again. "Shortcake," I whisper against her mouth. "Tell me to stop." She doesn't. "Michaela," I groan.

"Finn–"

My lips lightly dusk along the skin of her jaw to her ear. "Tell me to stop, and I will, but fuck... You need to tell me what you want." Shallow breaths fall from her lips as I nip softly at the sensitive spot where her neck and jaw meet. "Say it, Shortcake." I pull away to stare down at her, cradling her burning cheeks in my hands. Her blue eyes darker than ever before. "What do you want?"

It feels like an eternity before she whispers, "You."

I grasp the back of her head and pull her mouth to mine.

The kiss hungry and desperate, Michaela matches my intensity, like she's been craving it since the last time. She slips the coat from her shoulders letting it fall at our feet. An involuntary growl resonates deep in my throat when she twists her hands in my hair. My hands down her back and squeeze her ass lifting her feet from the ground and pushing her against the wall. Her legs wrap around my waist, and she grinds against me.

I pull away from her mouth and bury my face in her neck, the sweet scents of strawberry, raspberry, and rose fill my nose. She smells delicious. When I suck on the sensitive skin, a soft moan of approval shoots straight to my cock. Fingers slip beneath the hem of her shirt, skating across the skin of her abdomen as I tug lifting it over her head. She tosses her head back, fingers digging in my hair when my mouth meets her skin again. I trail down her exposed neck to the valley between her breasts. My left hand reaches behind her to undo the clasp of her bra but finds nothing.

A breathless chuckle, "Front clasp." Her manicured hands undo the clasp without hesitation letting the black lace article fall next to her shirt. My mouth waters at the sight. She gasps when I take her right nipple in my mouth, my tongue swirling over it. I gently tug on the peaked bud with my teeth, letting my tongue soothe over it before doing the same to the other.

"Where do you want me to fuck you, Shortcake?" I leave a trail of open mouth kisses up her neck. "Here?" I roll my hips into hers. "The couch?" A kiss against her collarbone. "The bed?" A lick along her jaw before a soft nibble on her ear. "The window?" I chuckle softly when she gasps at the suggestion. "What? Don't want everyone in the city to know who you belong to?"

"Are you saying I belong to you?"

The question sits between us – the mood shifting with each passing moment. I've backed myself into a corner without any idea how to get out of it. She *doesn't* belong to me, not yet, but fuck I can't help but wish she did. I'm not sure she wants that. Not sure she wants me the same way I want her. What am I supposed to say?

Michaela slowly drops her legs from my waist, the only sound is her boots against the wood floors as she finds her footing. This wasn't supposed to happen. We weren't supposed to do this again, or at all. I'm not supposed to like her, but somewhere in the past few months, things have changed. I've changed. She's not the annoying, bratty kid who gets in the middle of everything anymore. She's not *just* Josh's little sister. Just the thought of her makes me smile. "Michaela," I grip her wrist when she bends for her shirt, but she tugs away.

"Finn, don't." She pulls her shirt over her head. "I can't do this. I can't be some placeholder anymore." Finally, she meets my gaze, and the look in her eyes threatens to break my heart. "I get it, okay? You just needed someone to let a little steam off, and I was there... But, I can't be that for you. Not anymore. Not again."

"That's not–"

"I didn't mean for this to happen." Michaela pulls her coat back over her shoulders, "I should go."

Am I about to let her walk out after that? Feeling like she's only a placeholder in my life until something better comes along. Like some kind of toy that can be tossed aside. No, I can't. I won't.

Fuck, Josh is gonna kill me.

"I don't want this to be a one-time thing, Michaela." At my words, she freezes in the open doorway, her hand holding the doorknob. I grip her chin and force her to look at me. Confusion swims in her ocean eyes. Confusion. Fear. Hurt. Lust. It's all there. "I have no idea what this means, I am just as confused as you are, but I know I don't want this to be a one or two-time thing."

"Why now?"

"I don't have that answer for you. I wish I did, but I don't. I wish I could tell you that I've been in love with you since we were young, but...I can't." Tugging her hand, I gently close the door once she's back inside. I cradle her face in my hands resting my forehead against hers. "I can't let you walk out that door feeling like you are anything less than perfect. You are not a game, Michaela. You are so much more than that."

Soft, gentle pecks against her lips, but soon it's not enough. I need more, and so does she. I can tell by the way she pulls my mouth down on hers. Her laugh breaks the kiss when I lift her off her feet. It's only a brief moment before her lips find mine again and I carry her to my bedroom. Her legs slide down to stand stripping her coat and then her shirt, her bra...allowing us to pick up exactly where we left off.

Michaela falls on the bed as I reach behind my back grabbing a fistful of shirt and pulling it over my head. Her eyes brighten and her fingers reach out to trace my abdomen, "You're beautiful."

"I've been called a lot of things, but never beautiful." I smirk down at her.

"Take the compliment, Sheffield," she warns, tugging the waistband of my sweats, bringing me closer.

"Yes ma'am." She rolls her eyes when I mock a salute, and I laugh, bending down to kiss her. She opens her mouth in invitation, and I oblige, letting my tongue caress hers. A soft whimper when I pull away to settle on my knees in front of her. I tug the zippers of her boots before they fall to the floor with a *thud* – each one makes her jump slightly. "A little antsy, are we?" I grin up at her, but she's not the only one. I can't wait to get my hands on her, to feel her writhe underneath me as she comes undone.

"Finn, as much as I love the foreplay," she cups the back of my neck pulling me into a hard kiss. "I'd much rather have you inside me."

Holy. Shit.

Wasting no more time, my mouth fuses to hers. My fingers work the buttons of her jeans, and they're never-ending – okay, who brought back button-flies? But she brings my attention back to her nipping at my bottom lip, soft at first and then a little harder. Fuck, this woman is going to end me. I can't get enough of it. Finishing the buttons, I order her to lift her hips, hooking my fingers into the waistband of her pants and underwear to shimmy them down her legs.

"Drawer," I motion towards the floating nightstand. She obliges quickly crawling to search through the drawer for a condom. I stand shoving my sweatpants down my legs as she holds the foiled wrapper in the air like a metal. I chuckle, taking it from her and ripping the package before rolling it up the length of my straining erection.

I match the smile she offers when I finally settle between her thighs. It's a little nervous and I can't help but feel the same. Something is different this time. Every kiss, every touch, feels different. This isn't a one-and-done thing, it's the beginning of something new. We can both feel it, and it scares the shit out of me.

"I need you," Michaela says and wraps her hand around me, bringing the head of my cock to her entrance.

I cradle the side of her face and push inside her. She arches into me, taking me deeper. Each thrust deeper than the next, her moans go straight to my cock. The way she moves under me, the noises she makes, the way she takes me *oh so good...*it's too much, I'm not going to be able to hold back much longer. "Fuck baby," I murmur against her neck.

When I meet her blue-eyed gaze, I feel it, like a tugging deep inside—something I've never experienced with anyone else. The shine in her eyes in the moonlight tells me she feels it too. She reaches up to cup my cheek, and I turn into her palm, pressing my lips against her warm skin. Our bodies move together in tandem. I cover her mouth with mine, swallowing her moans of pleasure. Her hands roam my chest, my biceps, and my shoulders as I roll my hips into her, each stroke sending waves of pleasure through me. Fuck, she's so wet, so tight...I'm not going to last.

The gasp when I sling her leg over my shoulder, thrusting harder, tells me everything I need to know. Her eyes roll back into her head as she digs her fingernails into my back. "Finn," she whimpers. I swear I feel harder if that's even possible. "I'm close."

"Good, baby." I kiss the side of her face nibbling on the soft skin beneath her ear. "Come on my dick, Michaela. Go ahead, baby, it's all yours."

Her body spasms beneath me, and her thighs tremble as her muscles clench tightly around my cock. She cries out with each thrust, and I lose all restraint. I bury my face into her neck driving wildly with my hips, and with one last thrust into her, I come.

When I finally come down from my high, I slowly lift myself onto my forearms to alleviate some of my weight from her. A soft smile spreads across her lips as I stroke her face. She leans up to kiss me slowly and it's confident, thorough, all-consuming. I relish it.

And in this moment, I realize just how screwed I am.

"Stop staring at me, you creep," she murmurs against the pillow as the sunlight shines through the window of my bedroom. One eye pops open, and I smile down at her, pushing a golden lock behind her shoulder.

"Good morning, to you too." I kiss her bare shoulder,

letting my lips linger.

"Careful, you'll start something you have to finish."

"Is that a threat?"

She opens her right eye again, but I don't give her a chance to ask questions flipping her on her back and throwing the black sheets from her body. "Finn," she gasps when my lips meet her neck. I nibble at the skin and her body vibrates under me. I take my time kissing, licking, and sucking every inch of her, enjoying the sounds she makes. Every gasp, every moan is an encouragement to continue — a louder moan when I bite the sensitive skin of her hip. Another when I trace the pattern of her tattoo with my tongue. "Finn, I have to," a gasp as I ghost my fingers over her entrance, "go to the office."

"Says who?" I nudge her legs apart without a fight. "You can do everything you need to do," I dip my face between her legs, "right here."

"What's this?" Michaela asks walking out of the bedroom. My t-shirt hangs just below her ass, and it reminds me of the last time she was in one of my shirts. What was it...eleven, ten years ago? Josh and Nick had come over to the house and of course, Michaela followed. After a little too much sass, she ended up in the pool. In my defense, it was no one's fault but her own, she wasn't supposed to be there, and she couldn't keep her mouth shut about whatever we were fighting over. "You looked like you could use a dip to cool off," I laughed from the edge of the pool.

"You asshole!" She tried to send a wave towards me. I successfully dodged it, Nick did not.

Needless to say, she didn't have any clothes and my mother

would murder me if she came home to something missing from her closet, so I had to loan her some of mine. My shirt hung low on her body, hugging her hips in all the right places. I leaned against the doorframe watching as she tossed her wet clothes into the washer.

"See something you like, Sheffield?" she asked catching my stare.

"You wish, Shortcake."

She stepped closer and I straightened to my full height staring down at her. Her chest practically touched mine, and I tried to calm the thoughts racing through my mind — especially the one about the lack of a bra under my shirt. "I guess, I wouldn't mind." Her words sent a pulse straight to my dick. The silence around us deafening before she started giggling. "Don't think my brother would be too keen on you taking advantage of his little sister, though." She stepped into the pair of shorts I had given her before pushing passed me. When she was gone, I let out the breath I didn't realize I had been holding, but that wasn't the only problem I needed to address.

"You made breakfast?" she asks now stealing a piece of bacon from the plate.

"I made breakfast," I confirm.

"Finnley Sheffield knows how to cook, who knew?"

"Well, if you really want to know…"

"I don't," her kiss like a period at the end of her sentence. She smiles and takes the plate from my hands to start filling it with pancakes, eggs, bacon, and potatoes. "You have any… orange juice." She takes the jug I hold out to her with a smile. "You just so happened to know I'd want this?"

"You always have orange juice with your breakfast, never coffee."

"It's weird that you know that."

"We've known each other a long time, Shortcake. Whether

or not we were friends, we know things about each other."

"I don't know things about you, Finn. Not like that, not like only having orange juice with your breakfast."

"Well," I plant a soft kiss on her forehead, "there's plenty of time to learn. Though, I do have one question." She pops a piece of bacon in her mouth waiting for me to continue. "What's with the tattoo?"

Her laugh brings a smile to my lips. "Late night in college… I was trying to be spontaneous, so I chose dare instead of truth. I keep it hidden because Mom and Dad would lose their mind if they knew about it."

"Jimmy has them."

"Jimmy isn't their daughter." She hoists herself onto the counter and eats another piece of bacon. "I decided to go with the Pisces constellation because it wasn't completely basic, but it wasn't anything outrageous either." My hands grip the silky skin of her thighs spreading her legs so I can stand between them. Her arms drape around my shoulders lacing together at the base of my neck. "But, I'd like to keep it our little secret. Josh would probably freak out if he knew."

"You're a twenty-eight-year-old woman, Michaela. Why does it matter what your brother thinks?" I grip her chin lightly, bringing her eyes to mine. "You can't always worry about what they're gonna think, Shortcake. You have to be yourself." I press a gentle kiss to her mouth before wrapping her legs around my waist and stepping away from the counter.

"Finn!" Michaela giggles as I walk to the couch. When I lay her down on the chaise, she refuses to let go and pulls my mouth to hers, again.

"We need to eat," I mumble, and a pout forms on her lips when I pull away untangling her legs from my torso. She's quick to find her spot on the couch, bundling up in the green throw blanket draped over the back.

"Can I ask you something?" she asks as I grab both plates

and bring them back to the couch. "You started Sheffield House to help kids. Help them find a family, find a home… Kids who need a chance, like you, but…"

*Like me?*

"…you don't talk about your adoption. Why?"

It takes me a moment to register what she just asked.

"You could help so many kids by telling your story, I don't—"

"How do you know about that?" The words come out a lot harsher than I mean them to, and she recoils. There's only a handful of people who know the truth and I'm sure I know who it was that told her. My family doesn't discuss it because discussing it would mean admitting Oliver had failed at something. And he couldn't fail at anything. "Michaela, who told you"

"Josh mentioned it at Coney Island."

"Of course."

"Finn, I—"

"I don't talk about it," I interrupt her. "None of us do. Oliver and Hayley adopted me when I was five, and I was just happy to have somewhere to call my own. Happy to feel wanted after being in and out of different foster homes and group homes. And you know Oliver, how he is… The dream only lasted so long and as much as I came to hate him, as much as I got myself into trouble, I didn't care because at least I had a place of my own. And then, when I went to Bridgeport, I had a family with the Davises, so it wasn't too bad."

"Even with me around?"

Finn smiles, "Even with your pain in the ass."

# twenty-nine

## *Michaela*

**I HAVE ALWAYS WONDERED** why Finn preferred to hang around our family when the Sheffields had everything. Why would this kid who could have anything — literally, anything — in the whole world want to be around *my* family? We didn't have the money or the access they had. We didn't have a big, fancy house or a bunch of cars or a pool. We had your standard run-of-the-mill suburban middle-class home. The boys were always hanging out at either of the Davis households, very rarely did they take a trip to the Sheffields. And if they did, it was only because Oliver and Hayley were out of town. It never made sense to me, but now it does. He was still looking for the one thing he'd always wanted, the one thing he had hoped to find in his adopted parents, but instead, he found it in us.

Pulling up to the familiar house, I feel a newfound appreciation for what's inside. Unconditional love. Acceptance. Understanding. All of the things I needed while finding my way through this mess that I've created with David. I had been so worried my parents would be upset because my marriage didn't last as long as theirs, but recently, I've been reminded of who my parents truly are. They'd never judge me. They would be there for me and give me the support I need.

Mom steps out onto the front porch with a confused smile and a small wave. I didn't tell them I was coming. I didn't even know I was coming. I decided last night to surprise them and spend the weekend at home. I'd spend the weekend with them and when the time was right, I'd come clean about everything. I had no idea what I was going to say, but I knew it was time — it was long overdue. I promised Finn I would tell them before I left no matter what. He had asked me only once after that first night in his condo when I wanted to tell my family, but I didn't know. "Might be a little awkward if we start showing up together when I'm supposed to be married to someone else." I laughed, but even with the small smile on his lips, I knew he didn't find it amusing. They still didn't know about me and David, and could I (or should I) drop both bombshells at the same time? Even though he didn't push it, I know it's been eating away at him the past week — the sneaking around, the lying, especially to Josh. I promised him I would tell my parents everything before I left, no matter what. I'd tell them about him, about us.

A knock on the window makes me jump. Dad stands on the other side laughing. "Well, c'mon! Movin' slower than a Sunday afternoon."

I roll my eyes but climb out of the car. Guess it's time to get the show on the road...

I never thought I'd say this, but coming home was the best decision I've made in a while. Spending the past two days of uninterrupted time with my parents was everything I didn't know I needed. Homecooked meals, helping Mom clean the house on Saturday morning, working in the yard, and running errands before helping Mom make dinner and playing a game of Dominos. I didn't even balk at the idea of getting up for Church this morning. I almost looked forward to it. Living their mundane routine was a breath of fresh air compared to my normal day-to-day life.

The dirt currently digging under my fingernails is another reminder of what I'm missing in the city. Dad planted his garden two years before he retired, and tending to it has become his favorite thing to do on Sundays after Church. He spent the entire year before planting it, learning what would grow best in our region and how to properly tend to it. The first thing he planted was a small patch of Dahlias—Mom's favorite flower. Now, his garden is full of different flowers and veggies.

"Hey MJ, hand me those clippers, will ya?" Dad asks pointing to the pair of clippers in between us. Dropping the few weeds I had collected in his clippings bag, I planted the clippers in his open hand, watching as he gingerly chips away at some of the dead pieces on a Lavender plant. "Y'know, I wanted to ask you something."

"What's that?"

"Not that your mama and I haven't enjoyed you being home, been nice spending some time together, but what are you doing here?"

I knew this was coming. I could see the question behind their eyes the whole weekend, but they didn't dare ask, afraid it would scare me back to New York early.

"Can I not come home for the weekend?"

"Sure you can," he finishes cleaning the plant and stands. "But, you don't."

"I just missed you guys, that's all."

Dad quirks an eyebrow wiping his hands on his dirt-covered jeans, but he doesn't push it, he's going to wait until we're inside with Mom. "Run inside and wash up, I'm sure your mama is 'bout done with dinner. Wanna make sure you eat before you leave for the airport."

"Yes, sir," I grumble, already feeling sick at the thought of what's coming.

"So, tell us, how'd everything go with Finn?" Mom asks sitting a hot chocolate in front of me.

Nausea erupts in my stomach thinking about what I'm about to do. This might be the hardest thing I've ever done. I know they won't be mad, but I still don't know how they're going to react — especially about Finn. The only thing keeping me from chickening out is the thought of the man back in New York. If it wasn't for him, I'd still probably be pretending none of this was happening. I can't continue to lie to them.

"I assumed everything went well since we didn't see your picture on the news for murder. I tried to ask Josh about it, but he's been a little crankier than normal lately. Something must be going on with him and Elizabeth."

"Stay out of it, Jen," Dad warns.

"I'm not gettin' involved, I'm just saying. Am I not allowed to be a concerned mother?"

"Well, I'm just sayin', mind your business."

Mom rolls her eyes, and I make a mental note to bring it up when I talk to my brother. I did think it was a little strange that Elizabeth didn't show up to the Coney Island party, but I assumed she had a photoshoot. She doesn't do a lot of them anymore, but there is a select list of clients she will drop anything for.

"Quit stallin', how was it?" Mom's eyes light up with her question.

A blush creeps up my neck under her stare, and I shrug, simply trying to ignore the butterflies swarming my stomach. "Everything was fine, Mama."

"That's all I get? It was *fine*."

"He's not so bad, I guess." I smile thinking about the day Finn brought breakfast to the office all the way from Brooklyn. "Um, actually, there is something I've been wanting to talk to you and Daddy about." I adjust in my seat, stuffing my hands underneath my thighs and I tuck my feet onto the stretcher. It reminds me of when I was little — how my legs were never quite long enough, and my feet didn't touch the floor, so I'd swing them back and forth until they got tired and then rest them here.

"You know you can talk to us about anything, MJ," Dad says returning with a fresh cup of milk.

"Of course, I know, it's just—"

"What's going on, Sweetie?"

I swallow the nausea clawing at my throat. I can do this, I have to do this. I can't pretend anymore, once they know the truth, there's no going back. I take a deep breath and look between them, before the words tumble out, "David and I are getting divorced."

"Oh, thank Heavens," my mother sighs a breath of relief.

I'm sorry, what?

"I'm sorry, honey, but we've been hoping you'd wake up and leave him since you told us you were engaged." Mom touches Dad's hand and he envelops it with his own.

"Why didn't you say anything?"

"You wouldn't have listened. You were dead set on marryin' that boy," Dad says. "Thought you were gonna live your happily ever after."

"Then why did you give your blessing?"

"I didn't, he never asked."

But, he said… David promised me that he would ask my dad for his permission to marry me. What else did he lie about?

"Well, I for one," Mom takes a sip of her wine, "am glad we won't have to deal with him anymore."

"Mama!"

"What? He was a spoiled brat. You can tell he was raised to believe he walked on water."

"I'd like to buy him for what he's worth and sell him for what he *thinks* he's worth," Dad adds, and it makes me giggle.

"I'm so glad you finally came to your senses, MJ. Now, you need to find a good lawyer—"

"We've been separated since May," I say, interrupting Mom, and both of their eyes grow ten sizes. "I wanted to tell you, I did, but I just… I was scared. I didn't want you to think less of me because I couldn't make my marriage work."

Mom reaches over the table to take my hand in hers. "We'd never think less of you, MJ. Sometimes, what we think we want isn't what's best for us. But, you won't know that until you try."

"You guys have been married for so long, I didn't want—"

"You are not us, Michaela Jane," Dad stops me. "Your relationship is not ours, not your brother's or Nina's or anyone else for that matter."

Way to call me out, Dad.

"You gotta make your own choices, own mistakes. All we can do is be here to support you."

"We're sorry we couldn't be there for you during this," Mom smiles sadly.

"You've been separated since May," Dad confirms and I nod. "This thing is moving slower than molasses running uphill in the winter, what's taking so long?"

"It's my fault," I sigh. "David wants me to sell the condo and give him the ring. I've been fighting him on it. I know it's dumb, but I paid for that condo on my own and what does he need the ring for? I told him I'd give back the middle diamond since it was from his grandmother's ring, but... I don't know."

"What are you going to do with it?" Mom asks, and I shrug. "You have no reason to hold on to it, so give it back. Sell the condo, you can get a new one! The sooner you wash your hands of him, the sooner you get to move on with your life."

"What else?" Dad says after a moment of silence.

What does he mean?

"That's not everything you wanted to tell us, is it?" Dad holds my gaze, a knowing look in his eye.

I sigh and bite down on my bottom lip. Do I tell them that I have moved on and it's with my brother's best friend? That was the whole point of this weekend, wasn't it? To come clean about *everything*. I can barely hear my thoughts over the heartbeat in my ears, but I finally say, "I like Finn."

It's quiet for a moment before a wide smile breaks out on my dad's face. He laughs, "Well, that took longer than any of us expected."

"Excuse me?"

"We've known for a while, honey," Mom says. "I think everyone did except the two of you."

"We did not like each other!"

"Sure, honey." She pats my hand.

"Nothing ever happened before now. We were not interested in each other. It just...happened. I wasn't even looking for it. I was sure David and I would fix things, but—"

"Does Josh know?" Dad asks.

"No," I shake my head. "And please don't tell him, not about Finn. I want to do it, I want to be the one to tell him. He's going to have questions, he's going to be upset... This is not the kind of thing you do over the phone."

"You shouldn't hide this any longer, Michaela. That's not fair to Finn."

"I know. Finn has been extremely supportive about all

of this, but I need to do it the right way. I'll tell Josh, soon, I promise."

*thirty*

## Michaela

**COLOR ME SHOCKED WHEN** a delivery man showed up at my door with an oversized white box a few moments ago. A black ribbon elegantly tied with a small tag hidden underneath, Finn's handwriting scrawled across it: *I'll see you @ 8. - F*

Untying the ribbon, I dig through the box unsure what awaits me. A warm, gold color stands out against the white tissue paper. The material feels like butter against my fingers as I pull it out of the box — a dress. A fitted champagne-colored dress with a sweetheart neckline. That's not the only thing — there's a black YSL clutch and a shoe box labeled Christian Louboutin.

*Holy shit.*

He sent me an entire outfit? Holding the dress against my body, I look into the floor-length mirror. The tag on the side catches my eye, and I know I shouldn't, but I look anyway. My eyes bulge not only at the name but the price. Oscar de la Renta. *Is he insane?* Absolutely not. I will not be wearing this thing. It's going right back in the box and—

My phone dings. A text from Finn.

**Finn**

**Did you get it?**

I can't wear this.

**Why not?**

Finn, this is too much. Why would you spend this kind of money on an outfit? I have plenty of clothes to wear tonight.

What if I get something on it or rip it or... No, I can't wear it. I don't wear things like this. I can't afford them. That's not true, I could afford them every once in a while, but I'd rather spend money on other things...like food — a girl's gotta eat.

**Finn**

**The car will be there at 8pm.**

What happens if I don't?

I didn't realize dating Finnley Sheffield meant agreeing to let him run the show. Does he forget I just got out of a relationship like that?

No. Stop it, Michaela. Finn is not David. Far from it actually, this is simply a nice gesture on our first date.

*First date.*

The butterflies suddenly erupt in my stomach at the thought. A smile spreads across the lips of the girl in the reflection — my lips. This is my first date with Finn Sheffield. I never thought I'd say those words, but here we are. My phone dings again and for the first time, I'm nervous to read his reply.

**Finn**

**Guess we'll find out later if you decide not to behave.**

Tony extends his hand towards me when he opens the car door outside of the Met. The granite steps leading up to the museum entrance have never been more intimidating in my life. I've spent a lot of time on these steps — eating lunch, reading, sketching designs, and spending time with the girls — but, never have I been this nervous to stand here. There are only sixty steps between me and this new life and I'm scared.

Tony closes the door behind me, and I nearly jump out of my skin. "Better get inside, wouldn't want to keep him waiting too long," he says walking around to the driver's seat. "I'll be back to get you kids later. Have fun tonight, Miss Michaela."

*One...Two..Three...*

I count the steps, trying to keep my cool. My hands would tremble if not for the death grip on the chain of the clutch. Why am I so nervous? I've never been this nervous around him. This is no big deal, it's just Finn. I've practically known him my whole life, so why won't these fucking butterflies just die already?

*Seventeen...Eighteen...Nineteen...*

Deep breaths, Michaela. This is fine. You've had plenty of first dates before, this one should be a piece of cake. But it's not just any first date, this is a first date with Finn Sheffield. My first date with Finn Sheffield — sworn enemy and one of my brother's best friends. Once I walk through this door, things are never going to be the same.

*Thirty-five...Thirty-six...Thirty-seven...*

My fingers grasp the heart charm around my neck tracing the familiar pattern etched into it helps calm my racing heart. Things haven't been the same for weeks now. This solidifies the fact. But I've already seen him naked and survived the morning after. Nothing can be any harder than that, right?

*Fifty-seven...Fifty-eight...Fifty-nine...*

When I reach the landing, the middle doors open and a security guard steps out to greet me with a warm smile. The grand entrance, typically filled to the brim with tourists and locals alike, is eerily quiet. A variety of different candles cover the information desk flickering in the dim light.

"I guess you didn't want to see what happened if you misbehaved," his voice echoes through the great hall stepping out from the Greek and Roman wing. He adjusts the button of his royal blue suit walking toward me. The entire outfit consists of different shades of blue — royal blue suit, sky blue shirt, navy blue tie with some type of pattern on it. The only thing different is the pocket square to match the color of my dress. His stubble has grown into a full beard. *Fuck,* he looks good. I haven't seen him since I got back from Bridgeport two days ago, and it was a lot harder than I thought it would be.

Finn wastes no time pulling my mouth to his in a crushing kiss.

God, I missed him. Missed this.

"We could always skip this part of the date," I mumble against his mouth.

"Nice try," he laughs and gives me another quick peck. "We're doing this."

"What exactly is *this?*"

"Patience is a virtue, Shortcake." Finn extends his arm to me placing his hand on top of mine when I loop my arm through his. He guides me toward the Greek and Roman wing, the click of my heels the only sound besides the beat of my heart  It's so loud against my chest, I'm sure he can hear it. God, why am I so nervous? I've known him for over half my life, I shouldn't be this nervous to be alone with him. How can I not be? He rented out the entire fucking Metropolitan Museum of Art for our first date. Who does that?

We take our time strolling through the different exhibits that inhabit the wing. It's odd, the sense of familiarity between us, but at the same time, I feel like I know nothing about him. I know he transferred to Bridgeport High at the end of his freshman year because he was asked not to return to The Hills Academy. I know he was one of the better football players we had, alongside Nick. I know he dated a multitude of girls from all over Winchester and Bridgeport, but never more than one at the same time. I know he dropped out of three different colleges, including Rosecliffe. I know he, Josh, and Nick have been best friends since they met. I know he's been a big partier since high school; he spent years traveling Europe, always looking for the next party. Everything about Finn has always screamed complete asshole to me, but now I realize I may have been a little quick to judge.

We travel through Greek and Roman art, the African gallery, and the Italian Arts before Finn ushers me toward the Petrie European Sculpture Court. I gasp stepping through the archway. The courtyard is lit by candlelight. A pathway beckons us further inside through the multitude of statues. I recognize each one, even in the darkened space and it brings a heightened sense of comfort, like I'm not alone at the beginning of this new journey. A private table has been set up between Ugolino and Perseus. Candles litter the tabletop and a bottle of wine sits between two place settings. "Finn…"

He kisses my temple. "Like it?"

"Like it? This is…insane. I'm honestly surprised there isn't a string quartet." He blushes and motions behind me. When I turn, four musicians await their cues. "Spoke too soon."

Finn chuckles and the lead violinist nods towards the others. A soft melody fills the space. "May I have this dance?" Finn asks extending his hand to me.

"I never knew you were this cheesy," I smirk taking his hand.

"There's a lot you don't know, remember?"

Fair point.

"So," he pulls me into him, "how are Pat and Jenny?"

"They're great. Being home was better than expected."

"I take it telling them went okay, then?"

"We talked about this."

"Briefly, but I want to hear everything." Finn briefly spins me before pulling me back into his chest and the joke I had prepared catches in my throat when I meet his stare. I've always thought Finnley Sheffield was handsome, sexy even, but the word beautiful is the only thing that comes to mind right now. His strong features somehow look soft, yet sharp, as the candlelight dances across his face. Chocolate eyes look as black as the night sky above us, but I could stare into them for hours.

Surely, there's something to explain this feeling, but I can't think of it. Whatever this is, I've never felt it before. Not with David or any of my other boyfriends. It settles deep in my heart, wanting to consume me entirely if I allow it.

# thirty-one

*Finn*

**"I GOT YOU SOMETHING."**

"Please don't get me anything else," Michaela begged as we walked into the condo after our date at the Met. "You've done too much already."

It could never be too much. I wanted this to be different. I wanted to show her what it meant to be appreciated. I get the distinct feeling there weren't a lot of nights like this in her relationship with Asshole. Besides, being a Sheffield has its advantages, and it doesn't hurt to be able to make a sizeable donation to the museum when they're looking to make some changes. What's the old expression — money talks? "I had Paul make a spare for you," I said passing her a key.

"You're giving me a key?" She looked confused. "Why?"

"You're always welcome here, Shortcake."

"Finn, we've been dating less than two weeks."

"And? I've known you for over a decade. If you wanted to kill me, you would've done it by now."

"The jury is still out," she joked and I rolled my eyes but pressed the key into her hand. She continued to stare at it for about five minutes before she finally shoved it inside her clutch and followed me to the bedroom. Despite my lack of sleep the past week, I suddenly found myself wide awake.

That first date was perfect, and so were the two others since then, but I'm still struggling with having to hide our relationship from Josh. Michaela wants to tell him in person, and I respect that, but sometimes it feels like she's putting it off. She's been waiting for him to come into town instead of inviting him to visit or making sure to see him before coming home from Bridgeport. I get it, sometimes schedules don't align, but you'd think she would want to tell him about the divorce and start dropping hints that she is seeing someone new.

I don't push, though. I can never understand what she's going through, not really. When I broke up with Amanda it was much easier than I thought it would be — for me, anyway. This is going to sound terrible, but I'd grown tired of her. Don't get me wrong, I used to love a good party, but she was addicted to it. Eventually, it turned into something more sinister. I tried to get her help, I did, but she didn't want it. You can only lead a horse to water. It's up to them to drink it. Amanda didn't want anything to do with it. Everyone thought she was a good, wholesome girl — the girl I'd end up settling down with — and they were upset when I broke up with her after three years without an explanation. But, I knew they'd blame me for bringing her into our world, introducing her to this world of unlimited access with limited repercussions.

I blame myself too.

"Dude, get your head in the game!" Colin shouts towards Josh pulling me out of my thoughts.

"Okay, Wildcats," I snicker shoving Colin back a step. "Take a breather." I can't blame him, we've been getting our asses handed to us every time Josh goes anywhere near the ball today. It's pretty obvious something is on his mind, keeping him from being anywhere near the court and the other team is taking advantage of it. I'm curious what's eating at him because I know what it's *not*.

"Did you just make a *High School Musical* reference?" Knox looks appalled.

"Shut up," I laugh pointing a finger at him.

"Don't let him fool you," Nick chuckles. "He was a secret Disney kid."

"You're one to talk, Mr. Call Me Maybe."

Nick shrugs, "It's catchy, sue me."

"What is going on with you?" I ask Josh.

"Nothing," he snaps.

I share a look with Nick who subtly shakes his head. Now is not the time to get into this, whatever this is. My watch dings, a message. *Shortcake.* The name appears and I quickly dismiss the notification. The last thing I need is for Josh to see his sister's name in my notifications. I don't even want to think of how to explain that when we're not working together anymore, and he still thinks we hate each other.

**Shortcake**

**Lunch?**

benny's w/ the guys.

"You got somewhere else to be?" Colin asks. I look up from the dramatic gif she had sent in response to meet four curious stares.

*Thanks, Colin.*

"You've been checking your phone a lot," Josh adds with a knowing smirk. He knows me better than most and I'm sure he already has it figured out why I've been so preoccupied. The problem is, I don't want to be the one to tell him the who.

"Something you want to share with the class, Sheff?"

"Nope." I offer a tight-lipped smile locking my phone.

"It's my mom," Knox says quickly. I'm grateful the kid is quick on his feet. "She's wondering when I'll be home since she got off early today."

"You just said you could come to Benny's with us," Colin looks between us.

"Yeah, I can. He was confirming that with her."

"Why didn't she text you?" Colin motions towards Knox's phone in his hands.

"I wasn't answering," Knox shrugs. "C'mon, we gonna finish the game or what?" He returns to the court and yells the same thing to the other team. I follow him, ignoring the questioning stares of my three best friends.

# thirty-two

## *Michaela*

**I POUR A CUP** of coffee and lean back against the counter with a small sigh. In less than three weeks, this condo has become more of a home to me than my own. If you had told me when we started working together that I'd sorta-kinda-actually be in a relationship with Finn Sheffield, let alone sleeping with him, I would have called you crazy. Absurd. Delusional. The thought would have made me sick. Now, I can't believe I never thought about it before.

I have two hours before I meet with a new vendor, so I decided to sleep in and enjoy a slow morning with Finn before going to work.

The coffee warms my body against the slight bite of the air conditioner. It's the first week of October, and we're finally seeing the first signs of fall, each morning waking up to a chill in the air. However, by lunchtime, it feels like summer again. It's that awkward phase when you have to embrace being uncomfortable one way or another, and I'd rather be a little cold than too hot.

Sipping the steaming liquid, I step up to the windows

and take a moment to appreciate the view. The condo sits twenty stories above SoHo with floor-to-ceiling windows that showcase the beauty of Manhattan. You can see from Tribeca to the Freedom Tower with full-on views of the Hudson. This view is everything I've ever dreamed of in a New York City home. And now, I can call it mine (kind of). It's obvious Finn didn't do the decorating. There's a hint of a woman's touch in it. Mahogany wood floors stretch through the open floor plan of the condo. The cabinetry and doors throughout match the rich mahogany color, a contrast to the stark white of everything else. White walls. White furniture. White rugs. White marble island. White backsplash. Hell, even the bathrooms are almost entirely white marble. When he buys something of his own, we're gonna have a conversation about adding a little color to his life.

Looking over the Hudson, my mind wanders back to last Tuesday. Everything was perfect from the music to the food to *him*. "You know, this is my favorite place in the museum," I said, walking through the maze of sculptures, feeling like I was amongst friends. He stood on the other side of the La Crainte des Traits de l'Amour, a sculpture from 18th-century France, watching.

"I know," he said plainly, and when I looked over my shoulder a blush crept into my cheeks when our eyes met.

Finn is everything I always wanted David to be but never was — it's not even fair to try and compare the two.

Strong arms wrap around my waist before he kisses my temple. I lean back into his warm embrace, and he steals my mug taking a sip of coffee. "Finn!" I smack his chest ripping it back from his hands and holding it close to my chest. "Michaela doesn't share coffee."

"There's plenty in the pot, Shortcake," he mumbles against my forehead, and it's only then I realize he's fully dressed in a white button-down with black pants.

"Going somewhere?"

"Gotta meet Nina quick, then I'm all yours." Another kiss to my forehead.

"Nina?"

"I have a few things to go over with her. We're meeting at her office at Designs, then heading to the venue; she wants to walk it before the fundraiser next week." Finn shrugs a sand-colored blazer over his shoulders and uses the floor mirror in the hallway to double-check his appearance.

"I'm supposed to meet Josh for lunch," I say, wiping a piece of dust from his shoulder. "But I shouldn't be too long; I don't think he'll want to stick around for much conversation." He leans in for a kiss. Before our lips meet, three knocks sound through the condo. We share the same questioning glance. Paul never called to confirm whether to let someone up. The list of people allowed up without prior consent is very small… "I got it," I say tugging on the hem of his button-down from yesterday, but it's already reached max coverage. I pray this is just Paul bringing something up or a neighbor hoping to get a cup of sugar. I shouldn't assume it's someone we know, someone who doesn't know about us or my divorce. Opening the door, my heart stops. No fucking way. It takes a moment for the other person to register the scene before him – his eyes move from my face to the coffee mug in my hands to my clothing (or lack thereof).

"Who is it?" I hear Finn's footsteps behind me falter when he meets my brother's venomous gaze.

thirty-three

## Michaela

**"WHAT THE FUCK?" JOSH** practically growls, his eyes shooting daggers into Finn. He looks between us unsure who he should lay into first.

"Josh–"

"No," he stops me. "I don't want to hear your shit, Michaela."

Finn pulls me behind him trying to shield me from my brother's wrath.

"What the fuck is going on here, Sheffield?" The look on my brother's face breaks my heart. I don't think I've ever seen him look so hurt, so betrayed, so furious. "This better *not* be what I think it is."

Finn sighs, straightening his broad shoulders. He's preparing to take the brunt of this, but it's not even his fault. This is only happening because of me. Because I was too scared to be honest. Because I wasn't ready for everyone to know the truth. Because I waited to tell my brother about the divorce, about Finn. I half expect him to shake off my touch when I reach for his hand, but he doesn't. He accepts it, lacing our fingers together, and squeezes gently.

"You bastard!" Josh lunges, and Finn pushes me away before Josh's fist connects with his face.

"Josh!" I scream.

"How could you do this, Michaela?" His fury turns on me blocking me from Finn. And fuck, if the look of pure disappointment doesn't almost kill me right here and now. "How could you *cheat* on David?"

*How could I cheat on David?* Doesn't he know me better than that?

"Josh, what is wrong with you?"

"What's wrong with me? You're the one—"

"This is what I wanted to talk to you about at lunch."

"At lunch," Josh scoffs. "Michaela, this isn't something you casually throw out over some sandwiches."

"Get the fuck out." I shove him towards the door, but he plants his feet. "Josh, you need to leave, *right now.* If you don't get the fuck out, I'll call the police." He doesn't believe me; hell, I wouldn't believe me. Usually, I'd never even think about threatening my brother with something so drastic, but right now I'd do anything to get him away from here. He needs to calm down. Needs to breathe so he can think rationally. "You just assaulted your best friend, and for what? Your adult sister making adult decisions? You can't just come in swinging!"

Slowly, his grip loosens on my wrist, and I turn to check on Finn. I pull his hand from his face to examine the damage done — a bruise already forming on his left cheek near his jaw. There is some coverage from his stubble, but not enough.

When his brown eyes meet mine, my heart breaks in two. This is exactly what he didn't want, what he was afraid of. We knew Josh might have trouble accepting our relationship at first. I thought I could break it to him slowly and not with Finn around. Thought that would help lessen the blow.

"Josh, please leave," Finn's words are firm and demanding as he holds my stare. "Your sister will call you later to schedule a talk."

"Oh," my brother scoffs, "you speak for her now?"

"What did I say?" I threaten, but my eyes never leave Finn.

"Your place, two o'clock, Michaela. Don't be late," Josh warns before he slams the door behind him.

"Finn," I sigh. "I'm so—"

His raised hand silences me before he rubs the sore spot on his jaw. "Please just handle it." He doesn't say anything else walking out of the condo.

"Well, you're dressed, that's a good sign." Josh knocked on my door five minutes before two, and the arrogance of it instantly pissed me off. He most likely expected me to be late or not show at all.

The way he paces my living room tells me he still hasn't fully processed what happened this morning. I suppose that's fair, it's not every day you find your sister half-naked at your best friend's door. "Oh, don't give me that look, Michaela. I'm not the one in the wrong here," he says when I cross my arms tightly waiting for the lecture to begin.

"You're right, I forgot who I was talking to: Saint Josh."

"Don't be so dramatic, MJ."

"You're the one who threw punches this morning!"

"I'm not going to apologize! I came to see if my *best friend* wanted to grab breakfast before I met you, and what do I find? My *sister*, half-naked, answering the damn door of his apartment!" Josh shakes his head as if he's still in disbelief. "Don't you think you should have asked me if it was okay to fuck my best friend first?"

"I'm an adult, Josh. I don't need your permission to sleep

with someone, including your best friend."

"How long has this been going on?"

"That's none of your business."

"Not my business?" he scoffs. "You don't think I have a right to know when you're fucking around on your husband with one of my friends?"

"Okay, first of all, I'm not fucking around on anyone. And second, no, it's not your business. We weren't ready to tell you because of shit like this! Because of how you reacted this morning."

"How could you do this to David? And with him!"

"You're not listening to a damn word I say. David and I are *not* together. We haven't been together in months."

The words finally start to sink in. His brows furrow together as he processes my words, and the realization hits. His eyes meet mine, "You're not... What?"

"David asked me for a divorce...in Italy."

His eyes widen. "Italy? That was practically five months ago, Michaela!"

"I'm aware of when it was, Josh." I pull my cardigan tighter around me.

"Why didn't you tell me?"

"I don't know." I shrug as tears build behind my eyes. One slips down my cheek. "I guess, a part of me thought I could fix it before it was final. If I could fix it, I wouldn't have to tell anyone. It would be like it never happened, but..."

"Sleeping with Finn wasn't going to fix anything."

"Finn was an accident."

"I never meant for it to happen. God, Josh. It wasn't supposed to happen, but working with him on Sheffield House... I saw a side of him I never knew. I got to know him. I—"

"Do not say you're in love with him," my brother stops me. I swallow my words meeting his stare — it's not as cold, but he still looks hurt.

"No, but I think I could," I laugh softly.

## *thirty-four*

*Finn*

**"WHAT HAPPENED TO YOU?"** Wide green eyes stare as I fall into the chair across from her. "Babe, I have to call you back," she says into the phone hanging up without waiting for a response. "Finn, are you okay? Do you need ice?"

"I'm fine, Nin," I say, mustering my best smile.

"You get mugged or something?" Nina walks around her desk and grips my chin like a mother inspecting her child. I cringe when her fingers lightly graze over the bruise that extends from my jaw into my left cheek.

"Or something."

"Damnit, Finn. We have a meeting with your board tomorrow!"

"I know that, Davina."

"You can't walk in there like that. Find a way to cover it up because we can't push this meeting. Not when we have the fundraiser in a week." The way she looks at me is disheartening. I feel like I'm sitting across from Mom when I told her I dropped out of college, again. Nina is disappointed, rightfully so. Probably feeling a little letdown. I told her shit like this

219

wouldn't happen, I promised, and here I am, showing up the day before a meeting with a bruised face. This was supposed to be my fresh start, and from where she's sitting, it's just more of the same ole Sheffield bullshit. "What the fuck happened?"

"I think it's best if we don't discuss it, right now."

Nina lifts herself onto the desk and rubs her temples, mumbling something I can't quite make out in Italian. I hate when she does that. "You're lucky I don't have time for this shit today."

"What do you have time for, then?" I smirk, but her death glare is enough to shut up.

"You are ready, right?"

"Yes. Everything is done. You don't have to worry."

"Are you sure you're ready to handle this, Finn? Are you sure you can handle this? This isn't something you can toss aside when you get bored. This isn't Rosecliffe or the paper or Amanda. This is real..."

"I know."

"...This is *my* company, and I've stuck my neck out to ensure you got a fair chance here."

"And, I appreciate it. Truly, Davina. You've given me more than you know by helping me."

"What if they decide they don't like something you're doing?" My stomach sinks. "Are you ready to face them? To stand up for yourself and your decisions. Are you truly ready to be a business owner?"

No.

"Yes, of course." I can only hope she half believes me. I've never considered it like that, but the board members must like what we're doing, or they wouldn't have agreed to join. Regardless, I know she's right. I have to be ready for anything, including pushback from the board. I have no choice but to continue to win them over and ensure they approve the goals we want to achieve within the next year. "I'll always respect whatever decision the board makes. However, I don't see how they could turn this down. I mean, it's for the kids, right?"

"You don't know the board," she smirks and steps down from the desk. "Oh, how has Michaela been?"

"She's been..."

Wait, what? Surely, she doesn't know.

"I don't know; I haven't seen her since Coney Island."

"I have eyes all over this city, Finnley." That fucking smirk is back. Like she knows something I don't. She sits back in her chair and fiddles with her pen. "You know, I was happy to see that you guys had put whatever issues you had aside and decided to make the most of it."

"Well, we agreed to keep things strictly business for the good of the project."

Nina stares at me, chewing on her bottom lip like she's deciding whether or not to say what's on her mind. Finally, she sighs and lets the real question go. "Well, let's go. We need to meet Sasha downstairs and I want to see what you have for tomorrow before you leave."

I flip through my presentation slides, trying to concentrate on the words instead of the ache in my jaw. I'm waiting for the damn peas to refreeze so I can use them again. Tomorrow has to go well. I can't risk letting Nina down, instead of focusing on the presentation, my mind wanders to a condo seven miles away on the Upper East Side. I shouldn't be surprised I haven't heard from her. Part of me hoped I would have heard something by now, at least let me know how things went with Josh. I'm more worried for him than I am for her. I firmly believe she's capable of murder. The question is, would she call me to help bury the body? Probably not. She'd probably call Caitlin — I would, too.

Should I call her? I should check on her or at least text to make sure she's okay. Picking up my phone, my heart jumps at the new text notification. It falls just as fast when I see the name next to it: Oliver.

**Oliver**

**Be ready for next week.**

I roll my eyes and toss my phone on the table. What's that supposed to mean? I've successfully started the company. I've done everything he wanted. What else does he want? There's a lot I want to say back to him, but best to leave it. I consider calling her. Hell, I consider calling Josh. I need to apologize to both of them, but part of me thinks it might be best to give them both some time.

What the hell was that? I rub my eyes, scanning the room; the alarm clock reads *2:47 A.M.* Was that a knock? After a minute, I settle back into bed. Then, I hear it again. A knock on the door — who in the hell let someone up here at three in the morning? I've got to talk to Paul about letting people up here.

I swing the door open, ready to give whoever it is a piece of my mind, but every ounce of annoyance dissipates. Michaela stands with her arms wrapped tightly around herself. Dressed in her pajamas, hair is pulled up into a messy ponytail on top of her head, face makeup-free, and black-rimmed glasses sit on the edge of her nose. She won't look at me, eyes glued to the floor. Lifting her chin, my heart breaks at her eyes brimming with tears. I don't hesitate to pull her in my arms. Guilt gnaws at my insides. I'm part of the reason we're in this mess.

"I'm sorry for just showing up," she whispers. "I didn't want to be alone."

"Don't apologize. I told you, you're welcome anytime. You could've let yourself in, y'know." I kiss the top of her head and a small amount of relief floods my senses inhaling the familiar scent of her coconut shampoo.

"Finn, we need to talk."

"Michaela, it's three in the morning... Let's get some sleep and—"

"No, I need to get this off my chest. I just need you to listen. Okay?"

"Okay," I sigh and press a kiss on her forehead. "Let me make some coffee."

Michaela sits on the couch staring out over the city lights waiting for the coffee to brew. Her mind somewhere else barely registers the mug I extend to her and jumps slightly when I touch her shoulder. She takes it with a mumbled apology. I leave a little space between us when I finally sit down. I can't remember the last time I was this anxious to get a conversation over with.

"Finn, I know what happened was my fault. I should've been honest and told everyone about the divorce from the start. It was irresponsible and childish to keep that from them. I know that. I knew that, but I thought I could fix it. Make it all go away. Then, they'd never have to know about it." Michaela stares down into the dark liquid keeping a death grip on the mug handle. "I thought it was just a phase. Something we'd get past and everything would be fine again. But, I think, all along, I knew it wasn't." She sighs gnawing on the inside of her cheek. "And then you came along and messed everything up some more."

I try to hide the small smile that tugs on my lips.

"What happened this morning was exactly what I was afraid of. I knew Josh would be upset, He cares about us both, and I knew he'd need time to adjust. I didn't think it would happen like this. Selfishly, I wanted more time. More time to tell them about David, more time to get my life back together, more time to figure out what this is… You didn't deserve what happened. I'm sorry. I'm so, so sorry that it happened."

"This isn't your fault, Michaela. You're right. You should've been honest, but this isn't all on you. I'm at fault, too. What happened this morning was going to happen regardless of when Josh found out. You think your brother was going to be okay with there being an us?"

"Is there still an us? Because—"

"If the past two weeks have done anything, they've only solidified that I want this." Taking her mug, I place it on the coffee table and take her hands in mine. "I haven't felt this comfortable around someone in a long time; ever, maybe. You scare the shit out of me, more than your brother ever could."

A smile tugs at her lips. "We're a mess."

"We're going to get through this, I promise." I pull her mouth to mine in a soft, chaste kiss. "Might not be the easiest, but we'll figure it out."

"What did Nina say when she saw your face?" Her fingers lightly trace the bruise on my jaw.

"It's Nina, she doesn't ask too many questions."

"She probably already knew," Michaela laughs. "I swear, that woman knows things before they happen."

"That's her job." I kiss her forehead and settle back into the couch. She doesn't waste any time when I open my arms for her to join me. "She did mention I need to make sure I cover up my face for our meeting tomorrow, though."

"Need some concealer," she yawns.

"Oh yeah, I'm sure I have some lying around here

somewhere."

She smacks my stomach playfully. "You can use mine," another yawn, "my makeup is still here."

"I was wondering what that shit all over my counter was."

"It's the real reason I came back." Michaela beams a tired smile at me, and I roll my eyes.

"Get some sleep, Shortcake."

# thirty-five

*Finn*

**"DAYUMMMM," COLIN DRAWS OUT** the last syllable of the word catching sight of my face.

It has been three days since Josh unexpectedly knocked on my door, but the discoloration has shown little sign of retreat. The morning of my board meeting, Michaela spent a good thirty minutes applying (and reapplying) concealer and foundation trying to cover it. Luckily, no one on the board seemed to notice, and Nina seemed happy enough with Michaela's work when I walked into her office.

Colin sets the bag of to-go food on the island before coming closer to get a better look at me. "What happened to you?"

"Josh," I say. Josh and I still haven't spoken, and I suspect it's because Josh doesn't want to be first to wave the white flag and I don't want to get punched again.

"Let's just say my brother wasn't too happy when I answered the door the other morning," Michaela says walking out of the bedroom freshly showered and dressed in a pair of high-waisted jean shorts and one of my black t-shirts. She's supposed to meet Caitlin and Liv for lunch. I'm sure they heard through the grapevine that I'd shown up at Nina's office with a bruised face.

"You're joking," Colin answers with a hint of disbelief. His wide eyes move from her to me looking for confirmation.

"I wish she was." I lean over the island cradling my head in my hands. "Josh showed up Wednesday morning and Michaela may or may not have answered the door in my shirt."

"That's not *so* bad; at least she wasn't naked."

"*Only* in my shirt."

"Oh, dude," Colin laughs. "You're lucky you're not six feet under. I would've murdered you had it been me."

"In our defense," Michaela says over her shoulder pulling a water bottle from the fridge, "Josh showed up unannounced." She takes a long sip and kisses my unblemished cheek. "I'll tell Liv and Cait you said hi."

"Give them all the juicy details," I say.

She grabs her purse and gives me a quick kiss. "Behave yourselves, boys," she says before leaving.

When she's gone, Colin lets out a low whistle. "Can't wait 'til Knox hears about this."

"He can't make it today," I say tearing into the plastic bag, my mouth watering from the thought of Mr. Joseph's Panang curry.

"He can't make it, or you didn't invite him?"

The three of us were supposed to meet at the court for a game and head over to Benny's afterward for lunch, but considering my…condition, I decided it was best to stay in. I didn't want to risk further injury before the fundraiser next weekend and Colin seemed more than happy to swap a day in the sun for a day inside with take-out and video games. I told Knox we'd have to reschedule; something came up at work.

"He doesn't need to know about this," I say handing Colin his to-go container. "What kind of an example am I setting if he knows I got this for lying to my best friend about dating his sister?"

"Well, you wouldn't have to worry about it had you just told Josh," Colin shrugs digging into his Pad Thai. "I believe this is what they call fuck around and find out."

"I wanted to." I pull two beers from the fridge passing one to him. "I wanted to tell him, Nina, Nick…all of them, but Mic hadn't even told them about the divorce."

"Please tell me they know now." He puts his hands up in defense when I shoot him a glare. "I'm just asking."

"She told her parents but asked them not to tell Josh. She wanted to do it. I respect wanting to tell him in person, but— I don't know, it felt like she kept putting it off."

"Was she?" Colin lifts his brow taking a sip of his beer.

"I don't think so… I don't know. I like to think it was just bad timing."

"You sure she's totally over this ex of hers?"

"You met the guy," I laugh, but Colin doesn't.

"I'm serious, Finn. She's coming out of a marriage, that's tough shit. Are you sure she's not using you as some rebound?"

Dumping my rice onto a plate, I spoon some curry on top before taking a large bite. I can't lie, the thought has crossed my mind once or twice. I was there when she needed someone to get her mind off David, but she wouldn't have stuck around and told her parents if she wasn't serious, right?

"Finn—"

"Yes," I stop him. "I've thought about it, but— Colin, I don't think that's what this is. She's told her parents, and now Josh knows… We're going to Nick and Nina's wedding *together*."

"I hope you know what you're doing."

So do I.

*thirty-six*

## Michaela

**WHAT IS THAT SOUND?** It's so loud. Like a constant buzz against wood— Oh, shit. I blindly reach for my phone on the nightstand. A glance at the screen tells me I'm not getting back to sleep if I answer, but if I don't answer, I run the risk of him continuing to call until I do. "What do you want?" I yawn.

"Good morning, Sunshine," my cousin's voice comes through the phone. Why the hell is he calling me? "Stopped by your place, but the doorman said you didn't come home last night. Or most nights, for that matter."

Shit. Looks like it's time for *the* conversation. We haven't even fully recovered from Josh, now I have to face Nick?

"You're in town?" I stifle my yawn.

"Dee and I were visiting Romy and Enzo. They're in town to see his daughter. I figured I'd stop and see my favorite cousin before heading out to Haven."

Glancing at the clock, I groan and cover my eyes from the sunlight peaking through the blinds. "Nick, it's eight in the morning."

"Good thing I brought coffee then." Before I can ask what

229

that means, there's a knock at the door and he hangs up.

I groan and force myself out of bed, throwing a sweater on over my pajamas before running to the door. On the other side is none other than Nicholas Davis.

One cup is not enough for this conversation. I finished the coffee he brought in the time it took me to let him inside, brush my teeth, and wake up enough to try and have this conversation. I pour a cup from the fresh pot and offer him one, but he declines from across the island. He's probably already on his second or third. That's the only reasonable explanation for him to be this awake so early. I know why he's here, it's been six days since Josh knocked on our door. I haven't spoken to him since he left my condo that day, but Finn left this morning to go down to Charlotte, and I have a feeling he will be making a trip to Josh's office while he's there. "Josh told you?" I blow on the steaming liquid before taking a sip.

"Not sure what you're talking about."

"C'mon Nick, don't play stupid." I roll my eyes. "I know you're the second person he called after Elizabeth."

"Actually, he called me first, and then Elizabeth, but semantics."

"You're so annoying."

He laughs. "Why didn't you just tell us, Mic?"

"Which part?"

"All of it, really, but at least the part about David. I guess I understand not telling us about Finn this early, but—"

"Finn and I aren't—"

"Michaela, you're staying in his condo when he's not even in town. You open the door wearing his sweatshirt. And, according to your own doorman, you've barely been home. So, let's skip the part where we pretend you're only fooling around and not dating, okay?"

"What do you want me to say?" I sigh. "My life has been a shit show for the past six months. My marriage failed before we'd even been married a full year. We barely saw each other, which made it —"

"That's not an excuse, Michaela."

"Not everyone is you and Nina, okay? Not everyone is okay with being away from their partner for extended periods of time. Some of us like to be with them."

"You think we're okay with it?" Nick scoffs. "Being away from my wife is not easy. Do you think I like being gone weeks at a time, not knowing if she'll be there when I get home? Do you think I like only seeing her maybe once a week or once every couple of weeks? And when we do see each other, it's usually for some fucking event. Do you think I liked not knowing she's been going to the fucking doctor? No, Michaela. I don't *like* any of it, but like David, our careers take us away sometimes. And you have to make the conscious effort to make your marriage work regardless."

I take a large gulp of my coffee avoiding eye contact with him.

"I'm not saying you have to work things out with David. That's your decision and you have made the choice to move on, but you could've at least told us. Fuck, you could've at least told Dee."

"I was scared! I didn't think anyone would understand, especially not my parents."

"I don't think you give them enough credit. They want you to be happy, Mic. We all do. And if Finn makes you happy then—"

"Finn has nothing to do with the divorce."

"Maybe not entirely."

"I didn't cheat on David."

"That's not what I'm saying." Nick leans back in his chair with a slight grin. "But, Finn is one, if not *the* reason you're ready to move forward, am I right?"

Well, he's not wrong. I've never felt so comfortable with someone. I've never stayed overnight with a boyfriend this early in a relationship. Never slept over when they weren't home. Never had my own space and things at his place. Never borrowed his clothes. Never felt so comfortable to be myself.

"The other thing I don't understand is what's taking so long for the divorce to finalize. Josh said it's still not done. What's the hold-up?" Nick sips his coffee and his eyes dart to the clock on the wall before landing back on me.

"The ring," I mumble behind my mug. Nick cocks an eyebrow and I groan. "And, the condo. He wants me to sell it, and he wants the ring back, but I don't—"

"So, give it to him."

"What is he going to do with it? Give it to someone else? That's tacky."

"What are you going to do with it? It's not like you're going to wear it. So what if he decides to recycle rings with the next girl, that's his problem, not yours." His phone vibrates across the counter and a smile crosses his features when he picks it up.

I wonder if Finn does that when I text him.

"What's she doing this morning?" I ask, but I already know the answer.

"Working, what else?"

"She's wearing herself thin, Nick."

"Tell her that." He finally looks up when he hits send on the text message. "She wants to make sure everything is ready for when we're gone. The honeymoon will be her first real vacation since Ric passed and it's stressing her out."

"Kai can manage."

"Of course, he can. She knows that, but she's been overseeing almost everything since Ophelia was born."

"What's she gonna do when she gets pregnant? She won't be able to keep going like this."

"We'll cross that bridge if we get there."

*If we get there.*

The words feel like a rock in my stomach.

"But this isn't about us, it's about *you*. So, you wanna tell me how you went from hating Sheffield's guts to sleeping in his bed?" Nick leans forward resting his chin on folded hands and his eyes shine with mischief. "Was your hate just hidden desire this whole time?"

"No, you weirdo. Don't be gross."

"Oh, so it was him? He was the one who's been riddled with desire all these years."

"Oh my gosh, stop."

"Was it his dashing good looks – his luscious hair and bright, beautiful eyes? Or was it his charm — you know he's always had a way with the ladies."

"It wasn't any of that," I laugh.

"Well, don't leave me hanging, what was it?"

"I don't know. I guess, working with him I got to see a new side of him.."

"I thought he was an asshole."

"Seeing the way he was with the kids." I sigh, "He was an asshole, but there was just something about him. I don't know how to explain it."

"You sound like a love-sick puppy."

"That's rich coming from you."

"What can I say? I love my wife. No matter how crazy she makes me." Nick glances at his phone when the screen lights up again and frowns. "Shit, I gotta head out. I need to stop by the office before I head to the airport."

"Will I see you at the party?"

"You think I'd miss an opportunity to see my wife in a sexy dress?" He wiggles his eyebrows and pulls on his jacket.

"Ew, just... Ew." I shudder for dramatic effect earning a laugh from him. "What are you doing in Haven?"

"We're finalizing the sale. She didn't tell you?"

Did she? I can't remember. I think that's something I would remember.

"We're selling the old one and buying a fixer-upper a little further outside Haven."

"She loved that house."

"There's a lot of memories there and I think it will be easier for her to want to go visit if she's not surrounded by so many conflicting emotions."

"But, that's where you guys started."

Nick shrugs. "She wanted to do it. Talked to Kai and he seemed more than happy with the idea. They're both still healing, and I think this is going to help them. We can make new memories. Happier ones."

"Where's the new one?"

"About thirty minutes from the city. A little further from Sopris, but she'll live."

"Will she?" Sopris is her favorite mountain to hike, even if the rest of us complain the whole time. I refuse to go with her again, scratch that, I refuse to go hiking in general. I'd prefer to take a quick spin class than go hike a mountain or go for a run in the city.

He laughs, "As long as she can get there, that's all that matters."

## thirty-seven

## Michaela

**FINN LEANS AGAINST THE** SUV his hands shoved deep into the pockets of his black suit. A smirk grows on his pink lips when I step into view. "You should've worn the other one," he says placing a hand on my hip. "I don't like this one."

My brow quirks in suspicion, "You picked it."

Another dress courtesy of Finnley Sheffield had shown up on my doorstep this afternoon. When I asked the delivery man if he could return it, he refused with a tight smile before disappearing down the hall. Cursing under my breath, I closed the door with my foot tossing the box on the table. Finn answered the phone on the second ring, and I didn't give him a chance to say anything, "Stop doing this."

"Stop doing what?" he asked innocently.

"I already had a dress to wear tonight."

"I'm aware."

"Was it not up to your expectations?" I undid the black bow and shook my head when the name Dior came into view.

"A little presumptuous considering I haven't seen it."

I dug through the white tissue paper and a black-colored

dress came into view. "What's a little presumptuous is buying me one when you haven't seen the one I already have."

"Wear whichever you prefer," Finn said before whispering to someone on his end of the phone. I assumed it was one of the construction guys since he had been gone the last two days and went straight to the Brooklyn building when he landed in the morning. "I thought I'd give you options."

David would never have given me the option — if he felt like I needed to wear something in particular, I was wearing it. I thought that was normal. Appreciated it even because I didn't want to embarrass him or myself. Barnes had thrown a Christmas party last year and I felt an enormous amount of pressure to look and act perfectly considering not only was it the first time I'd be meeting his boss, co-workers, and staff, but we had just gotten married. I had spent the entire day getting dolled up: hair, makeup, nails…I had even hired a stylist to pick out my dress.

"Michaela Reed, you've outdone yourself," I said staring into the mirror. "Pretty as a peach, Daddy would say." The elegant, off-the-shoulder velvet dress fit like a glove, hugging me in all the right places. I had specifically asked for an emerald color to match the tie I had gotten David for the event. He had been with Barnes most of the day, which left me to get ready without interruption.

"Mic, I'm back!" I heard him enter the apartment. When he had gotten the job with Barnes, we decided he should get an apartment for when he was in Washington, and let's say, it was obvious a woman didn't live there full-time. It was more of a bachelor pad than the actual bachelor pad he lived in before we moved to New York. The only semblance of a relationship was one of our wedding photos that sat on his desk. Stepping out of the bedroom, I prepared myself for some kind of reaction that would tell me just how good I looked. "Where are you—Oh, what is that?"

"What?" I looked down at my outfit hoping I hadn't gotten anything on it already.

"*That.* The dress. Why are you wearing it?"

"Because we're going to a Christmas party."

"Yes, I know, but why are you wearing that dress? I got one for you; it's hanging in the closet." He never told me he had bought me a dress. I followed him back into the bedroom and watched as he pulled out a simple, short-sleeved burgundy-colored dress.

"Oh," was the only thing I could say. "You don't think this is a little more...appropriate?"

David looked between them before letting out a deep sigh, "I suppose it's sufficient."

*Sufficient?*

"I mean, I guess I can wear that instead, I just—"

"I want you to be comfortable, y'know? I think you'd be a lot more comfortable in this."

I took the dress from him and walked into the bathroom hanging it on the back of the door. I sat on the edge of the tub and stared at it. Under normal circumstances, I'd think it was pretty and I might even buy it, but this wasn't a normal circumstance. Not only was this party the first one I'd been invited to, but it was our first one as a married couple.

A knock on the door after a few minutes, "You 'bout done? We have to go."

When I opened the door, David's lips pulled into a small smile, "There, doesn't that feel better?"

"Yeah, so much better. You were right."

He pulled me to him and kissed my forehead. "Let's go, we don't want to be late."

When we walked into the party that night, I wasn't surprised to see every other woman in a dress similar to my emerald one, hell some of them were dressed fancier. I'd felt extremely underdressed in the dress he chose, but David didn't seem to notice. His hand never left its place on my lower back all night, guiding me through the crowd and introducing me to his friends, colleagues, and finally Senator Barnes. Despite the smiles and polite interactions, I couldn't shake the looming feeling I was the talk of the party — and not in a good way.

"You mean that?" I asked Finn, pulling the dress out of the box, unsure if he really meant it or was trying to coax me into changing into this insanely gorgeous black one-shouldered dress with an incredible asymmetrical neckline that transformed into a cape off the right shoulder. Talk about a showstopper.

"Of course," Finn said. "You can wear whatever you want, Shortcake. Either way, it'll end up on the floor."

"Finn!" He chuckled before hanging up without another word leaving me to face the impossible decision of what to wear. Was it a test, or could I wear the one I had picked out? I hung the black dress on the closet door and stared at it. *It's not a test,* I told myself, *he just wants to do something nice for you.* That was something I wasn't used to.

"And, I want to rip it off and ravage you right here in front of all of New York City," Finn says, his breath hot against my ear as his right hand trails down my hip to the slit in my thigh. His fingers are like fire on my skin when they slip under the material. "Show them who you belong to." My small gasp urges him on, and his hand travels closer and closer to my throbbing core that has been craving his touch since he left three days ago. Fingers graze the material of my underwear before pushing it aside.

"Sir," Tony clears his throat and Finn's hand retreats. Damnit, Tony. "If we don't leave now, we'll be late. Traffic is a nightmare."

"You ready?" Finn asks as if he wasn't about to finger me on the sidewalk. I nod, unsure I trust myself to speak at the moment.

# thirty-eight

## Finn

**BEFORE TONY CAN COMPLETELY** roll up the partition, I pull Michalea's mouth to mine. Fuck, I missed her. I missed her more than I want to admit. I was only in Charlotte for three days, but it felt like an eternity. I've never felt like this about someone before, not even with Amanda. I thought I loved her, but I've realized what I felt for Amanda was far from love.

My hand accidentally tugs the earring dangling from Michaela's left ear and she yelps in pain. "Shit," I release my hold on her, "I'm sorry."

"I know they weren't the ones you picked," she laughs and pulls the earring from her ear, "but maybe we don't rip my ear in half trying to get them out, huh?"

My cheeks burn with embarrassment.

"Should I leave these out or—"

"Maybe for the car ride." I wink and this time it's her cheeks burning red. I take her hand tugging her forward and lift her dress when she straddles me. She kisses me and our tongues collide. My hands find her hips grinding her against my lower half. "Up," I command against her lips, tightening my grip to help her lift off my lap before I make quick work of my belt and trousers.

"Finn," she hisses stopping me from pushing down my legs. "We can't do this, Tony is right there!"

"Tony can't hear a thing," I smirk and push her underwear out of the way. She gasps when I push a finger inside her, and fuck, she's already so wet for me. I hum and crook my finger, which must have hit a sensitive spot the way she whimpers. I pull my fingers from her and suck the taste of her from them. Damn, she tastes so good. I can't wait to get her home so I can take my time with her. "Take those off, Shortcake."

"Am I supposed to go commando?"

"Is that a problem?" Our faces are mere inches apart, and her chest rises and falls against my own with each breath. "Take them off."

Michaela narrows her eyes before she falls back into the seat across from me. She hooks her fingers into the band of her underwear tugging them down. My eyes never leave hers. When she finally unhooks her underwear from her foot, I hold my hand out and she hesitantly hands them over. I grip her hand tugging her back to me and stuff the thong in my front pocket before I kiss her.

I groan when she pulls away falling to her knees on the floor of the SUV. She tugs the waistband of my briefs putting my cock on full display. I follow her every movement and see her eyes light up seeing me in such a vulnerable position — she'd never admit it, but I think she likes being in charge, just a little. Her finger lightly traces the thick vein down my shaft and her gaze meets mine when she replaces her hand with her tongue. Mother of God, this woman is going to kill me. Drawing back, she runs her tongue over my head, lingering for a moment before sucking.

"Fuck," my head flies back against the seat and my hips spring forward when she cups my balls and squeezes gently.

She switches between deep sucks and long strokes of her tongue. "Shortcake, you keep that up and I won't last much longer." I dig my hands into her hair and try to slow her tempo, but she refuses. It's been days since I've had her and I refuse to come in her mouth. I tug a little harder, but she doesn't budge. My hand slides down her jaw and to her throat and squeezes gently; she finally releases me with one last pull of her mouth. I force her eyes on me, "As much as I love seeing you on your knees, I haven't had you in days and I want to feel your pussy around my cock when I come."

My hand still wrapped gently around her throat, I bring her mouth to mine in a hard kiss — it's all tongue and teeth — and I taste myself on her tongue. She crawls back into my lap and I align myself with her entrance before pulling her down. She gasps dropping her forehead against my shoulder.

"God," I sigh in relief. I've been waiting for this since I landed at JFK this morning. "You feel so good." Warmth fills my belly feeling her pulse around me. She begins to rock back and forth and it pulls a moan from me. This woman is going to be the death of me. The way she can turn me into a beggar with one look is like nothing I've ever known before. My appetite for her is voracious and greedy, a man starved. I don't know how I'll ever grow tired of her.

Our eyes connect and her entire body clenches around me. My left hand tangles in her blonde waves and tugs. I lick a stripe up her neck before biting the skin behind her ear. "I thought of you every night I was gone, Shortcake," I whisper in her ear and roll my hips into her. "Thought of you riding me, just like this, and as much as I wanted to touch myself — I didn't because I didn't want to come unless it was inside *you*."

She whimpers.

"Close baby?" Her movements are more jagged and haphazard. She nods but I want to hear her say it. I force her eyes on me and say, "Use your words, Shortcake."

"Y-yes," she gasps and my thumb finds her clit. I glance down where our bodies become one. I almost come at the sight. My fingers tremble slightly against the skin of her hips. I do most of the work for her when I feel her begin to slow. Her breathing is heavy and she's right on the edge. My lips graze the exposed skin of her left shoulder up her neck. Pleasure crawls up my spine, and I'm trying not to come before she does, but fuck it's getting harder with each stroke. "Finn," she moans.

"Go ahead, Shortcake. Come for me," I whisper, nipping gently on her eat, and she does. Her body shakes as the high rushes through her. My movements become sloppy, losing control as she comes undone above me. My body trembles beneath her as I reach my own climax. Her head drops to my shoulder again, exhausted, and I kiss her temple. "We better get cleaned up." Michaela hums in response before I help her off my lap. After I clean myself up and resituate my trousers, I pick her earrings up from the floor and hold them up to her, "Don't forget your earrings."

Michaela shoots me a playful glare before taking them. "You have lipstick on your face."

"You think it's my shade?"

She rolls her eyes and takes a handkerchief from her purse. Opening a water bottle, she wets it and begins to wipe the shade of red from my face. "You ready for tonight?"

"As long as I have you by my side, I won't need anything else. Tonight is for you too, y'know." Blue eyes meet mine before she smiles and returns to her work. "It is, I wouldn't have been able to do this without you."

"Well, I'm happy to have been of assistance, but tonight is about your hard work — don't let anyone take that from you."

*thirty-nine*

## Michaela

**I FORGOT HOW TIRING** these things are. Shaking hands, kissing ass, having to remember everyone's name – or pretend to – I don't know how Nina does this all the time. Then again, she's usually on the other side of it. I watch her smile and nod along to whatever story the man in front of her tells – Jason, was it? She laughs at the right times and sips her champagne occasionally, never once looking away from the conversation. And she looks gorgeous doing it, dressed in a high-waisted blush pink bandage dress with a slit up the front. The light above her reflects off the rhinestones that make up half of the ruched bodice when she moves to greet another man who joins their conversation.

"She makes it look easy, huh?" Nick offers me a fresh glass of champagne.

"She makes it look *very* easy. They both do." I glance at Finn who's doing the same thing with a group of older gentlemen sipping on old fashions.

"They were raised to do it. Makes me kind of happy our family wasn't rich," Nick laughs behind his beer.

"You have no idea." I was never more grateful for my parents than when I started hanging out with people like Nina and Finn. I can't imagine growing up in this world, being born and bred to run with the elite from day one.

"Wouldn't trade it for the world though." Nick smiles and offers a subtle wink when he catches his wife's eye. She excuses herself and makes her way through the crowd. "How's Jackson doing?" Nick asks when she finally reaches us.

Jackson! That's it. Well, I was close.

"Still pushing for a Villa-Hope collaboration. Apparently, Kai told him I'm the biggest ocean nerd out there."

"You hate the ocean," I say.

"That's the point."

"Hey Nin," Kai joins us, wrapping an arm around his sister's shoulder. The biggest shit-eating grin I've ever seen on his face. "How's Mr. Hope doing?"

Oh, I get it. She and Kai fuck with each other, it's how they keep themselves entertained during these things. That's brilliant.

"Oh, fuck off, Kai." Nina shoves him away earning a hearty laugh from her brother.

"Tossing her to the wolves again, Kai?" Finn asks placing a gentle hand on my lower back. Nina's eyes flicker to the movement briefly then to me and then to Nick who wets his lips and smirks behind his beer. Butterflies erupt in my stomach, and I have to remind myself not to step away from his touch. Why am I so nervous? Everyone here knows about the divorce, they know about me and Finn, so why do I still feel like a teenager in a secret relationship?

"I just like to have a little fun," Kai says. "Besides, she makes it too easy."

Sasha's assistant appears whispering something to Finn. He turns back to the group, "Showtime."

"Go bring in the big bucks," Nina instructs.

Finn laces our hands together bringing the back of mine to his lips. "When I'm done, we'll get out of here. Sound okay?"

"I could go for a hamburger."

"That's my girl." The blush rises in my cheeks at his words. *My girl.* Finn smiles and kisses me, hard, before following the assistant toward the stage.

When he's gone, I turn to meet the smirk of Davina Villa and she motions to the hallway off the bar. *Shit, we're going to do this here?* I sigh following her. When we reach the quiet space, I hold up a finger and say, "Hold on, let me down this before we start." I down the remainder of the champagne in my glass. The smirk never leaves her lips even she takes a sip of her own. "Okay, go ahead."

"So, Finn…"

"Nina, I swear, I didn't mean to, I—"

"Michaela, I don't care. I just hate that you felt like you couldn't come to me, about any of it. Why didn't you tell me about David?"

"I guess, I wasn't ready to admit it out loud." Glancing out of the hallway, I meet Finn's stare, and he does one of those small waves when you're trying not to be too obvious. This side of Finn is nice, it's the person I wish I had known years ago, but I'm glad I've gotten to know now. A smile tugs on my lips and I wave back before turning to Nina. "Saying it out loud made it real and…I wasn't ready for it to be real."

"Well, it's his loss." Nina places a soft hand on my arm. "How exactly did this thing with Finn happen? I thought you couldn't stand him. What was it you called him? Jabba the Hut? That's an insult in your Star Wars lingo, right?"

I know she knows what happened. Nick is a gossip when it comes to telling her things — you can't tell him anything you don't want her to know — but she wants to hear it from me. I shouldn't tell her that Finn and I slept together in the office. I mean, she is technically my boss, and it was technically her office, and this is technically a work event, so she's partially in Davina boss-mode, not one hundred percent Nina friend-mode. I'll just admit to the kiss…keep it PG. "After the bagels—"

"From Brooklyn."

"Yes, from Brooklyn… Things took a weird turn. We were getting along and working well together, and then naturally turned back into normal Finn. One thing led to another, and we kissed."

"That's all?"

"Davina Bay, what kind of girl do you take me for?" I touch my heart in fake offense. "I would *never* do anything more than that in the office."

She mumbles a faint acknowledgment behind her champagne glass.

"Then he ran into me and David fighting and…when he came to check on me a few days later, we slept—"

"All I need to know is, are you happy?"

"Yes," it comes out before I can even think about it.

"Good. That's all that matters."

"You're not mad?"

"Michaela, why would I be mad?" Nina laughs. "Finn is a great guy, a little rough around the edges and kind of a dick sometimes, but I adore him. And he seems completely infatuated with you."

I bite down on my bottom lip.

"Have you spoken to Josh?" Her brow quirks and hearing my brother's name makes my stomach sink. I haven't spoken to Josh since he left my condo a week ago. Mom called to check on me a few days later but made no mention of him or about knowing what happened. "I'm going to take the look on your face as a no."

"He was pretty upset when he found out."

"Can you blame him?" Nina takes a sip of champagne. "How would you feel if your little sister opened the door half-naked at your best friend's house?"

"He didn't have to punch Finn."

"So the bruise *was* from Josh, I had a feeling." She taps her finger on her glass, she steps towards the doorway eyes roaming over the room. They land on Nick who beckons her to the stage. "We'll finish this conversation later, okay? Come to my office at corporate on Tuesday morning."

"Not Monday?"

"Kai will want to be there. He can't do Monday." Nina glances over her shoulder again to meet Nick's impatient stare. "Tuesday, okay?" She squeezes my hand gently before disappearing into the crowd.

I thank the bartender for the glass of champagne turning to face the sea of people. A petite man in a pastel pink suit steps up to center stage. Jeremy, Finn's new assistant, taps the microphone gaining the attention of the audience. He introduces himself and begins thanking everyone for coming with open pockets to support the foster youth of the area. I wade through the crowd to get closer to the stage because once Finn is done with his speech, I'm sure he will want to get the hell out of dodge. I find my place on the outskirts of the room leaning back against the wall with a clear shot of the stage. Finn scans the crowd until his gaze lands on me. I watch his shoulders rise and fall with a deep breath. "Good luck," I mouth and smile before Jeremy introduces him on stage.

He's nervous, I can tell by the way his voice wavers slightly at first, but most people probably don't notice. I keep my eyes on him half-listening to the story he tells, I've only heard it one hundred times in the past two days, until I notice Oliver walk by, Hayley on his heels. He talks to an older couple in hushed tones, and I try to control myself, it's not my business. Whatever they are talking about in such a secretive manner is *not my business.* I try to stay focused on the man on stage, but I'm too nosey and something is telling me to follow.

I keep a distance between us and hand my half-empty glass to a server who walks by. They stop short of the entrance to the lounge, and I stop another waiter who carries a tray of fresh glasses. I turn my back to them, and it looks like I'm watching the stage, but my attention is focused on the conversation behind me.

"He's had a good turnout tonight," the other man says.

"Thanks to Davina," his wife scoffs.

"Now Gladys, that's not fair."

"Let's not pretend it's not true," Oliver chuckles. "He wouldn't have been able to do this without her. That boy should've never been able to pull this off and yet somehow he did."

My jaw tightens. Oliver is such an ass.

"I think we all know how he did it, I'm just curious as to why. I can't think of one thing he could offer Davina in exchange for her help."

I keep my eyes on the man onstage — he's more comfortable than he was minutes ago, wooing the crowd with jokes and flirtations.

"I mean, I told you why he did this, didn't I, Gary?" Oliver asks.

Gary and Gladys, how original.

"I'm sure, but I don't remember," Gary hums.

"One too many bailouts. I told him to shape up or I was taking the money. He'd gotten into some trouble, real trouble down in Mexico, and I had to pay to make it go away, again."

My heart drops.

*Taking the money.*

The whole thing, all of it, was all so Finn could keep his inheritance. I swallow the lump forming in my throat. No, that can't be right. He cares about the kids, he wanted to do this for them…

"I wouldn't have been able to do this without the help of some very special people," Finn's voice breaks through their conversation. "First and foremost, Davina, you've been instrumental in making this whole thing a success." A bright spotlight shines in her direction, but I can't see her. I can imagine the look on her face though, she hates being called out like that. Hates the spotlight being put on her unless she wants it.

"He went to Davina because he knew she'd made sure it happened," Mr. Sheffield continues.

Nina knew? No, there's no way. She would've told me.

"You taught me so much about being a business owner. I am eternally in your debt," Finn continues.

There must be some other explanation. Finn might hide something like this from me, but my best friend certainly wouldn't. I glance over my shoulder at the older group and see Oliver smirking at his son. Part of me can't help but believe what he's said — it's exactly something he would do. Dangle the money he promised his son in front of him like a worm on a hook. Another part of me hopes I'm wrong.

"Sasha," Finn continues, "without your expertise, we would've never been able to pull off these amazing events. Please give her a hand because she has worked tirelessly to make sure this gala went off without a hitch." Everyone does as Finn commands, except me. Don't get me wrong, I love Sasha and she's done an amazing job, but right now, all I can think about is the information bomb dropped.

"So, what now — you just handed it over to him?" Gary continues their hushed conversation.

"I unfroze his accounts," Oliver says. "Left him with a little in one to get by while he was working with Davina, but now he has access to it all — including the money my father left him a year ago."

That would explain the sudden influx of grand expenses.

"I'm surprised he has any of it left," Gladys huffs.

"I don't expect this will last too long. Finnley doesn't know what it takes to run and foster a business, especially one like this. He'll grow tired of it like he does everything else, and he'll leave a mess for Davina to clean up."

"Have a little faith, dear," Hayley tsks.

"That boy has never stayed interested in one thing for very long, he'll drop this eventually, just like he'll drop his newest fling when he grows tired of her."

"Oh, I don't know, she might be the one who makes it."

"That's what you said about Amanda. Look how that turned out, he left her high and dry when she needed him most."

"You have no idea what you're talking about," I finally say earning confused glances from all four of them. Shit, I should've kept my mouth shut, but I couldn't take it anymore. As his girlfriend, I'm supposed to stand up for him...right? "You have no idea what your son has accomplished nor what his plans are for the future of this company."

"And who might you be?"

They don't recognize me. I'm not sure whether to be offended or relieved. I shouldn't be surprised, we've only met a handful of times.

"My girlfriend, Michaela Davis," Finn's words are met with warmth on my back — the spotlight. I glance over my shoulder to meet Finn's beaming eyes on stage. His smile widens, and but his gaze moves behind me to his parents and his smile falls before forcing it to return. A hint of suspicion remains in his gaze even when he turns back to the crowd. "She's a little shy," he chuckles along with the rest of the room before continuing with his speech.

"Am I supposed to know who you are?" Oliver looks me up and down and I can't lie it's somewhat intimidating, I refuse to cower though.

Hayley leans in to whisper, "The Davis girl, she's the assistant Davina hired to help Finnley, dear."

"Assistant?" he scoffs. "I should've known he'd be sleeping with the help." Oliver snickers earning a chuckle from Gary and Gladys. I'm surprised Hayley doesn't join in, instead offering a small smile to the group.

Tears prick the corner of my eyes, but I swallow them back. These people will not see me cry. I won't give them the satisfaction. Instead, I take a deep breath and stare Oliver Sheffield dead in the eyes to say, "Your son has done an incredible thing by starting this company. You may not see it, but everyone else does. Regardless of *why* he started, he's doing remarkable things here. I just hope you pull your head out of your ass before it's too late."

Hayley's face falls, but she recovers before her husband notices. Her eyes wander toward the front of the room. The longing look of a mother who misses her child, even though it's her fault he is so distant.

"What's that supposed to mean?" Oliver scoffs.

"If you have ask, then it's already too late."

A hand grazes my hip squeezing gently before he presses a kiss to the crown of my head. "Mom, Dad…you know Michaela," his voice steady, staring down his father.

"Wonderful speech, sweetheart," Hayley beams.

"I wasn't sure you heard any of it seeing as you've all been busy bothering my girlfriend." Finn stares each of them down before turning to me. "You ready to get out of here?"

Yes, but no.

The warmth in his eyes spreads across my skin like fire, but it only makes me anxious instead of the comfort it usually brings. I finger the locket around my neck before offering him a slight nod. I don't trust my voice not to give away the anxiety mounting in my system. Finn takes the champagne glass from my hand and threads our fingers together, his thumb tracing small circles on the palm of my hand, before bidding his mother goodnight.

"Finnley," Oliver says. Finn looks back over his shoulder, his hand gripping mine a little tighter. "Try not to mess this up, we wouldn't want to get back in the same situation, would we?"

Finn narrows his gaze but swallows the words just behind his lips and ushers me towards the door.

*forty*

## Michaela

**"WHAT'S ON YOUR MIND,** Shortcake?" Finn asks enveloping my left hand. He draws it away from my necklace to his lips. I knew this was coming the moment we walked through the door. Since we left the party, I've tried not to seem distant, but it's not hard to tell something is on my mind. I don't think I've said more than fifteen words. I haven't been able to stop thinking about what Oliver said. Can you blame me? I don't understand why Finn wouldn't tell me about the deal with his father. That's something you tell the person you're dating, right? "We had a fun, successful night. What's there to be anxious about, hmm?"

"I'm not anxious."

"Nice try, Michaela, but your tell is showing."

What's that supposed to mean?

"You always play with your locket when you're nervous… it's your tell." He pulls me close and pushes a piece of hair behind my ear, "Michaela, we had a good night. A *great* night. I'm sorry if my parents said or did something. You know how they can be, but I don't want that to ruin our night. It's still early, we can—"

"I need a minute," I interrupt him stepping out of his grasp. I retreat to the bedroom and close the door, but it isn't enough space between us. I grip the edge of the bathroom sink and take a deep, shaky breath trying to regain my composure. I'm losing it with every passing second. The knot in my stomach has grown ten times since we left the party. I feel nauseous and light-headed and shaky. I'm two seconds from implode because this is all too much. Finally looking up, I meet the eyes of the girl in the mirror. We both know what the right thing to do is, but one of us doesn't want to, and the other knows we have to. After a long moment, we nod in understanding.

I rip the dress over my head before digging through my drawer and changing into a pair of leggings and my old Rosecliffe sweater. Heels exchanged for a pair of Converse, I pull my hair into a messy bun and open the door to find Finn with his hand raised to knock. He takes in my appearance, "Going somewhere?"

"I'm leaving."

He chuckles softly. "Did something happen? Is everyone okay?"

"Everyone's fine, it's me." I push my way out of the bedroom and snatch my purse from the kitchen island. Finn stands with his hands shoved deep in his pockets and I can see the gears turning as he tries to piece together the events leading up to this moment. Trying to understand what's happening. I take a deep breath and move toward the door. "I have to go."

"Hold on a second." Finn grasps my wrist not allowing me to step outside. "Talk to me." I try to look away from his intense stare, but he pulls me back. "Shortcake, I'm trying to understand. Did I do something? If I did, just tell me, and I—"

"Finn, I can't do this. I can't— I can't pretend like everything is okay when it's not."

"Pretend... What are you talking about?" Finn pulls me

back inside, closes the door gently, and caresses my cheek with his thumb. I hate that I lean into his touch, but it's soft and warm and inviting. I want nothing more than to curl up on the couch with him, but I can't. Not right now, I have too much on my mind, too much to think about.

"I'm so proud of you, Finn." His eyes narrow in confusion. "And, I know you're going to do great things, but—" I take a deep breath and recenter myself because I need to do this. I remove his hand from my face, and he looks genuinely hurt. "I don't want to be a part of this — *us* — anymore. I told you, I am done being a pawn in people's game."

"What do you— This isn't a game, Shortcake."

But, it was a game, a competition put on by his father. Win, and he gets to keep the life he's always known. Lose, and he loses everything. He won the competition with my help, and getting in my pants was a bonus.

"Don't call me that."

"Okay, *Michaela*. This is not a game. Now, would you please explain what is going on? I'm a little lost."

"The fucking bet, Finn!" My voice carries through the condo and the silence that follows fills my stomach with knots.

"What bet are you talking about?" He tugs on the ends of his sandy-brown hair. "You're not making sense!"

"Your inheritance!" Brown eyes widen. "The sick game you and your dad play. I know about your fucking money, Finn. I know that your dad put you up to all of this... He made you start this company. It wasn't because you wanted to, it's because you *had* to." Tears burn my vision, but I won't let them fall. I promised myself ten years ago I wouldn't let Finnley Sheffield be the cause of any more tears and I intend to keep that promise. "Was that all this was to you?"

"No! No, Michaela. I mean, yes, in the beginning, of course, it was. I didn't— It didn't stay that way."

"So, helping these kids, it doesn't mean anything to you. It was just a means to an end."

"These kids mean everything to me."

"Because they got your inheritance back."

"Because I care about them. Because I've been them! I want to help them. I know what it means to—"

"Save it, Finn. You are exactly who I always thought you were. All you've ever cared about is yourself. This proves it." I try to open the door again, but his hand holds it shut.

"Yes, initially, I had to start a business to prove to Oliver that I'm not some screw-up — not completely, anyway. But, it didn't stay that way. I found something that I'm good at. Something I didn't think I was capable of before." He stoops down to eye level and takes my face in his hands. "When I decided to start Sheffield House… Michaela, the money didn't matter anymore. And *this*, you and me, was never part of that."

The tears threaten to spill over staring into his eyes. He looks hurt and sad, but right now, I don't have it in me to believe him. He lied about the truth of this business, and he lied about why he wanted it so badly. How do I know he's telling the truth now?

"Finn, please let me go."

"No, because if I do, I'll never see you again, and I'm not going to accept that."

"Finnley," the sound of his full name shocks him. "If you do care about me and I'm not part of this game, then you'll let me go." At first, I don't think he's going to, but after a moment his grip loosens until his hands fall to his side and he stands to his full height. "I hope it was worth it," I say and step into the hallway closing the door between us.

forty-one

## Michaela

**"SURE, COME ON IN,"** Nina says when I pass her to enter the penthouse. She's still dressed in her gown, which means they haven't been home long. She yawns rubbing her eyes, "I wasn't expecting you 'til Tuesday."

"We need to talk *now*." I've spent the past hour trying to figure out how I missed the memo about this whole thing being a sham to help Finn keep his inheritance. I planned on talking to her at the office before we meet with Kai, but I can't wait. I need to know the truth. Now.

"Oh, hey, Mic," Nick walks down the hallway. "I was about to order pizza. Want some?"

"No," I say sharply turning back to Nina, "we need to talk."

"Whatever it is can wait until Tuesday. We had a great night, let's not ruin it with—"

"This is important."

Nina sighs and I wonder if she already knows what this is about. I watch her face transform from Nina to Davina in a matter of seconds. Her lips press into a firm line, and her shoulders straighten slightly. She turns to Nick and tells him not to wait for her before leading me to the office

Nina leans back in her chair. She doesn't say anything, only watches as I pace the length of her desk. Back and forth. Back and forth. Repeatedly. Trying to compose my thoughts. I have to do this; I have to know how much she knew and why she didn't tell me.

"Did you know?"

She doesn't react, "I'm going to need a little more information."

My heart drops. "You did," I scoff. "How could you do this to me, Nina?"

"What exactly did I do to you, Michaela? From where I'm sitting, I only offered you an opportunity to try something new. Get out of the rut you had put yourself in."

"I wasn't in a rut! I had life shit going on."

"Shit you chose not to tell any of us. You chose not to tell *me!* I'm supposedly your best friend, but you still hid it from me. So, from my standpoint, it was either give you a change of pace or fire you." I swallow the lump in my throat under her burning gaze. "I chose the former because I didn't want to fire you. You left me no choice. And it's not my fault you decided—"

"But, you fucking knew! You knew about the wager with Oliver, and you didn't tell me."

Nina straightens in her chair, "It wasn't my place, Michaela. I cannot gossip to you about confidential business matters."

"That's not a confidential business matter, Nina!"

"Yes, it is!" Her words echo in the space around us, the first time she's raised her voice since we stepped into her office. She sighs and pinches the bridge of her nose, the light reflecting off the emerald on her finger. "I'm sorry, I am, but it wasn't my place to out his business. I knew how you felt about him, and I didn't want to give you any ammunition, especially something he told me in confidence."

"When you knew we were sleeping together—"

"I didn't, though!"

"Oh, come on, Nina."

"I had my suspicions, but you were a married woman. I didn't want to assume. Then, Josh told Nick about walking in on you and… Michaela, I didn't think it mattered. Why does it matter what got him here? All that should matter is he's here!"

"It matters, Nina. He *lied* to me. He didn't want to help kids, he only wanted to keep his money."

"You're wrong," she says matter-of-factly. "When Finn decided to move forward with a nonprofit, he knew it was a risk. Oliver isn't exactly the type to care about things like this, but Finn did it anyway. He knew he might not earn the money back and did it anyway."

Nina doesn't understand. She can't understand.

"I get it, you feel betrayed, but—"

"You don't get it!" Her eyebrow raises. "You're Davina *fucking* Villa. You don't have to worry about things like this happening to you. You get everything handed to you on a silver platter."

"Are you forgetting who I'm fucking married to? What we went through?"

"That's not the same," I sigh.

"No?"

"No," I shake my head. "It's not the same because Nick loved you!"

"Finn loves you!"

"Don't say that."

"He does, Michaela," Nick's voice interrupts us. He leans

against the open doorframe freshly changed into a pair of sweats and a T-shirt.

"Get out," I hiss towards my cousin. "This is an A and B conversation, so C your way out of it."

"Oh, very mature."

Nina visibly rolls her eyes before walking towards the door. She places a hand on her husband's chest and urges him out of the doorway. "Just... Give us a few more minutes. Please?"

"You may not be ready to say it, but the feeling is there," Nick says over her shoulder.

"Nick, please, you're not helping."

This time, he finally gives in when Nina urges him away. She closes the door turning back to me with a softer expression than before. I freeze when she steps forward and gathers me in her arms. I'm not expecting it, Nina isn't a big hugger, but it's comforting, and I feel myself relax. She squeezes me gently, and I hug her back taking a deep breath of her warm magnolia-sandalwood scent.

"Michaela," she pulls away and wipes a tear I hadn't realized fell down my cheek. "I wish I could say I'm sorry for not telling you, but I'm can't. His private matters are his own; the only reason he told me was out of desperation. He knew I'd never take him seriously unless I knew *why* he was doing it. I promise you, in the end, this meant more to him than getting his inheritance back. You mean more to him than getting his inheritance back."

"I don't know why I thought someone like Finn and I could make it work. We were doomed from the start."

"You're being a little dramatic."

"Says you." I roll my eyes and fall into one of the blue toile armchairs on this side of her desk. "What am I supposed to do, Nin?"

She shrugs, falling into the other chair. "Talking to him seems like a good place to start."

"I'm not ready yet."

"Then take a few days — nothing wrong with that."

I rub my eyes, a wave of exhaustion falling over me as the adrenaline begins to subside. All I want now is to go back home and crawl in bed next to Finn. But, I know I shouldn't because I'm not over this and I don't want to cause more problems with my conflicting feelings. Then I remember who I'm sitting next to. "How did you do it?"

Nina looks at me, confused, "Do what?"

"How did you decide you could be with Nick again after… everything? He lied and—"

"Oh," Nina says. She wets her lips and laughs softly. "Well, I guess, I always knew his secrets had something to do with Brina. I couldn't blame him for not—"

"What about Rosecliffe?"

"It's not his fault I didn't recognize him, right?" Nina folds her hands over her stomach. "I knew I loved him, and I knew the only reason he hid certain things from me was to protect me. He *tried* to tell me, I just— I didn't let him. It was never the right time to have those conversations. As upset as I was after everything, I still wanted him. I was so thankful he was the one who found me when Daddy died…and despite our argument, he was the only one I wanted there. My heart already belonged to him, and as if I needed any more confirmation, when JJ tried to weasel his way back into my life all I could think about was how I wished Nick was there."

My shoulders rise and fall with a sigh.

"It's okay to want him, Michaela. And, it's okay to be upset, but don't hold on to that. Don't lose something good because of a misunderstanding. We're not kids anymore. Talk to him. Take a few days and then talk to him."

I find myself nodding without thinking about it — Nina's right. I'll take a few days to think about things, and then… then, I'll talk to him.

*forty-two*

## Michaela

**"NO, YOU CANNOT FAKE** sick," Caitlin said standing outside my door at eight-thirty with coffee and bagels. When she received my text feigning illness last night, she decided to be at my condo before my first alarm. She ushered me back inside and picked out my outfit while I showered. She was determined not to let me skip this meeting, no matter how much I wanted to. Despite my protests, I dressed, did my hair and makeup, and walked out the door. Because of her determination, we arrived thirty minutes early, and I decided to get another coffee — maybe a shot if I could find a place willing to do that sort of thing this early in the morning — because I was going to need it to make it through what awaited me on the other side of that door.

I have successfully avoided it for the past week, and I'd do anything to keep things that way for a few extra minutes. This new client is a friend-of-a-friend of none other than Finnley Sheffield, and something tells me he will show up to the meeting today. He gave me a few days before he tried to contact me, but when I saw his name flash across my screen the first time, I hit ignore. Then I blocked him. Was it childish? Probably. Did I care? Nope. I know I said I would talk to him, and I will, but I need more time to figure out where we go from here.

"Oat milk latte," the barista calls out setting a black to-go cup on the counter. Refreshing my email for the millionth time, I step up to the counter and reach for it without looking.

"That's mine," a man says behind me.

That voice. There's no way.

I look up from my phone to meet the stormy eyes of my ex-husband. Instinctively, I take a step back. Great, just great. I needed this run-in like a hole in the head. What are the chances David would be at the same coffee shop in Brooklyn today? Apparently, pretty damn great. "What are you doing here?"

"Barnes had a meeting in the city."

The barista sets another cup on the counter, "Oak milk latte." Before I can, David grabs both coffees and thanks the barista. He moves away from the counter leaving me with two options — follow him or pay for a new one. A glance at my watch tells me I don't have time for either option, but I don't have time to wait in the line that has now formed.

"I'm glad I ran into you." David uses his back to open the door and holds it open for me. I don't have time for this shit. I will be unprofessionally late if I don't leave in the next ten seconds. I reach for the coffee, but he keeps it just out of reach.

"I don't know what game you're playing, but I don't have time for it. I have a meeting in ten minutes and I can't be late. I'm signing the papers on Thursday. You can have the—"

"That's actually what I wanted to talk to you about."

"Have your attorney call mine," I say and snatch the coffee from him. "I can't do this rig—"

"I want to get back together."

My grasp falters, sending the cup plummeting to the

ground, but David is quick to grab it before it hits the sidewalk and ruins my brand-new pants. "I'm sorry, I must be hearing things," the words fall out in a stutter. "Did you say you want to get back together?"

David hands me the coffee once again with a sheepish smile. "Is that so hard to believe?"

"Um, a little, yeah." My phone vibrates in my hands, and without looking, I know it's Caitlin.

"Look, I know you were seeing someone, but I thought— Well, I don't know." David sighs running his fingers over the lid of his coffee cup. "I thought maybe you'd be open to at least talking."

My phone begins to vibrate again and I know I have two options — one, go to the meeting and risk seeing Finn, or two, tell Caitlin to handle it and let David explain himself. "Hello?" I answer the phone.

"Where are you?" Caitlin asks.

"Cait, something came up. I'm not going to make it."

"What do you mean? Michaela, you need to be here, this is—"

"Can you please handle it? I have to deal with something. Call me when you're done, and we can—"

"Michaela," Caitlin sighs. Her voice lowers when she speaks again, "I know you don't want to see Finn, but you're going to have to face this at some point."

"It's not because of him," I say meeting David's stare. "Just handle it."

A toothy grin spreads across David's face when I hang up, "I take it you're free?"

# forty-three

*Finn*

**MY STOMACH PLUMMETS WHEN** Caitlin follows behind Meredith *alone.* She briefly glances at me flashing a quick smile before turning back to Meredith, who continues to babble about what she wants this space to "represent." Caitlin makes confirming noises and nods at all the right times taking notes and drawing small sketches on a pink legal pad. I hang back a few steps, hoping that her partner is running late. As time ticks by, it becomes obvious she isn't coming. I shouldn't be surprised; it's been a week since she left my condo. She has done everything to avoid me, including blocking my number and putting me on the blacklist at her building. When I tried to stop by a few days ago, her doorman regretted to inform me that I was no longer allowed in the building. I considered showing up at DV Designs, but Nina would kill me if I caused a scene there. However, just because I couldn't show up at the office didn't mean I couldn't show up for the meeting with the client I gave them. I'm guessing Michaela had the same idea, which is why she sent Caitlin solo.

"What do you think, Finnley?" Meredith asks from the

other side of the space.

"Say again, Mere." I move closer to them and notice the sketch on Caitlin's notepad of a wall that doesn't currently exist closing off the kitchen from the rest of the space.

"Were you even listening?"

"Of course. You want to add a wall to the room, but I think that will eliminate that open feeling you have going on. I thought that's what you liked about the place?"

"Well, I do, but—"

"I can do a few different mockups to give you an idea of what different plans would look like," Caitlin says.

"Why don't you ask Caitlin what *she* would do with the space?" I suggest earning an eye roll from Meredith. "Wasn't that the whole point of this meeting? You wanted a professional opinion of what should be done."

"Yes, but—"

"So, let the professional do her job."

Thomas warned me that Meredith might be a challenge; she had already run off two different contractors because she couldn't commit to anything. They would start work on one idea, and she would get a wild hair up her ass wanting to change things as soon as they started. When she said something about hiring a professional designer, Thomas mentioned I might have an in with one of the top designers in the country.

"Well, you promised me Davina, this isn't Davina," Meredith says looking Caitlin up and down.

"I promise, Caitlin is more than capable," I say earning a grateful smile. "Neither Davina nor Michaela would send someone incapable of handling such a high-profile project."

Meredith glares at me for a moment before rolling her eyes and turning to Caitlin. "Fine, what would *you* do with the space?"

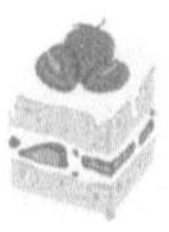

Knox scrapes the plastic spoon along the wall of the paper cup to get every last drop of the chocolate chip gelato. There hasn't been much conversation today — neither of us seems to be in a talkative mood, but that didn't stop us from devouring a cup of gelato with an extra scoop each. However, I wish we had picked a different spot to indulge in our desserts because sitting on the steps of the Met is the last place I want to be right now.

"What's got you in such a mood today?" Knox asks.

"I'm fine. What's your deal?"

"I asked first," he says sucking the last of his gelato off the spoon. "Michaela finally break up with you or something?" It's meant to be a joke, but his tone turns serious when I don't laugh along. "Wait, did she?"

"Knox—"

"What did you do?" His outburst causes a few heads to turn in our direction.

"Keep your voice down, would you? The entire city doesn't need to know about it." I sigh, letting my folded hands fall between my knees. The gray clouds rolling in above us look a little extra puffy. They cover the sun bringing a cool breeze with them. We should start heading North before it rains, but I hate to rush him.

"What happened? I thought things were going well. Last week, you said—"

"Yeah, well, things changed."

"What changed?"

"Just things. Look," I check my watch, "we should probably start heading towards your place. It's getting kind of late and about to rain."

"Finn—"

"I won't talk to you about this, Knox." I stand from my place on the steps, and the building looms over me. I can't be here any longer. "My problems aren't your problems. You have your own stuff to worry about."

"I liked her," he says looking up at me.

"Yeah, me too, kid." I reach my hand out to him. "Now, c'mon, let's go before the sky opens up." Looking up at the sky, he finally takes my hand, and I pull him to his feet.

We walk down the steps in silence, but it doesn't last long. Knox pushes the topic further, "So, why don't you try to get her back?"

"She wants to be left alone, Knox."

"How do you know?"

"I just do."

"Doesn't seem very Finn Sheffield of you to give up this easy."

"I'm not giving up," I say hailing a cab. "Not yet. I'm just giving her some space." When Michaela didn't show up today, I took that as my sign to wait until next weekend. We'd be in the same place to celebrate Nick and Nina's wedding, and she wouldn't be able to avoid me all weekend. I'd wait until after the wedding, of course, because I wouldn't take away from Nick and Nina, but I refused to let Michaela leave without talking to me.

# *forty-four*

## *Michaela*

**BUTTERFLIES ERUPTED IN MY** stomach the second the cab stopped in front of SoHo House Chicago, and they have only gotten more irritated as the elevator doors finally draw open. My feet drag, my body trying to avoid the conversation awaiting me on the other side of the door at the end of the hall. She's going to have questions, a lot of them. I don't have the answers — I'm still trying to process it myself. So much has happened in the last two weeks.

I contemplate turning and running when I reach the door, but I can't. I have to do this. A moment after I knock, the door swings open to reveal Nina with the phone pressed to her ear, "Mic! What are you doing here?"

I chew on the corner of my bottom lip, "I need to talk to you."

Her smile falters slightly recognizing my tone of voice. "Fossette," Nina says into the phone before relaying some message in Italian alongside my name. She retreats into the room to grab her blazer from the arm of the couch. "Sì, sì, sì," she agrees after a moment, "ti amo." She hangs up and turns to me. "I was about to grab some dinner. You hungry?"

"Nin, I—"

"I have a feeling this conversation is going to call for carbs and wine. Am I wrong?" I swear she can see right through me. When I don't respond, she nods. "Thought so."

As the waitress walks away, the pit reforms in my stomach. It feels like deja vu sitting across from Nina, the quirk of her eyebrow beckons me to start the conversation, but I suddenly feel nauseous. I hate the thought of disappointing her more than I already have. Isn't that why I'm here? To avoid doing just that. "I'm leaving the company," it comes out as a whisper. I almost don't hear myself, but I know she does from her sigh.

She swirls the red liquid in her glass. "I wanted to talk to you about that."

"You decided to go ahead and fire me?"

Nina laughs, "No. No, not firing you. Listen, I love having you work on designs, but Mic, I know you're not happy. You did a great job with Finn; the change of pace was everything you needed to get back on your feet. I think you'd be happy working full-time at Villa Inc. That's what Kai and I wanted to discuss in the meeting you postponed. We wanted to offer you a consulting or developmental team position."

"No."

Nina's head tilts ever so slightly like she's trying to make sure she heard right. "No?"

"I'm leaving, as in everything...DV Designs...Villa Incorporated...New York."

"You're leaving New York." She repeats my statement and her eyes narrow slightly tossing the idea around her mind.

"And *where* are you going?"

The words get stuck in my throat, but I force it out. "Washington."

Nina takes a long sip of her wine, "What's in Washington?"

"Nina—"

"Michaela. What's in Washington?" She annunciates each word perfectly.

"David," I whisper and half expect her to react, but she doesn't. Her fingers trace the rim of the glass as she lets his name sink in.

"Michaela…"

"He's my husband, Nina. I need to—"

"You were in love with Finn not even two weeks ago," Nina says and I roll my eyes.

"I wasn't in love with him."

"We'll pretend that's true," she scoffs. "You expect me to believe you're happily going back to David because of a stupid misunderstanding with Finn? That doesn't make sense!"

"Y'all keep telling me I need to grow up, right?" Everyone, including Nina, has been telling me I need to grow up. Consistently late to work? Grow up. Hiding things from everyone about my personal life? Grow up. Sneaking around with my brother's best friend? Grow up. Everything led back to one thing… I needed to grow up. Running into David seemed like fate working its magic when I was trying to decide what growing up looked like. "That's what I'm doing. For better or worse, Nina — that's what David and I promised each other, and the adult thing would be to honor that. This thing with Finn has been—"

"He left you, Michaela!" There's a small silence after her outburst, and Nina takes it to recenter herself. She takes a deep breath and continues in a quieter tone, "David left you, and he's been a total dick since. Now he wants to come crawling back, and for what? What is he getting out of this?"

"It's not like that, he…"

"No?"

"…missed me. Being apart made him realize he was wrong."

Nina scoffs. "And somehow, you're back in the same impossible situation as before, except this time, you're going to do whatever he wants — example, moving to Washington."

"Being there is the only way this is going to work."

"Oh, stronzata!" I swear her entire body goes into the eye roll. "That's bullshit, Michaela, and you know it. You've worked your ass off to get where you are. Even if you leave the company, you could get a job anywhere."

"That includes Washington."

"Are you going to get a job in Washington?" The question hangs between us. "All it takes is one phone call, and you'll have a job tomorrow."

"I don't need you to do that."

"But I would." Nina touches my hand gently. "Michaela, what are you going to do in Washington?"

"I don't know yet, but I'll figure something out."

Nina scoffs and licks her lips. "Why do you have to make all the sacrifices for this relationship to work?"

"He's making sacrifices, too."

"Name one."

My fingers instinctively reach for the metal heart dangling from my neck. What is he sacrificing? I can't think of one thing. I'm selling the condo. Leaving my job. Leaving my friends. Packing up everything and moving to D.C. I'm doing all of it with the knowledge that my life is about to do a complete one-eighty because that's what he wants. What he's always wanted. If this marriage is going to work, Washington is where I have to be. Short term pain for long-term gain. Once the dust settles, I'll start looking for a job, there has to be *something* out there that I can do.

"Exactly." Nina reaches for her phone. I hadn't even

realized it had been vibrating between us. She checks the name and contemplates answering before double-clicking the side button setting it upside down. "Look, if you want to throw away everything you've worked for to be with someone ready to throw you away like a doll he was tired of playing with, be my guest. Don't expect the rest of us to be happy about it."

"I can't just walk away, Nina."

"Two weeks ago, you were on the road to divorce. You were dating Finn. *Finn Sheffield.* A man who doesn't open up to anyone. Who helped you grow out of the rut you've been stuck in. Now, you want me to believe you're going to live happily ever after with the man who put you there? Who has been treating you like shit for the last five months! Over a fucking engagement ring and selling your condo."

"He's my husband," I sigh unable to look her in the eye. "You should understand what that means."

She swirls the red liquid in her glass, "David is no better than Brina."

"Oh, please. That's a little unfair, don't you think?" It was unfair. David didn't cheat on me. He didn't date any of my exes. He wasn't a terrible person, he just liked things a certain way. There's nothing wrong with that. Nina likes things a certain way, too.

"Did you know he was dating someone else, too? Someone named Karina Miller."

Of course, he'd run back to her. Karina was his high school sweetheart, the girl he always went back to when things didn't work out with any of his other girlfriends. She's the girl his mother wanted him to marry. It doesn't surprise me he'd run back to her. I pinch the bridge of my nose, "Nina, for the love of God, Please tell me you didn't have him investigated."

"Something seemed off." Nina shrugs nonchalantly. Of course, she doesn't see an issue with it. She never does. "Michaela, they've been together practically since the day the divorce was filed. Don't you find it a little weird he was dating someone else until he asked you to get back together?"

Yes.

"No."

Nina shakes her head, "You're smarter than that, Mic.

"Nin, I—"

"Michaela—"

"You're not listening to me! Nina, it doesn't matter what you say, I'm doing this. I'm giving this another shot. I owe it to my marriage, to David, to me."

"You're running away. You're scared of what you had with Finn, so you're choosing to—"

"Nina! Damnit!" I interrupt her, and it comes out harsher than I mean it to, but fuck…she's not listening to me. Taking a deep breath, I massage my temples an ache beginning to form between my eyes. "I love you. I appreciate everything you have done for me, but for the sake of our friendship, you have to let me do this." I sigh and meet her unwavering stare as she swirls the glass on the table between us. "You have always been there for me, making sure I don't fall on my ass, protecting me. You gotta let me make my *own* decisions or mistakes. Whatever this is, you have to let me do this. I need to prove to myself, to you, to everyone, that I can be grown up."

She starts to say more, but stops and downs the rest of the wine her glass in one sip. "Fine," she says. "If this is what you really—"

"It is."

"Then I support you, regardless if I agree or not." Nina stands from her seat and goes to the bar mumbling something along the lines of needing another drink.

"I need this to stay between us," I say stepping through the front door of SoHo House. "I don't want this getting around, not yet. And, if you tell Nick, he's going to tell Josh, and Josh is going to tell—"

"I thought you were going to be to be an adult about this," Nina says a few steps behind me. When I turn around, the knot in my stomach lessens noticing the smirk on her lips. She's teasing me.

"What will you tell Nick when he asks why I showed up in Chicago?"

"That you missed me, duh."

"I have missed you." It's true. I do miss her. I didn't realize how much until recently. Nina and I have been friends for ten years, and before the move, we were together almost every day. We have barely seen each other since I moved to New York, and when we do, it's usually work-related. Sure, we grab dinner afterward, but it hasn't been the same.

"At least you'll be a little closer in Washington." A black SUV pulls up to the curb. I'm grateful she was loaning me her car for the trip back to the airport. I was not looking forward to the cab bill out of downtown. Her features are more serious when she turns back to me, "I promise I won't say anything, only if you promise to do it as soon as the wedding is over."

I nod accepting her terms. I couldn't ask anything more of her. A silence falls between us and that knot forms in my stomach again. "Nin, I'm doing the right thing, right?"

"I can't answer that for you, Michaela. Only you can decide what's right for you."

"But—"

"Are you having second thoughts?"

Yes.

"No," the lie rolls off my tongue easier than it should. But, isn't it normal to second guess a decision like this? To be afraid of the unknown.

"Then, I'd say you're doing the right thing." She greets the driver before turning back to me. "Everyone is going to have something to say about this, Michaela," she warns. "Regardless of what anyone thinks, you have to do what is best for you."

"And do the grown-up thing at the same time."

"The grown-up thing," she shakes her head with a soft smile. "Oh, Mic. I love you, even when you get on my last nerve."

"I love you too, Nin."

"Good, then don't bring David to my wedding."

I laugh, "Wasn't even an option."

# Part Three

*You're gonna make it.*

*- Psalm 23*
*(simplified)*

## forty-five

## Michaela

**"THIS IS THE NASTIEST** combination, who thinks of this?" I grimace as Raeanne crosses the threshold of the suite.

"Davina Villa, that's who," Rae laughs. She clings to a bottle of Dom Perignon and two bags of Chick-fil-A trying not to get any grease on her dress. Grease and chiffon don't mix well.

"Where have you been? She's about ten seconds from ripping my head off."

"I had to wait for the food, it's a Saturday! Do you know how busy CFA is on a Saturday afternoon?"

"If only she had decided to get married on a Sunday."

Raeanne stifles a giggle as we walk into the living room of the enormous suite. The living room boasts one-eighty-degree views of the Alderidge estate grounds and the surrounding mountains. Vintage-style floral paper covers the top half of the walls, met with warm mahogany wainscoting. A deep navy-colored couch with cream toile pillows sits across a coffee table from two khaki armchairs. A new desk made to look old with a cream chair behind the couch is littered with last-minute Villa Inc. things she had been working on this morning. I swear, the woman never stops working. An oversized oriental rug sits beneath it all covering the deep mahogany floor. A kitchen off the living area features a breakfast bar with navy bar stools — it's built out of the same wood as the wainscoting, and the wallpaper carries over. Navy drapes have been drawn to allow the October sun to warm the room. A glow surrounds Nina as she stands in the center and thumbs the pendant around her neck. Her long dark hair loosely braided has been pulled back into a bun, with a golden leaf headdress resting on top. She pushes a stray piece of hair from her eyes weaving across the letters on the page in her hands. "Everything okay, Nin?" Raeanne asks when Nina wipes a tear from her cheek.

"Nick wrote her a letter," Romy says walking out of the bedroom.

"I don't know how I got this lucky." Nina folds the note and tucks it in her purse on the breakfast bar. "You have the stuff?"

"What are we, drug dealers?" I joke as Raeanne raises the goods in the air, and a smile spreads across Nina's burgundy lips. I pop the champagne and let bubbles fill the flutes before handing one to the bride as she shoves a chicken nugget in her mouth. "Seriously, what made you think Chick-fil-A and champagne was a good idea?"

"You're not pregnant, are you?" Rae asks. She's joking, but under normal circumstances, I'd probably think the same.

Nina's body stiffens. You'd hardly notice if you weren't looking. She recomposes herself. "Alcohol," Nina says raising the glass of champagne to her lips.

"Nina!" Elizabeth's voice carries down the hall. "Please tell me you're ready. It's 2:45."

"Shit!" Nina downs the rest of the bubbles.

"I'll go help." Romy follows her into the bedroom muttering something in French. I was surprised when she walked into dinner on Thursday, not because she was here, but because she was with Enzo. Yes, Enzo Vitali, co-owner of Bacami

Estate! Elizabeth said they've been seeing each other. They hit it off when we visited back in May. Nick later confirmed that he told me they were in New York a few weeks ago — a fact I must have completely glazed over considering everything that has happened.

I hand Elizabeth a glass of champagne and fall on the couch with a heavy sigh. This weekend has been nonstop, I don't know how Nina is still standing. From the moment we arrived Thursday afternoon, we've had a full schedule — "we," meaning Nina and the girls. From spa trips, salon trips, vineyard tours, hikes, and multiple meals a day…our schedule has been packed. I'm not sure how Nick and the guys managed to get out of it, but I'm kind of jealous. I shouldn't complain, it has kept me away from Finn. I haven't seen or talked to Finn in a little over two weeks, I was sure he was going to jump at the opportunity to talk, but he's kept his distance. I'm not sure if I'm more disappointed or relieved about that fact.

*Relieved.*

That's the right answer. David and I are back together. He was a little disappointed I wouldn't wear my ring this weekend. He understood why I couldn't though, I think. I'm not supposed to want Finn to talk to me.

After the rehearsal dinner last night, the bride and groom treated the wedding party to a night out, resulting in only a few hours of sleep before the makeup and hair team arrived this morning. Once again, something the guys didn't have to worry about. Lucky bastards.

"You okay, MJ?" Elizabeth breaks through the light sleep I've been drifting in and out of and I notice Eileen and Lydia have finally joined us.

"Where is she?" Eileen asks. "We have to get going."

"Getting dressed," I yawn, "she's been too busy crying."

"It hasn't even started yet," Lydia laughs and pours champagne for them.

"Nick wrote her a letter," Raeanne explains trying to stifle her own yawn.

"And if he messes up Sarah's work she'll kill him," Elizabeth grumbles.

The double doors swing open to reveal Romy with a proud smile and twinkle in her eye. "May I introduce Mrs. Villa-Davis."

When she steps aside, I feel a prick in the corner of my eyes watching Nina glide through the threshold. The chiffon boatneck dress has a short train that trails behind her bare feet. Long flowing sleeves end a few inches above her wrists with ivory lace trimmings that match the outline of the backless design. She looks like a Greek goddess. (Sorry, Italian. Roman? You get the idea).

"You look stunning," Eileen smiles.

"If Nick doesn't cry, I'm suing," Lydia jokes behind her glass.

"Hush," Nina laughs and steals another fry. She pulls her shoes from the box on the table — red-bottomed stilettos, ivory-colored mesh houses a simple floral pattern, and the heel wrapped in suede. "You guys, I'm nervous. I know we've been married for two years, but... What if I mess up?"

"You're gonna be fine," I reassure her holding out my hand so she can step into the second shoe. "You've already done it, and besides, we're all gonna be up there with you."

"Your brother is waiting," Eileen looks up from her phone, "impatiently, might I add. You ready?"

Nina lifts a finger and downs the rest of her champagne, taking a deep breath. "Okay, now I'm ready."

I meet the nervous stare of my cousin at the end of the aisle and give him a reassuring smile as his brother squeezes his shoulder. The groomsmen wear burgundy bow ties and pocket squares to match our dresses. I'm extremely grateful they didn't pair us to walk down the aisle. My partner would have been Finn and I'd like to avoid any kind of interaction a little longer. A subtle movement near the end of the groomsmen line catches my attention. Even though I tell myself not to, I meet his stare and he offers me a soft smile, the slightest uptick in the corner of his mouth, but I don't return it. I turn and take my place next to Eileen. Elizabeth follows, giving Nick a thumbs up before taking her place as Matron-of-Honor.

There's a moment of silence, and I swear I hear Nick's heart beating before the melody shifts. He straightens and pulls his lips between his teeth as his wife steps into view, when their eyes meet, he visibly relaxes. A wide smile stretches his face matching the one on her own.

God, I want what they have.

Nina tosses her head back laughing at something Kai whispers for only her to hear. "Shut up," she giggles a few steps from the altar.

"Take care of her," Kai warns handing his sister over.

"Always," Nick answers, never taking his eyes off her. She wipes the corner of his eye, and he kisses the back of her hand. "You look beautiful."

"Looks like you won't have to sue," I hear Rae whisper to Lydia earning a giggle from the bridesmaids.

"You're not so bad yourself," Nina whispers and they turn to face the priest.

I should be paying attention to the ceremony, but my mind wanders to the man on the other side of the aisle. The countdown is on. I promised Nina I would tell him about David — tell everyone about David —after the wedding, and I have to keep that promise. David is handling everything in

New York. I've let him take the lead, it's easier that way. The condo is already on the market as of Thursday, and he says there is an open house today. My personal things have been packed up and shipped to Washington, but he decided to sell the condo furnished since he has everything we need. When I leave here, I'll be going straight to Washington.

"The couple has prepared their own vows they'd like to share," the priest interrupts my thoughts.

"If someone had told me when we were younger that we would be here, I would've told them they were insane," Nick starts. "You have helped me grow so much in the last few years. I wish you had asked me to be your fake boyfriend sooner," Nick says and I can practically see the whole body eye roll from Nina. "I'm so grateful for you and your love. You've helped me learn to open myself up to the unknown. You've taught me how to love again. Just the thought of you makes me smile. I promise to always love you, even when you're stubborn and thick-headed."

"I thought this supposed to be nice," Nina laughs.

"I'm getting there," Nick teases. "I know things won't always be easy, but being able to wake up every morning knowing I have you by my side makes it worth it. I promise to always support you, honor you, and love you unconditionally. I love you so much, Dee."

Nina wipes under her eyes, laughing. "I was trying to get through this without ruining my makeup. Sarah is going to kill you."

Nick kisses her cheek.

"We're not there yet," the priest whispers, earning a laugh from the audience.

Nina takes a deep breath before she begins, "Nicholas, I'm sorry I have always been stubborn, whether at home or work. I wish I could tell you it will change, but—"

"It won't."

"No, it won't." She shakes her head. "Asking you to go to Haven was one of the best decisions I ever made, even if I didn't think so initially. I was scared we wouldn't be able to pull it off, but I guess we pulled it a little *too* well."

"You think?" I mumble earning a look from both bride and groom.

"Sometimes, I wish things had worked out differently, that we had known each other in high school or stayed in touch at Rosecliffe. I wonder what our lives would be like had that been the case. The truth is, I wouldn't change a thing. We are right where we're meant to be."

"I don't think things would've worked out in school if Alex had anything to say about it."

Alex blushes, "Shut up, dude."

"You don't always believe me when I say it, but Nick, you are the most amazing man," Nina sighs. "You have the biggest heart and the most giving spirit. I can't wait to spend the rest of my life with you, to start a family, and experience the world together. I love your loyalty to me and our relationship. It's something I've never experienced before. I promise to work on my patience, even if it means having to hold my tongue, to always support you, honor, and love you unconditionally."

Well, that proves it, I'll never have what they have.

*forty-six*

## Michaela

**STRING BULB LIGHTS ILLUMINATE** the front lawn of the Alderidge Estate — it looks more like a fairy tale castle you'd find in France than the Blue Ridge Mountains of North America. It's one of the largest homes in the country built by the Alderidge family as a summer home over one hundred years ago. Underneath a large chandelier, several guests glide across the dance floor, others sit at tables and lounge areas scattered across the lawn. I sway to the beat of a slow tune with the groom. "So, what's it like?"

"What?" Nick asks.

"Officially being a married man."

"It wasn't official before?" He laughs, but he's not wrong. Their city hall wedding over two years ago wasn't what anyone would have predicted, especially not from Nina, but I think it's the best thing they ever did. "She's my best friend," his stare moves behind me to find his wife. "It couldn't be any better than that."

"I'm happy for you guys. I'm just glad I was able to witness it finally."

"I couldn't wait for her to plan it," Nick shrugs. "I mean, look how long this one took."

"I think we all forgive you after the weekend we've had."

"Would you have expected any less?"

"Absolutely not," I laugh, but it fades when I meet Finn's stare from the edge of the dance floor. He stands with Josh and Dean half-listening to their conversation. Damn, he looks good.

"Why don't you talk to him?" Nick asks looking to see what caught my attention.

"I'd rather shit bricks."

"A little dramatic, but okay." Nick spins me under his arm.

"There is nothing more to say."

"I'd say there's quite a bit. You guys seemed to get along pretty well, there was just some miscommunication."

"Well, none of it matters anymore," I scoff.

Nick shakes his head with a small chuckle, "Did you ever ask him why he was doing it?"

"One would assume you're starting a business because you want to, not because you *have* to. Not because if you don't, you'll lose your inheritance and way of life."

"I'm just saying, you and Finn—"

"Nick," I stop him. "Not everyone can be you and Nin, okay? We can't all have an epic love story."

"Now you're really being dramatic. Stop putting us up on some pedestal, Mic. You can't always compare yourself to us, to Nina."

I roll my eyes.

"I'm serious, Michaela. If you would just talk to him, I'm sure you could figure it out."

"I don't think it's that easy. Besides, things have gotten more complicated the past few weeks."

Is complicated the right word?

"What's that supposed to mean?" He asks, brows raised.

My shrug isn't the answer he wants, but he doesn't have time to push because a manicured hand grips his arm.

"Mind if I cut in?" Nina asks with a knowing smile.

"I wasn't finished," Nick argues.

"Yes, you are. There will be no more interrogations tonight."

"But—"

"I will fill you in when we don't have an audience," Nina says kissing him lightly. "It's time for the last bit of fun before we leave, and then real fun begins." She winks at her husband before wiggling her eyebrows.

I fake a gag. "You guys are disgusting," I say earning a small smile from my savior.

"Is this the part where I go up your dress in front of everyone?" Nick asks pulling her close a smirk tugging at the corner of his mouth.

"Don't be such a perv." Nina smacks his chest playfully.

"I haven't had enough alcohol for either of these conversations." I quickly take the opportunity to escape before the DJ welcomes the single ladies to meet in the middle of the dance floor. I find my way to the bar ordering a new glass of wine.

"Shouldn't you be out there?" Warmth blooms across my skin when I hear *his* voice. I refuse to look at him as he leans casually against the bar as the bartender pushes the glass my way.

"Shouldn't you?" I reply from behind the glass.

"You've been avoiding me."

"Great observation, Sheffield. You went into the wrong business, you should've started a private detective service, instead. You have the pretending part down."

His hand grips my arm when I try to walk away. His touch sends a shock through my system. "I wasn't pretending, Shortcake."

*Shortcake.*

My resolve melts a little at the nickname.

"It never came up, and maybe that's my fault, but I didn't think it mattered."

"Of course, it mattered, Finn!" The outburst catches the attention of a few guests nearby, but they're not the only ones — my brother's narrowed eyes from the edge of the dance floor dare me to cause a scene.

"Come with me." Finn grips my hand pulling me into the night.

# *forty-seven*

## *Finn*

**"FINN, STOP." MICHAELA TRIES** to free her hand from mine, but I continue down the path around the side of the mansion and into the garden. God, this place is so big. Why is it so big? It feels like we've walked a mile before the sounds from the party begin to blend with the night. "Would you please let go?" She asks again, but I maintain my hold, my thumb grazing across the skin on the back of her hand. "What do you want?"

"I didn't lie."

"You can't be serious," her scoff cuts through me and I release her hand when she tries to pull away again. I didn't lie, though. And, I wasn't hiding anything. It wasn't like I was going to walk around with a big sign saying: *Will work to save my inheritance.*

"You never asked, Michaela. I would've told you."

"No, you wouldn't. You barely spoke to me when we first started. You weren't ever going to tell me the truth or you would've come clean when we started dating. This was all to keep your inheritance intact. Nothing more. You only did it because Daddy was going to cut you off."

"Was the initial reason to save my own skin? Yes. I don't deny that, I never have. But it's not the only reason I started Sheffield House."

"Finn, I don't care. Okay? It doesn't matter. You got what you wanted and then some. You got your money back and some ass while doing it. Sleeping with me was just a bonus, right?"

"No! Michaela—"

"Something to wet your whistle until you could get back to the big leagues."

"That is not true, Shortcake." I brush a strand of hair that had fallen into her face and cradle her cheek. A slight tug on the corner of my lips when she leans into my touch. "I want this, I want you. Fuck everything else. I'd let it all go if it meant you'd give me another chance."

"David asked me to reconsider the divorce." The words tumble out at a rapid speed and her confession sits between us briefly before it starts to sink in. Reconsider the divorce? She can't be serious. My hand falls from her cheek taking a step back. She no longer looks me in the eye when she says, "He wants to try again."

"You cannot be that stupid." I regret it the second I say it. Her blue eyes shine in the moonlight — tears filled with hurt and disappointment. *Shit.* I shouldn't have said that. Saying that makes me no better than Asshole. I want nothing more than to pull her in my arms and beg her not to do this. She can't do this. Instead, I keep my hands stuffed in my pockets. The comforting job is no longer my responsibility; it's reserved for another man.

"You're an asshole," she hisses.

"I'm an asshole?" I scoff and look toward the Heavens for some kind of answer. All I receive is a twinkle of a nearby star. "You're telling me, David gets a pass to be a narcissist for four-fucking-years, but when I call you out—"

"He's still my husband," Michaela cries. "Finn, I'm sorry, but we have so much history and–"

"You know what, Michaela? I get it."

Except, I don't get it. I don't understand how she could even consider going back to that asshole. I guess it's not for me to understand. As long as she does, that's all that matters. At least, that's what I'm going to tell myself.

"I want you to be happy." I lean in close, our faces mere inches apart, and I can hear the small hitch of her breath. "Is getting back together with your ex-husband going to make you happy?"

"He's not my ex-husband," she stutters. I'm certain there's a tinge of red in her cheeks, but it's too dark to tell.

"Pretty damn much." She takes a step back into the stone wall when my voice rises, and I pinch the bridge of my nose. "Is that going to make you happy, Michaela?" I look up to meet her gaze. It's wavering and conflicted. It tells the truth even though she won't. This isn't what she wants, and I know it, she knows it, but she's too damn stubborn to admit it. I take the two steps between us, caging her against the wall with my arms, and lean in, my breath on her lips. "Is it?"

Michaela hesitates.

Her lips barely brush against mine and I'm about to close the gap between us...

I step back.

"You'd like that, wouldn't you, Shortcake?" I shake my head. "You want me to kiss you, to make the decision *for* you. I'm not going to make it easy on you this time, Michaela. You wanna know something? Old me would have fucked you up against this wall in front of the entire guest list." Her breathing ragged as if I had done just that. "But I'm not going to do that, and I will not make this decision for you. You want to say you've grown up?" I lean forward, my lips ghosting the shell of her ear earning a small whimper. "Prove it." I pull away and turn on my heel without looking back.

I hasten my steps through the garden trying to get out as fast as possible, everything in me screams to turn around. Go back into that garden to *show* her why this is not a good idea…

I can't believe she's going to do this — go back to David. Has she forgotten the past few months? Has she just erased everything he's said and done to her?

*He's still my husband.*

What a bullshit reason to—

"Dean, stop!" A feminine voice says and a giggle follows the soft command. "Someone could see us."

"Don't worry, sweetheart. No one is gonna come looking." Across the landscape, I see Dean catching up to a woman in a burnt orange colored dress.

"Not even that girl you were dancing with?"

"What girl?"

"That one bridesmaid."

"Rae?" He chuckles. "No, she's just my best friend."

I roll my eyes at Dean's antics. Of course, he's sneaking away with some girl. Too bad he can't see what's right in front of him. It's only a matter of time before Rae gets tired of his shit.

Dean pulls the girl close, but she whispers something and takes off again leaving him behind. He chuckles to himself before catching my eye. He smirks and shrugs with such nonchalantness, it makes me queasy. It reminds me of… Well, it reminds me of a younger me. I force a slight nod and keep moving.

"Where the fuck is Josh?" I mumble. I need to get out of here. Scratch that, I need to get a drink and then get out of here. I need to— "Shit! I'm so sorry, I— Nina?" Not exactly who I expected to see coming back from our little escapade, but I'm not entirely shocked either. I clear my throat and step back, "What are you doing out here? Shouldn't you be enjoying the final moments of your wedding?"

"Oh, I needed some air." Nina offers a knowing smile, "Care to join me?"

I want nothing more than to decline her offer and get out of here, but despite the growing pit in my stomach, I can't refuse. She takes my arm when I extend it and leads me alongside the garden's edge.

It's quiet for a beat until she asks, "You okay?"

"Of course, why would—"

"Finn, I know…about her and David." Of course, she does. It doesn't surprise me Michaela would tell her first. What does surprise me is how okay she seems about it. "She told me a few days ago. She was going to tell everyone else tomorrow."

"Why didn't you tell me, Nin?"

"It wasn't my place." Nina sighs, a sad smile tugging on her lips. "I wanted to, trust me, but… You have to let her do this. We all do."

Scratch that, maybe she's not okay with it.

She's right, I know she's right, but fuck if it doesn't hurt.

"He's just going to hurt her all over again," I sigh.

"Maybe." She pulls me into a tight hug, and tears start to form behind my eyes. I take a deep breath pulling them back from the surface before we part. "But, if he does, we'll be here to pick up the pieces." Nina squeezes my hand gently before glancing to her left, "Nick is over there if you want to say goodbye. Josh, too."

I press a quick kiss against her cheek. "Have fun on your trip, and try not to think about work."

"You try not to get into any trouble. I don't need any extra messes to clean up when I get back."

I raise my right hand, covering my pinkie with my thumb, "Scouts honor."

Nina chuckles and I expect her to join me in my return

to the party, but she stays in the same place waiting for me to leave and join the boys. She's waiting so she can return to the garden and find Michaela. Because while I have to walk away, Nina doesn't.

# forty-eight

## Michaela

FUCK.

*forty-nine*

*Michaela*

**THE ALARM BLASTS THROUGH** my phone speakers on the nightstand across the room, but I'm already awake. I have been most of the night. I spent about five hours tossing and turning before finally giving up. I made a cup of coffee and sat on the balcony overlooking the estate and the Blue Ridge Mountains. We have one more item on the wedding agenda — brunch — and I'm dreading it. The thought of facing Finn after last night… Facing my brother *knowing* Finn told him about David before I could. I know I should've told them before now, but this weekend was not supposed to be about me. It was supposed to be about Nick and Nina — the only way that would happen was if no one knew about my life change.

I stop the alarm and notice I have two text messages, both from David.

**David Reed**

**How was the wedding?**
**Did you tell Josh yet?**

**We have 3 offers.**

My stomach drops at the second message.

*Three offers.*

That means there's a good chance one of them is good enough to settle on. The reality of what that means hits me like a ton of bricks. Until this moment, I don't think I had fully accepted what putting the condo on the market meant. Or I wouldn't let myself accept it. Now that we're this close to accepting an offer...

A rush of warmth spreads through me. Blood pounds in my ears as my heart tries desperately to escape its cage. I try to take in a breath, but my airway is constricted, and there is a pallet of bricks on my chest. I force myself to walk the small distance between the bed and the balcony. I grip the railing. I try to take in a deep breath of fresh air, and it helps a little, but not enough. I lower myself onto the ground and plant my hands next to me soaking in the morning chill of the cement.

Deep breath in.

Deep breath out.

Repeat until the tightness in my chest begins to subside, and the warmth begins to dissipate, but now my body feels like it's vibrating. I close my eyes and take another deep breath. I haven't had an attack in a long time. It's only stress from the last few months finally reaching a head. I know after today it will get better. Things will be better...

After a few more breaths, I roll my shoulders trying to relieve some of the tension they hold. It doesn't work, but I have to get ready. Brunch starts in twenty minutes. I need a shower, I can't show up looking like I haven't slept all night — even if I didn't — or like I just had a mini freak out — even if I did.

"Has anyone seen Finn?" Dean plops down in the seat next to me stuffing a cheese Danish in his mouth. "I gotta talk to him about Christmas."

"I haven't seen him since the bouquet toss," Alex says from behind his coffee mug. Sunglasses hide his eyes from the brutal sunshine beating through the windows. He didn't slow down after I left last night. The proposal rejection is still eating away at him, but I can't say I blame him. Can't imagine it's easy seeing your brother re-marry his wife not long after you propose to your girlfriend, and she rejects you. I still can't believe she said no.

"Finn left last night," Josh answers from his place next to Alex not looking up from his plate.

Dean rolls his eyes. "What the hell for? We're supposed to hang out today." His eyes lock on Raeanne when she walks into the restaurant. He follows her every move, even tries to motion for her to sit next to him. She ignores him. She seems to be actively avoiding his stare even when she sits at the end of the table. Weird, normally she'd sit next to Dean.

"Had some family shit to take care of," is all Josh offers.

Family shit? Yeah, okay.

"Oh, Michaela, you're here?" Romy asks with a mimosa in hand and a smirk on her lips. Enzo pulls the chair next to Alex out for her. "I didn't think we'd see you."

"And, why's that?" I ask.

"Well, when you disappeared with Finn last night, I figured you'd be a little indisposed this morning."

Josh drops his fork catching everyone's attention. He pushes back from the table without a word. Conversations around the table have paused at the sudden commotion, all eyes on him as he walks out of the dining room.

"What was that about?" Dean whispers.

"I find it best not to ask anymore," Alex groans taking a large gulp of water.

Elizabeth sighs, folding her napkin, and she moves to follow him, but I stop her, "I got it."

Josh paces the edge of the patio. He tugs on the ends of his hair, shaggier than usual — his entire appearance is a little rougher than he usually keeps it. Has he looked like that all weekend? Did he look like this a few weeks ago? I can't remember. Have I been so busy worrying about Finn that I didn't even notice my brother looks like a complete mess?

"Josh—"

"Don't." He stops abruptly pointing a finger in my direction. "Don't you fucking start your bullshit, Michaela."

"My bullshit? You're the one acting like a child stomping away from the table like that."

"Unbelievable," he scoffs. "You're like a toddler who can't decide which toy she wants, so you just take them all until you're tired of them."

Yep, he definitely knows about David.

"I didn't mean for any of this to happen, Josh. I thought I was over David. I thought we were done. I mean, we *were* done, but then–"

"Forgive me if I don't give a fuck, Michaela Jane. You know, I thought Finn would be the one to hurt you, but turns out I was wrong. You're the one who ended up breaking his heart."

"Broke his heart?" I scoff. "Josh, do you hear yourself? A month ago you were pissed at the thought. Now you're defending him?"

"I'm tired of your shit. Don't fucking bring David around because I don't want anything to do with him or your 'marriage.'"

"He's my husband, Josh! That has to count for something."

"What makes you think this time will be any different?"

"You're choosing *him* over me?" I ask, but he doesn't say anything. "I'm your sister! Does that mean nothing to you?" He crosses his arms tightly over his chest, and his jaw clenches a little bit harder. "You're really choosing Finn? I'm back to the annoying kid sister left behind while you *once again* choose your friends over me. You don't want to include me in your shit, but you feel just guilty enough to let me stand on the sidelines and watch you with your perfect friends, in your perfect life, having your own perfect marriage… While I'm expected to be the good little girl who is seen and not heard — that's what you want, right?"

"You didn't answer the question, Michaela. What's going to be different?"

I don't know if it will be different. But what if it is? What if we're able to make it work? Doesn't that mean I owe it to our marriage – to the agreement we made – to try and make it work? "He's my husband."

"Y'know, Finn was wrong when he said you were *acting* stupid."

"Fuck you, Josh."

"Hey, can you two wrap it up?" Elizabeth steps out the door looking between us. Normally, she'd be able to calm the situation, bring us back to our senses and make us apologize to one another… Not today. Today, her presence only increases the tension. "Nick and Nina just got here."

"We're done." My brother finally rips his glare from me allowing it to soften when it lands on his wife. Wait, was that a hint of sadness? Maybe Mom was right. Maybe something is going on between them. His pace is quick as he retreats inside because we both know it's better if Nick and Nina don't know what's happening out here.

Elizabeth gently touches my arm, "You okay?" I nod with

a weak smile. "There have been quite a few...changes to digest recently. He's confused, we all are."

"So am I."

"I believe that." Her smile is genuine. "You need to do what's best for you, MJ. But, that doesn't make it any easier for your brother to see you go back to someone who hurt you so much. On top of being hurt that you didn't come to him with any of this."

I swallow the lump in my throat and try to ignore the stinging behind my eyes. She's right. I didn't go to my brother with any of this. I didn't go to her either. Elizabeth is the sister I always wanted growing up. I loved having my brother, and we were close, but I always wished I had someone like me, someone who could understand what it was like to be a girl. I'm not sure when it happened, but it feels like we've all been hiding things from each other.

"We want you to be happy. It's a little surprising, is all. You seemed adamant about Finn—"

"He lied, Elizabeth."

Her brow quirks. "All I'm trying to say is, if your happiness means trying again with David, then do that. But if that means signing the papers and moving on...do that."

# fifty

## *Finn*

### *ONE MONTH LATER*

**WALKING INTO THE HOUSE,** I immediately look for the one person who will make today bearable. I find him in the corner of the sitting room, scotch in hand as he speaks with one of Oliver's friends — Sam, I think? He looks relieved when we make eye contact and excuses himself from the conversation. "Thank God, you're here," Uncle Jack says. "I was starting to think you were going to bail on me."

"And let you have all the fun?"

"Where's your girlfriend? I was hoping to meet her after hearing about your parents' little run-in with her at the party. Sorry, I couldn't make it, by the way. I was caught up in London with—"

"We're not together anymore." I down the scotch from the bartender in one sip, offering a tight-lipped smile. "She decided to go back to her ex-husband."

"Well, that's good news." The sound of Oliver's voice makes every nerve stand on edge. Uncle Jack subtly shakes his head, signaling me not to start the fight. This is not the time or place, and it should be handled privately after the luncheon is over. He's right, this should be done without an audience. Rolling my shoulders, I turn to greet my father, and the amusement on his face reignites the flame I had dimmed seconds ago. "You can do better than sleeping with the help, son."

*"The help?"*

"That girl was just a convenient piece while you were busy putting your little project together. We all know it," he says. "We knew it wouldn't last. She was far too worried about fitting in, and that was never going to happen."

"Honey," Mother says and loops her arm through mine. "You'll never guess who I ran into the other day." She tries to pull me away from the scene, but my feet are planted. "Amanda! She is back and—"

"Is that what you said to her?" I ask never taking my eyes off my father.

"I didn't tell her anything other than the truth," he says with a simple shrug.

"You told her the only reason I started Sheffield House was the money! You told her—"

"Is that not the truth?" A smirk spreads across his face when I don't respond. "You did start this business solely because you—"

"Okay boys," Uncle Jack cuts in, "I think we need to move this to a more private place." He smiles at both of us motioning toward the crowd around us. Oliver huffs before turning to the eager guests wanting to see what happens next. "Excuse me, everyone. I need to have a quick conversation with my son. Lunch should be ready in just a few moments." Uncle Jack grips my shoulder and pushes forward when Oliver walks out of the sitting room toward the club.

The moment the door closes, my back is against the wall with a stubby finger in my face, "How *dare* you, boy." His blue eyes burn with a fury I know all too well, and suddenly, my anger disappears and I'm the same little kid who has always cowered to the man before him. The man who was supposed to protect him and love him. I look away from my father's fury, but he grips my chin roughly and forces me to meet it again. "Who do you think you are?"

"Oliver—"

"Jack, stay the fuck out of this," Oliver hisses without looking. "How dare you come into *my* house filled with *guests* and start a fight. Your mother has worked tirelessly to make this day perfect, and you come in here thinking you can ruin it. Absolutely not. You will go out there and *apologize* to her immediately."

"Yes, sir," I say between gritted teeth.

"Oliver, it wasn't that bad, you started—"

"Jack, I said stay *the fuck* out of it." Oliver turns back to me, "When everyone is gone, we will discuss how you're going to rectify this. Do you understand?"

I meet Uncle Jack's disappointed stare before turning back to my father, "Yeah."

"I'm sorry, what was that?"

"Yes, sir."

Satisfied, my father takes a step back from me and straightens himself, adjusting his suit before offering a nod and walking out of the room.

I finally release the breath I had been holding and scrub a hand down my face. I hate the way I turn back into the scared little boy who used to walk on eggshells trying not to set his father off. I'm a grown-ass man, for godsakes; I should be able to stand up for myself, tell him to fuck off... I never can, though. I do what I have to in order to survive and try to avoid the alternative.

"Finn—"

"Thank you for trying." I straighten my jacket and brush

invisible dust from the sleeves. "We should get out there, don't want to give them any more reason to talk."

Rejoining the party, I'm met with knowing glances telling me word of the family squabble in the sitting room has made its rounds and everyone has their idea of what happened. Mother stands with a group of friends, including Gladys, and her smile brightens when she sees me. "Oh Finn, darling! I'm glad you're feeling better. Your father said—"

"Yes," I say quickly. "I apologize for my display. It must have just been the lack of food." The women chuckle, and Mother loops her arm through mine excusing us from the group.

"Now, as I was saying, I ran into Amanda the other day and invited her to join us today."

"Mother—"

"I told her you would be so thrilled to see her. You just needed a little break, some time to get your head on straight. Now that you have your project complete, you'll have time—"

"Mother." I pull my arm from hers and take a step back. "I'm not getting back together with Amanda."

"Honey, she's cleaned herself up. She is—"

"I don't want Amanda."

"Oh, Finnley, is this about that Davis girl?" She waves her hand and tries to take my arm again, but I don't allow it. "Finnley, you will stop acting this way this instant."

"Michaela is—"

"The help. Nothing more. Those Davises are not meant for this world. I don't know what Davina sees in them. Brina is *appalled* by the way her daughter has handled everything since Alaric's death, and frankly, we are too."

"Are you fucking kidding me?" Mother reels back at my words, her brown eyes wide in appallment. "How dare you talk about them like that. Those *Davises* have been more of a family to me than the Sheffields ever have."

"Honey, they're just plain people; there's nothing wrong

with that."

"Everything okay over here?" Oliver clamps his hand down on my shoulder and gives it a hard squeeze.

"Of course, dear," she smiles at him. LIke she always does. Always turning her head to look the other way.

"Actually, I was just leaving," I say, stepping out from his grasp.

"Don't be silly," she says giving me a stern look. "You and I were just discussing how he intends to go speak with Amanda."

"I am not going to talk to her. I have nothing to say. And, you know what? You both can take your money and shove it where the sun don't shine."

"Finnley!" Hayley gasps.

Oliver pats me on the back, hard, and grips my shoulder again. He smiles looking around at the guests, who have started to stare before meeting my gaze. "Do we need to go have another conversation? I don't think the last one stuck."

The anxiety starts to creep into my veins, but this time I force it back. I swallow the massive lump in my throat and shrug his hand from my shoulder. "If this is what your family looks like, then I think we'd be better off strangers."

"This is what happens when you sleep with the help," Oliver scoffs. "You lose any lick of sense—"

"Michaela is not the help!" My outburst brings everything to a halt. "Michaela was not and is not the help. She did more in making Sheffield House what it is than I can ever repay her for and I will not let you speak about her that way."

"If she's so wonderful, then where is she? Oh, that's right, she left you for her ex-husband. I'm not sure if that says more about her or you."

"Sheffield!" A voice echoes across the gas station. Glancing over my shoulder, Nick and Josh walk toward me. "I didn't know you were in town," Josh says when he embraces me. I haven't seen him since the wedding over a month ago, I haven't seen any of them. I didn't tell Josh or Nick the truth before leaving the reception. I couldn't bring myself to do it. However, when I ran into Josh at the hotel before I left, and we had a drink. I may have slipped that his sister was going back to her soon-to-be ex-husband. And he may have had a few choice words.

"Yeah, I came in for the day. Oliver and Hayley requested my presence at the annual Thanksgiving luncheon. I'm about to head out, though. I'm supposed to help out at the center tomorrow afternoon."

"How'd that go with your parents?" Nick asks.

"I may or may not have told them to take their money and shove it up their ass." After Oliver was finished trying to decide who was more to blame for Michaela running back to David, he tried to drag me back into the club for another chat. When I refused, he started to lose his temper despite his guests being there. Somewhere between reminding me that no one wanted me and calling me an ungrateful brat that no one will ever love, I mustered up the biggest smile I could and told him I'd rather be alone than call him 'Dad' another second longer. "Things may get rough for a bit, but I'll be okay."

"They're not going to cut you off," Josh says.

"I have no doubt about it after today, but I don't care if they do. I made it without them while working on Sheffield House, I'll do it again."

"Going to be a little weird keeping the name Sheffield House now, isn't it?"

"Gives me the chance to redeem the name."

"I tried to call you last week to invite you to dinner," Josh says, "but I never heard back."

"I've been busy with the center, getting things ready for

the holidays. I meant to call you back, but time got away from me." That was true, but I also didn't call back because I didn't want an obligatory invite. I wasn't going somewhere I wasn't wanted. I didn't think I'd be welcome after what happened. I figured the wedding was the end even after my talk with Josh. I guess that's why I decided to attend the annual Sheffield Thanksgiving Luncheon. I wanted to feel part of some family, even if it meant dealing with Oliver. And well, after today, I don't think I'll be invited to any more luncheons, or Sheffield functions for that matter...

"Well, you're in town. Come to dinner," Nick suggests readjusting the case of beer in his hands. "We're doing it a day early since Nin and Kai have to be in New York tomorrow. Y'know, I could probably swing by the center while they're at their luncheon."

"You sure Nin will let you out of it?"

"Supporting the nonprofit she helped start or hanging out with a bunch of businessmen for lunch," he uses his hands to weigh the options before the one indicating the nonprofit wins by a landslide.

"Fair point. Well, I appreciate the dinner offer, but I don't think everyone there would enjoy my company at your Thanksgiving meal."

Their smiles fall before Josh says flatly, "She isn't gonna be there. Michaela will be spending her holidays in Montana from here on out."

"You say that like it's a permanent thing." The look on his face tells me I might just be right in that assumption. "You can't be serious."

"She's making it work, man." Josh shrugs. "I guess part of that means spending all the important days with his family."

Walking into the Villa-Davis house, I'm met with a chorus of various greetings, and it makes me regret not returning Josh's phone call. I would've hated to miss this. Without them, I'd be spending my holiday eating Thai take-out and watching some rerun of a show I've seen too many times.

"I'm glad you decided to come," Nina says wrapping me in a tight embrace, and I kiss her cheek.

"He didn't think he was welcome," Nick calls over his shoulder from the pantry.

"You're always welcome at the Villa-Davis household." Nina squeezes my arm before handing me silverware. "Now, go set the table. You can manage that, right?"

"Yes, ma'am." I salute before taking the silverware to the black farmhouse table in the bump out to the left of the kitchen. The sounds of holiday dinner preparations begin to fill the silence and wrap around me like a warm blanket.

"Who wants wine?"

"Is the turkey almost done?"

"Alex, get your feet off my table!"

"Dad, do you mind grabbing more firewood?"

"Ophelia, no cookies until after dinner."

"Nin, you guys have any tea around here?"

The Sheffield house was never filled with these kinds of sounds growing up; it was always quiet and cold. Hayley never made a meal. When I ate at home, it consisted of sandwiches — mostly peanut butter, and occasionally I got wild adding strawberry jam. If there was a meal at our house, it was always prepared by someone else. Come to think of it, Mother's parents were the same way, so it shouldn't be a surprise she turned out the same way. When I met the Davises, I learned what it meant to be a family, and over the years, this group has become more of a family to me than Oliver and Hayley ever were.

"You okay?" Nick hands me a beer, and I nod. "I'm glad

you came, man. You're always welcome here, even if Michaela decides to pull her head out of her ass and come back home for a holiday or two."

"Thanks for the invite." I smile sadly. Part of me hoped she would be here, but a bigger part of me is glad she isn't. Imagine *that* dinner. Michaela, David, and I sitting around the table — that'd be a sight to see. But, I know she's made her decision, and I have to respect that.

"I know it doesn't mean much, but I was rooting for you," Nick says. He pats my back briefly before going to help Nina — pulling the turkey out of the oven before she can. She rolls her eyes, commenting something in Italian — something about how she could do it herself, I'm sure. Nick ignores her, sets it on the counter, and kisses her temple. He whispers in her ear and she smiles reaching up to drape her arms around his neck and kiss him briefly.

"Get a room!" Alex shouts over the back of the couch. Nick flips his brother off before swatting Nina's ass and picking up the turkey to bring it to the table.

## fifty-one

### *Michaela*

**"WE'RE SO GLAD YOU** chose to join us for the holidays instead of spending another year out in the boonies," Helen says with a smile so sweet it makes me sick. This isn't the first time we've been in Montana during the holidays, but it is the first time we'll spend the entire season here. Normally, we spend one holiday in Winchester and the other in Montana or Richmond, going home in between, but not this year. David said his mother hoped we could stay longer since they hadn't seen much of him this year, and he was more than happy to oblige. Glad to know he will carve out time for his mother but not his wife.

Stop, Michaela.

You're supposed to be making this work.

"Oh, be nice, Mother," Hannah says across the living room. Hannah is the one saving grace of the Reed family. She might be the only person who hates her mother more than I do. I swear she lives to find ways to annoy Helen; like right now, Hannah sits in one of the armchairs, her feet resting on the hand-painted brass inlay trunk that's supposed to be a coffee table. It's one of Helen's favorite pieces, and she visibly cringed from her armchair when Hannah's feet touched it. "Winchester is cute."

"Winchester is cute, but Bridgeport is—"

"Better be careful. Bridgeport is the epitome of small-town America, the thing Daddy ran his campaign on years ago."

"It's a little run down, I'm not saying it's a bad thing."

I hide my grimace behind my wine as they go back and forth. David walks through the front door. *Finally,* is all I can think. He's been gone the past two days overseeing some business back in Washington while I was left to bond with the girls. "It'll be good for you," he said packing up a small travel bag moments before he walked out the door with a small peck on the forehead.

"Darling!" Helen exclaims. "How was Washington?"

"Fine, just finalizing a few things before I hand everything over to Jonah." David leans down over the back of the couch and kisses the crown of my head. I don't miss the harsh look from his sister that follows him into the kitchen. Only when she meets my gaze does she offer a small smile before getting up from the couch to follow. Hushed whispers come from the kitchen, the sounds of a sibling argument I know all too well.

"Is Jonah going to be ready to take over?" Helen asks.

"He has no choice," David says and tosses a pretzel in his mouth. When he returns from the kitchen, he looks more annoyed than moments before. Jonah has worked with David for a while, and David has been setting him up to take over as Chief of Staff. Why you ask? Because David is running for Congress. Yep. His sisters dropped *that* bombshell two days after we got here. They were unaware David hadn't told me himself. He said he was waiting for the "right time" because he didn't want to scare me away

David falls onto the couch beside me but leaves a small space between us. Just enough that someone else may not notice, but I do. Whenever we sit next to each other, there is always the slightest gap with room for one of us to take the first step, but neither has yet. *Yet,* because surely one of us will.

"Tay says dinner will be ready in ten," Hannah reappears from the kitchen with a full glass of wine. "Not sure if we're ready for whatever she's concocting, though."

"I heard that!" Taylor shouts. Taylor, the youngest of the Reed siblings, recently started culinary school. She was adamant about cooking all of our meals. Most everything has been delicious, but some things have been a little questionable — like that duck pâté inside of some kind of dough thing she made three nights ago. David's father had pizza delivered not long after dinner was served that night.

"I better go get your father," Helen says grabbing her jacket from the coat rack. "He's been fiddling with that old truck all afternoon." James does that a lot — finds a project to keep him busy when the family gets together. This time, it's a 1956 Ford pickup truck that he purchased from a local shop where it has sat in the back lot for the last ten years. His project has kept James safely tucked away in the barn, and away from his family for the last weeks. Helen tells Hannah to set the table before walking out the front door.

"So, David—"

"Don't start, Hannah." David drapes his arm around the back of the sofa, his fingers graze the base of my neck, and as much as I want to pull away, I don't. His touch feels...weird. Foreign.

"Whatever do you mean?" Hannah smirks. "I was going to say it's nice to have you back. Things were getting a bit bland here, weren't they, Mic?" A twinkle in her eye tells me there is more to this conversation than just letting her brother know how bored we've been. Hannah and I tried to escape to town — Kalispell is only twenty minutes away and perfect for a day of shopping and gossip — but Helen put a stop to that.

"That's one way to put it," I say earning a laugh from her, but an eye roll from David.

"Now that David is back, maybe Mom will let us go into town tomorrow. What do you say?" Hannah sits up in her chair planting her feet on the floor, that twinkle in her eye still there.

"Sounds like a date." I down the rest of my wine standing from the couch. Hannah joins me to start setting the table. "I'm not very hungry, don't worry about setting a place for me. I think I'm going to go take a bath instead."

"I'll sneak you some later if it's edible." She winks, and I laugh thanking her before heading upstairs.

Two days after we arrived in Montana, I found myself in Taylor's room waiting for Hannah to join us so the younger Reed sister would spill the beans about her new boyfriend. She had casually mentioned it while we were baking cookies and it put a stop to our baking immediately. Hannah wanted to know everything about this secret boyfriend, and I was just here for the gossip — anything to make the day go by a little faster.

Hannah returned with three mugs, handing one to each of us before flopping on the bed next to me. When I took a sip, a cough surged from my throat, not expecting to taste bourbon with a dash of apple cider. Taylor did the same. "Damn, Han," I chuckled, "you like a little cider with your bourbon?"

"Keeps you warm in the winter," Hannah shrugged sipping her own. "So, Washington, huh?"

"We're not here to talk about that."

"Oh no, we are," Taylor said with a smirk, and I looked

between them rightfully confused. We were supposed to be talking about Taylor's boyfriend, not me and David.

Hannah sighed, "I know this isn't my place, but why are you doing this? Not that I don't love having you around — it's nice to have someone else who doesn't enjoy being stuck with my family as much as me…"

"Hey!" Taylor interjected, but Hannah ignored her.

"…but, you *hate* it here."

"I don't hate it."

"Michaela," Hannah quirked a brow. "Be serious."

"I don't hate it," I said simply. "Do I enjoy being away from my family? No, but you're brother and I are trying to make it work, and right now, that means me being here with all of you."

Hannah scoffed, "Is that what he said?"

When I shrugged, Taylor whispered, "He's such an asshole."

"Look y'all, sometimes making it work means having to make sacrifices. I know that, I was prepared when—"

"Weren't you dating someone else, though?"

"I—" How do they know about that? "Yes, but it ended right before David and I got back together. And with everything falling into place like that, it felt like the universe was giving us the chance to fix this." My thumbnail ran across a blemish on the handle of the coffee mug, and soon it became the only thing I could focus on. "So, that's what we're gonna do."

"Who are you trying to convince?" Hannah said taking a sip of her cider.

"Hannah," Taylor warned.

"I'm just curious," Hannah smirked. "Has our dear brother told you what he's been up to in Washington?"

"What do you mean? Barnes always keeps him busy with—"

"Oh God, he hasn't told her," Hannah said to Taylor who sighed. Between the two of them, Taylor was the less confrontational one. She liked to give everyone the benefit of the doubt. While she may have been a part of this conversation, it was Hannah's idea. Taylor only wanted to feel included, but she knew better than to let anything spoken in this room leave it.

"Would someone tell me what is going on?" I begged.

"David is running for Congress."

The bathroom door glides open, bringing me back from the memory. I keep my eyes closed hoping he gets the hint. Just a few more minutes of alone time is all I want — alone time is a rare occurrence with the Reed family, and I take advantage of the little bit I get. "I had Tay make a plate for you, figured I should bring it to you since it's obvious you're not going to be rejoining us tonight."

"Sorry," I sigh. "I had a headache; the bath seems to be helping." I sink a little lower into the warm water thankful for the bubbles lingering. Part of me feels the need to cover up in front of him, even though he's seen every part of me, touched every inch of my skin. Knows every intimate detail of my being... It feels wrong.

"Look," David sets the plate on the sink and sits on the edge of the tub. "I'm sorry I had to work, but Barnes is counting on me—"

"He always is."

"Michaela—"

"I know, I know." I sit up a little taller and notice his eyes waver between the tops of my breasts that come into view over the bubbles and the floor. "I'm sorry. It's this headache, it's making me grumpy."

"You should eat something. It'll help," he says as standing from the tub. David keeps his back to me as he walks toward the door, pausing before stepping out. He adds over his shoulder, "We're all trying to make this work, Michaela. You need to do the same."

## fifty-two

## *Michaela*

**THE WOMAN IN THE** mirror shrugs her shoulders and straightens her back. Her long blonde hair has been straightened and pulled into a high bun with delicate tendrils that frame her face. A soft, neutral makeup look paired with red-colored lips. Both professionally done by the hair and makeup team her husband hired to get her ready for his former boss's annual Christmas party. Even her dress and shoes have been picked out for her — a long-sleeved crew-neck emerald dress paired with gold heels. She should be grateful, and she was to a certain extent because it meant she didn't have to worry about disappointing him, but she felt like a stranger in her own skin.

I feel like a stranger in my skin.

A hand gently grazes my hips when David appears behind me in the mirror. He smiles and kisses my temple. "See, this one is perfect," he says looking down the length of the mirror. The dress he had picked out arrived this morning on the arm of the hair stylist while we were, *calmly,* discussing how I should act at the party tonight. On the plane ride from

Montana last night, I suggested running to CityCenter and finding something to wear since I didn't pack anything, but he informed me that wouldn't be necessary — his team had already done it. *His team.* That was something I still couldn't get used to. "Remember what we talked about," he says meeting my eyes in the reflection.

"Proud and supportive wife."

"Good girl."

*Good girl.*

His words make me nauseous. *He* isn't supposed to say that. He doesn't say that. Everything about it feels…wrong, but I force myself to lift the corner of my mouth in response. "The car will be here in five minutes."

When he's gone, I finally take a deep breath and let my shoulders fall. The metal locket is warm against my fingers from being trapped beneath the neckline of the dress, but its touch brings me some comfort. At least there's one piece of me left.

*Your tell is showing.*

Finn's voice echoes in my mind, and I can almost feel the ghost of his lips on my skin. I drop my hand from the necklace like it will burn me if I touch it any longer. Finn would have been happy to let me go to CityCenter and pick out a dress. He would have let me wear something in my closet if I wanted to. There wouldn't be a script to follow, nothing to make sure I was reminded of my place. And he definitely wouldn't have hidden the fact he was running for *Congress.* It would have been a discussion, not a statement.

*David is running for Congress.* Hannah's words had caused quite a stir. I waited until everyone had retired to their rooms to confront David about it. He promised he had intended to tell me before the beginning of the year, but he didn't want to ruin our holiday season. He knew it would upset me since it meant he would be busier than ever. He was wrong, though; it made me more relieved than upset — which is what bothers me most. The next morning his mother was ecstatic when she could finally talk about it, and trust me, she *talked* about it.

Finn wouldn't have kept that a secret. He would have told me, he would have—

What am I saying? Of course, he would have kept it from me. Finn is exactly like David. They both have secrets to keep and only feel the need to share them when it's convenient.

David calls up the stairs that the car is here. I shake my head, hoping it can remove any thought of the brown-eyed man who still visits me in my dreams. "Proud and supportive wife," I murmur snatching my purse from the bed.

Because if there's one thing I've learned, better the devil you know than the one you don't.

Walking into the party earlier, I was more than a little relieved to find out I wasn't the most underdressed person this time. My dress is similar to the ones worn by most of the other women, excluding Marsha Barnes, who is dressed in a red ball gown making her easy to spot in the crowd. After dinner, Senator Barnes and Marsha invited their guests to dance and mingle in the ballroom steps away from the dining hall where two long tables hosted the feast. Since then, David has been schmoozing the room while I stand to the side like some kind of mute — nothing more than his arm candy. Listening to these conversations, I realize I have nothing in common with these people. They didn't even like the dinner and I thought it was amazing, the food anyway. The conversation was dull. However, I was pleasantly surprised by how nice everyone pretended to be at the table compared to last year. Still, I've felt more like one of those valet girls who walks wrestlers down to the ring, not someone meant to mingle in a room of politicians. David would do better with someone like Finn on his arm.  At least he was raised for this kind of thing.

Marsha works the room with such grace; it reminds me of Nina and my heart aches at the thought. I miss her. I miss my brother. I miss my family. I miss the craziness that being around them brings. I should call Nina, it would be good to catch up with her. But, she will want to know how things are going. I can't tell her the truth.

"Oh David, I'm so glad you made it!" Marsha greets him and pulls him in for a hug. Her bright blue eyes light up when they land on me. "Oh my goodness, Michaela! We haven't seen much of you. Where have you been hiding?" She pulls me into an awkward hug pressing a kiss to my cheek.

"I've been—"

"She's been finalizing some things in New York," David interrupts. He offers me a tight smile before turning back to Marsha. "She moved down to Washington before Thanksgiving."

"Goodness, that's wonderful! You'll be able to join the campaign trail."

"Can't wait," I say with as much enthusiasm as I can muster.

"Don't worry, this life...it gets easier," Marsha assures me. "Just follow whatever talking points Cindy gives you. She's a godsend. Helped me so much the first time Andrew ran for office." Her attention quickly diverts to someone on the other side of the room, and she excuses herself. If everyone pretended to be as pleasant as Marsha, then I could totally do this.

David tugs me in the direction of a group of people standing near one of the oversized Christmas trees. Dressed in silver decor The only person I recognize is Jonah. He looks me up and down before meeting my gaze with a smile, but it doesn't reach his eyes. It makes my skin crawl. "Good to see you, Mrs. Reed," Jonah says with a small smirk. He gives me another quick once-over. When I don't respond, David nudges me.

"Nice to see you," I say with my best customer service voice. Jonah asks me something else, but I don't hear him because my attention is on the server trays flooding the ballroom. Each one holds miniature plates with a dessert on them. Two small biscuits with a white fluff in the middle and topped with fresh strawberries and sauce…Strawberry Shortcake. "You've got to be kidding me."

"Michaela," David says stepping in front of me.

"Huh?"

"You blatantly ignored Jonah. He asked you a question."

"Oh, Jonah. I'm so sorry." I try to ignore the desserts floating past me and keep my gaze on him, but when a server saddles up next to me, I excuse myself without waiting for permission. I hustle towards the doors to escape this shortcake-infested room.

"There she is," Jonah exclaims when I return ten minutes later. "Everything okay, Michaela? You looked like you'd seen a ghost."

Felt like it, too. What are the chances the Barneses would choose the exact dessert matching the nickname given to me by the man I'm supposed to be forgetting? Apparently, very high.

"I apologize for my abrupt departure; I was just a little overwhelmed."

"Too much wine," David jokes, earning a laugh from the

group.

"Overwhelmed? Didn't you use to work with...what's her name?" Jonah asks. "Oh, Villa. I've heard she's tough."

"That wannabe businesswoman?" A woman I haven't been introduced to scoffs, and I glare at her. Who the hell is she?

"People like Nina are hard to deal with," Jonah explains. "This should be a walk in the park compared to *that*."

"What's that supposed to mean?" My voice comes out shrill, and I hate that it makes me sound whiney. David tightens his grip on my bicep, squeezing gently — a warning. I don't care, these people aren't going to talk shit about my best friend.

"Nina is an acquired taste," David laughs along with them. "She always held Michaela back — it's one of the reasons we felt it best that Michaela leave her position in New York." When I start to dispute the comment, he pats my arm and starts to pull me away from the group. "If you'll excuse us, we're going to take a turn on the dance floor." David practically drags me onto the dance floor. He pulls me dangerously close a death grip on my hand. "What was that?" His tone betrays the smile on his lips.

"You just talked shit about my best friend, openly."

"Mic, that group is—"

"That *group* is my family, David." When I try to pull away, he refuses to let go. "My family has never been anything but kind to you, including Nina. What is your problem?"

"My problem is they keep you plain, Michaela. They hold you back. All of them. And Nina," he chuckles, "she has to be the center of attention and will always keep you in her shadow. You're better off without them."

"Have you always felt this way?"

He shrugs but doesn't deny it. When he spins me out, he pulls me back in closer than before, whispering in my ear, "Smile, Michaela. Everyone is watching."

# fifty-three

## *Michaela*

### *TWO MONTHS LATER*

**ROYAL BLUE STANDS OUT** in a sea of pink and red, and it transports me back to a night in New York City that I've kept under lock and key for almost four months now. The heat travels up the column of my neck and flushes my cheeks. I'm sure the man next to me can feel my pulse pick up speed, but if he does, he doesn't say anything. He's still preoccupied with a conversation about taxes — *yawn.* I try to keep my attention on their conversation, but it diverts every time there is a flash of blue in my peripheral.

*What is he doing here?*

"What is he doing here?" David reiterates my question as if he can read my mind. He turns to me, "Did you know about this?"

"Yes, David. I invited him." My husband glares at me. "I don't know why he's here. Probably something to do with the company."

"Well, he won't find any support here."

"Mr. and Mrs. Reed," Robert Niven, a senator from North Carolina, calls to us with a wave. He whispers something to his counterpart with a small chuckle. The senator waves us over again, but David's feet remain planted in the same spot.

"Don't be a child, David," I hiss with a gentle shove.

"There you are. I haven't seen you all evening, where you been hiding, Reed?" Robert shakes David's hand before he presses a kiss to the back of mine. "Always a pleasure, Michaela. You look ravishing this evening."

"You flatter me, Mr. Niven."

"Reed, I've been looking for you. I wanted to introduce you to a friend of mine," Niven says and starts walking, expecting David to follow. "He started an amazing program for kids in the system up in New York and is in the process of bringing it down to the Carolinas. I thought it might be a good opportunity to add some philanthropy to your campaign over in Virginia."

You've got to be kidding me.

"We've been working with—"

"David," Niven interrupts him, "trust me, this is the one you want. You have less than a month before the primaries — you gotta show 'em you're not all business." Royal blue comes into view again just before Niven waves him down. A smile spreads across his face before he realizes *who* is with Niven. "Finn," Niven exclaims. "Always one to stand out in a crowd."

"Pink isn't really my color." His voice wraps around me and sends a shiver down my spine. It's warm and inviting, the opposite of the look in his eyes. There's a wall between us that I've never known before, not even when we were younger. His entire demeanor is cool and indifferent. "Mr. and Mrs. Reed, nice to see you."

"Oh, you know one another already?" Senator Niven asks.

"My wife actually helped Mr. Sheffield with his...project."

Senator Niven's eyes widen when he looks between me and Finn. "I had no idea she's the one you were talking about.

Well, this is marvelous. It won't be any trouble to get this off the ground in—"

"Actually, we already have a cause we've been putting some time into," David stops Niven before he can get started. "We're extremely passionate about education reform."

"We don't want to get ahead of ourselves, Robert," Finn adds. "We're still a freshman company."

Robert looks between the two men before his gaze lands on me. I hope he doesn't notice the blush creeping into my cheeks or the sweat building on my brow. There's a quirk in the corner of his mouth then he nods accepting whatever he believes he has figured out. "Well," he extends his hand to David. "I look forward to seeing how you fair in the election, Dave." He kisses the back of my hand, "Always a pleasure."

When Robert turns to Finn, I take the chance to give him a once-over, and when my gaze finally reaches his face, his eyes bore into me. His gaze softens — a small crack in the wall — but he turns away when Robert claps him on the back.

"Is your Uncle Jack with you?" Robert asks.

"He is, c'mon, he'll be happy to see you." When Finn turns back to us, the crack has been reinforced, and the wall fortified. He extends his hand to David, and after a moment of hesitation, David takes it. An unspoken conversation between them before they release. Finn turns to me. "Mrs. Reed," he says almost too politely. Warmth rises across my skin when his hand touches mine. The wall is down when his warm gaze meets mine from under his lashes, and my breath catches. He brings the back of my hand to his lips setting my body ablaze. Fire spreads across my skin as if I'm drenched in gasoline. Every touch we've shared flashes before me. It feels like hours until he releases my hand, and when he's gone, I feel cold. He stands tall and takes a step back, the wall rebuilding before my eyes. "It was nice to see you again."

David offers them both a tight-lipped smile as they walk

away, but his smile begins to fail, and is replaced by a narrow-eyed glare. I touch his hand to get his attention, but he pulls away and walks outside without a word. I'm expected to follow, but right now, I want to do the opposite of what I'm expected to do. I reach for the heart charm that normally rests on my chest, but it's not where it should be — actually, there's nothing there. My heart drops. Then I remember *why* it's not there: Cindy. Cindy is the head of David's team, and last month, she showed up on the doorstep of David's townhome ready to give me a makeover. The last part of that makeover just so happened to be my choice of jewelry.

"Absolutely not," I said when she told me to take my locket off. I glared at the middle-aged woman in front of me. She drew back in shock. I'm not sure if it's because it was the first time I had spoken since her team arrived that morning or because I told them *no*. I don't think that's a word they hear very often. I had let them poke and prod me, go through my closet before resigning to a simple navy-blue three-quarter sleeve, boat neck dress saying they'd send over a new wardrobe the next day, do my makeup three different times, and change my hair twice. I drew the line at removing my locket. "The necklace stays on."

"It doesn't go with the outfit."

"It goes just fine."

"Michaela."

"Cindy."

We were at a stalemate.

Cindy and I have been like oil and water, but I guess that's my fault. Under normal circumstances, I'm sure she is a nice person and very helpful to the wives of future politicians who need a little help. Bless her heart, I couldn't do what she does, but I don't need her help. I've spent the past ten years around the Villa family, I think I can hold my own. That doesn't seem to matter because she has taken a particular interest in me since the Barnes Christmas party two months ago.

"David, please speak to your wife," Cindy called over her shoulder and David appeared from the kitchen.

"Michaela, whatever it is, just do it," David said without looking up from his phone. "Don't be so difficult."

"David, it's my locket, I never—"

"It's only a necklace. It's not that big of a deal." He waved me off continuing to stare down at his phone. Not that big of a deal? This was the same necklace I'd worn every day since I turned eighteen — a gift from my family. He knew that.

Cindy smiled triumphantly. She stuck her hand out in anticipation. As much as I wanted to argue the topic more, I didn't. My hands trembled as I undid the clasp and laid it in her palm. My heart leaped when she tossed it to one of her assistants. She tousled my hair lightly, letting a few pieces hang over my shoulders. When she is satisfied, she took a small step back so I could look at myself in the floor-length mirror they had brought with them. My fingers grazed across the skin where the locket *should* be, and my throat tightened. "See, doesn't that look better?" Cindy beamed behind me, proud of her work. "Now, you look like a congressman's wife." I barely recognized the woman in the mirror.

I may look like a congressman's wife, but it's not how I feel. Every time I walk out of the house, I feel like I'm just playing a part, checking a box for David's campaign. My nails trace the skin where my locket should be as my eyes scan the room for Royal Blue, but don't find him. There's no sign of him amongst the colors of love that fill the room to the brim. If it weren't for the glare of the man standing by the door, I might think the last ten minutes were just a figment of my imagination. David beckons me, and I take a deep breath before heading towards the choice I made.

# fifty-four

## *Michaela*

**STANDING AT THE KITCHEN** sink, I scrub the remnants of my coffee from the mug. There's a heavy weight on my shoulders that I haven't been able to shake — not surprising since there hasn't been a single moment of peace since joining the campaign trail in January. The last three months have been a blur of luncheons, dinners, parties, flights, and campaign stops. "Get used to it," Cindy said earlier when we got into the car. We spent most of the day outside the polls talking to voters — shaking hands, kissing babies, that kind of thing. "When we win this, you'll always have somewhere to be," her words made me sick to my stomach. This wasn't what I wanted. Now, I didn't have a choice. I reached for my neck but found it empty. Instead, my fingers tugged on the neck of the dress staring out the window. Where one would expect their husband to offer a reassuring hand-hold or leg squeeze, I got nothing. David remained securely in his space with his nose in his phone.

That's how it's been. I might be standing next to him physically, but mentally he is somewhere else entirely. I'm an accessory to toss into his drawer when the night is over. When I'm not on his arm, I'm expected to be at the club with the other wives or doing something philanthropical (is that even a word?). That's how he prefers it — when I'm not there — unless there is an event, I've barely seen him. Last night was our first chance in a month to have some alone time, but what did he do instead? Run off to the office. We should be embracing the opportunity to be alone together.

Tonight is the primaries. I don't understand why, but they're treating this like the general election. His parents (Helen) are hosting a small party for the staff while we await the results — even though we know he's going to win. According to Cindy, we won't get much time alone once he's elected (surely, it can't get worse than it already is). *Oh, don't worry, he will be,* she said when I questioned what if he *didn't* win. The thought terrifies me. Despite whatever plan they might have cooked up, David is well-liked in his hometown community. I know he'll be elected. David winning the election means I become a congressman's wife.

*Congressman.*

I don't know that I'm cut out to be a congressman's wife.

I didn't want this. I don't want this. I didn't sign up to be a politician's wife... Running for office isn't the kind of thing you decide on a whim, which means David *knew* about this when we ran into each other in Brooklyn. He knew when he asked me for a second chance. I can (almost) guarantee he didn't tell me this was part of the plan because he knew I'd say no. Immediately, the answer would have been no.

"You ready?" David walks into the kitchen fiddling with his cufflinks, and I have to do a double-take. He's dressed in the freshly tailored suit that arrived this morning, but he had left it in the garment bag and tucked it safely in the closet until now. The royal blue color reminds me of Finn. My coffee starts to creep its way back up my throat.

"I can't do this." I barely register the words, but as soon as I say them,  the weight lifts off my shoulders.

"What are you talking about?" David glances up at me but still fiddles with the cufflink. "It's going to be an easy night."

"David, I—"

"Are you sick or something?"

"No."

"Then you have to go. How is it going to look if I'm there by myself?"

"I don't want this."

There's a brief pause, and it feels like the air is slowly being sucked out of the room. My hand reaches toward my neck but still finds nothing. The metal heart is no longer there when I need it. Instead, my fingers grasp the kitchen towel, wringing it through my fingers.

"I can't do this, David."

Confusion is written across his features. "Michaela, what the hell do you want from me?"

"I'm done. With this…us. I thought this was what I wanted. I thought I wanted to make this work, but… I don't, and I don't think you do either, not really."

"Michaela, you can't be done. I need you! I can't run this campaign without you."

"I don't give two shits about your campaign," a breathy laugh escapes my lungs. "I'm not some accessory to make you look good. I'm not here to be the perfect little housewife who spends her days cooking, cleaning, going to brunch with other wives… That's not me. But, that's all this is to you, David. It was never about making things work between us. It was about you looking good to the public."

"C'mon Michaela, don't do this. We can make this work. We—"

"The thing is, I don't want to. I get it. You're busy with the campaign, but do you realize until yesterday we hadn't spoken since last Thursday? We were apart for three days and didn't speak one time."

"We text each other."

"And in those brief texts, you never once asked me how I was doing or if I was okay."

"I've been busy, I—"

"I know, and that's okay," I say softly, "but this life is not what I want."

"You were willing to accept the same kind of life with Finn Sheffield, though."

My face falls at the mention of his name. "Don't bring him into this."

"I can't bring up the man who was sleeping with my wife?"

"Finn has nothing to do with this."

"He has everything to do with this!" David's palm slams against the island and his eyes are like southern storm clouds just before they unleash a heavenly downpour. If we were outside, there'd be a rumble of thunder in the distance. The air growing more humid and damp, with a distinct smell of earth and ozone one can only know as the coming sign of a summer storm. "I will not have a divorce scandal in the middle of this campaign!"

I wet my lips tasting the matte lipstick coating them. "The truth finally comes out."

David squares his shoulders, and his lips pull into a tight line, but he doesn't deny it.

"I will get you through tonight, but after that, I'm done. The votes are going to go how they're gonna go. I've played my role, and I've played it well, but...no more."

Personally, I think tonight was my best show yet. One-thousand-watt smile. Tender touches. Perfectly timed laughs, but never too loud or obnoxious. Listening intently as if every word was step-by-step instructions on how to cure cancer. Applause, feigned shock, and an appropriate kiss on the cheek when the results were called. David had won the primary election, and now it was time to go home.

Walking through the kitchen door, there's a heaviness in the air. Before I can make a break for the stairs, his voice cuts through the silence. "Don't do this, Michaela." His voice is soft, almost defeated. "Don't…Don't leave."

"Don't leave? You didn't even want me to begin with!"

"That's not true, I love you. I do, I—"

"You don't love me. You haven't for a long time. Sometimes, I wonder why we even got married, because we knew things weren't going to work. When you got the job with Barnes, we said we would figure it out. We said we wouldn't let it come between us. I didn't realize you already had this plan for us… our life. Even though you knew I'd never be able to give it to you."

"I just wanted us to be together."

"That's why you asked for a divorce?"

"It was the only option! You wouldn't come here, and I couldn't be in New York. My job is here, Michaela. I'm not the only one at fault here."

"But I did, David. I finally gave you what you wanted. I left everything behind. I moved to Washington. I haven't seen my family, my friends in months…" Tears prick the corners of my eyes. They threaten to fall when I take a shaky breath. "And it's still not enough."

"That's not true."

"I thought I could do this. I thought coming here and doing all the right things would make you happy. I thought it would fix things, but it hasn't. We might be in the same place, but we're still living separate lives!"

"Michaela—"

"The difference is, you got to keep your identity, I lost mine. I can't keep pouring from an empty cup and pretending to be okay, David." I wipe a tear that breaks the surface and falls down my cheek. "It's time for me to finally choose me."

"You mean Finn."

"Stop bringing him into this!"

"But that's what you mean; you're just choosing him over me."

"You didn't want me! You were dating Karina up until the moment Cindy told you that you needed me instead of her." Her name makes his stormy eyes grow ten times their size.

"Karina? I haven't— I haven't seen her—"

"Oh, save it." I roll my eyes. "I know you've been seeing her."

"Michaela," he scrubs his hand down his face, "please, I can't do this without you. After the election in November, we can do whatever we want. You want to be with Finn? Fine. You can be, just not publicly."

"Do you hear yourself?" I scoff and slip the ring off my hand. I feel like I can finally breathe without it on my finger. I set it on the counter between us; as relieved as I am, a small part of me hurts to see that diamond sitting there. David looks between it and me. His eyes grow more desperate with each glance. I almost feel bad for the man across the kitchen, but I have to walk away, even if it means losing everything I have left. The past five months have proven we've only been putting off the inevitable, and someone else is meant to live this life. "Goodbye, David."

*fifty-five*

*Finn*

*TWO AND HALF MONTHS LATER*

**"WHERE'S ELLIE?" I ASK,** taking the beer from Josh when he returns to the backyard. He invited the me and the boys over for a pre-Memorial Day BBQ since everyone was going to be in town. I haven't seen the Villa-Davis clan since Thanksgiving because I spent Christmas with Dean and his friends in North Carolina. Though, I probably should've opted for another VD holiday. The tension between Dean and Raeanne finally came to a head, and it was not pretty. That's practically twenty years of sexual tension and hidden feelings that spilled over and ended with Raeanne leaving without saying goodbye.

And I thought *I* had problems.

Josh joined us for New Year's at Jeremy and Lola's home in Los Angeles, but only because Dean bugged him until he said yes. Elizabeth wasn't with him, which I thought was odd. He said she was spending the holiday with Nina in New York, which I didn't think was odd.

"She's back in Charleston." Josh runs a hand through his

337

hair, longer than he usually keeps it, tugging on the ends. It's starting to look like a sophisticated mullet. He sits back in the bright blue lawn chair and cracks open his beer, taking a long drag.

"Been gone a lot, hasn't she?" I share a questioning glance with Nick across the fire pit. He knowingly raises his eyebrows, taking a drink of his beer instead of offering a verbal response. "Everything okay with you guys?"

"Sure, why wouldn't it be?"

The sound of the doorbell echoes outside; and at first, no one moves. When it sounds again, Josh finally gets up to answer it with a long sigh.

"What in the hell is going on?" I ask Nick and Alex.

"You think I know?" Alex sighs, "No one tells me anything."

Nick rolls his eyes, "Just a bit of a rough patch. They're working on things. He doesn't want it getting out, if you know what I mean."

"Well, as long as he doesn't tell Michaela, he'll be fine," Alex says, and they share a laugh, but my smile fades behind my beer. There's a pang in my chest at the mention of *her*. I haven't seen her since the Valentine's Day dinner when Robert tried to introduce us. I know he was trying to help me get Sheffield House out there. He doesn't know our history, how could he? But, I spent the entire night avoiding contact with them on purpose. I had heard David was running for office, I should've known they would be there, but Robert insisted I tag along. I had been doing okay after everything, until that night. Seeing her on David's arm, a polite smile on her lips, nodding along every once in a while, but never actually being part of the conversation... It wasn't right. It wasn't her. Her eyes had dimmed, they didn't sparkle when she laughed. Instead, she looked like she was trying to contain herself. It made me sick. She didn't deserve to be his arm candy, she's so much more than that. She made her choice, I reminded myself about two hundred times that night. It's what she wanted.

"Divorce papers finally came," Josh says holding up a manila envelope. "Signed, sealed, delivered."

Divorce papers?

"Finally," Alex says nonchalantly. How are they so calm? Josh just received *divorce papers.* I thought Nick said he and Ellie were working on things.

"Whose divorce papers?" I question as though about to step over a landmine.

"My sister." Josh rips the envelope open and pulls the documents out scanning over them. "We've been waiting for these. David and his attorney took their sweet time sending them over."

"Probably thinks he can convince her to come back," Alex laughs.

"Wait, Michaela left him?" I ask. Why didn't anyone tell me?

"About two months ago," Nick answers with the smirkest smirk I've ever seen. "And she's been Eat, Pray, Loving it all over Europe since."

Josh tosses the envelope on the table between us. Beneath it, I notice a second envelope, but he doesn't seem interested in that one. Instead, he reaches for the item that hangs out of the first envelope. A necklace.

"Is that her locket?"

"Yeah, David has been holding it hostage since she left," Josh says. Sunlight reflects off the silver piece. "His campaign manager made her take it off because it didn't go with the aesthetic they were creating for the wife of the future Congressman."

Of course, it all makes sense now — the real reason he wanted her to come back. He needed her to save his image. There couldn't be a divorce scandal amid running for office. "I wondered where it was the night of the Valentine's Day dinner," I say, and all heads turn toward me.

"What Valentine's Day dinner?" Alex asks.

"Oh, we were at the same event and ran into each other."

"And you're just now telling me this?" Josh accuses.

"Nothing happened." I shrug. "I don't think we said two words to each other. David made sure of that."

"Did Nina know about this?" Josh asks Nick.

"Don't think so. They've only started talking again after she left him." My face must display the *what the fuck* going through my mind because Nick says, "Apparently, he didn't want her involved with Nina. He told her that our family is plain and Nina was holding her back."

"He's such an ass," Alex mumbles under his breath.

Josh raises his beer, and we join him in cheering, "Here's to never seeing that asshole again." He stands from his chair and excuses himself to call his sister. "She'll want to know she's officially a free woman," he says and walks back inside with both envelopes and the necklace.

I still can't believe his team convinced her to take that locket off. She never takes it off, not even for the Sheffield House gala. She has worn it every day since her eighteenth birthday. Watching her open it, I remember feeling a certain sense of happiness. She loved it. She loved something I had done for her, but she had no idea the truth behind it. No one except Josh knew I picked it out. We figured it was best not to let her know since we didn't exactly get along.

"You picked that out, didn't you?" Nick asks me.

"How'd you know that?"

"Josh told me, made me swear not to tell MJ, though."

"He went to Finn to help pick something out for Michaela?" Alex questions. "Why didn't he ask one of us?"

"Your brother was a little busy handling things after your mom died." I shrug, "I was here, and I have a knack for buying gifts."

"You mean you had a knack for buying all of your girlfriends gifts to keep them happy."

"I didn't have *that* many," I say rolling my eyes.

"You had enough," Nick says.

Okay, so maybe I had fun in high school, and the small amount of time I spent in college, sue me. At least I was gentleman enough never to date more than one at a time.

Josh returns looking extra annoyed and falls back into his chair with a huff. "She's out of her damn mind. She wants me to overnight the damn things to *Estranei.*"

"Estran-what?" Where in the world is that? What in the world is that?

"You remember Romy and Enzo from the wedding? Enoz's family owns a vineyard in Italy. Nin's great-grandfather used to work there. Mic has been staying in the vineyard guest house," Nick explains. "She added it to the end of her little trip of self-discovery."

"She's supposed to leave in two or three days. Even if I overnighted it, it'll never make it in time."

"You know who his wife is, right?" Alex points towards his brother.

"I don't even think Nina Villa could get it there that fast."

"You'd be surprised by the things she can do." Nick licks his lips with a wide smirk. Alex grimaces, and Josh and I try to ignore the obvious thoughts going through his mind.

"She's just gonna have to wait until she comes home." Josh shrugs. "It'll be waiting for her with the rest of her shit in the guest room."

# fifty-six

## *Michaela*

**I SMILE AS THE** warmth of the Italian sun kisses my face. The ends of a curly bob tickle the top of my shoulders as the breeze blows through the vineyard. The almost two weeks I've spent here with Romy and Enzo have been the perfect way to end my two-month sabbatical.

What have I learned in the past two months? First, I'm a people pleaser. I want people to be happy, I want them to be proud of me, and I want to make sure their expectations are met...even to my own detriment. Second, I compare myself to others. My life is deeply rooted in the lives of people vastly different from mine. Lord knows I have to stop worrying that my life doesn't look like theirs — I'm sure it's easy to guess who I'm talking about. Nina is my best friend, that will always be true, but we are not the same. We don't have to be, nor do I want to be. Third, I lead a privileged life compared to most of the world, but still not as privileged as some. I'm still trying to figure out what that means, but I know that I want to use these past few months to make some changes in my life. And finally... I shouldn't have been mad at Finn (not *as* mad).

He didn't *have* to tell me about the agreement with his dad, though it would have been nice to know what I was getting myself into. It wasn't my business. It was before we started dating. Therefore, he didn't owe me any explanation. Coming to that conclusion a few weeks ago, I decided I would talk to him when I got home — apologize, at least, for how I acted.

My phone rings from inside the bedroom, but I don't move. I only have two more days to take in as much of this view as I can, and I'm not going to miss a moment. The guest villa sits in the middle of the vineyard with surrounding views of the fields and mountains. It's quite literally peace on Earth.

When I asked Nina to contact the Vitalis about coming to the estate, I wasn't sure if they'd welcome me back after how David acted the last time we were here. I hoped they'd be willing to give me a second chance without his presence. Instead of an answer from Nina, I received a call from Romy. I knew it was her immediately from the accent. "Michaela! You have to join us at the vineyard. We have the guest house you're more than welcome to occupy while you're here."

"Oh, I was going to rent a—"

"Nonsense. You'll stay with us. Camilla and Enzo wouldn't have it any other way."

"Are you sure they're okay with this? After the last time, I—"

"They were ecstatic to hear you'd be back. Nina called Camilla, but she is on vacation and won't be able to greet you. Enzo and I will be here, though. You're welcome to join us for as long as you wish." Romy refused to hang up until I promised to cancel my room at the hotel and stay at the vineyard. That's how I found myself extending my trip an extra week.

My phone rings again, and I roll my eyes before padding back inside. I should answer it, or at least see who it is.

*Alex.*

Alex has checked in with me every other day while I've

been away, even if I don't respond. I have avoided my phone as much as possible, even telling Elias to handle the divorce. I'd be fine with whatever he did because I didn't want anything. David could have it all. The only thing I did want was my freedom. Did he want an annulment instead? Done. Money? Here's a lump sum. Whatever it was, I didn't care. I'd do anything to be done with that part of my life.

**Alex**

**Call me.**

Busy. Can it wait?

The three dots bounce up and down briefly before disappearing and returning a moment later. I watch them gyrate around before disappearing altogether. I guess it wasn't that important after all.

"Oh, Michaela, I forgot to tell you," Enzo says as we walk toward the tasting room. Enzo and Romy had taken me to dinner on my last night in Italy. I was sad to leave, but it was time to go home. Time to face reality and start putting the pieces of my life back together. "Annamaria said a package arrived for you. Let me see if she left it here or took it to the villa already." Enzo disappears into the darkness of the tasting room, leaving me and Romy alone for the first time tonight.

"I'm glad you could join us on your trip," Romy says with a smile.

"Romy, I'm sorry for how I acted last year." I pull the clip from my hair and shake it out, I'm still adjusting to this new length, but I think I could get used to it. "Even at the wedding, I wasn't very nice to you."

Over the last two weeks, I have gotten to know Romy better and understand why Nina gravitated toward her so easily. They were extremely similar, yet completely different. Where Nina was a total workaholic, Romy was more free-spirited. She worked hard, but work wasn't her life. She had grown up in France and was the embodiment of the French lifestyle, especially when it came to her style. She dressed to impress regardless of what she was doing (including working the vineyard). When I asked about Enzo, she couldn't hide the blush on her cheeks or the giddiness that bubbled inside her. Romy told me she had visited the estate about a month after we did, and Enzo invited her to stay in the guest villa. While she was here, they got to know each other, becoming friends first, and fell in love. She packed up and moved to Italy three months later. Now, she helps Camilla run the business side of things, mostly working on broadening distribution.

While I had spent time getting to know her, I still felt bad because I hadn't once apologized to Romy for my behavior last year, it was long overdue.

"You had a lot going on, Michaela." She waves off my comment. Her bright green eyes shine under the light of the lantern above us. "Besides, I'm sure I came off a little strong. I do that sometimes. You were just being a good friend to Davina."

Truthfully, I think a part of me knew things with David weren't going well. I just didn't know how bad it was. Unfortunately, I decided to focus that energy on Romy instead of figuring out my own life.

"How are you feeling about going back home?"

I shrug. "I'm ready, I miss everyone, but I'm also dreading it. Going back means having to face everything I left behind."

Romy wraps her arm around my shoulders and leans her

head against mine in a warm embrace as we walk to find Enzo. "And what of Finn?" Her words stop me in my tracks. This is the first time she's mentioned him. I'm not surprised she knows; I'm sure Nina told her everything about why I had taken this trip. If she did, I appreciated Romy's feigned interest when I told her what happened with David.

Just before we can open the door, Enzo steps outside. He has nothing in his hands. Shit, did Josh not send it? Dammit Josh, but he said he did. Before I can ask why Enzo's not carrying a package, someone else steps through the door, and my heart stops.

"Why the long face, Shortcake? Not happy to see me?"

# fifty-seven

*Finn*

**THE GENUINE SHOCK ON** her face tells me she had no idea I'd be here, though I do wish she looked a little more excited to see me.

At least we know Josh can keep a secret, unlike his sister. When he was done ranting about his sister wanting the impossible yesterday, I suggested I could bring the locket to her. Two of them laughed, but one of them didn't — Nick. I've always known he was a secret romantic, but he hasn't been very good at hiding it the last few years. Not since he met Nina. He offered me a small smile while the others continued to joke about me taking the locket to Italy. Because according to him, it was ludicrous to think about doing so.

"Wait, you're serious?" Josh asked.

"Why not? She wants it, I can get it there before she leaves—"

"Because she's in Italy!" Alex laughed.

"So? I've jumped on a plane a lot for less." That was true, but this wasn't just jumping on a plane for a quick rendezvous. "Look, she's been without it for months, and we all know how much it means to her. If I can make this happen, why not?" I shrugged, trying to act like it wasn't a big deal, but inside my heart raced at the thought of seeing her. Being the one to return this piece of her.

"What are you doing here, Finn?" Michaela questions. The greeting is a *little* harsher than I expected, but at least she hasn't told me to fuck off yet. Her hair is shorter than before — chopped to just above her shoulders, tickling the strap of her white button-down. Buttery, tanned skin from months in the European sun on display from the top few buttons left undone.

"Just wanted to make sure this got here safe and sound." I pull the locket from my pocket and let it dangle between my fingers.

Her eyes widen. "Why do you have that?"

"Josh may have mentioned you wanted it back as soon as possible."

She tries to snatch it from my grasp, but I move away. "I'm not playing your games, Finn. Give me the necklace."

"All in due time, Shortcake."

Michaela groans trying to reach for it again, but I pull it away. We're close, closer than we were at the Valentine's Day dinner, and almost as close as we were at the wedding. The energy radiating between us only builds the longer we're like this. Her chest heaves with an annoyed huff before she turns on her heel. Whether she wants me to or not, I follow mumbling a quick thank you to Enzo and Romy, who wear matching smirks. "Finn, I'm not doing this. Please, I have somewhere to be."

"Drinks with some local. Yeah, I know."

"How do you— Nina," she sighs. "Of course, she told you."

"It was Nick, actually. Your cousin thinks you deserve a little payback for meddling in his love life."

"Well, they were being stubborn idiots."

"Says the most stubborn woman I've ever met."

She spins back around, and blue orbs glare up at me. Her finger jabs into my chest, "Give me the necklace, Finn."

"I will, but first, we need to have a conversation."

"I have nothing to say."

That's a lie.

"You're telling me you spent the last two months eat, pray, loving it, and you have nothing to say to me? Nothing at all." She doesn't respond. "Exactly. Now, let's go."

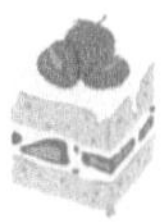

The guesthouse is as big as the typical home you'd find back in the States. The foyer opens to an large living space with a sitting area, a huge kitchen, and a dining room. Dark stained wood arch doors lead from the living space to a covered patio. Step through the tall arches of the patio, and you'll find a courtyard overlooking rolling hills of the vineyard. This place has at least four bedrooms and an office and a gym...they really thought of everything. The Vitalis have created an oasis at the center of their expansive estate, and I wish I had found the courage to join her sooner — if only I had known. Had I known, I would've jumped on the first flight.

Michaela stands in the center of it all with her arms crossed. Her eyes narrow in annoyance, and her nostrils flare, but I find the whole display cute. She's trying to be upset because she feels like she should be. "What do you want, Finn?"

"I'm sorry."

She huffs paired with the biggest eye roll, I'm surprised her eyes don't fall on the floor.

"I know you think I lied and hid things from you, I'm not going to sit here and dismiss how you feel, but... Michaela, I didn't tell you because I didn't think I had to. Looking back, yeah, I should've told you everything, but I didn't think it mattered."

"Of course, it mattered, Finn!"

"Why? That deal with Oliver had nothing to do with you. It happened before we ever started dating."

"Because."

"Because, why?"

She searches through an index of answers, but can't quite find the right one. "Just because!" She throws her hands up walking into the kitchen.

"We weren't dating, Michaela. I didn't owe you an explanation about anything. We weren't even truly friends yet. You were just the person Nina put on the project in her place."

Michaela fills a kettle with water and puts it on the stove, but she doesn't turn back to me. Her eyes stay trained on the stove.

"Why would I tell you? I didn't even want to tell Nina, but I had no choice." And that's the truth. I knew I couldn't do it without Nina's help so, I had to tell her because it was the only way she'd take me seriously. Even then, she was skeptical until everything was approved. Can't say I blame her with my track record. "I'm sorry if that's not what you want to hear, but it's the truth." Finally, her eyes meet mine. "We slept together, and I knew it was a mistake— Don't make that face. It *was* a mistake. I took advantage of you. I'm sorry for that. You and I have always had a complicated relationship, but sleeping together made it even more so. On top of that, I didn't think we'd see each other outside of the occasional family gathering. I thought we could manage. Until I saw you at Coney Island and then on the street with David... Something was different. I thought it was because we'd slept together, but I knew it was more than that. I cared about you, despite what you think, I always have even if you got on my last nerve. But this, this was different. I felt the change, but didn't understand what that meant."

"So, why didn't you tell me the truth?"

"When I got into the trenches of what we were doing with Sheffield House, keeping the money was no longer the most important thing. It was helping the kids, giving them the support they need. I just wanted to make sure Sheffield House happened. Why does it matter what jumpstarted the whole thing? Michaela, you're not even mad that this 'bet' — if you really want to call it that — was the catalyst for me starting the company. You're only mad that you weren't aware."

"That's not true."

"Yes, it is. You're the nosiest person I've ever known. You always have been. And, if you truly thought I had lied to you, you would've never let me walk through that door tonight." She turns back to the kettle, but I pull her back to face me. "I should've fought harder when you told me about David, but I was heartbroken. You were choosing him over me and it hurt." I gently wrap my arms around her. "I know you're scared. I'm scared too. I can't promise everything will be perfect. Knowing us, it'll be far from, but we can be perfectly imperfect together. I love you, Shortcake."

My confession makes her body go rigid in my arms, and she tries to take a step back, "Finn—"

"I do, I love you." I had never considered this an option until last year. Michaela had always been Shortcake, Josh's little sister, the annoying kid who never left us alone, but she did offer entertainment value on occasion. Sure, I felt a little protective over her, but looking back, I don't know if it was because she was my best friend's sister or because there was always an underlying connection between us. "I wish I had realized it sooner. It could have saved us both a lot of heartache."

Her blue eyes glisten under the warm lights, and for a

second I think she's going to close the gap between us. The kettle begins to scream breaking the trance. Michaela pulls it off the burner and gathers the ingredients for tea — dried roses and some other spice — stuffing them in a metal tea bag holder. "Finn, I'm not living in New York anymore. I sold the condo, I don't have a job, I don't have—"

"You can stay with me."

"Be serious," she huffs.

"I am," I say without hesitation. "If you want space, you can move into the guest room, but... Michaela, stay with me."

Michaela chews on her bottom lip, considering my words. This is a lot, I know it's a lot, but I can't go another day knowing she isn't mine. I'll give her *anything* she wants as long as it means bringing her back home with me. She takes a deep breath meeting my stare, finally uttering, "I love you too, Finn."

# fifty-eight

## *Michaela*

**FINN PULLS THE LOCKET** from his pocket, "Guess I should give this back now, huh?"

"Please," I sigh and turn so he can put it on.

"Little unknown fact," he says, bringing the chain around my neck, and my hand instinctively reaches for it. A tidal wave of comfort hits me when my fingers grasp the small metal heart. It's like walking into your parents' home on Christmas. "I helped your brother pick this out."

Why would he have picked this out? It was a gift from my parents and Josh for my eighteenth birthday. He wasn't even home when I got it.

"Your parents sent him on the mission to get something for your birthday, and we were supposed to hang out. Your brother is good at many things, but picking out gifts is not one of them. I truly believe Elizabeth buys her own gifts and just says it's from him." His fingers light a fire on my skin. Securing the clasp, he gently rests the chain around my neck and presses a delicate kiss where the two meet. He turns me to meet his stare and continues, "I suggested jewelry. What girl wouldn't love jewelry? Then when we got to the store, he kept picking out these weird pieces. Finally, I saw this one… And, it just seemed like you."

"So, you picked out the locket that I've worn every day since I got it on my eighteenth birthday."

"Sure did," he nods with a proud smile.

"You never told me that."

"Suppose I had, would you have kept it?"

"Point taken." I laugh because I probably would've thrown it in the garbage had I known. Eighteen-year-old me wouldn't want something that had Finnley Sheffield's imprint on it.

I stand on my tiptoes and wrap my arms around his shoulders, but he leans in before I can and kisses me. The first one is quick, but after the third one, it changes tempo. Too many months of longing and wanting have led to this moment, and it feels like coming home.

A squeal escapes me when he lifts me over his shoulder carrying me into my bedroom like a caveman. This is the opposite of what one would expect from Finnley Sheffield — the man who always seems so refined and dignified. I love when he lets his guard down and sheds the years of *Sheffield* training. This side of him is something most people don't have the pleasure of knowing, it's reserved only for a few people, but it's what made me fall in love with him.

I giggle when he tosses me on the bed shedding his suit jacket and shoes, climbing onto the bed. A blush creeps into my cheeks under his intense stare. "I missed you," he whispers pushing a strand of hair from my face.

"You have *no* idea," I say, leaning into the warm touch of his palm. His thumb and forefinger grip my chin bringing my lips to his. The kiss is gentle and inviting, his tongue prying open my mouth and moving in languid strides. It's all-consuming and there's a desperation in his touch that matches how I've felt since the night he left me in the garden.

"Baby." Finn stops me when I begin to undo the buttons of his shirt. "You have no idea how badly I want this, but I don't want to push anything. We just—" He grunts when I push him back onto the bed and straddle his hips — a genuine look of surprise on his face. "Careful, Shortcake, you'll start something you have to finish."

Holding his gaze, I undo the buttons of my shirt letting it fall down my shoulders, unhooking my bra, and tossing it aside. I cover his body with mine, and lean in close to whisper, "I'm just finishing what *you* started."

"Fuck," he groans and a shiver runs through him as my mouth skates across the tanned skin of his neck. The earthy scents of his cologne fill my nose when he shrugs out of his shirt. I move down his chest leaving open-mouthed kisses. "Michaela," he stops me, lifting my chin, "as much as I'd love to see you on your knees while I fuck that pretty mouth of yours, I'm not in a waiting mood." Finn undoes his belt and shoves his dress pants and underwear down his legs before I even get my jeans to my ankles.

"Someone's eager," I laugh kicking my clothes off the bed.

"*You* have no idea," his breath is hot against my ear and I feel his hardness press against my ass. *Damn,* he's already so hard. His mouth sucks the skin just beneath my ear and his right hand caresses the side of my abdomen. He squeezes my breast, kneading the doughy flesh before his fingers find my nipple — pinching at the same time he bites down on my neck and it sends a jolt straight to my core. He groans when I arch my backside into him. His fingers move at a slow, frustrating pace getting closer and closer to where I want him before he dips two fingers inside me. "Fuck, you're already so wet for me." His palm against my clit creates some of the friction I need, but it's not enough. My hips move against his fingers, his palm, anything to ease the ache for release. I need more. I need him. Now.

"Finn," I moan, "I need you inside of me."

His fingers toy with my clit before he releases me and I ache from the loss. "Back on top, Shortcake," he commands and a wave of hesitation hits me, but I push it aside straddling his hips. Finn wastes no time positioning himself beneath me and shoves himself in.

I gasp at the sudden fullness when he bottoms out inside me. His fingers dig into the flesh of my hips as my back curves and my head rolls back with a soft hum of pleasure. My hands grasp his thighs as my body adjusts to the newfound fullness. I'm not usually the one on top — David wouldn't let me, and it wasn't something I was ever comfortable doing with my other partners. But with Finn...he makes me feel confident and sexy. Except, now that I'm in this position, I'm not feeling as sexy. Noticing my hesitation, he persuades my hips to move, and the sounds he makes encourage me to continue on my own.

"That's right, baby. Keep riding me." His hands move from my hips to my breasts, his fingers gently pinch my nipples and it sends me into a spiral. He moans as I move my body in rhythm against his. "Fuck, just like that."

I feel *every* inch of him as I lift and drop back down on his cock. Sweat begins to form on my hairline and my legs burn from the constant motion, but it's worth the sore muscles I'm sure to have in the morning.

"You ride me so damn good," he growls, breathlessly. His fingers reach between us to find my clit and my body shudders in response. Holy fuck. Without warning, he grasps the back of my neck and pulls me down to meet his lips. "You're close, I can feel it," he whispers and takes a fistful of my hair. He pumps into me, hard; each one pushes me closer and closer to the edge. "You want to come on my dick, Michaela?" I nod, but I know that's not enough. He wants to hear me say it. Before he even has to ask, a soft *yes* flows from my lips. "Good girl. Show me how bad you want it."

Instead of increasing my movements, I slow them down, letting my body move like a wave against his. Each stroke of his cock builds the pressure in my belly. I'm so full of him, it's becoming too much. Right before I take the first step over the edge, he kisses me, swallowing my moans as my orgasm rocks through me. He thrusts his hips up a few more times before he spills himself, filling me up.

We stay like that for a while, trying to catch our breath. For how long? I'm not sure, but it's not long enough when he starts to move, rolling me off him. He kisses my forehead, the tip of my nose, each cheek, and finally my lips. "That wasn't part of the plan," he chuckles, breathless.

"I'm not complaining."

"I didn't come here just for this, Michaela." He pushes hair from my face and offers a small genuine smile. "I want you to know that. I love you, and as soon as I heard you left David, I didn't want to go another moment without you."

Pulling the sheet tighter against my skin, I pour fresh hot water into two mugs. Tonight feels surreal — Finn showing up in Italy was not on my bingo card for this year, and neither was his love confession, but I'll take it.

Lavender fills my senses taking a sip of tea. I hate that I let myself take two steps backward when I first saw him tonight — before he showed up, I was ready and willing to talk about everything that happened. Accept that he didn't have to tell me about his father's challenge. Ultimately, it doesn't impact me or Sheffield House. He still did the work, got the business up and running, and continued to lead the charge daily. After everything I've experienced the past two months, after all my healing, I hated that I was so quick to let the anger take over when he showed up. Seeing him reminded me of the hurt, but I had to remind myself it wasn't his fault. It was David. It was Finn's parents. It was *me.* None of it was because of him, not really. I only took it out on him because I wanted someone to blame other than myself.

Walking back to the bedroom, Finn stands with his back to me. I take a moment to admire him, the way his muscles pull taunt under his skin. When he turns, I see the phone up to his ear. Who in the hell is calling at this hour? Finn kisses my temple, handing me the phone, "Phone call."

I look at the name and roll my eyes. "This better be good."

Alex sighs, "What does it take to get you to answer the damn phone?"

"Well, considering I'm still on vacation, a lot." I look at the time, "Alex, just spit it out — it's like three in the morning here."

"Considering Finn answered the phone — and don't think we're not gonna have a conversation about that later — I know the time of day is not an issue."

"Alex."

"Okay, okay… Have you talked to Josh?"

"Is that really why you're calling me at three a.m.?" I roll my eyes. Of course, I've talked to my brother.

"Michaela, I'm serious. When did you talk to him last?"

"He called me the other day about the divorce papers and—"

"No, I mean, yes, it is about divorce papers, but not yours."

What does that mean?

"Elizabeth filed for separation."

## *fifty-nine*

*Josh*

*FOUR MONTHS LATER*

**THERE'S AN ENVELOPE TUCKED** away in my desk drawer that arrived four months ago, and I still haven't opened it. The contents confirm what I know has been coming, but I never expected it to hit me this hard. We have been living apart for almost eight months, even though it goes against the terms of our arrangement. It doesn't matter though, because now we are *legally* separated and the countdown to filing the divorce papers is on (thank you state of South Carolina divorce laws). We have eight months until that day comes and I know she's counting down the days. Me? Well, the jury is still out on that one.

"Sorry," Finn says, walking back from the kitchen and I mute the Yankees game. I had spent the weekend in New York helping move Knox and his mom into the ~~penthouse~~ condo Finn and Michaela had recently purchased on Park Row Avenue. Knox's mom refused to let Finn hire movers. *I can do it myself,* she said. But, he wouldn't allow it. So, they compromised — Nick, Alex, and I were elected to join Finn over Labor Day weekend to move the Taylor family from East Harlem to the Financial District. Alex left this morning, he needed to prepare for his new client meeting on Tuesday, and Nick flew home last night after we finished so he could be home with his wife and their ten-day-old daughter. "Knox's mom is adamant I let her cook dinner, so she made Knox take her to the store, even though the doctors told her to rest—"

"Let the woman do what she wants," I say taking the cold beer he offers. "Besides, you're going to turn down a homecooked meal? When's the last time you had one of those?"

"I cook, and so does your sister, on occasion."

"Finn Sheffield cooks? Yeah, okay." I've never known him to cook a meal a day in his life, except that one time Mom made him help her cook breakfast because "everyone should know how to cook eggs."

Finn rolls his eyes and flops down onto the oversized gray couch. The entire condo has floor-to-ceiling windows, but the ones in the family room have a direct view of the Woolworth Building, One World Trade, and the Hudson. There's a bar on the same wall as the seventy-five-inch flat screen where the Yankees are currently up by two in the ninth inning, but bases are loaded, with two outs, and the Rangers just sent García up to bat. The penthouse has two floors, five bedrooms, six bathrooms, four terraces, a library, and just under six thousand square feet (exactly forty-four less, my sister said). I think Michaela just wanted to say she had something Nina didn't (i.e. a bigger condo), but that's none of my business.

"So," Finn says, sipping his beer.

"So?"

"You wanna talk about it?"

"Talk about what?"

"Oh, c'mon Josh, don't play coy."

I know what he's asking — he wants to know about Elizabeth. He and everyone else want to know what happened because our separation seemed so out of the blue. They never expected *us* to be the ones who didn't make it, but that's because they don't know the truth.

"There's nothing to talk about." I shrug. "We just...grew apart."

"Don't feed me that bullshit. What happened? I thought you guys were working it out."

Since Elizabeth filed the separation papers, I've kept myself buried under mountains of work, even earned the promotion that I (and everyone else at the office) was sure Jackson Holmes had secured. But, on Warren Hendrix's second-to-last day, they said my name instead, earning me a brand new office and an assistant. Working so much has given me a reason to avoid everyone. I'm sure they think it's because of the separation and part of it is, but what right do I have to be upset about something that wasn't anything more than a business transaction? That's all this was to her. That's all it should be to me too, but—

"Save your breath if you're going to spew more bullshit about how you 'grew apart' or are better as friends," Finn says. "I want to know what's really going on."

I chew on the inside of my bottom lip, I can't tell him the truth. I haven't told anyone the truth, not Nick, not Michaela... The only people who know are me, Elizabeth, Mom, and Brina, though I'm sure Elizabeth has told Nina by now. Whether she told Nick or not...I can't be sure, but I'm certain he would've said something by now.

Finn starts to say something else, but I cut him off, "Fine, I'll tell you, but no judgment."

"You remember who you're talking to, right?"

"Elizabeth and I...we're in an arranged marriage."

The bottle falls from his hands onto the stone gray carpet

soaking it with beer. His eyes are ten times their normal size, and his mouth opens and closes trying to get out whatever questions are flooding his mind.

"Yes, arranged marriage." I scrub down my face and roll my shoulders as a small weight lifts off them. It feels good to finally say it out loud, to no longer have to keep this secret from everyone. "And, at this point, I just want the whole thing to be over."

Even if it means losing her. But can you lose something that was never really yours in the first place? Of all the things I expected from our arrangement, I never expected to want to keep her.

# Thank you!

Did you enjoy *Strictly Business*? Please consider leaving a review on Amazon, Goodreads, etc!

Interested in more from Jensen Parker? Scan the code below to sign up for the newsletter

# WHAT'S NEXT?

The *Strangers* Series will continue with an arranged marriage romance featuring Josh and Elizabeth.

Where to begin...

They say your second book is your hardest and they (whoever *they* are) were right! Part of the struggle I faced with writing *Strictly Business* was my pregnancy. With everything going on, there wasn't much energy or mind power left for creativity. It made me sick. It forced me to slow down. It made me *loathe* writing. I felt like I had a fog surrounding every bit of my person and I was scared I'd never get back to normal... Then, I had my baby girl and it was practically instantaneous! I swear, I felt the fog lift and I could see and think clearly for the first time in almost a year. Even though it was one of the hardest times of my life, and set me back practically a year workwise, I wouldn't trade it for the world.

Being a writer and a mom is difficult because you no longer have the freedom you had before the baby came along. You have to be good at time management and very intentional with your time. I wouldn't have been able to do this without the help and support of my mom and husband.

There were times I never thought I would get here, but I made it! Every sleepless night. Every tear. Every bottle of wine. Every cup of coffee. It was all worth it because I finished my *second* novel!

First, I need to thank the good Lord above. I know I started with Him last time, but a girl has to give credit where credit is due. Without Him, none of this would be possible. He has blessed me with an incredible gift and I'm happy to have the opportunity to share it.

Second, I need to thank my husband. His patience during this whole process have been above and beyond - even when I was on the brink of a breakdown (once or twice). His support and love has been above and beyond. I truly couldn't do this without him. ♥

Third, I need to thank my mom. She has supported me so much since the release of *Until Now*. She has helped me with the baby while still working her day job so I could try and get uninterrupted work time. Did it always go as planned? Well, let's just say, Baby CJ is a mama's girl, *but* my mom does what she can to help.

My editor, Kate. Girl, you're a gem. You have helped me turn this into what it is today and pushed me to be a better writer.

Claire, I'm so blessed to have met you at a random signing last year. Your friendship and support during this journey has been incredible. Not only in writing but in stepping into motherhood, as well.

Holly, thank you. Not only your knowledge and advice but your friendship.

The group of ladies (IWC) I met after moving back home... You are lifesavers. Our (almost) weekly meet-ups to write, chat, and just get a break from the world came into my life exactly when I needed it.

My family and friends, your love and support means more than you know. Even those of you who thought *Until Now* was a little... "racy." (P.S. If you thought that was racy... You didn't stand a chance in *Strictly Business,* oops!)

My team, I love our chats. You guys have been so supportive and encouraging. Thank you for letting me ask random questions and get feedback from you. ILY

There were so many of you who showed support during this journey, I can't even begin to name all of you, but just know I appreciate and love you.

Finally, my baby girl, Baby CJ. You've shown me a love I never knew before. Even though my deadlines got pushed (and pushed again) because my body was focused on creating you, I wouldn't change it for the world. You are the best thing I've ever done.

Next year is looking to be a *very* busy year. Filled with signings, conventions, and new books... I can't wait to share more details with all of you soon!

- Jensen

# about the author

Jensen Parker is a wife, mother, and contemporary romance author. Her hobbies include coffee, wine, travel, and books. A former retail store manager and real estate professional, but her heart has always belonged to writing. She recently moved back to her home state of Indiana with her husband, daughter, and their zoo. When she isn't writing, you'll find her reading, playing with her daughter, cooking new recipes from scratch, or planning a vacation.

For sneak peeks, giveaways, and more... Sign up for Jensen's newsletter! https://www.jensenparker.com/subscribe

Follow her on social media!

Instagram : instagram.com/jensenparkerauthor

Facebook : facebook.com/jparkerauthor

Threads : threads.net/@jensenparkerauthor

Twitter : twitter.com/jensenpauthor

Goodreads : goodreads.com/jensenparkerauthor

Amazon : amazon.com/author/jensenparkerauthor

TikTok : tiktok.com/@jensenparkerauthor

*"I urge you to live a life worthy of the calling you have received. Be completely humble and gentle; be patient, bearing with one another in love."*

*- Ephesians 4:1-2*

*#MadeforMore*

www.ingramcontent.com/pod-product-compliance
Lightning Source LLC
Chambersburg PA
CBHW031845310726
48972CB00005B/1412